THE STEPPES OF PARIS

THE STEPPES OF PARIS

Helen Harris

Hodder & Stoughton
LONDON SYDNEY AUCKLAND TORONTO

British Library Cataloguing in Publication Data
Harris, Helen, *1955–*
  The steppes of Paris.
  I. Title
  823'.914[F]

ISBN 0-340-51337-3

Published by Hodder and Stoughton,
a division of Hodder and Stoughton Ltd,
Mill Road, Dunton Green, Sevenoaks, Kent TN13 2YA
Editorial Office: 47 Bedford Square, London WC1B 3DP

Typeset by Hewer Text Composition Services, Edinburgh
Printed in Great Britain by St Edmundsbury Press, Bury St Edmunds, Suffolk
and bound by Hartnolls Ltd, Bodmin, Cornwall.

Contents

Edward

He had hoped it would be South America. The whole city smelt of perfume on the late summer evening he came to live there and as he walked the dense boulevards, scorning the scented women and their apparently equally scented dogs, it seemed to him that instead of travelling somewhere crude and vital which would invigorate him, he had been consigned to a florist's shop, full of elegantly rotting memories, where he would inevitably be smothered.

The newspaper had kept him in the dark right up to the last minute: Sao Paulo or Lagos, Harare or Lima. For weeks, he had been over-eating, over-drinking, and generally indulging in every lush and decadent comfort London had to offer, in nervous anticipation of the imagined hardships ahead. Mentally, he was already living in bare, once white rooms where mosquitoes, outsize ants and cockroaches whirred and clattered in a re-enactment of a nearby war. When, in the end, they had told him Paris, he could barely believe his ears. He had walked out along Fleet Street in a stricken daze. The opaque windows of the last remaining newspaper offices looked down on him in jaded amusement and, holding their drainpipe arms akimbo, hooted with laughter at the casual but ridiculous cock-up some only relatively senior editor had just made of his life. For it was merely, he knew, a snap decision, made by some burdened bureaucrat between breakfast and lunch. Whether Wainwright was sent to La Paz or Paris was a matter of supreme indifference to everyone but Wainwright.

Briefly, the space of pavement between one confectionery and cigarette shop and the next, Edward considered chucking it in. The satisfying style of the gesture would not make up for the year's training in London: the dreary word-processor courses, the bullying condescension from older journalists whom he considered in every way his inferiors, the salary which could be divided, humiliatingly, more than twice into those of his university friends who had gone into the City. There would be a brief burst of admiration – "Hey, did you hear what old Eddy did?" – but then there would be un-employment, disillusionment or even disgust with his chosen profession, and the difficulty of settling for something else, which he might turn out to be stuck with forever, as second best.

He wished he smoked. He would have liked to go and stand on Blackfriars Bridge then, drawing deep on a slim white shaft. He would inhale and exhale steadily, his almost imperceptibly shaking hands the only sign of his distress. Instead, after half an hour's directionless walking, he went into a fug-filled café at Ludgate Circus and ordered a black coffee and, on second thoughts, a fried-egg-and-bacon sandwich and thought about the immediate although less serious difficulty of telling his friends his farcically undignified destination.

The more he thought about it, chewing, the more angrily disappointed he became until, in a paroxysm of fury and frustration, he wondered what option he had other than to hate the place. In Paris, he would surely find nothing to compete with the fantasies which had sustained him at the word-processor. In Paris, there would be no Amazon and no Andes; no machine-gun-toting revolutionaries with faces like icons, saintly with the right of their cause; no obese cigar-smoking dictators ripe for overthrow; no mean colonels in sunglasses with whom Edward would argue wit-tily, trenchantly for his press pass and his justice; no poet-prophets with whom he would somehow obtain exclusive interviews and dispatch them back to London, thereby making his name in literary circles as well as press. There would

4

be no larger-than-life Hispanic dramas of absolute evil and absolute good: shrieking and tearing of hair and beating of large, flapping breasts; no natural cataclysms – earthquakes, landslides – in whose aftermath Edward, notebook in hand, would witness human suffering that would etch its lines and whittle down his still-too-youthful, podgy, fresh face.

In Paris – it really did not bear thinking about – he would wake in the mornings in some cushioned apartment and there would be no alien dawns outside his window, no new winds or rains, no sounds or smells or tastes he did not know by heart already. There would be no encounters with rampant women soldiers who would seduce the Englishman with their khaki-rimmed cleavages and unshaven armpits. The egg yolk clogged Edward's throat and he had to put down his sandwich and stand up and leave the café. He went out into the street where, although it was mid-July, a steady mildewing rain was falling, and he walked back to the newspaper office to face his colleagues' reactions.

He was quite alone in his disappointment for the older men on the paper all made jolly, envious comments to him when the news came out. They reminisced, as they browsed through files of tired clippings for their next pieces, about favourite restaurants and favourite meals. For them, Paris, indeed the world, Edward frequently thought, was nothing but an immense dining-room. They didn't remember wars, historic happenings or meetings with great men when they recalled their younger, more active selves. They remembered *tripes à la mode de Caen* and 1961 Nuits-St-Georges. The fine profession of journalism was for them, or at any rate their journalism was for Edward, nothing but a means to eat the most meals in the most restaurants at someone else's expense. And Paris, as a city exceptionally well supplied with excellent restaurants, naturally rated highly as a destination on their scale of priorities. There weren't many four-star restaurants in Lima. They licked their pendulous lips at Edward's luck. One of them, a man Edward particularly disliked for his habit of ruthlessly mocking the less pretty secretaries with a barrage of sexual suggestion, even called Edward a "jammy bastard". Edward hated them all.

5

A small but especially galling footnote was that Foster was to be sent to Khartoum. Jas Foster, Edward's fellow-trainee for the past year and pet hate, had evidently entered journalism because he saw in it an opportunity to develop his alcoholic inclinations to the full. On the few occasions he was by chance quite sober, he expressed complete cynicism for the ideals and principles of the profession which had appealed to Edward. Whether drunk or sober, he subscribed boisterously to the school of thought that the goodies of the world were now his to be consumed, at somebody else's expense. Free drinks, free meals, free junkets here and there; that was what journalism was all about and Wainwright was a poor fool not to know it. Edward could all too easily imagine the life Foster would lead in Khartoum: an idle round of government offices for the useless officialese briefings, and the rest of his days spent propped at the bar of the press hotel, lamenting with his cronies the dearth of decent restaurants in town. He would sweat and grumble every time he had to go anywhere sandy in a Land Rover and at the end of his time in the Sudan he would still not speak more than a word or two of the local language. (What language, Edward suddenly worried, did they speak in the Sudan?) The one consolation in which Edward could uncharitably take comfort was the likelihood of Foster's contracting some nastily exotic and perhaps penicillin-resistant strain of venereal disease. He couldn't help but rage at the fate which had wafted undeserving Foster out to the Sudan and sent him to fester in Paris. It was bad enough for the fate which directed his future to take the form of a middle-aged incompetent in a London office. But for that fate to be both arbitrary and unjust was more than he could swallow.

He was beset by humiliating comparisons with "pretend" childhood journeys as he went through the small rituals of preparing for Paris: a five-year-old Edward on a beach some-where, bested in argument by his older brothers and sisters, and setting off staunchly with his bucket and spade to dig his way away from them through to the other side of the earth. He remembered a miniature green rucksack, which his mother would fill with egg sandwiches and Kit Kats for him when he wanted to go "exploring". He would set out, sternly wearing the rucksack, to go and eat his picnic by himself on

6

a piece of overgrown and jungly "wilderness" adjoining the family garden.

In the weeks which preceded his departure – August, with Fleet Street invaded by Crimplene-clad, immensely buttocked Americans looking for Dr Johnson's house and the Cheshire Cheese – Edward developed a slow-burning grudge against the paper. He decided he would have his revenge by taking from them all that he could in the form of training and experience and, after a year or two, when he would be a more desirable acquisition, he would move to another paper, to a more prestigious position on another paper, and they would send him to Santiago. It was all very well publicly to save face by repeating what a good move Paris was career-wise. As far as he was concerned, in Paris he would regrettably, but it now seemed inescapably, just be marking time.

His friends greeted the news with a variety of equally irritating reactions: some said promptly that they hoped he would get a large and comfortable apartment so they could come and stay often. Others, who had always privately felt he was far too confident of his own success, jeered, "Bit of a let-down from Ouagadougou, what?" and a girl called Rosie, whom he had been looking forward to leaving far behind when his Varig-Aerolineas Argentinas-VIASA plane taxied for take-off, clasped both his hands in a wine bar and breathed, "Oh, Eddy, thank God, thank God, thank God." Even though Edward really wasn't all that keen, his friends decided they would hold a goodbye party for him.

The stuffy warm embrace of the party brought home to him what a non-event this departure was. Instead of awe and excitement at the distance Edward was to travel, and the titillating dangers he was to face, there was cheery indifference. Instead of raising their glasses in toasts which should long be remembered, his friends went in for a lot of "Ooh-la-la-ing" and, late in the evening, a roistering all-male can-can. Those who saw nothing to rage against in being sent to Paris (frequently female) annoyed Edward by listing the city's trite attractions. Those who, in his place, would also have been disconsolate (frequently male) rubbed in his disappointment with jokes about Nicaragua and hiccuping cries of "Olé!"

As the evening advanced and, one after another, his friends' faces ballooned out of the dancing to hoot, "*Au revoir*, Eddy!" and "*Bon voyage*, Eddy!", he retreated further into apparently drunken remoteness.

His best friend Roland and his best friend Guy were sitting out on the stairs, drinking from a secret cache, and abandoning the party, he went to sit there with them. From this perch, he surveyed the party ebbing around them and willed it to be over.

He did take a small, smug pleasure in the number and enthusiasm of the acquaintances who had come to clap him on the back and kick up their legs in fun at his destination. Only he wished he were sorrier to leave them. The *bonhomie* seemed devalued by his impatience for it all to be over, and by his pervasive regret that there would not be wider oceans than the English Channel to separate them. Rosie spent the evening noticeably always in a different room, publicly reproaching Edward for his desertion, now he had made it clear her visits would not be called for. Her attitude convinced him more than ever that, in the long term, she would have been no good as a companion. In any case, as far as he could see, there had been no way of handling the problem gallantly. He and Rosie had been sleeping together intermittently for the best part of a year but, on this Edward was adamant, there had been no agreements made between them. Rosie came to his house, her nylon sausage bag slung over one shoulder, or she came without the bag, or she didn't come at all. But none of the three options was supposed to signify anything beyond the day on which it occurred. Sometimes, when Edward woke early in his room behind the insufficient curtains, he did not know without turning his head whether Rosie was beside him. And Rosie's feelings for him had, until now, never much concerned him either; she seemed, in her cheerful way, to be quite contented with their arrangement. If anything, she seemed perhaps too contented. Edward didn't like to find trailing items of her underwear forgotten under his bed or a blue box of Tampax tucked prudently in his chest of drawers. He never went as far as saying anything to Rosie about not becoming too much of a fixture. After all, she knew perfectly well that when his training period was over, the paper would send Eddy to the ends of the earth.

Although Rosie was generous and sweet-natured, obliging and affectionate, there was no doubt in Edward's mind but that would be the end of it. For he had known all along, and had some trouble reconciling with his image of himself as someone who behaved well to women, that there would be no room for Rosie in South America.

Her attempts to treat his demotion to Paris as a happy pretext for prolonging their partnership infuriated him. He realised it would be asking too much of someone with Rosie's aspirations to share his disappointment. But her open joy offended him. Instead of bringing what there was of a relationship to a painless close by simply putting several thousand miles between them, there had to be tedious explanations, pressure, scenes and tears. This, on top of all the other irritations of his last weeks in London, contrived to destroy any remaining affection he had for her.

He sought and found consolation in the inebriate company of Roland and Guy. The three of them had been friends since university and, in any sort of adversity involving women, tended to close ranks. The most frequent refugee, as a matter of fact, was Roland, simply because he risked his neck the most often. Fortunately, he was also the one who generally cared the least about the outcome. He had surprised everyone by getting a much sought-after job as a television researcher a year or two out of university and, assigned to a salacious late-night chat show, had quickly found his naturally promiscuous inclinations legitimised. Guy who, before admitting defeat and becoming a stockbroker, had waged a long and bitter battle to get a job somewhere civilised as an English lecturer, was altogether more reticent in his approach.

Sitting blearily between them, Edward concluded that these were the only two individuals whom he would be sincerely sorry to leave behind. But, at the same time, he congratulated himself on being the one who was leaving. Guy and Roland were both already on predetermined paths whereas he, by going away, had the whole world ahead of him. He had a vision of himself squatting between them; popular, yes, laughing, yes – at a girl called Sophie who was blowing joke kisses up at him from the hall – not bad looking, the man most likely. He was meant to stride away from them all now, wearing wide shorts

9

and a cocky smile, and only reappear years afterwards, with a tanned skin and a wise expression.

As the party wound down, Edward shut himself in the lavatory and sat, confounded by the pointlessness, the sheer stupidity of it all. Why, for God's sake, generate all this noise, this shouting and music and stamping, when, really, he was not going anywhere?

His first night in Paris, he dreamt there was a fan whirling round above his head. He woke to find he had left the light, and therefore the extractor fan, on in the bathroom cubicle and now, at half past two, it was rattling away, driving itself into a mechanical frenzy. He got up and turned off the light and dropped back into bed, where he lay and listened to the last wheezes and croaks of the machine in its death throes. It was, in derisive miniature, a perfect symbol of the let-down.

In the filtered half-light coming in from the street lamps, his hotel room looked ancient and ghostly. You could only see the old-fashioned shapes of the furniture: the arthritic paws of the bedside table, the frilly-edged frosted glass lampshades on the wall lights, the gleam of the perfectly ridiculous wardrobe brass door-handles. It was too dark to see how worn and soiled they were, proving, however deceptive their shadows, that many years had passed since their installation; that it was no longer 1900.

Once awake, the press of his preoccupations stopped Edward from going back to sleep. He lay sprawled diagonally across the undulating double bed and, trying not to focus on the furniture which oppressed him, considered his predicament.

"I've booked you into a reasonably decent hotel I know," his new boss, Henry Hirshfeld, had told him. "It's not the

11

George V, you understand, but since you may be there for some time – I thought we'd let you choose your own apartment. We do have the place in Neuilly you could take, of course, but you'd have to move again in four months because the lease runs out. Take a look at it, if you want. It's a functional kind of a place, I guess; smart, modern, *une machine à habiter*." He hesitated. "Some of your predecessors have preferred somewhere a bit more – Parisian."

On his way back from viewing the paper's apartment in Neuilly, Edward felt extremely grateful to Henry Hirshfeld. He had gone there straight away his first afternoon. "There's no point your pretending to do any work for a day or two, is there?" Henry had said amiably. The apartment was on the fifth floor of an anonymous de luxe block, hygienically sealed off from any trace of local colour by double glazing, air-conditioning and an entry-phone. Edward had been just momentarily tempted by all the plush accoutrements: the closed-circuit television screen which enabled you to see who was down at the front door, the infra-red cooking rings under a see-through slab in the kitchen, the champing garbage guzzler. He had briefly imagined having his friends from London to stay there, and how impressed they would be by the rich lifestyle he had swiftly attained. But he had stood in the silent living-room, looking out of the tinted-glass sliding windows which occupied one wall, and he had experienced a dismal sensation of being nowhere. He was sealed in an unnatural quiet: no traffic noises, no remote sound of human voices. Judging by the synthetic climate and the view from the window of an utterly undistinguished, well-to-do, suburban street, he might as well be anywhere. He would be tucked up in a sleek grey box if he moved in here. He would not even be in Paris. This impression was reinforced by the traces of the apartment's present occupant, a visiting American journalist who was a friend of Henry's. He had left, strewn around the various see-through coffee and bedside tables, copies of *Time* and *Newsweek*, a disconcerting array of bottles of prescription medicines, and, in the kitchen, several boxes of American breakfast cereals, expensively priced in French francs.

This was what was likely to happen, Edward concluded, if you chose to live in a place like this. He imagined himself installed there, reading his *Guardian Weekly* in one of the black leatherette easy chairs, his hi-tech kitchen stocked with Marmite and English staples from the Marks and Spencer he had already noticed on the Boulevard Haussmann. Sooner or later, he would give in to the memory of Rosie and her relative proximity and, prompted by the clinical emptiness of the apartment, ring her and invite her for a weekend.

He was about to help himself to a cup of coffee (instant and decaffeinated) from the kitchen when it struck him that this could be the first small step in succumbing to the easy comfort of that life. He replaced the jar. He would go out and drink a real *café crème* sitting at a small round table in a real café. It was while he was looking for the keys, which he had inadvertently put down on a piece of furniture somewhere as he arrived, that he noticed the hum. The whole building, or everything in it, was infested by a high, continuous hum: the air-conditioning hummed, the strip lights, the security system, the deep freeze and, for some inexplicable reason, the window panes. In winter, doubtless the central heating would hum as well. Edward was so horrified by it and by the thought that he might not have noticed it and unknowingly moved in to live alongside the hum, that, having found the keys, he hurried to leave. He forgot the ferocious static electricity from the door handle, which had snapped at him as he came in, and he grabbed it, to receive a stinging charge in the palm of his hand. Swearing and nursing his smarting hand under his left armpit, he rode down in the big, matt metal box of a lift. Outside, where it was once again a warm late summer's afternoon, he decided to skip the coffee in his haste to get well away from the humming apartment house. He caught a bus back into the centre of Paris, although a taxi would have been legitimate, and on the way he offered appreciative thanks to Henry Hirshfeld for having sensitively given him the option not to live there.

He had been rather favourably surprised by Henry Hirshfeld. From the name, which he had been told in London, he had imagined someone so much less likeable that, when he met Henry, he had had to struggle with complete disorientation, as well as the natural apprehension associated with meeting the man who would be his boss for the next year or two. He had been glumly expecting a jowly cynic. He thought Hirshfeld would be the American counterpart of those desk-bound diners he had so raged against in London; a complacent, chauvinistic armchair traveller, content just to finish his career in comfort and roundly dismissive of any innovations or enthusiasms which Edward might come up with.

He sprang to his feet when Edward appeared in the doorway of his office.

"Mr Hirshfeld?"

Henry Hirshfeld stretched out not one but both big hands and shook Edward's extended one in a protracted double clasp. He appraised Edward with a pair of shockingly piercing bright blue eyes and then pronounced in a rumbling voice, as though it were a conclusion he had come to, "Pleased to meet you, Edward."

He was built on a big scale, a thick-set man with short-cropped iron-grey hair, but everything else about him confounded Edward's expectations. He took Edward out to lunch, at a Japanese restaurant.

Disconcerted by the geographical distance between the interior of the restaurant and the pavement outside, Edward took a while to adjust to this unexpected new personality. Across the low table from him was not a jaundiced habitué of expense accounts and business-class travel, but a man still avidly alive, exhibiting keen, almost boyish enthusiasms, which glimmered through his surface traits of silver-rimmed spectacles and calm, wry irony.

He began by outlining humorously to Edward how the office worked. There were five of them: himself, Edward, whose official job title, he observed drily, might be assistant to the bureau chief, but who would find himself running the bureau pretty much single-handed during Henry's frequent absences. There was Monsieur Marchais, whose role was, he smiled, "not easily categorisable". Monsieur Marchais had been with the paper in some undefined capacity for far too many years to get rid of him, now that he had outlived any original usefulness. He came in erratically two or three times a week and it was wisest simply to regard him as a part of the fixtures and fittings. "Above all," Henry twirled a little pink piece of raw tuna judiciously on his fork, "I would suggest you keep off the topic of the French Communist Party. Our Monsieur Marchais hates to be reminded of good old Georges."

Edward could not help giving him a short, startled look. Apart from his general good humour, there was absolutely no sign of a joke on Henry Hirshfeld's broad, crumpled face.

The rest of the paper's staff consisted of the telephonist-receptionist and the secretary, Marie-Yvette and Aurore. "So far as they're concerned," Henry said, "I have no cause to poison your mind with prejudice."

He said nothing about work. Edward, who was eager to know something about the extent of his responsibilities, if he would have his own by-line, how many trips he was likely to land, was a little dismayed. But it seemed crass and priggish to raise the subject when Henry didn't. So he sat and listened, in growing astonishment, to Henry discoursing knowledgeably on art and architecture, the very real threat posed by the rise of the National Front, and Zola's *J'Accuse*. Edward felt increasingly uneasy. Here was a man he would actually like to impress. But, out of pique, he had done almost no background reading on France before he left London. He hadn't even taken the elementary precaution of reading through Hirshfeld's pieces. He must find a decent bookshop, he decided, at the first possible opportunity.

In response to a later question from Edward, Henry also explained how it was he had come to spend the last fifteen years of his life in Paris, and why, if fate so willed it, he would quite contentedly finish his days there.

He had been around. He used the phrase with a smile. He had rolled up in Paris at the very end of the Sixties, when the memory of '68 was still fresh and the municipality was busy replacing the cobble stones with concrete. As well as the sentimental lure of Paris for any even mildly literate American, there was a real feeling of ferment in the air. It was an exciting place to be. In the course of researching a book – Edward did his best to look as if, naturally, he knew what the book was and Henry, modestly, didn't tell him – he had met, fallen in love with and pretty quickly married a young Vietnamese art student. One year had

15

followed another, they were putting their child through school here, until eventually Henry realised that, even if he had wanted to, it was too late to return to Chicago.

At the end of the meal, Henry brushed aside Edward's offer to come and begin to familiarise himself with the office.

"Plenty of time for that later," he declared. "Go out and choose where you want to live. Take a look at Neuilly and decide if it's what you want. If it isn't, your first assignment will be to find somewhere to live."

As he walked through central Paris in a largely apricot-coloured evening, after he had been to Neuilly, Edward's mood vacillated unsteadily between depression at the concrete evidence that here he was, settling in Paris, and a completely unexpected, bracing anticipation of possible exploration ahead after all. For this, he knew he had only Henry Hirshfeld to thank. For a man as exceptionally impressive as Hirshfeld to have chosen to live here when, with his credentials, he could live anywhere, the place must have something challenging going for it. Henry had straight away understood Edward couldn't possibly live in the humming apartment house in Neuilly when he brought the keys back to the office at the end of the afternoon.

"I'll call the *comptable*," he said simply. "Let's just check how much rent you're allowed."

In totally fluent although unmistakably accented French, he had had a brief telephone conversation with a Monsieur – was it possible? – Rat. He handed Edward a sheet of office notepaper on which he had scribbled some sums and the addresses and telephone numbers of two accommodation agencies.

"Happy hunting," he had said. "And it's an important decision, remember. Take your time."

Henry Hirshfeld's "reasonably decent" hotel was in a narrow grey side street off the Boulevard Saint Germain and as he walked back towards it via a leisurely route, Edward was surprised to find himself registering a number of places where he thought it might actually be quite fun to live. He crossed the Pont des Arts and followed the *quais* as far as the Boulevard Saint Michel. He could live behind one of those stiff, po-faced façades looking out over the river. The caramelised yellow surface of the Seine would chug past on a summer's evening, always consoling. Or he could live somewhere very high up, looking out over a roofscape: irregular grey slates and lurching television aerials and chimney pots. He caught himself; one day in Paris and he was succumbing to the chocolate box. Next, he would be reminiscing fondly about pitchers of *vin rouge* on café terraces like those old codgers in London. Determinedly sullen, he ploughed his way up the Boulevard Saint Michel. He overtook crowds of pedestrians of flamboyantly assorted nationalities, all strolling at a slow, self-conscious dawdle. Only a lot later that evening, eating, alone, a deliberately parsimonious pizza in a modest Italian restaurant, did he think that, now he was unavoidably here, surely the right thing to do was to enjoy it. If he acted intelligently, exploring the possibilities of Paris *à la* Henry Hirshfeld, then it wouldn't be a selling-out. It would be a journey made against all odds.

Around him in the dim bedroom, the furniture challenged this momentary optimism. His walk had ended in the Jardin du Luxembourg and there depression and disgust had threatened to win out. A chirruping crowd of Parisians, pigeons and little dogs filled the garden. The air was saturated with perfume and the sound of unsuitable footwear clipping over gravel. Edward had considered the jumble of green metal chairs, the statuary and the bulrushes and reflected that the park was, if possible, even more citified than the boulevard outside. A portrait gallery of Parisian intellectuals sat on the green metal chairs, reading – or perhaps only affecting to read – a selection of slim journals about philosophy, literature, music, art. He had been gripped by a ferocious physical and mental claustrophobia.

It was the lace curtains, he decided drowsily, which he found most oppressive. The street light came through them where he had not completely closed the thicker brown ones, intensifying the pattern of curlicues and unimaginative flowers. They were redolent of primness, inhibitions, repression. Living behind that kind of curtains would be

17

like trying to breathe with your head inside a polythene bag.

Just as he was falling back to sleep, he became aware of the noise of two people starting to make love with considerable gusto in the room next door. It seemed to Edward they were laughing in Portuguese.

In the morning, the hotel pipes blew like a hunting horn. Edward felt for his alarm clock, saw it was seven o'clock, and decided to make a good impression on Henry Hirshfeld by arriving at the office as soon as possible after eight.

His shower put the first damper on his resolve; it petered, rather than anything else, out of the old shower rose so that, instead of beginning the day as he liked to with his normal all-over blasting of hot water, he was simply wettened. He dressed for the office, relieved that Hirshfeld, who had the day before been wearing corduroy trousers, a brown belt and brown shoes, was not a tie man. He kept an unbelievably battered old sports jacket on the back of his door and, at lunch time, he had simply shrugged it on, whereupon it fell into place about him like a baggy skin.

There seemed something immature about having breakfast in the hotel, so Edward went out into the warm just faintly misty morning, intending to stop for a coffee and a croissant somewhere on his way. The pavements of the Boulevard Saint Germain were already quite busy, mainly with smart but grim-faced women, walking briskly like well-finished automatons to work. The few men about looked to him by contrast sorry; Lowry figures, hunched, with bent heads, scurrying. Aware of his own leisure – Henry had actually said to show up at

19

the office only when it fitted in with his house-hunting – Edward enjoyed the walk. At the corner of the Boulevard Saint Michel, he chose his café, bought a paper, and went in, intending to sit for a good ten minutes on the glassed-in terrace, having a soup-bowl-sized cup of coffee and one or maybe even two croissants, while he turned the pages of his paper and watched the smart women snapping past. OK, it was a pose but, stuff it, a harmless one. He hadn't noticed that most of the terrace chairs were still up-ended on the tables and when he tried to sit down on one of the few which weren't, a waiter bad-temperedly mopping the floor shouted at him that the only place he could have coffee at that hour was standing up at the bar. Even the minor thrill of noticing that two of the men at the bar were drinking red wine for breakfast and one, for God's sake, brandy, didn't make the bar an appealing proposition. The same scene was repeated, although less bad-temperedly, at a second café he tried lower down the boulevard so, as it was after eight o'clock already, he ended up drinking a foul-tasting black coffee standing in a totally Americanised fast-food joint with large illuminated pictures of the hamburgers and milk shakes it served, and caught the Metro at Saint Michel.

The office was deserted when, at a quarter to nine, he let himself in, with the master key Henry had given him. It wasn't until gone nine o'clock that he heard another key wrestling with the lock and Marie-Yvette, to whom he had been briefly introduced the day before, fumbled her way in and gave every sign of severe shock at seeing him there.

In contrast to the sleek, hard-faced women on the Boulevard Saint Germain, Marie-Yvette was anything but smart, and Edward couldn't help wondering if it were Henry who had hired her. He thought, with a feeling that was very close to the beginning of affection, that it would probably be typical of Henry Hirshfeld to have employed someone so resolutely un-smart.

Marie-Yvette had short, bedraggled henna-red hair. The day before, she had been wearing jeans and two unironed T-shirts one on top of the other, one navy blue and one white with a slogan. Today they were maroon and black. Edward had already noticed, and faintly reproached himself for noticing, that she had virtually no breasts. As she went through the office, switching on the lights, he also noticed that she was wearing open-toed sandals and not a scrap of make-up. Her pitted skin gleamed a little.

She was looking him over at the same time. Despite her homespun appearance, she evidently wasn't at all shrinking. When she had cleared the telephone answering machine of the night's messages and taken a couple of sheets off the telex, she invited Edward to join her for a cup of coffee, which she began to make at a murky percolator installed in a corner of the main office.

"Ed-ward?" she pronounced carefully. "Not Eddie, like Murphy?"

Edward hesitated. He was, he recognised, childishly particular about who used which version of his name. Eddy was only for intimates, for his very closest friends; he was Edward to everyone else. He opened his mouth to reply firmly, 'Not Eddie, like Murphy or anybody else,' but found himself instead answering incautiously, "Different people call me different things: I'm Edward, Eddy, Ed, Ted, Teddy, Ned. Take your pick." He supposed it must be the keenness of the new boy to ingratiate himself on the staffers which made him answer so unguardedly; that, and the unexpected intimacy of sitting drinking a leisurely coffee in an empty office with a girl who turned out to be – it came up in the conversation – exactly his own age and who reminded him, with her scrappy looks and stern standpoints, of a grim feminist with whom he had once shared a house in London.

He asked her in return, "Are you always Marie-Yvette?" and she answered snappishly, "Always, always. No abbreviations."

They had been chatting for five or ten minutes when Aurore, the office secretary, who had been out on an errand when Edward came in the previous day, arrived in a whirlwind of concern at her lateness. She was a tall, very pretty young black woman from Martinique; all vivaciousness, ebullience, deep giggles, and a quite extraordinary contrast to stern, drab Marie-Yvette. She shook Edward's hand formally but then tut-tutted teasingly over the difficulty of pronouncing his name: "Ed-ward, Ed-ward. Ts-ts-ts-ts-ts. Before we have How-ard, now Ed-ward." She sighed in mock exasperation.

"You can call him Eddie," Marie-Yvette told her in French.

Aurore looked Edward up and down. "No," she declared. "It does not suit him. He is, *hélas*, Ed-ward." And, hanging up her jacket, she went off into a volley of provocative giggles.

Marie-Yvette shrugged. She put her hand on the telephone receiver to answer the first call of the day, which had been flashing for some moments on the switchboard, and retorted, "You create your own problems, Aurore."

Ed-ward concluded, as he sat down in the small room which had been allocated to him, that he was stupid to have wondered if Henry Hirshfeld had been responsible for employing the paper's present staff. Only Hirshfeld, he thought, smiling, would have picked such unlikely characters from among the city's ranks of well-finished female automatons. He felt a brief moment's warm anticipation at the prospect of working for the man.

Henry, arriving soon after ten, was astonished to find Edward there and only refrained from ticking him off for a completely unnecessary display of keenness when he heard him making appointments on the telephone with the two accommodation agencies.

Edward spent the best part of the next three days looking for a place to live. He had heard that it would be a problem; by the second week of September a lot of places had already been taken. But, even more than the limited number to choose from, it was the sort of apartments the agents were showing him which dismayed him.

Although he had imagined, before he came here, that he didn't care at all where he lived, that being in Paris was a death sentence to adventure, and the shape or form or shell it took was immaterial, he had realised nearly at once this was wrong. His only hope lay in finding the right flat, one which would let him into some authentic layer of the city and enable him to travel, as Henry Hirshfeld had, simply by living there. This was precisely what the glass cube in Neuilly would not do.

The estate agents showed him three more cubes on Tuesday and Wednesday. They seemed convinced that a journalist on a prestigious paper, even if only a young trainee journalist, must want to live in a modern block. They glossed over the undesirable, virtually suburban locations: Porte de Choisy, Porte de Châtillon, Vincennes. They dwelt in each case on the newness, the shiny kitchen, the anonymous, still paint-smelling hall. Edward told them three times, increasingly unpleasantly each time, that he wanted to live somewhere old, didn't they understand, prior to 1914 at least, somewhere with a bit of character. Where was the problem? In the whole of Paris, crammed as it was, if you believed the literary stereotypes, with crummily picturesque locations, surely they could find somewhere a little less soulless for him?

By Thursday, they claimed to have understood what Monsieur Wainwright had in mind and the long-suffering woman from the agency drove him out to the extreme edge of the sixteenth *arrondissement* to show him what she said was the ideal property. It was in a solemn, grey stone street opposite the Bois de Boulogne, a street whose absolute silence oppressed them as soon as they opened the car doors, and where they did not see, arriving or leaving, a single pedestrian. The apartment was on the sixth floor of a chillingly grand apartment house. The entrance hall had a singularly ugly marble, which reminded Edward of nothing as much as lino, on the floor and walls, and two chandeliers. The lift was, rather embarrassingly for the estate agent, out of order. (The term on the card which hung from the lift door handle, Edward was delighted to notice, was *"En Dérangement"*.) As they laboured up the six floors, nothing but their own shoes disturbed the almost invalid silence except, at one point, an inexplicable lady-like "A-hem" issuing from an invisible source. The flat itself was a chamber of horrors of unstable little white and gold chairs, upholstered in yellow ochre plush, and a bedroom where every piece of furniture, including a sizeable dressing-table, was decorated with a large pink flounce. Despite the scale of the building, the flat itself was a minute three-room affair. Even the view of the yellowing autumn Bois did not compensate. It was, as Edward offensively told the estate agent on their way downstairs, just right for a very short can-can dancer.

The last straw was discovering in the course of their conversation on the drive back that the flat cost 750 francs a month

23

more than his rent allowance from the paper, a sum which the woman from the agency had smilingly assured him she would in no circumstances exceed.

Arriving at the office, distinctly depressed, Edward found on his desk a scribbled invitation to dinner the following evening from Henry Hirshfeld. There was no sign of Henry himself and Marie-Yvette told Edward in an offhand way that Henry had gone out to interview a mad priest and wouldn't be back any more that day. Edward left a note of acceptance on Henry's desk. He was slightly ashamed of how glad he was to accept, having rather to his disgust managed to get fairly lonely and miserable over the few evenings spent on his own. That was not how he saw himself; he was resilient, enterprising, by now he ought to have engineered an adventure or two. But the sort of adventure he might have engineered in London – drunken dares, hoax phone calls, the public embarrassment of an old friend – required companions or at least an appreciative audience to come home to. The mundane repetition of a meal alone followed by a walk or a film, and then going to bed by himself in what he termed his geriatric bedroom, with no prospect yet of any change, had very quickly got him down. He couldn't help dwelling, too, on the nights he should have been spending, tropical nights, with the windows open on a non-stop street-life and insistent music. He would welcome, he thought sullenly, climbing under the pink candlewick, the disturbed sleep, the mosquito bites, the sweating.

The hotel played a nasty trick on him. He was woken in the night by two voices crying out in passion in the room next door. After their quite phenomenally noisy crescendo, Edward could hear them panting and chuckling and commenting to one another. His second night, he heard quite distinctly that they were speaking Portuguese. Wherever they were from, their stamina couldn't fail to impress him when he was woken by a repeat performance, this time with a climactic cry of *"Senhora da Gloria!"* only a couple of hours later. Sleepy and irritated, he pulled the pillow over his head, but in the morning they were at it again, less energetically this time, it was true, but he could still clearly hear whoops of female laughter and the sound of flailing limbs knocking the wall. Crabbily and uncomfortably, he soaped himself hard in the

24

shower. He used the pretext that he had not yet found a local café ready to serve him a comfortable breakfast at eight o'clock to stay in the hotel for breakfast and try to identify the couple. No likely candidates appeared and it wasn't until Friday morning, when he happened to meet them leaving their room and travelled down in the lift with them and their luggage that he realised they had been at breakfast after all but they were such an unlikely pair that he had failed to identify them. They were short and fat and very far from beautiful; a dark and hirsute pair with prominent, fleshy features and stubby, gold-laden fingers. Edward put their age admiringly at around fifty. He saw their suitcases were plastered with Varig labels and, because they were preparing to pay their hotel bill, they were holding in their stubby, jewelled fingers green Brazilian passports.

Henry Hirshfeld lived in the Marais, an area Edward had not really ventured into on his previous trips to Paris, for all that he thought he knew the city, and he was a bit put out to find that it seemed to be one of its most beautiful districts. Following Henry's brief but accurate directions, he came out of the Metro at Saint Paul, took a left, second right, another left, another right, and found himself on the corner of the street Henry had written down for him. He was about twenty minutes too early. As he walked around the neighbourhood to fill in time, he was astonished to find himself in the middle of something virtually mediaeval. Although it was still quite light, the narrow streets seemed to hold their own darkness. For some reason Edward couldn't fathom, nearly all the shops were closed and shuttered and there was almost no one about. As he admired, despite his stubborn intentions, the crooked façades and deep courtyards, he suddenly noticed two stars of David painted on the windows of one of the few unshuttered shops. 'Oh,' he thought dimly, 'a Jewish shop.' But then he noticed there were stars of David and what he was pretty certain were Hebrew shop signs the whole way up and down the street. Taken aback, he retraced his steps. He had just walked unheedingly through what seemed to be an entirely Jewish neighbourhood. Since the twenty minutes were more than up, he turned in the direction of Henry's address, but he was still shocked by what he had failed to notice. Those streets in the summer twilight were somewhere a long way away. He had crassly overlooked it, but they weren't in Paris at all. And as he found the corner of Henry Hirshfeld's street again, he wondered in an uncertain groping way if it were out of some sort of tribal loyalty that Hirshfeld had chosen to live there.

Henry's home was at the back of one of those deep court-yards, a courtyard which had been considerably smartened up, certainly, but which, despite its scrubbed stone and ultra-modern lighting, retained its venerable character. Edward was impressed by the weighty wooden double front doors, through one of which you stepped into the renovated courtyard, which came as something of a shock behind the unassuming dark façade. He climbed to the second floor up a broad, immaculately white stone staircase and then stood for a few seconds, feeling ridiculously unsure of himself and eager to make a good impression, in front of the bell marked "Hirshfeld/Nguyen".

Henry opened the door, still in the same checked shirt and cords he had been wearing at the office and Edward felt a fool for having changed into a fresh shirt and a tie. Henry showed him through a short corridor, hung with so many paintings Edward did not manage to focus on any single one, into a large, comfortably furnished living-room. Almost at the same moment as they entered the room from the corridor, a small figure whom Edward took to be Mrs Hirshfeld came in at the other end. Although Edward had registered that Henry's wife was Vietnamese, he hadn't actually stopped to consider what she might be like. If he had given her any thought at all, it was to expect that she would be a sinewy, self-confident modern American woman inside a Vietnamese shell. The woman who walked towards him, smiling and holding out both hands, surprised him so much that he was worried he might have momentarily gaped at her. She was extremely small, and seemed, if possible, even smaller beside her lumbering husband. She had her hair scooped strictly into a perfectly round bun, like a neat silk pincushion on the top of her head, and through it she had stuck what Edward thought of vaguely as a single lacquered chopstick. She was wearing

27

black cotton ski-pants, bead-embroidered cloth sandals and something rather like a smock in whose abstract pattern there seemed to be a dab of every bright colour known to man. She greeted Edward just as her husband had by taking his single politely held out hand in both of hers and Edward wondered briefly which of them had had the gesture first.

"Hi, Edward," she said in twangy Oriental American English, "I'm Mai."

They sat and had drinks in the pleasant living-room. Side by side on one of the two low settees, Henry and Mrs Hirshfeld formed such a total contrast that, at first, Edward had a little difficulty concentrating on the conversation. Just before they went to table, the child of this most unlikely couple came into the room. She had her mother's glossy hair and Oriental complexion but although she was only, Edward guessed, about ten, she already showed signs of growing tall like her father. She stood rather gawkily in the doorway and confronted them from under her fringe, possibly a bit put out, Edward thought, to see the visitor.

Henry introduced her. "This is Dina, also known as Dinh. We gave her a name which adapted equally well to both sides of her heritage. It's very convenient for her; some days she's one, some days she's the other." And, not in the least patronisingly, but perfectly seriously, he asked his daughter, "Which are you today, honey?"

The child shot Edward a short but he felt on the whole uncomplimentary look before answering shortly, "Dinh."

The meal was easy, not in the least taxing. The subject of work and the paper only came up once or twice in a relaxed, tangential way. The Hirshfelds' horizons clearly extended far beyond the recurring themes and vocabulary of journalism. Even when a phone call for Henry from the New York office disrupted the main course, nobody seemed particularly interested in using it as a pretext for bringing the conversation back to work and Edward's expected contribution to it. They talked about the euphoria that had greeted the Socialists' victory at the last elections, the dancing that had gone on for most of the night at the Place de la Bastille, the planned cultural developments in the capital, and, at one point, the subject having been arbitrarily introduced by Dinh, they all talked perfectly seriously for at least ten minutes about the sadism of spinster teachers.

Edward decided to walk back to his hotel. The evening had contradictorily both cheered him and further depressed him. Naturally he was pleased at the prospect of having at least one place in Paris where he knew he would spend further educational evenings. But, at the same time, the family scene had reinforced his feeling that he was stuck in a stolidly bourgeois city, where life was lived according to the same old encrusted patterns. For all their appearance of unconventionality, the Hirshfelds were after all just a middle-aged married couple, leading a comfortable, settled life. And if there were one thing Edward could not stand the thought of, it was marriage. The mere idea of tying yourself to the one person forever and, even worse, voluntarily giving up your freedom to take off into the blue, to do as you liked, made him shudder. He thought marriage was a kind of communal madness and every time one or another of his acquaintances succumbed to it, he saw it as another manifestation of the herd instinct, the terror-stricken lemming rush over the cliff, to which he intended to remain forever immune. It was the early signs of this distressing aberration which had made him so very relieved to part from Rosie.

After a fortnight, Edward had forgotten all about his early attempts at optimism. The last of the summer weather was appropriately succeeded by low grey skies and a spiteful diagonal drizzle, through which he went resentfully to and from the paper. Almost all his leisure hours were devoted to trying to find a place to live and he got so discouraged by the end of the second week that he even considered moving into the box in Neuilly after all. It was not that there was any pressure on him to move out of his hotel; Henry, when the subject came up, said easily, "Oh, give it at least a month." But Edward was sick of his bedroom furniture, of the lace curtains, of the limply trickling shower. He was fed up too with what he felt to be the reception staff's faintly condescending *"Bonjour, Monsieur"* and *"Bonsoir, Monsieur"* every time he went in or out. He was fed up, above all, with the lack of autonomy brought about by not having a place of his own.

The search for a flat did nothing to endear Paris to him. Of course, he had not been brilliantly well-disposed towards the place from the day he arrived when, in a moment of far-fetched global gloom, he had seen in a *charcuterie* window all his ambitions put to rest on a bed of aspic, glazed, reduced to a miniature *hors d'oeuvre*-sized spoof of a journey, and trimmed with cross-sections of stuffed olives. He had come to Paris,

30

already disliking it, not only for what it was but for all that it wasn't. In that first fortnight, the city exceeded even his dire expectations.

His first weekend would be memorable, he realised, even while he was getting through it, for its gloom. With the estate agents shut, he decided to have a look on his own. He bought several papers and tried telephoning some of the numbers given in the property columns. Out of six numbers he ringed, two were estate agents' answering machines informing him in bright metallic voices that their offices were closed on Saturday, two of the flats were already let and the final two, which he managed to make appointments to view on the Saturday afternoon, both led him to such grotesque and unpleasant encounters that he was faintly shaken.

He took a taxi to view the first one which was in the fifth *arrondissement*, near the Jardin des Plantes. Three times, the driver flew into vicious shouting altercations with other drivers: someone had run someone else too close, somebody had braked too sharply, somebody else didn't know left from right. When the traffic slowed to a complete standstill, the driver explained to Edward where the problem lay, bawling his abhorrent theory at the top of his voice above the battery of furious car horns: the fault lay with the immigrants from backward countries. That wasn't just his opinion; it was a recognised fact. In the first place, there were too many of them, which in itself caused congestion; it was obvious. But the real trouble started when they got behind the wheel of a taxi; they had no road sense at all. What could you expect; they came from countries where there weren't proper roads, just dirt tracks, for the most part, and they had no idea how to drive in a modern metropolis. They drove here, around the Etoile and the Place de la Concorde, as if they were still in the bush and, not surprisingly, there were straight away accidents and terrible traffic jams. And the worst of it was you weren't allowed to say a thing. If you stood up in public and reproached them with anything, there were immediately howls of "Racist!" It drove him mad. He wasn't a racist, there was nobody less racist than he; he just believed in everybody in their proper place, that was all. He had nothing against those Mohammeds back in Sidi-bel-Abbès. It was when they

31

came over here that he began to see red. Would he go and set up as a taxi driver in Sidi-bel-Abbès and take away their livelihood? They were ruining the reputation of taxi drivers, the way they carried on.

He deposited Edward at the address he had been given. His abuse, provoked by the reproachfully small size of his tip, followed Edward across the pavement until, losing patience and taking out on the driver the steadily mounting hostility he felt towards the entire city, Edward turned and stuck two fingers in his direction.

He had liked the idea of being near the Jardin des Plantes. Judging from his admittedly brief exposure to Paris parks, he doubted if it would be of any use for any of the normal purposes of parks: jogging, lying on the grass, relaxing. But the location was promising and the rent well within the limits sanctioned by the accountant, Monsieur, it turned out, not Rat but Rapp. He was a bit discouraged to see that the house seemed to be the most run down in the whole road; next to it was a building site, still at the early stage of being a rubble-filled pit, and it looked as though this house might any day follow suit. Dispiritedly, Edward rang the front door bell and pushed the dark green front door, which had clicked open in response. He found himself in a small, dark but very strong-smelling entrance hall. Someone had been boiling vegetables in the vicinity for a number of years. As instructed, he climbed the ill-kept round staircase to the third floor and rang the bell of the left-hand flat. Almost at once, the door sprang open, as though the flat owner had been listening to his footsteps coming up the stairs, and Edward was confronted with one of the most grotesque human beings he had ever seen.

For some seconds, he was unable to decide if the person in front of him was a woman or a man. Its clothes, not to mention its physical attributes, indicated clearly that it was a woman: a tight-fitting green skirt and a peach blouse filled with a fairly hefty bosom. It had light red hair, elaborately styled and set. But there was something in its bold stance as it stood, legs slightly too far apart, on the threshold, and continued to hold onto the door handle with one large hand, which was unmistakably male. Its voice, when it spoke, put an end to any doubt.

"You've come to see the flat, I take it?" he asked in a scratchy but not unpleasant tenor. *"Entrez, Monsieur, s'il vous plaît."*

Edward hesitated on the landing. "Are you Monsieur Comblat?"

The person laughed, a high-pitched, strained trill.

"Madame or Monsieur, whichever you prefer." He took a step back and beckoned again to Edward to come inside. He added confidingly, "I prefer Madame."

Ninety-nine per cent of Edward wanted to stay out on the landing. But some tiny perverse hunt for a story persuaded him to go in. Besides, it was a bit difficult at that stage to think of a polite reason not to.

The small flat looked as if the owner had no intention of moving out in the near future. It was stacked from floor to ceiling with records and yellowing back numbers of distinctly odd magazines. A tailor's dummy sporting garish theatrical make-up dominated the living-room.

After a guided tour in which he successively mocked each of the cluttered rooms with a disproportionately grandiose commentary, the owner explained cautiously to Edward what he had in mind. He wished to let the flat but not completely, as it were; he had just got a new job which was going to involve a lot of touring – he was, he informed Edward airily, in *"le showbusiness"* – but he wanted to hang onto his Paris base. What he proposed was that Edward rent the flat, complete with all his trappings and weird magazines, but at an exceptionally low rent, on the understanding that every fortnight or so he would be free to come back and spend a couple of nights there to "recharge his batteries". Edward declined the offer to stay and reconsider his decision over coffee, which followed his prompt refusal. He gave Monsieur Comblat an unnecessarily wide berth in the front hall and still shuddered at his hard, vindictive handshake halfway down the stairs.

He was so very relieved to be out of the house and safely in the street again that he didn't take note of where he was going. He found himself walking beside the railings of what was presumably the Jardin des Plantes. Suddenly he was shocked by a perfectly hideous, inhuman cackle. Only after a moment of extreme alarm did he notice the netting of a big aviary beyond the railings and realise that inside was the zoo.

After that, he thought that whatever the second flat had in store for him would be an anti-climax. He was tempted, in fact, to give it a miss altogether. He was tired and he couldn't believe that Paris had anything worthwhile to offer him, that weekend or at all. But the flat was almost on his way back to the hotel and he thought that he had nothing better to do with the rest of his afternoon.

He found the rue Guynemer for the second time on his flapping *Plan de Paris*. It ran alongside the Luxembourg gardens and until he saw its stern, shuttered houses, he thought it might be rather an agreeable place to live, lying as it did at almost the dead centre of the map. He was greeted by a small but visibly ferocious old lady, dressed in a raincoat and holding a furled frilly umbrella. For a moment, he thought she was going to tell him that the flat had already been let; she was only waiting for him to arrive to go out. But it turned out that, although she had given him her address over the phone, the flat to let was actually off the rue Guynemer, a few minutes' walk away. She didn't allow Edward so much as a glimpse of the inside of her own flat. She whipped the front door shut behind her and double-locked two locks at the top and bottom of the door. As they bustled over to the other flat – the old lady's heels rapped severely on the pavement – she cross-questioned Edward about his credentials, shooting sharp sideways looks at him as they scurried along. She appeared displeased that he was a journalist. She repeated several times, approvingly, that the previous tenant had been a gynaecologist. She asked Edward which paper he worked for and, when she hadn't heard of it, to tell her the French equivalent; was it *Figaro* or *Le Monde?*

The flat was desolate; it was at the back of another sombre apartment house like her own, high ceilinged and spacious but almost without natural light. Its rooms, which all opened off to the right of a long, sinister hall, looked out onto an adjacent blank wall where a scrawl of etiolated ivy only underlined the bleakness. The room smelt unpleasantly of mothballs and the furniture was mostly hidden under opaque plastic covers, two of which, the old lady informed him, she would ask him to keep on to protect the better armchairs. The bathroom finished him off; it was a skimpily partitioned slice of the hall, without a window, into which were crammed what looked like half a bath with an indecent little step to sit on, an antiquated washbasin, a bidet and a monstrous water heater which, when the old lady switched it on momentarily to show him how the system worked, started to pant horribly with steadily mounting hoarse breaths. The old lady chose this moment of maximum horror to tell him that there had been a misprint in the advertisement. The figure given for the rent was too low; where they had put a five, there should of course have been a seven. Edward turned to her, pleased with his outward calm. "I know plenty of more cheerful cemeteries where I could stay for a lot less," he said.

Later, in the evening, he went out to find something to eat and some entertainment if he could. He found himself drifting back towards the Marais where he had had dinner the night before. The streets which had been closed and silent had somehow or other come back to life. They were full of the most exuberantly un-Parisian people bustling to and fro and the shop window shutters had been raised to reveal equally un-Parisian displays of seven-branched candelabra and silver tasselled shawls. He found a shabby North African restaurant in a backstreet which was pleasingly unlike the smart expense account sort of place he could have been eating in. Although half the items on the menu were unintelligible to him – *Brik à l'œuf, Merguez* – he managed to have a reasonable meal amid the high-pitched Oriental music and the constant coming and going of the owner's acquaintances for what seemed to be free glasses of mint tea. He took as long as he decently could over his dinner to stay in the restaurant's social embrace, although he was forced to give up on a deathly sweet pastry which seemed to set all his fillings jangling like alarm bells.

Afterwards, he couldn't find any entertainment he wanted to see on his own. With Roland or Guy, he might have gone to jeer at somewhere like the Crazy Horse but on his own it seemed profoundly sordid. He walked back to the hotel through the party-going crowds of a Saturday night, feeling like the classic outsider from French A-level, and Sunday,

35

when he couldn't make any business appointments to reduce the time available to stew, was even worse.

On Thursday or Friday of the following week, as he came back into the office from some specious errand he had invented to make himself seem busier than he yet was, Marie-Yvette told him he had had a phone call from Mrs Hirshfeld. She handed him the number and added, "It was something to do with a flat."

Edward's heart plummeted. The last thing he wanted was for the paper to get involved in his accommodation arrangements. The more elusive his Paris flat became, the more convinced he was that it would be his only hope of redeeming his time here. Above all, he didn't want that slender possibility appropriated by the paper too, so that his single remaining chance of displacement was removed.

He went into his office and sat there for a while, feeling disgruntled and also apprehensive, before he lifted the receiver and dialled Henry's home number.

The phone was answered by Dinh. While she was fetching her mother, Edward prepared a polite explanation of why he could not take up Mrs Hirshfeld's proposition, whatever it might be. Her bright, "Hi, Edward" interrupted his train of thought.

He mumbled, "Oh, hello, Mrs Hirshfeld. I was told you telephoned while I was out. I'm sorry I wasn't here to speak to you. I'd just gone off for a bit to deal with some bureaucracy."

Her laugh was high and concise like a wind chime. "Don't worry, Edward. Have you found a flat yet? Henry told me the other day you were still looking, you were having a lot of problems."

"I've sort of got something in mind," Edward lied.

"You have? That's great. Where is it?"

Edward thrashed around. "I haven't seen it yet. It's just the estate agent told me this morning she had something a bit more promising sounding. I'm afraid I don't remember the address exactly."

Mrs Hirshfeld marked an infinitesimal pause. "Well, take down this number anyway," she instructed him. "It might not be what you want. But I think it is worth looking into."

36

The number, she explained, belonged to another teacher at the school where she taught art. By a complete coincidence she had been talking to this other teacher in the staff room a few days previously and she had happened to mention that a flat which she and her family rented out was standing empty. It was the last chapter of a long story involving an unsatisfactory tenant. Anyway, she, Mrs Hirshfeld, hadn't given it another thought until a couple of days ago Henry had quite by chance spoken at dinner about Edward's difficulties and she had remembered Mademoiselle Iskarov. She had spoken to her about it again that morning when she went into the *lycée* and it seemed the flat was still vacant and the Iskarovs, who only let it via personal contact and not through advertisements, would be happy for Edward to come along and have a look at it.

Drearily, Edward took down the address and then the difficult name as well. Mrs Hirshfeld spelt it out, "I-s-k-a-r-o-v", and then she added enthusiastically, as though it were a recommendation, for some reason preferable to teaching maths or gymn or biology, "She teaches Russian."

Edward decided he would wait for a few days in the hope that the choosy Iskarovs would have found somebody else by the time he rang. He had to ring, of course; his initial brief temptation to lose the piece of paper with the address and the telephone number was not an option. If Henry didn't think to ask why he hadn't been to see the flat, the Russian teacher was bound to.

That weekend he had too much to drink; on Friday night in an Indonesian restaurant and on Saturday night in an Afro-Caribbean night club. He had spotted the club just a few streets away from his hotel and put its closed door and red light bulbs in the category of places to steer well clear of. But he had already drunk enough to have shed a few preconceptions as he walked back to the hotel on Saturday night and, seeing the door flick open to admit a group of loudly protesting West Indians who had been beating on the locked door, he gave way to a moment's fatalistic curiosity and followed them inside.

Downstairs, where the air was thick with heat, tobacco and other smoke, and the insistently thudding rhythm of a five-piece band, white customers were in a self-conscious minority. Edward bought another drink and squeezed into a seat rather too close to the pounding *"Soleil du Sénégal"*. Although hardly anyone looked at him and no one spoke to him, he felt peculiarly pleased to be there. Resolutely turning their back on the European city outside, the West Indians were creating a concentrated version of what they were homesick for; more tropical than the tropics themselves.

The address intrigued him. Finally, the following weekend, he could not put off any longer contacting Mrs Hirshfeld's teacher friend. He had seen two more impossible flats in the course of that week, and a third which was to all outward appearances perfectly acceptable but, he knew, totally wrong. It was in a large, beige, slab-like block built, according to the date stamped at the bottom left-hand corner of the façade, in 1927. Its entrance hall and stairs had marbled walls which looked like cross-sections cut through an immense pudding. As you climbed the stairs, you could identify darker veins which looked like trickles of a syrupy sauce. Unless he could find an alternative fairly soon, he saw he would end up living there.

As he ran his finger over the seventh *arrondissement* on the map, trying to find the puzzlingly named street in which the Iskarovs lived, an unmistakable sensation of defeat settled over him. It had been ridiculous to suppose he could set out on a worthwhile journey within a stationary city. He might as well reconcile himself to living inside the pudding, where he would spend a pampered, stifled, utterly pointless year. For he had no intention of renting anything from a colleague of his boss's wife.

However, if only for the sake of good manners, he had to

go through with it. Once he had located the Cité Etienne Hubert, a blunt cul-de-sac off the Avenue Duquesne, he tried telephoning. There was no reply on Saturday morning and he was considerably relieved. He spent the best part of the day wandering the grimy northern reaches of the Boulevard Barbès and La Chapelle. Henry had let drop in the office that those neighbourhoods were the closest you would come to the Third World in Paris. Edward thought maybe he could write a piece about them; a spoof travelogue as a rather dismal private joke. But the misery, bitterness and hostility he thought he could read in the inhabitants' faces were not conducive to a jokey treatment. Besides, he was propositioned too often for comfort by some spectacularly stomach-churning prostitutes. On the Boulevard de Rochechouart, he came upon a loathsome rubber doll in a brightly lit glass case; when a passer-by inserted a coin, the doll's vacant eyes and lumpen breasts rotated mechanically for thirty seconds. A surreptitious coin dropped as Edward approached drew an immediate small crowd.

In the late afternoon, he tried the Iskarovs' number again and he was a bit put out then that there was still no answer since viewing the flat would have been a convenient way to fill in the time before the evening.

On Sunday morning, there was again no answer. By then, it seemed clear they had gone away for the weekend. Edward didn't try again and spent most of the day, it was wet and cold, reading on his bed: a couple of hours each of Theodore Zeldin's *The French*, Richard Cobb on France's war record, and Borges. Consequently, he was more than slightly indignant when he rang one last time out of boredom at half past six and was immediately told by the woman who answered the telephone that they had been waiting for him to ring for days.

"Come over and look at the flat now," she suggested. "I'm not busy."

Edward leant across from the bed and lifted a corner of his lace curtains. Long ropes of rain were slapping against the window and it was almost dark. He said, "I think I'd rather see it in the daylight, if you don't mind."

To his irritation, the woman at the other end positively snorted. "There is electric light there, you know."

Edward thought, 'If you're not going to bother to be polite, I really don't see why I should either.' But, mindful of the constricting connection with the Hirshfelds, he ad-libbed, "It'd be difficult timewise too tonight. I've got a dinner appointment later. Could I come and see it during the week?"

There was a clatter at the other end and then a long silence as though the receiver had been accidentally dropped.

"Hello?" said Edward. "Hello? Hello?"

He was wondering whether or not to hang up and also whether or not to bother to redial afterwards when the woman returned.

"I'm not teaching on Wednesday or Thursday mornings," she informed him. "Or on Friday afternoon. Could you make any of those?"

"Wednesday morning would be fine," Edward said. "What sort of time?"

The woman gave a gusty sigh, as if contemplating many weary hours filled with a round of unwelcome chores. "Eleven?" she suggested.

"Fine," Edward agreed. "Fine, I'll be there. Eleven o'clock on Wednesday. Number Nine, Cité Etienne Hubert."

"It's the last but one house in the street," the woman said. "On the left, the last but one."

Edward reflected, as he dressed against the rain to go out and get some dinner, that the Russian name and Mrs Hirshfeld's enthusiasm about it seemed distinctly irrelevant. The woman had sounded to him like a typical, hard-hearted Parisian bitch.

He made sure to mention to Henry where he was off to on Wednesday morning although, to be fair, Henry didn't seem in the least interested. He asked the taxi for the Avenue Duquesne, since the Cité Etienne Hubert was such a small street, and being in good time, he got down at the southern end of the avenue and strolled up.

It was a grey day and there was little difference in colour between the weighty apartment houses on either side of the wide avenue and the sky. The brightest things in the streets were the yellowing autumn leaves, which were just beginning to fall, and reflected a cheering yellow radiance off the

41

pavements as he walked along with his head bowed. Until he reached the corner of the Cité Etienne Hubert, everything ran along predictable, ornate Parisian grooves.

It was hardly a street at all; that was his first thought as he confronted the high wall in which it ended so abruptly only a few hundred yards away. There were about six apartment houses on either side, all of the same stolid mould, and then, immediately, a towering blank wall which ran from façade to façade of the two end houses and blocked off all perspective, views or passage. It rose to fourth-floor height at least, covered completely by a flourishing dark green ivy whose tentacles were just beginning to encroach on the adjacent houses.

'No wonder,' Edward thought, feeling his first inkling of sympathy for Mademoiselle Iskarov, 'no wonder she had made such a point of not living next to the wall.' The closer he came to it, the more overbearing it seemed; the last two houses looked grimly overshadowed.

Number Nine, like all the other houses, was a pompous seven storeys of stone wreaths and stone fruit: pebbly grapes and fossil pineapples. Because he had been looking at Paris apartment houses for nearly three extremely long weeks, Edward noticed it had been built, like its neighbours, in 1901 and the architect was one F. AD. Bocage. Bocage! Small wood or copse? Edward felt a sudden warmth for the man who had covered his otherwise dull creations with his own bucolic symbols. That, surely, must be the explanation of the stone greenery up and down the street: Bocage's trademark across Bocage's façades. In the moment before he arrived at the front door and rang the brass bell coldly labelled "Ring then Push", he indulged in a very brief but entertaining fantasy in which houses built by Monsieur Rat were adorned with rodents, by Monsieur Dubonnet with appropriate bottles and by Monsieur Lamour with erotica. It was the sort of joke which, if Guy and Roland had been there with him, would have gone on for days. It put him, as he rang then pushed the immensely heavy glass and green ironwork front door, in the first spontaneous good mood he had been in for a fairly long time.

The lift was at the ground floor waiting for him so, as Mademoiselle Iskarov had told him her flat was up on the fifth floor, he took it and, as it rose, shivering and giving out a weird mechanical moan, he thought that he wouldn't mind living in this building at all. Immediately, even before the lift had travelled another floor, he remembered that the flat he was coming to view was, of course, somewhere else entirely.

The door was opened by a handkerchief. Or at least that was Edward's first impression, as a muted honking noise behind the door gave way to a small woman obviously suffering from an outsize cold. Her face was almost entirely covered by a man's checked handkerchief. Apart from her watering brown eyes, he could not see anything of her looks or even particularly of her age. He registered vaguely that she was wearing a rather fashionable and dramatic black and maroon knitted outfit, which did not, to his taste, go awfully well with her tinted auburn hair.

He said, "Oh dear, I'm Edward Wainwright. It doesn't look as if I've chosen an awfully good day to come."

After a severe spluttering cough behind her handkerchief, the woman let out a dramatic groan. "I completely forgot you were coming." She hesitated, one hand on the edge of the door and the other still clamping her burka-like handkerchief to her face. "I'm afraid I can't possibly come over there with you. I've got the most terrible cold."

"I can see that," Edward answered, he was aware, a trifle ungraciously. "But can't you give me the key and tell me how to get there? I mean, I've taken time off work specially to come over here and see it."

The woman eyed him up and down and, unexpectedly, considering her indignities of streaming eyes and spluttering, Edward felt at a sudden disadvantage for she was so protected by the handkerchief.

"Come in," she said, evidently not needing any further persuasion, which he couldn't help but be marginally flattered by. "I'll find the keys and I'll explain to you how to go there."

She shut the door behind him and led him through an overfurnished hall, sneezing so explosively, he really did feel rather sorry for her.

He said, "Gosh, I hope you're treating yourself to a couple of days off work with this."

43

She nodded miserably and then said quite distinctly through the handkerchief, with surprising vehemence, "That *lycée* is the source of every sort of sickness."

She showed him into a huge living-room and said formally, "Please sit here. I'll go and get the keys."

Like the hall, the living-room was crowded well beyond the point of cosiness with dark bulky furniture, overloaded bookcases and dressers and standard lamps trailing a tangle of flexes across Oriental carpets. At first, as in any house he might have found himself in, Edward got up to look at the view from the living-room windows, but since it was only a mirror image in the form of Number Ten, Cité Etienne Hubert across the street, he turned his attention back to the living-room. It struck him as an inappropriate backdrop for someone as relatively young and dynamic as Mademoiselle Iskarov; it must surely be the family home. She was distinctly too old, though, however old she was, still to be living at home with her parents. Edward began to examine the contents of the living-room considerably more closely. Whereupon it dawned on him, belatedly, that a high proportion of the objects in the room were indeed Russian: there was a silver samovar and some old photographs of bearded men in boots and smocks on one of the dressers; some of the pictures turned out on proper investigation to be icons and, yes, all the books in the bookcases were in Russian.

When Mademoiselle Iskarov came back, she had changed her handkerchief. She had also, Edward was astonished to notice, combed her hair and pulled her knitted top and skirt into shape so that he could see, whatever her indeterminate age, she had a well-endowed if round figure.

She held the keys out to him. "I've written down the address for you. It's not difficult to find. It's off the rue Saint Dominique. You can either go up the Boulevard de Latour-Maubourg or Avenue Bosquet. Bosquet is less direct but more pleasant, I think, less – " she hesitated and squared her shoulders, "less designed for victorious military processions, you know."

Edward laughed. "I know exactly."

He unfolded his map and Mademoiselle Iskarov pinpointed the rue Surcouf. It all sounded excellent: two bedrooms, a

44

good-sized sitting-room, the rent was reasonable. Edward thought what a pity it was that if the flat were even halfway decent, he would still feel obliged to turn it down because of his scruples about mixing work connections and housing.

As Mademoiselle Iskarov showed him to the front door, he thought he heard a very faint noise somewhere off the hall. Through an open doorway, he thought, but wasn't certain, he caught a grey blur of movement. He must have looked concerned for Mademoiselle Iskarov raised her voice to call something in Russian in the direction of the open doorway and she explained to Edward: "My grandmother." While they stood at the front door and clarified the final details of locks and keys and *concierges*, Edward became clearly conscious of a quavering voice holding forth uninterruptedly from the unseen room.

He had his hand above the ground-floor button of the lift when he heard the door of the Iskarovs' flat flung open. With one of the worst pronunciations of his name he had yet heard, Mademoiselle Iskarov called, "Mister Wenwright! Mister Wenwright! Please stop!"

Edward pushed open the lift door and said, "Yes?"

"You don't cook a lot with curry, do you?" she panted and then, seeing the exasperated bemusement on his face, explained, "Our last tenant was an American follower of Hinduism. He made the most awful mess of the kitchen. The neighbours complained of his smells. We had to tell him to leave. Well, he was mad too."

"No," Edward answered shortly. "I don't."

"Very good," said Mademoiselle Iskarov. "Then, if you wish, you may rent our flat." And, in a flurry of horrible coughing, she vanished behind the front door.

The appropriateness of the rue Surcouf was obvious as soon as he turned the street corner. The Iskarovs' flat was only two or three houses along, in a low, by Paris standards, shabbily off-white house. Its neighbours were a similar house and a small, workaday baker's shop. He had come via Mademoiselle Iskarov's recommended route, walking along the bustling commercial length of the rue Saint Dominique. The neighbourhood seemed to him much closer to what he was looking for than anywhere else he had yet been. Behind these

45

façades, he could imagine muzzled poodles and simmering *tripes à la mode de Caen*, but not marbled stairwells or bidets on silver-gilt paws. When he identified the house, he felt almost frustrated that somewhere so eminently appropriate had to be out of the question because of his scruples.

Standing in his future living-room, he abandoned them. For everything about the flat delighted him: it consisted of three partially inter-connecting rooms, with double doors between them, like a jigsaw puzzle or some elementary set of children's cubes. He walked through them, enjoying the clever satisfactory way the living-room led into the elbow-shaped kitchen, and from the further bedroom you could look back at the living-room windows. The flat was on the ground floor; overshadowed but not gloomy, it took up the right-hand side and half the back of a small, dingy courtyard and the left-hand side was occupied by someone whose name on the letter-box was Dupont. Edward found it all thoroughly cheery and authentic and congenial. He grinned at the lingering curry smells in his kitchen and the burnt-out joss sticks by the front door and felt positively grateful to the American "follower of Hinduism" for having had himself evicted at such a timely juncture. A straight choice between this flat and the marble pudding was no choice at all.

When he rang the front door bell of Mademoiselle Iskarov's flat to return the keys and to tell her, to his surprise, that he would like to rent the flat, there was at first no answer. He rang the bell again and waited for a long time. Maybe in her scatty way she had gone out and forgotten about him? Or maybe she was bombed out of her mind with the French equivalent of Night Nurse? He began to scribble a message on a sheet of his pocket notepad. On the other side of the door, there was an undeniable rustle. Remembering the possibly crazed old grandmother, he shouted, "It's me, Edward Wainwright. About the flat."

Mademoiselle Iskarov's voice answered him. "You can't come in."

'What now?' thought Edward. And what on earth was going on inside? Mademoiselle Iskarov was in no fit state to have got herself into any compromising situation. Maybe the aged grandmother had run amok?

46

He shouted, "I've brought the keys back."

"Put them in the letter-box downstairs," Mademoiselle Iskarov replied in a muffled voice.

"But I have to talk to you," Edward protested. "I want to rent the flat. We need to discuss arrangements and things."

"Good. I'm very pleased you're going to take it," came Mademoiselle Iskarov's voice. "But I'm afraid I can't let you in. We'll discuss it all on the phone."

"Why can't you let me in?" Edward exploded. "It'll take three minutes."

There was a very long pause, such a long pause that he wondered if he hadn't blown it. Goodbye, rue Surcouf.

"I realise you're not feeling well," he added placatingly. "But, really, it won't take any time. I'd just like to have it all settled before I go back to the office."

Behind him, he was aware of inquisitive footsteps coming to the door of the flat opposite.

Lowering his voice, he said, "Listen, I don't want to be a pain. So long as it's definite I can have the flat." And lastly, a bit guiltily, he asked, "Nothing's the matter, is it? You are OK?"

Inside, there was a noise which was either a cough or a laugh. "I can't let you see me in this condition," Mademoiselle Iskarov answered. "It is too disgraceful."

Edward had fairly serious doubts as he walked away down the Avenue Duquesne about whether he ought to get any further involved with this family. Considering he had seen Mademoiselle Iskarov in her full-blown "disgraceful condition" only an hour beforehand, he found her sudden onset of vanity largely comic but also faintly disconcerting.

A month after his arrival in Paris, Edward moved into the rue Surcouf. He didn't have much to move; he prided himself on travelling light. A taxi ride liberated him from the lace curtains and the dribbling shower and he found himself and his two suitcases inside his own front door, with an angular void to fill.

He did have a low patch immediately after moving, but it was short-lived. The door-slamming certainty of being settled in Paris, which the flat in the rue Surcouf represented, provoked another sad little flurry of comparison with all the other places where he might have been. The Duponts' macaw, which warbled advertising jingles from their window-sill – "*Orangina – à la PULPE d'orange*" and again and again "*Felix Potin – on y revient*" – caricatured the narrow domestic horizons he feared he was now confined to. He had never had any time for domesticity. He hurried through the necessary procedures to take over the flat and the uninteresting but essential household purchases. Much as he liked the flat, he didn't put up any pictures or do anything to improve the decoration, beyond taking down the last of the American's unnerving posters. That would have been too frank an admission of long-term residence. He concentrated on ignoring the things which triggered the worst of his wanderlust: the slanting sun stripes falling through the shutters first thing in the morning, which should have been from a real sun, the Portuguese *concierge's* wife singing a throaty folk melody as she washed the flagstones of the courtyard. He viewed this as a reverse Pavlovian-dog training and he was quick to learn. Relatively fast, he reverted to resignation, for the primary obstacle which had stood in the way of his embarking on Paris life was gone. Without any more flat hunting, he was free to make of the city whatever he could.

Neither Henry nor Mrs Hirshfeld made any further reference to the role they had played in helping him find his home. They had him to dinner a second time about a week after he moved in and, although he arrived thanking Mrs Hirshfeld profusely for her thoughtfulness, she did not take him up on it.

He had not expected to be left quite so much to his own devices. Of course, he didn't want to be overseen either. But Henry's completely *laissez-faire* managerial style left him pretty much on his own. Henry was kept busy with his weekly *Letter from Paris* and it was obvious that any really big stories which broke Henry would cover. In the first few weeks, Henry took Edward along with him to meet the best press officers, the most useful sources. But once the introductions were over, Edward didn't really have that much to do. He felt it would show a lack of initiative to speak about this to Henry. All he had to do, Henry would surely think, was go out there and find the stories. But Edward wasn't yet well enough acquainted with Paris to know where to find her weak spots. He went to press conferences and dealt with urgent calls for information from the paper's other bureaux. He tried not to cross swords with eccentric old Monsieur Marchais, about whom Henry had warned him. When Monsieur Marchais came in for his querulous couple of hours compiling what he called his *"Rubrique Culturelle"*, Edward would more often than not invent an errand and wander out. It seemed to him more than once that he was wasting his time here on the work front too. He hadn't expected the cinema drama of shrilling phones, chattering telexes, sweat-glistening men rushing in with shouted news of world-shattering events. But he hadn't, frankly, expected such slow motion either.

49

He observed Henry, contentedly going about his worthwhile business of telling it how it was, setting the record straight, and after a while it struck Edward that, for all his apparent nonchalance, Henry was observing him too. The neglect, the casual address was deliberate; Henry was waiting to see what Edward could generate for himself. Edward had no intention of following in the footsteps of his predecessor, one Howard Knapman now at the Wellington bureau, who seemed to have spent his idle hours here elaborating a multi-coloured index card system of Paris contacts. He wanted to show Henry that he understood and was worthy of the blind eye that was being turned to him. But, first of all, in order to land the scoop which would cause Henry to congratulate him, he had to get his bearings. And Henry seemed prepared for him to spend as long as it took to get them.

He had more leisure time than he had anticipated. In London, he would have filled it, no problem, drinking with his friends and he would have been temporarily happy doing that. But here he didn't have any friends. Moreover, he had not yet seen a way of ever acquiring any. If one thing was clear to him about Paris, it was the city's mollusc-like nature; its hard and shiny lips clamped shut on its salty inner workings, it excluded disdainfully all foreign bodies. The house in the rue Surcouf illustrated this principle in microcosm. Edward liked the house, he continued to like it. He came home to it along the rue Saint Dominique sometimes repeating "Surcouf, Surcouf" to himself like the yapping of a little dog. But inside the house he was totally ignored. After nearly a fortnight, he had still not spoken to any of the other residents, apart from the *concierge*, whose French was so rudimentary it was hard to consider what they had a conversation. He had seen Monsieur and Madame Dupont going in and out, a wizened pair with sour, mistrustful, elderly faces. Once he had seen Monsieur Dupont on a sunny Sunday morning cruelly taunting the macaw by offering it scraps of food held just beyond the reach of its beak. The residents of the other flats he had barely seen. There was a middle-aged spinster lady living above him, who came down smartly to complain the day he celebrated the arrival of his first delayed month's salary by buying a stereo cassette player and renting a TV. She made almost no noise at all, although once or twice Edward heard her little pop-eyed dog giving shrill, strangulated barks overhead. Otherwise, the house was unusually quiet. It was enough of an event to hear voices in the courtyard for Edward to slip sheepishly over to a window and snoop outside. Sometimes it was just the macaw giving a particularly life-like eulogy to "*Rasoirs Bic*". Sometimes it was Monsieur or Madame Dupont exchanging parsimonious civilities with the *concierge*. Once, it was an itinerant knife-grinder braying out an offer to sharpen anyone's knives. Edward spent a good many evenings just sitting in the atmospherically lit living-room, savouring the freedom of his flat and speculating with nothing like urgency how he was going to fill future evenings.

To begin with, it was all harmlessly entertaining. He wrote some biting satirical cards about his new lifestyle to his friends. He even, although he would have been reluctant to admit it, derived a certain desultory amusement from establishing his neighbourhood routines: where he bought his paper, where he bought his milk, the identical exchanges he had in the next-door bakery every time he bought a *baguette*. He found himself a launderette, a dry cleaner which did ironing. He invented nicknames. But he knew this game couldn't last; it was only a matter of time until he exhausted the entertainment value of the here and now. Ultimately, it was far too cramping and frustrating to envisage for long.

Next, he specialised in drunken walks. Late at night, after finishing a bottle of cheap Nicolas wine, he would set off across the empty stretches of the grander seventh *arrondissement* and watch what alcohol and street lighting could do for the Eiffel Tower and the Esplanade des Invalides and the Ecole Militaire. Brilliant, facile insights would come to him as he walked the deserted avenues, venting his frustrations on the farcical, spotlit monuments. Walking around London at night, he would have been able to look in at the living-room windows of two-storey terrace houses and snigger at rubber plants and enamelled ducks in flight. Here, he walked between immense shuttered apartment blocks. The metal shutters were clamped fast over whatever amusing scenes went on behind them. Only sometimes on the top floors were the shutters left open and Edward could see single yellow squares of light high up

51

above the trees. His exclusion was total and he satirised the monuments because there were hardly any people on the streets to take his unhappiness out on. Occasionally, one of Paris's small bowed men would emerge from the chandelier-lit entrance hall of an apartment house, taking his wife's perfumed dog out for a last piddle. But otherwise Edward had the avenues to himself.

He found a late-night café ideally suited to thinking jaded thoughts. It stood at the junction of three broad avenues, its bright façade already attractive from a long way away. Inside, it was always busy with a faintly disreputable, almost exclusively male clientele. There was a boisterous solidarity between them; people out on the town when everyone they knew was at home, guzzling home-cooked *tripes* and preparing for the marital duvet. Raucous jokes, shouted just too fast for Edward to follow them, flew across the room. He was, in any case, not part of their party; sitting by himself at a pricier terrace table, alternating liqueurs and coffees in a steadily queasier and costlier sequence. He contemplated the *habitués* condescendingly from his alcoholic elevation. Their hunched shoulders above the bar signalled to him that he was an utterly uninteresting foreigner and he signalled back with a glazed world-weary smile that they were buffoons.

One night, an American girl came in and sat at a table close to him and started talking.

Edward asked her, "How did you know I was English?"

She answered, "Oh, easy; sitting on your own like that, looking pissed off. You had to be a foreigner. And you look pretty English."

This vision of himself, pitiful and self-pitying, irritated Edward considerably and even though the girl, who was moderately good-looking, freely volunteered her name and telephone number, he didn't get in touch with her.

He did try briefly pretending that he was happy to be there; acting the part of the young Henry Hirshfeld arriving in Paris, full of sincere enthusiasm. He spent a few weekend afternoons in obscure bookshops, staffed by stooping characters of early middle age whose clothes and hair length – if not luxuriance – were fixed forever in the late Sixties. He went to independent cinemas showing the most unlikely films. He even, once or twice, tried reading a slim volume with uncut pages at a café table. But it was naturally difficult to ride on the pretentious merry-go-round he was simultaneously scoffing. He appeared to himself and felt ridiculous. He persevered for longer than he respectably should have, in the unreasonable hope that he might somehow alight on an intelligent method of living in Paris. All he did was seriously undermine his self-esteem. His whole set-up seemed a pathetic parody of an aspiring foreign correspondent's life.

The first of November was a public holiday, All Saints' Day. It fell on a Monday, giving Edward his first taste of three consecutive days' holiday alone in Paris. By Sunday evening, he was ready to risk anything as a diversion. He had gone out in the late afternoon for a somewhat pointless walk along the silent avenues. At the main intersections, florists' stalls were selling the matt maroon and sombre bronze chrysanthemums which Marie-Yvette had told him were the flowers traditionally put on graves. He tried cheering himself by repeating ghoulishly, *"La Fête des Morts"* but without much effect. As he walked back towards the rue Surcouf through an appropriately low and ghostly mist, it occurred to him that he had been on his own for nearly two months. Short-sighted as it might seem, he had never really thought about loneliness when he planned his exciting life abroad. Now, in the supremely dismal November dusk, it closed in on him. He realised that, since arriving in Paris, he had not spoken to anyone between leaving the paper one day and returning there the next. His evenings and weekends were filled by walks and films and meals and reading, all undertaken in a joyless determination not to give way to depression. He had begun to live according to little, set, single-person's routines. He had caught himself talking to himself in the shower.

There was something else he had gone without for two months also. He walked unconsciously faster to counteract the ache of deprivation which started up as soon as he thought about it. Would he have to go a whole year, or two if they kept him here for two, without as much as a stray passing fuck? The prospect was too grim to contemplate; he was bound to find somebody co-operative sooner or later. But, reviewing the few women he had met so far, he had disturbing

53

doubts: not counting, naturally, Mrs Hirshfeld, they consisted of the predatory American female in the café, Marie-Yvette and Aurore. Aurore was, according to Marie-Yvette, more or less married. The idea of suggesting any such thing to Marie-Yvette or of her consenting, was so ridiculously unattractive that he at least cheered himself up slightly by laughing at it as he turned the corner of the rue Surcouf. The wistfulness stayed with him, though, all evening. When he went to bed, the bed seemed to him for the first time uncomfortably wide and empty. He lay for a long time still aching for lack of anybody there beside him.

It was humiliating to be so pleased to go back to the paper on Tuesday morning. Maybe Henry guessed his loneliness, maybe it showed; he invited Edward out to lunch to try a new local restaurant.

As they walked there, Henry asked him, apparently casually, how he was making out. Edward thought he sensed a paternal concern and, over-hastily, he answered, "Oh fine, fine."

To his surprise, Henry laughed. "You are? Well, you must be a man of iron, Edward. Most people find this city pretty tough going at first."

Edward grinned awkwardly. "Maybe I didn't have terribly high expectations."

"Let me tell you something," Henry said disarmingly. "You may well find this city is better training in survival techniques than some of the wilder places you might have liked to be sent. I don't know where was your heart's desire. But in South-East Asia, you know, in some of those African capitals, everyone bands together. You go out hunting in a pack. Someone gets a lead and you all follow it up. There's not so much scope for the individual. Whereas here, paradoxically, you can make of it what you will."

The restaurant was Lebanese. The owners, eager to woo their new clientele, lavished them with dozens of small dishes to sample, the lunch became extended and their conversation franker than Edward had anticipated.

Henry asked him if he had any friends in Paris.

Edward shook his head. In a moment's honesty which he immediately regretted, he admitted, "That side of things does look a bit bleak at the moment."

54

Henry looked thoughtfully at the bread basket. "It's a strange business, I know, setting yourself up somewhere when you know you're just passing through."

Before Edward could even wonder what was an appropriate reply, which neither absolutely agreed with nor absolutely refuted Henry's assumption, Henry pushed a dish of *hummous* towards him. "Here, make some inroads into this. You're young enough not to need to worry about cholesterol."

He supposed, with hindsight, that he had thought it was a bit too good to be true not to have heard anything out of the Iskarov family for the first three or four weeks he lived in their flat. Certainly, when they did make contact, he was conscious that he had been waiting for it, "braced for it" was the term.

One evening, into the semi-permanent silence of his living-room, the telephone rang. He was so little expecting it that he actually jumped, a reaction which disgusted him because in all his previous existences the telephone had always rung for him with healthy frequency. Expecting that it could only be Henry, or perhaps a call from England, he answered in English, "Hello?"

"*Allo? Allo?* Mister Wenwright?" came Mademoiselle Iskarov's flustered voice.

"Ah," he said awkwardly. "*Bonsoir.*" Did she always sound, he wondered, as though things were falling in chaos about her ears? Her fluster was infectious.

"*Bonsoir,*" she replied, he felt just a trifle stiffly and sorely, as though she had interpreted his formality as a rebuff. "I hope I'm not ringing at a bad time?"

"No, no, it's fine." And then, completely unnecessarily, he found himself adding, "I've been out quite a bit. I hope you haven't been trying?"

"No, no, I haven't. In fact, I did mean to ring you before, but I've been so busy. I wanted to ask how you were getting on. Is everything all right in the flat?"

'No,' Edward retorted to himself. 'No, it isn't. I've set up a Buddhist temple here, you see, and there have been a few complaints about the chanting.'

"Yes, fine," he answered shortly.

There was a pause. "Will you be in later on? Are you busy? I'd like to come round if you're not in the middle of something."

Edward controlled his indignation. "What's the problem?"

"No problem," Mademoiselle Iskarov said laughingly. "I just want to see that everything's all right, that's all; that you have everything you need. I would have come before only I've been utterly snowed under. I've got a second set of keys for you, in case you need them, and some spare bulbs for those old lamps in the living-room. They're a funny kind; you'll never find them anywhere."

While he sketchily cleaned up the living-room, and the remains of more than one day's dinner from the kitchen, Edward reproached himself for his immediate acquiescence. It went, of course, without saying that Mademoiselle Iskarov was coming to check up on him; the keys and the light bulbs and the salt which she had rather bizarrely mentioned were a transparent pretext. He would put up with it this once, for the sake of harmonious relations, but he was not going to let her make a habit of it.

He was spared the complicated decision of whether or not to do anything to improve on his appearance by the front-door bell ringing a bare five minutes after he had put the phone down. He had expected half an hour or so's grace, the time it took to walk the distance, but obviously Mademoiselle Iskarov must have come by car or taxi.

She stood on his doorstep, smaller than he remembered her, and rather stylishly swamped by a bulky red fur coat. Almost in the same instant that he admired the effect of the fur, it occurred to him that it really wasn't quite cold enough for fur and that if she had come by car it was, in any case, ridiculous.

Her arms were loaded with packages. She gasped at him

urgently. "Take them, take them. I'm about to drop the light bulbs," and as he gingerly extricated the top parcels from her pile, she explained wryly, "I brought a few things I thought you might need."

He showed her into the living-room and, somehow she was the sort of woman to whom you did that, he helped her a bit self-consciously off with her enormous coat.

"Do sit down," he said and, he realised afterwards, with something close to curtness, "Or d'you want to look round straight away?"

Mademoiselle Iskarov ignored him. She stood and gazed around the tidied living-room, which now looked as though there were no one living there at all.

"It is funny," she said, "to see Volodya's furniture but no Volodya."

"Sorry?" said Edward.

Mademoiselle Iskarov caressed the back of the armchair Edward had been sitting in. "This was his favourite chair," she said. She sat down in it and abruptly shut her eyes.

"Would you like some coffee?" Edward offered somewhat helplessly. "And, forgive my asking, but who is Volodya?"

Without opening her eyes, Mademoiselle Iskarov said, "Dyadya Volodya was my favourite uncle. This was his flat. He lived in it after he got divorced from my Aunty Ada, who was my least favourite aunt. In Russian *yad* means poison. When I was little, I used to call her Aunty Yada." She opened her eyes to ask him, "Can you understand couples like that? One of them the sweetest, nicest, kindest person you could ever hope to meet and the other – a cow." Without waiting for an answer, which Edward would, in any case, not have been able to give, she closed her eyes and continued, "He was a replacement father for me when I was growing up; he was better than a father. Certainly better than *my* father would have been if he had stayed around." She stretched out both her arms and laid them palms down along the arms of the chair. "Volodya went to America and he was killed in a car crash. I ask you; survive everything else and then that. It was so stupid, so stupid; how could he have let it happen?"

Her eyes sprang open and, seeing Edward's fazed expression,

she burst into disconcerting laughter. "What am I doing? I mustn't give you ghosts."

She bustled out of the chair and over to the heap of packages which lay tipped on the settee. "Here, look, these are the keys and these are the light bulbs. They don't click in, you understand; you need to twist them. And I've brought you a change of tablecloth. You can't keep on using that green one all the time; it'll get disgusting. And this is a lampshade for the bathroom. There isn't one, is there? Something unfortunate happened to the last one. And this, laugh if you like, is a traditional Russian house-warming gift, rather late, I'm afraid: bread and salt."

She took the last two bundles from the heap and thrust them at Edward. "Here you are. I wish you health and happiness in your new home."

"Well, thank you," said Edward. He looked uncertainly at the two brown paper parcels. "Am I – are we supposed to have it now, or what?"

Mademoiselle Iskarov shrugged. "That's up to you." Then she seemed to thaw a little and added, "Though why not? You suggested coffee, didn't you? We can have a mouthful with coffee."

She followed Edward into the kitchen. "Well, you keep it cleaner than your predecessor, I'll say that."

Edward repeated, with perceptible irritation in his voice, "Do have a look round, if you want to."

To his surprise, Mademoiselle Iskarov seemed to take offence. "I didn't come on a tour of inspection, if that's what you think." But, almost immediately, her offence seemed to vanish and she asked him, "Please put in a bit more coffee than that. I like it very strong."

It was embarrassing to realise, not having entertained any guests in the flat before, that he had no sugar, since he himself didn't take any, and when he opened the fridge to get out the milk, he had to reveal that there was nothing inside it but a quantity of wine and a single piece of distinctly aged-smelling cheese.

Largely to distract attention, he asked Mademoiselle Iskarov, "Would you like something a bit stronger with your coffee? I've got some whisky and some liqueur."

She clapped her hands. "Oh, thank goodness. You are a normal person with normal weaknesses; not a dreadfully proper young English gentleman with no known vices."

Edward felt provoked to childish annoyance. He was at an undeniable disadvantage, squatting in front of his evil-smelling fridge, and it galled him excessively to look up and see Mademoiselle Iskarov condescendingly laughing at him.

"I don't know what on earth gave you that idea," he retorted crossly.

Mademoiselle Iskarov snorted with laughter.

Edward finished making the coffee in silence.

Mademoiselle Iskarov said contritely, "I've offended you, haven't I?"

"Not in the least," said Edward, hoping to make it plain through the screen of a foreign language that Mademoiselle Iskarov was of such minimal importance, she would be hard put to offend him.

They went back into the living-room. Following him, bringing her bread and salt, Mademoiselle Iskarov repeated gloomily, "I have offended you, I know I have. I'd forgotten how easily you English people get offended."

Laughing, Edward said, "Look, you haven't offended me. But you haven't answered my question either. Would you like a drink?"

Mademoiselle Iskarov nodded. "We must. Drink and make up."

"We don't need to drink and make up," Edward said. "Would you *like* a drink?"

Mademoiselle Iskarov replied with a wordless beam.

While he was in the kitchen, getting the bottle and glasses, one of which was sticky and needed to be swilled out under the tap, he heard her get up and move around the living-room. When he returned, she was standing with her back to the window surveying the room with a sad expression.

Edward asked, "Does it make you unhappy to see someone else living here?"

"Oh," she said, "not you, Mister Wenwright. You seem to appreciate the place. Not like that awful American. I think Volodya would have been happy to know you were living here. No, you know, it's just for me the place is full of his absence."

Edward nodded, he hoped eloquently. Unable to think of any other response, he passed Mademoiselle Iskarov her coffee and her whisky. He asked, "How do we deal with this bread?"

Mademoiselle Iskarov came out of her reverie. "Of course, it should be black bread," she said. "Not one of these stupid *baguettes*." She took the bread from its paper and wrenched off two ragged chunks. Then she delved into the salt package and liberally sprinkled each chunk. She passed the bigger chunk to Edward and proceeded to munch contentedly on her own.

Edward went more slowly. In combination with the ferociously strong coffee, it tasted to him a pretty noxious mixture.

When the bread ceremony was disposed of, they sat and sipped their whisky. Mademoiselle Iskarov asked him about his job and he wanted to reciprocate by asking her about her job but he couldn't think what questions to put to a Russian teacher. The questions he could think of, nothing to do with her work, seemed perilously indiscreet and intrusive.

Soon enough, an uncomfortable silence settled over them. To break it, Edward determined to overcome his unprofessional hesitation. He started to interview her.

"How long have you lived in France?"

Mademoiselle Iskarov looked astonished. "What do you mean? I've always lived here."

"Always? Were you born here?"

Mademoiselle Iskarov bridled visibly. "Of course I was born here. Do you think I speak with an accent or something?"

"I'd hardly be the one to comment on it if you did," Edward said conciliatingly. "No, you just seem so Russian; you know, your flat and what you've told me of your family and this bread business. I just wondered."

Mademoiselle Iskarov shrugged and spread her palms helplessly. "Of course I'm Russian. It's not just something you discard like a pair of stale socks, you know. We keep our traditions, our language."

"I suppose you're completely bi-lingual?" Edward asked.

"Of course," answered Mademoiselle Iskarov. She smiled affectionately at something within her and explained, "Russian

61

is my mother tongue. French was only my father's tongue," and she pulled a comically disparaging face.

"Your father was French?" Edward said. "But you've got a Russian name."

"It's my mother's name," explained Mademoiselle Iskarov. "My father walked out when I was still a baby and my mother changed my name back when she changed hers."

"I didn't know you could do that," Edward said.

"My mother could," replied Mademoiselle Iskarov. "Why should I be blighted by the name of a criminal?" She laughed, making fun of her own melodrama. "I like this name. If I ever get married, I shall call myself Madame Iskarov Something or Other."

Edward couldn't help being secretly startled that she should still openly consider marriage an option. She was definitely well into her thirties although now, sitting in the weak-tea light of the standard lamps, animated and chattering, she could pass for younger. The combination of her job, Mademoiselle Iskarov the Russian teacher, and the alienating fact that she was his landlady had led him to put her in the category of confirmed spinster. She evidently saw herself quite differently.

She lifted her heavy amber necklace and considered the glossy beads thoughtfully under the light. "I suppose you're thinking I've left it a bit late to be talking about marriage?"

"Of course not," Edward said. "People get married incredibly late nowadays," and, promptly, both of them burst into embarrassed laughter.

"How old are you?" asked Mademoiselle Iskarov warily.

"Twenty-six," Edward answered.

Mademoiselle Iskarov clapped her hand to her lips with a little shocked amused exhalation.

"Am I allowed to put the same question to you?" Edward asked.

Mademoiselle Iskarov considered him coyly. "Probably better that than me telling you to guess and you guessing awfully wrong. I'm *thirty*-six. Now tell me I don't look anything like that old." She kicked her heels coquettishly and laughed.

"I would have guessed early thirties," Edward said honestly.

"That much?" Mademoiselle Iskarov exclaimed mock tragically. "I'm heart-broken." She grew serious. "I don't believe in the importance of age. My mother had magnificent love affairs till the end of her days. She was fifty-five when she died and she had more broken-hearted admirers at her funeral than most women could have hoped for in their twenties."

"She sounds amazing," Edward agreed.

"She was," Mademoiselle Iskarov said fervently. "She was. And my grandmother, too, before she started to – And my Great-Aunt Elena. I was brought up entirely by Russian women. They made me strong and capable of standing on my own two feet. I think that's why I find the majority of men somewhat weak and unsatisfactory."

"I see," Edward said teasingly.

"Well, I'm sorry," Mademoiselle Iskarov said sternly, "But I do. I exclude you, naturally, since I don't know you, but my experience of men has on the whole not given me a high opinion of them."

As he looked at her, tilting her chin defiantly towards him and twisting her right foot in a taut provocative circle, Edward suddenly, unmistakably sensed that her experience of men had been vivid, dramatic and extensive.

He was wondering when she might leave. To his disappointment, she accepted his offer of a second glass of whisky and as he reached out for her glass, he noticed on his watch that it was already half past eleven. He told himself, 'Time, gentlemen, please' and he decided that he would not offer another round when this one was finished. He had to admit that it was to Mademoiselle Iskarov's credit, though, that he had no doubt at all she would undauntedly drink it.

A short while afterwards, she looked at her little gold watch bracelet, however, and gave a loud groan. "Oh no, I can't bear it."

"What's the time?" Edward asked with studied indifference.

"A quarter to twelve," exclaimed Mademoiselle Iskarov. "And at nine o'clock tomorrow morning I have to be back in that lousy *lycée*, face to face with my *beloved* pupils." She pulled another extravagant face.

"Some time," Edward said politely, "not now, you must

tell me something about the *lycée*. I'm still pretty ill-informed about the French education system."

Mademoiselle Iskarov seemed to mistake his politeness for a genuine desire. "Of course," she said. "You must come round and have dinner. I've been meaning to ask you, in fact, ever since you moved in. But my time isn't my own."

She scrabbled around for her bag and her gloves and her silk neck scarf.

"That's awfully kind of you," said Edward. "But, really, I didn't mean – "

"Now, please," Mademoiselle Iskarov interrupted him. "Don't be English. I really can't stand that sort of thing."

"But I know you're incredibly busy," Edward said. "I don't want to put you to trouble."

Mademoiselle Iskarov wagged her forefinger, now clad in a black leather glove, at him and declared in unusually accented English, "Where there's a will, there's a way."

"Oh," Edward exclaimed. "Do you speak English?"

"Certainly," she answered, still in English. "But not infallibly."

"Huh," joked Edward. "To think I've been sitting here, labouring away in French all evening."

"It's good for you," said Mademoiselle Iskarov. Promptly, she reverted to French. "So, when are you coming to dinner? Except we're not just going to talk about the French education system."

"When would suit you?" Edward asked helplessly.

Mademoiselle Iskarov thought for a moment or two. "Well, things always wind down a little towards the end of term," she said. "The Christmas holidays start in just over three weeks. Nothing much happens in the last week of term. So why don't you come not next Friday but the one after?"

"Um, the seventh?" said Edward, looking in his diary for appearances' sake.

Mademoiselle Iskarov shrugged. "If you say so."

"Yes, that's fine," said Edward. "Well, thank you very much."

He called himself a couple of richly deserved rude names as he wrote the date in his diary; talk about asking for trouble.

When Mademoiselle Iskarov had left, he got ready for bed

absent-mindedly. The novelty of having a visitor in the flat seemed to have changed it somehow. In his pyjamas, he went back into the living-room and had a look at it. Instead of imagining the room peopled by the numerous new friends he was going to make – dinners, parties – he found himself wondering about its earlier inhabitant – what had she called him? – Dyadya Volodya. What had he been like? Good taste in flats but, if Mademoiselle Iskarov was to be believed, poor taste in wives. What had he looked like? And, after his divorce from Aunty Arsenic, what sort of a life had he led here?

Thanks to the powerfully strong coffee, he couldn't get to sleep. He thought over the way Mademoiselle Iskarov had talked about Volodya. He wondered whether their relationship had ever gone beyond that of uncle and niece, although he knew he was only speculating in that direction because it made the whole scenario more interesting. Most probably, Volodya had been a gloomy old Russian with a bushy beard and a taste for vodka. At least the flat's tradition of alcohol consumption was being kept up.

He cursed Mademoiselle Iskarov for keeping him awake. There was no doubt about it, the woman was a menace. It was funny, when he had first met her, when she had that cold, she hadn't really seemed to him at all threatening. She had seemed, if anything, slightly to be pitied; so swamped by life and its miseries. Restored to health, she was quite definitely a woman to steer clear of. He resolved not to pursue the acquaintance any further than he had to. He tossed on the wide, empty bed. He wondered how much action it had seen in the days when Volodya slept there.

His social life, if you could call it that, consisted of Henry's and Mai's invitations. The third time he went to have dinner with them, he had begun to feel a little pathetic and uncomfortable and he wondered whether he ought unfailingly to accept. Maybe they were only including him out of pity and he would actually go up in their estimation the day he couldn't come. Otherwise, he was getting nowhere. He had struck up a conversation with a young German journalist on a press trip to the construction site of the new Cité des Sciences at La Villette and the German had given him his business card. (Edward's weren't yet printed.) After letting a respectable week go by, Edward telephoned him and Dieter, sounding somewhat startled, agreed to meet him for a boozy lunch. That was all very well but it didn't solve the problem of the unending series of empty evenings nor bring any female company his way. Over lunch, Dieter volunteered the information that he was married with eighteen-month-old twins, as far as Edward was concerned the ultimate definition of a domestic nightmare. The ringed eyes and muzzily weary look which Edward had singled out on the press bus as the signs of a prospective fellow-carouser were thanks to the twins. For the rest of their lunch, he worried that Dieter might invite him home for a meal but, luckily, all he did was apologise that his wife was far too busy to entertain. He seemed obscurely puzzled

66

by Edward's approach as if all his capacities for social contact were exhausted.

Edward spent more time on his own than ever in his life. For all that he lived in a classically Parisian house and went to work at the city's bustling commercial centre, he was effectively as excluded as if he were living in a different city entirely. The indignity of it bothered him nearly as much as the loneliness. If he couldn't cope with Paris, how did he imagine he would have coped with Peru? The ready answer, that in Peru the shutters would have gaped open on avid faces, didn't satisfy him. If he were as self-sufficient as he fancied, then he ought to be self-sufficient anywhere. Simultaneously, as he searched for an instrument to prise open the city's shell, his dislike for it increased because it was making him appear a wimp in his own eyes.

Because of all this, he did not feel quite the dread he had anticipated when the Friday of Mademoiselle Iskarov's dinner invitation arrived. If nothing else, it was one evening filled. She hadn't told him a time at which to come so, at about seven o'clock, he telephoned her to ask when he should show up.

The telephone rang for so long he wondered momentarily if he had somehow managed to get the day wrong and she was out. But at the last moment, just as he was about to ring off, she snatched up the receiver and answered, *"Allo?"*

"Hello, it's me," he said, "Edward Wainwright. I was just ringing to ask what time I should come over?"

"Oich!" gasped Mademoiselle Iskarov. "When I heard your voice, I thought for a minute you were ringing to say you couldn't come. I would have wept; I'm making you such a wonderful dinner."

Edward, rather taken aback by this candour, stammered, "Oh, gosh, don't go to any trouble."

He heard what he termed an "Iskarovian snort".

"I shall be disappointed," Mademoiselle Iskarov told him playfully, "if you continue to act the proper English gentleman with me." And when Edward, now quite at a loss, didn't straight away answer, she said, "When d'you want to come over? When would suit you?"

Edward looked across at the elderly carriage clock on the bookcase which was a handsome oddity but hard to decipher.

67

"I could be over there in about half an hour if you like. Or – "

"No, no, my God," cried Mademoiselle Iskarov. "I'm up to my ears in butter. Give me at least an hour."

"OK," said Edward, mentally adding, 'Why *ask?*' "I'll be there between eight and half past."

He imagined he heard a last flustered gasp just before the receiver slipped too quickly from Mademoiselle Iskarov's buttery fingers.

The idea of her labouring to create an elaborate dinner for him was somehow quite unexpected. He hadn't thought of her as someone who would gladly get to work in a kitchen. He wondered whether she was also a good cook and what she might be cooking for him. He got dressed slightly more smartly than he would have to go to Henry and Mai's.

As he walked over to the Cité Etienne Hubert, as well as the pleasant anticipation of a good meal, he felt a faint childish triumph; like the smug passers-by bustling along with their bottles of wine and bunches of flowers and caricatures of *baguettes*, he was on his way to a *rendez-vous* behind the mean metal shutters.

Mademoiselle Iskarov swept the front door open, giving a jaunty parody of a gracious society hostess. "Ah, good evening, Mister Wenwright. Do come in."

"Ooh good," Edward said. "Are we going to speak English this evening?"

Mademoiselle Iskarov spread one upturned palm in an exaggerated your-wish-is-my-command gesture. "If you desire."

She had certainly made an effort, Edward noted. She was wearing an imposingly chic pink dress which gave an initial impression of being a shiny metallic sheath but as Mademoiselle Iskarov moved, it displayed an expensive ability to dimple and fold along with her, clearly suggesting every asset beneath it.

Edward admired this effect from behind as Mademoiselle Iskarov led him across the hall to hang his coat in a walk-in cupboard. It was remarkably clever, really; all the dress seemed to consist of was four long triangles of fabric, two front and two back, plus two sleeves, yet its repertoire of shimmering and clinging was quite amazing. Edward supposed it must be

68

the creation of some ultra-fashionable Parisian designer; he frankly didn't remember Mademoiselle Iskarov being anything like as elegant as she looked this evening. He appraised her covertly while she opened the cupboard, reached for a hanger for his overcoat and tried to clear a space for it inside. He was tickled to notice, just quickly, that the cupboard was crammed with a convincingly Russian collection of substantial fur coats and solid boots. Mademoiselle Iskarov held the coat hanger out to him. Edward decided that he wasn't quite sure about the colour of the dress. He certainly wasn't used to women wearing such an uncompromising shade of pink; a very bright, tough, grown-up pink, he thought, no relation at all of the soft, little-girl pink of Rosie's favourite track suit. It seemed to him a somewhat dicey combination with Mademoiselle Iskarov's auburn hair.

He remembered, belatedly, the small box of chocolates in one of his coat pockets and he had to fumble for it as Mademoiselle Iskarov held his coat on the hanger. He was slightly annoyed that she didn't make the effort to seem more pleased, just taking the box matter-of-factly and putting it on a nearby chest. Maybe she was already preoccupied with something else because she announced, "Now we have a little ceremony to go through; you must meet Babushka."

Edward remembered his previous visit to the flat; he remembered how he had become conscious of the voice holding forth from the unseen room and how he thought he had seen a grey blur of movement as they passed the half-open door. He actually wasn't sure that he wanted to meet Mademoiselle Iskarov's grandmother.

But she led him across the hall, pausing at the door of the same room to whisper, Edward worried, perfectly audibly, "Don't be concerned if she says anything unusual." Without elaborating, she walked into the room, announcing clearly as she went, "I've brought a gentleman to meet you, Babushka."

For the first moment after he entered the room, Edward couldn't actually see the grandmother amid the cluttered quantity of cushions and pouffes and padded settees; she was herself just another unobtrusive rounded object among them. When he had distinguished her, he wondered with slight dismay what medical condition had made her quite so uniformly round: her small rotund body and her circular face, surmounted by a perfectly spherical bun, were one thing, but even her hands and feet were swollen, inflated-looking, and hung somehow helplessly at the end of her limbs.

Mademoiselle Iskarov went on in the same over-articulated voice. "He's the new tenant of Volodya's flat, remember? Mister Edouard Wenwright from England."

The grandmother looked back at them absolutely blankly. There was no sign on her aged face that she was even aware of their presence.

Just slightly louder, Mademoiselle Iskarov continued, "You can speak English to him, Babushka. He'll like that."

Perhaps, imperceptibly, the grandmother's face turned towards Edward, who said uncomfortably, "*Bonsoir, Madame. Enchanté.*"

"No, no," Mademoiselle Iskarov hissed. "Speak English. It may stimulate her."

"How do you do?" Edward said.

Surprisingly, Mademoiselle Iskarov nudged him fiercely. "Go on."

Falteringly, Edward said, "I like the flat a lot, you know."

He was convinced he caught the grandmother's filmy blue eyes flick back and forth from him to Mademoiselle Iskarov.

Raising her voice a fraction more, Mademoiselle Iskarov repeated, "Did you hear that? Mister Wenwright is very happy in Volodya's flat."

Still, the grandmother did not respond.

"*Bon*," Mademoiselle Iskarov concluded, a little roughly, Edward thought, "If it's like that – " She motioned to Edward. "Let's go and have our *apéritif*."

"Nice to meet you," Edward murmured rather helplessly as Mademoiselle Iskarov ushered him out. The grandmother watched them go impassively.

"She has times like that," Mademoiselle Iskarov explained in the hall. "There's no point in persisting."

Edward felt Mademoiselle Iskarov was being rather hard and unsympathetic. But, when he thought it over, there did seem something faintly perverse in the way the grandmother

70

had chattered uninhibitedly when there was no one there and clammed up irremediably when she had visitors.

"What can I offer you to drink?" Mademoiselle Iskarov asked brightly. "You've done your duty now; you deserve it."

Edward looked at the pleasingly well-stocked drinks cabinet. It was the old-fashioned sort which lit up when you opened its rounded walnut doors. "What do you suggest?"

Mademoiselle Iskarov tilted her head to one side and said coquettishly, "Vodka?"

Only at this point did it occur to Edward to wonder whether other guests were invited too. He had somehow assumed all along that the invitation was for him only; come over for a meal, quite casual, I, Mademoiselle Iskarov, will do my welcoming bit for a forlorn young foreigner. But now everything, beginning with the dress, was out of all proportion to such an occasion: the little black and red lacquered trays of cocktail titbits set out on the low table, the promise of the elaborate dinner prepared for him. Surely, he thought, with the start of an unformulated panic, there must be other people coming too?

The bottle of vodka which Mademoiselle Iskarov took out of the drinks cabinet bore no resemblance to any vodka Edward had ever seen; it was in a thickish blue-glass bottle at the bottom of which something spidery but plant-like was suspended.

He must have looked concerned because Mademoiselle Iskarov explained, "It's home-made, a present from some friends of ours. Have you ever drunk vodka with green herbs?"

Edward hoped he could keep the apprehension out of his voice. "No, I can't say I have."

Mademoiselle Iskarov gave a gleeful chuckle. "Ah, you're about to have an unforgettable experience."

"I suppose," Edward said light-heartedly, "It's going to knock me out completely?"

Mademoiselle Iskarov passed him a generous measure. She giggled and, with a very accurate imitation of flirtatiousness, she answered, "No, not completely; just the right amount."

She matched his drink and sat down in the high-backed armchair opposite him, sinking luxuriantly against its cushions. She lifted her glass. "Well, *Na zdorovye.*"

71

"Cheers," said Edward.

One mouthful of the vodka was enough to let him know what was what. He reached hastily for something from one of the cocktail trays, which turned out, rather unpleasantly, to be a piece of marinaded fish. He gulped it down quickly and then, rather hopelessly, took another swig at the vodka to wash the taste away.

Mademoiselle Iskarov was watching him from the depths of her armchair. She had crossed her legs and, indolently, she was drawing circles with one sharp black shoe. "Well," she asked him, "how do you like it here in Paris?"

"Not much," said Edward. The combined attack on his senses by the vodka and the herring had temporarily distracted him from the worrying situation in hand. Now, as Mademoiselle Iskarov bestowed a high voltage smile on him and replied, "Ah good; we have something in common," his apprehensions returned in force.

"What don't you like about it?" he asked absent-mindedly.

Mademoiselle Iskarov heaved a tremendous sigh. Her dress, Edward couldn't help noticing, even though he didn't want to, gave a tremendous follow-up. "It's cold, it's unfriendly. You can live here all your life but they'll never accept you. My mother came here when she was a baby, you know, but they still called her Russian till the end of her days."

"But I thought," Edward said tentatively, "from what you were saying the other day that you kept it up deliberately; that you *liked* being Russian."

"That's not the same thing at all," Mademoiselle Iskarov reproved him. "Of course I 'like being Russian'; I'd rather be Russian than some silly *chi-chi* little *Parisienne*. But I resent being an outcast because of it. Look," she leapt up and beckoned Edward, concerned to find that he was already not quite rock solid on his feet, over to one of the windows. Dramatically, she yanked back the curtain and gestured across the street. From the fifth-floor apartment opposite a single yellow patch of light spilled out. The rest of the building was shuttered in darkness. "They don't always close their shutters. Neither do we. How far away do we live from one another? Fifty metres? In the summer, with the windows open, we can sometimes hear one another's voices. And how many times, do you suppose, in all the years that we've lived here have we had a friendly wave or a nod from our *neighbours? Parfaitement*; not once." She smacked the curtains closed again. "That's what the Parisians are like; they live in their little hermetically sealed homes, thinking blinkered chauvinistic thoughts in their hermetically sealed minds and unless you're one of the *zenfants de la patri-uh*, unless you belong, you're a nobody. Not, of course," she concluded erratically, "that I would wish to be part of that *milieu*. Are you ready for some more vodka?"

"Oh gosh, I'm not sure," said Edward.

"You want to keep your wits about you?" Mademoiselle Iskarov asked mischievously. "Why bother?"

Edward wasn't sure whether the slight unsteadiness from the vodka downed too fast was responsible; in a remote but accessible region of his brain a figure from a strip cartoon, with inky hair standing on end, leapt to his feet crying, "Aaargh!" and fled.

"Well, are we waiting for other people?" he asked abruptly.

Mademoiselle Iskarov's face collapsed into an expression of immeasurable offence. "I beg your pardon?"

"Are you expecting other people for dinner?" Edward repeated brutally. "I mean, if we're waiting, yes, sure, I'll have some more. But otherwise I think, on the whole, maybe I'd rather not."

In the icy silence, Mademoiselle Iskarov drew herself upright. "What am I supposed to understand by that?"

"Only what I said," Edward persisted uncomfortably. "This vodka's pretty strong stuff. I don't think I really ought to have another glass without a good reason."

"I see," Mademoiselle Iskarov commented haughtily. "And an enjoyable dinner with just the two of us presumably isn't a good enough reason?"

To his embarrassment, Edward felt himself about to start giggling; her dignity was so ludicrously overdone. "Oh, come off it," he pleaded. "You know I didn't mean it like that."

Mademoiselle Iskarov considered him for a moment. She was standing with the bottle at the ready. In Edward's strip cartoon, which continued to flicker intermittently at the back

73

of his brain, she might at any moment swoop as a female fury brandishing a rolling-pin. But, against all the odds, she grinned.

"Are you famished?" she asked him. "I'll go and get our first course ready."

In the living-room doorway, she stopped and turned back to him. She pulled a teasingly reproachful face, culminating in a quick display of the tip of her pointed pink tongue.

The meal was superb. Whatever Edward might hold against Mademoiselle Iskarov on grounds of excessive touchiness, her culinary skills were flawless. They began with a deep red, peppery soup on which a clod of cream floated unashamedly. In Edward's experience, women who were lavish cooks were usually not much to look at. In England, certainly, the best-looking girls weren't interested in eating much more than salads. Mademoiselle Iskarov was the first woman he had come across whom you wouldn't mind walking down the street with, who also evidently enjoyed a good spread. It was true there was just a little too much of Mademoiselle Iskarov, but she carried her surplus with undeniable style. In fact, without it, the pink dress would probably not have been nearly as eye-catching.

She had reappeared in the doorway after a good five minutes, during which Edward had wandered blurrily about the living-room, looking at the family mementoes. He had also, unwisely, taken an extra nip of the vodka after all, to stoke his courage. But when Mademoiselle Iskarov came back, her indignation seemed to have subsided. She gave a little mock bow in the doorway and said, "*Le dîner est servi, Monsieur.*"

She led Edward into a small, very full dining-room: a large dark dining-table filled most of the room and into what was left there were squeezed a quantity of matching straight-backed dining-chairs and a sizeable serving trolley. It must have been the noise of the trolley which had made Edward giggle nervously a few minutes earlier. He had heard the steady horror-film creaking and imagined another even older and frailer relative being wheeled out of the way.

The preparations which Mademoiselle Iskarov had revealed already ought to have prepared him for the sight of the dinner-table. But he was still so taken aback by the silver candlesticks and the white cones of starched napkins that,

74

in combination with the talents revealed by the soup, he became too overwhelmed by the dimensions of the dinner to carry on a conversation. Mademoiselle Iskarov herself seemed, uncharacteristically, to have become rather inhibited. They drank their soup almost in silence. It was only when Edward offered to help clear the plates and Mademoiselle Iskarov protested, "No, no, you're my guest; you just sit looking elegant and useless like an English lord," and then added, "Listen, shall we drop this silly Madame-Monsieur business? My name is Irina. May I call you Edouard?" that, on the surface at least, things relaxed a little.

The main course was an incredibly complicated combination of roast meat wrapped around minced meat and rice and mushrooms and capers. Together with the accompanying heavy sauce and volume of vegetables, it created quite a challenge. Mademoiselle Iskarov, he knew it would be some time before he could think of her as Irina, kept his glass topped up from a bottle of excellent red wine which had been breathing on the trolley, and that helped. But it was as much as anything else to give himself a respite that he worked considerably harder at keeping up the conversation.

"Do you cook on this scale quite often?" he asked her. "Or am I the lucky one?"

Mademoiselle Iskarov went through a little rigmarole of fluttering her eyelashes at him. "I don't entertain a great deal," she said. "It's difficult, you see, with Babushka. When Mama was alive, we used to have parties here quite often. But since – " she shrugged.

"Well, anyway, it's wonderful," Edward said hurriedly.

To his embarrassment, Mademoiselle Iskarov exclaimed, "Ach, you're sweet." She reached across the table as if she were about to pat him gratefully on the hand but at the last moment her hand halted a few inches above his and gave a symbolic pat to the air.

"Tell me something," she asked. "Would you say you were a typical Englishman – of your generation?"

Edward gave her an amused smile. "Why d'you ask?"

"Well, I've never really known any Englishmen very well, apart from once, one very old one, and I just wondered. I mean, outwardly you seem, forgive me, very typically English and I just wondered if what I'm going to discover within will also be traditionally English?"

"I see," Edward said jokingly, although he was actually a little disconcerted to be appraised so matter-of-factly as a specimen of English manhood. "You've really only invited me here for research purposes, is that it?"

Mademoiselle Iskarov guffawed, as though he had said something genuinely funny. "Yes," she agreed. "Strictly for research purposes."

Edward chose not to pursue what it might be about her answer which made him feel obscurely uncomfortable. Muzzily, he considered the question of whether or not he was a typical Englishman of his generation. He came to the sobering conclusion that he probably was; even his longing for distant horizons followed a well-trodden tradition. He felt, uneasily, that Mademoiselle Iskarov was beginning to gain the upper hand; nobody could possibly call her a typical young Frenchwoman.

Over the cheese, he asked her some more about her family. It turned out he had already heard of almost all of them: her mother, her grandmother, her Great-Aunt Elena, Dyadya Volodya. There was no one else to speak of; they were, as Mademoiselle Iskarov put it, becoming extinct. They had been a big family once, a *Forsyte Saga* she said, but somehow in the upheavals of history a lot of them seemed to have got lost. Mademoiselle Iskarov was the only member of her generation.

Edward, afflicted with what he had always considered a particularly second-rate collection of siblings and cousins, considered her situation with a mixture of envy and zoological fascination. She really was a rarity; the last surviving specimen of a vanishing breed. It gave her, he concluded, a mournful but not necessarily off-putting aura.

"Why are you looking at me like that?" asked Mademoiselle Iskarov.

Edward smiled self-consciously. "Sorry. I was just trying to imagine what it must be like to be in your position; you know, the last one left."

"You were looking at me," Mademoiselle Iskarov reproached him, "as though I were some unusual but not biting furry animal stuffed in a museum." She shuddered distastefully.

Edward laughed. "I'm sorry. I said I'm sorry. But you must see it's rather fascinating for someone like me," he added ingratiatingly, "coming from a typical English background."

"Oh sure," Mademoiselle Iskarov agreed bitterly. "It's fascinating." She propped her chin on one hand and contemplated her own predicament with what looked like gloomy pride.

Edward couldn't help being impressed, though, by how swiftly she seemed to shake off her bad moods. A moment later, she jumped up, saying briskly, "Time for dessert," whereupon Edward inadvertently groaned.

"I'm so full," he explained. "Couldn't we wait a bit?"

Mademoiselle Iskarov beamed with contented pride. "You mean my aim is achieved; I have overpowered you with my *cuisine*?"

Edward grinned. "You certainly have."

Mademoiselle Iskarov rubbed her hands naughtily. "Now I have you in my clutches. I shall put you into a trance with some very special liqueur and you won't even be fit to walk home. Shall we forget the dessert?"

Edward had managed to keep at bay for most of the meal the possibility that there might be a strand of seriousness behind Mademoiselle Iskarov's parody of a Parisian seductress. The later it got, the more real the risk became.

He said firmly, "I certainly wouldn't mind some coffee."

He asked the way to the toilet while Mademoiselle Iskarov went to the kitchen to make the coffee. As he emerged from the bathroom, he saw outlined in the light coming from her room the blurry, round shape of the grandmother, whom he had assumed to be long tucked up in bed. He had to walk past her to get back to the living-room. She was obviously unsteady on her feet for she was holding onto the door jamb with both hands and it was impossible to tell whether the vivid concern in her eyes was caused by the sight of Edward still there so late in the apartment or by her own precariousness. He gave her a cheery "Hello" as he walked past and even though he knew it was unreasonable, he couldn't help feeling rebuffed by her staring silence. He didn't say anything to Mademoiselle Iskarov about having seen the grandmother; he reckoned it must be trying enough having to live with your crazed grandmother at the age of thirty-six without being reminded of her presence at inopportune moments.

He couldn't be sure but he thought Mademoiselle Iskarov had topped up her perfume while she was preparing the coffee. He caught a great gust of it as she bent to give him his gilt-edged cup and to offer him sugar and cream. Actually, it was not unpleasant; he just wasn't used to such decibels of femininity.

He sat deliberately upright as he drank the coffee; opposite him, Mademoiselle Iskarov reclined in her armchair, her legs lengthily crossed. Against his better judgement, Edward had also accepted a glass of the special liqueur. He told himself every few sips it would be the only one.

Mademoiselle Iskarov's matter-of-fact conclusion caught him unawares. "Well, I'm very glad I changed my mind and didn't let Volodya's flat to that Norwegian woman."

"Sorry?" said Edward.

Mademoiselle Iskarov smiled smugly. "Yes, you don't know, do you? You very nearly didn't get Volodya's flat. A couple of days before you came to look at it, we had somebody else interested, a Norwegian girl, and she seemed like a good tenant. We were going to let it to her. In fact, I'd completely forgotten you were coming to see it. We were just waiting for her bank reference. Only I preferred the look of you."

Edward's embarrassment was matched by his irritation; he didn't at all like the thought that he had been an unwitting pawn in Mademoiselle Iskarov's machinations.

"Well, I only hope you won't be disappointed in your judgement," he said brusquely.

"Oh," Mademoiselle Iskarov replied archly, "I doubt it."

As soon as he had finished his coffee, Edward announced, almost in a rush, "Well, thank you very much. It's been a lovely evening. I really must go."

To his relief, and slight surprise also, Mademoiselle Iskarov didn't try to detain him. She accompanied him to the hall cupboard to retrieve his coat and to the front door.

At the door, they both stopped uncertainly.

"Well, thank you very much," Edward repeated. "I did enjoy this evening."

"So did I," said Mademoiselle Iskarov. She had one hand on the lock but she didn't unlock it. She was waiting for something.

"It was very kind of you to go to so much trouble," Edward ventured.

Mademoiselle Iskarov smiled tartly; he was heading in the wrong direction.

"And it was nice to meet your grandmother."

Her smile became perceptibly sourer. Something in her attitude spelt it out; face upturned, she was waiting for him to kiss her good night. Promptly, almost in self-defence, his hand shot up to shake hers instead. Her smile vanished. As she extended one hand to meet his ungracious gesture, her other was already opening the front door. Before Edward could think up some propitiating goodbye line, which might make up for his churlishness, he found himself, by the sheer force of her displeasure, being propelled out into the liberating dark.

In a pulsing, Latin American night club, Edward found himself incongruously dressed in heavy winter clothes. It was stiflingly hot and he felt sweaty and even a little sick. Somewhere, in the explorative excitement of arriving in a new country, he had eaten a pretty dicey dinner. He thought he would be OK, if only no one asked him to stand up. But his outlandish clothes had begun to attract attention; he was dressed, to his profound embarrassment, in a pair of enormously baggy cords and a brightly lozenge-patterned Shetland pullover he hadn't worn since he was at least fifteen. The people around him, all of whom were ultra-developed and deeply tanned and dressed in very little, started to point him out to one another, openly giving him incredulous looks and giggling. Obviously, the thing to do was to find the toilets and take off as many as possible of his embarrassing layers. Only he couldn't get up. He tried to once, tentatively, but his head spun round or the room spun round, one or the other, and all the ultra-developed dancing couples flew up into impossible horizontal and upside-down positions like a flamboyant surrealist painting. He clamped himself to the seat of his chair with sweaty hands. The horizontal and upside-down smiles had been truly revolting. His main concern became to avoid a repetition. A woman who, even upright, had contrived to keep

80

her perpendicular smile, started to manoeuvre closer to him. She was dancing, nominally, with a short, dapper man but every time they turned in the right direction, her mascaraed eyes signalled vigorously to Edward over her partner's low shoulder. Edward looked coldly – except how could he do anything coldly? – in another direction. Only he couldn't have been looking hard enough because he could still see her. She was herself not tall but her body had compensated by thrusting out tremendously in various directions; she had large active breasts which were carrying on a command performance under her bright dress, and an energetic bottom of substantial proportions. Putting all this apparatus into play, she was closing in on Edward. He sweated even more. Inside his head now, the samba music was pounding relentlessly. The woman broke away from her partner and made for Edward, raising her dancing arms to reveal twin copses of dark, matted, underarm hair. It was an unmitigated relief to wake.

His head was still pounding and he had an overwhelmingly urgent thirst. As he stumbled to the bathroom, unable to find any of the light switches along the way, he realised that being sick was actually a possibility. He bent over the wash-basin, gulping water from the tap, and then stood there for a time, unsteadily, waiting for the possibility to recede. As he returned to bed, it filtered through to him dimly that in the morning he was going to have an all-time hangover.

He did, and as he lay in bed, wishing he could disown his body, memories of the evening before contributed to his overall queasiness. He thought he had total recall of the dinner but it seemed so improbable that he wondered if he didn't still have to disentangle it from the nightmares of the intervening night. Mademoiselle Iskarov was after him; it seemed so extraordinarily unlikely. It filled him with a new and sweaty panic. He stayed in bed for most of the morning, only going once, carefully, to the kitchen to make a pot of tea. For any number of reasons, bed seemed an eminently safe place to be. As he lay there, weakly monitoring the state of his symptoms – reeling head, dry mouth, uncertain stomach – he replayed the evening anxiously again and again, hoping he would discover that he had got it wrong; that this wild idea was only the product of alcoholic paranoia. But it wasn't, and as, around midday, he timidly got up and restored himself a little further with a shower, he realised that he had to devise a strategy to deal with it.

The idea of lunch was repugnant but he thought a walk might do him good so he set out into an exceedingly wintry afternoon to breathe in a lot of fresh air and to walk off, if possible, some of his impotent exasperation.

He walked up to the Quai d'Orsay and followed the gloomy river round to the Quai Anatole France. The sky was bulging with low, deep-grey clouds and, across the river, the trees of the Tuileries looked, he thought, singularly stark and claw-like. Taking a perverse pleasure in his bad temper, he crossed the river by the Pont Solférino to walk under the depressing trees. One thing was clear, of course; he was not going to co-operate. Whether or not Mademoiselle Iskarov made a habit of going for men ten years her junior, he had certainly at no time had a taste for the older woman. In fact, far from thinking a taste for older women was a sign of sexual sophistication, as a number of his friends did, Edward had always considered it distinctly dubious. As far as he was concerned, older women meant your mother and he knew he was not that way inclined at all. He would have to adopt a policy of total avoidance, which naturally would not be easy. There were bound to be sulks and probably scenes along the way but he didn't see what other alternative he had. It was, of course, highly unfortunate that Mademoiselle Iskarov should be his landlady; they were obliged to have a certain number of unavoidable dealings. And he must take care not to alienate her to such an extent that she started to take sharp, landlady's reprisals. It seemed just too much bother to move again, after all that house-hunting, but he did briefly consider it. While he was considering it, and the welcome weight of arguments was stacking up against it – the bother, the awkwardness of explaining to Henry and Mai why it was he had decided to move again – a grey figure approached him out of the empty park and said something which he missed.

"*Pardon?*" he asked automatically.

The figure, a deeply sad-faced man in a raincoat and a floppy brown hat, seemed to be trying to interest him in a small brown packet.

"Have a look," he was saying. "It'll cheer you up. *Ça va vous remonter le moral.*"

"I don't need cheering up," Edward said huffily. He walked a little faster.

To his distaste, the man laid a hand on his sleeve. "No, look," he said urgently. "They're not the usual junk. Looking won't cost you anything." From the packet, he pulled a black and white postcard on which an unspeakably fat middle-aged man was doing unspeakable things to a small blond boy.

Edward pushed the man's arm away. "Fuck off!" he bellowed, so loudly that the man took fright and scuttled away between the bare trees. Edward quickened his pace towards the sanctuary of the tourist buses parked around the Louvre. For several hundred yards, he detested Paris.

On his way back, reinvigorated by the freezing afternoon and by his indignation, he stopped in a café at Saint Germain for a coffee and an experimental omelette. His insides were ready for it. As he sat over a second coffee, flipping at speed through the pages of the boring Saturday papers, he put a lot of his panic down to the hangover. Now he was fully restored, he wondered a little how he had managed to get so worked up about it. Pursuit by Mademoiselle Iskarov wasn't such a nightmarish prospect. In some murky corner of his brain, he was even passingly flattered that he was capable of arousing the desire of a worldly-wise Parisienne of thirty-six years of age. But, above all, he felt nonchalantly confident that he could cope. What had seemed earlier that day like the start of an appalling persecution now seemed more of a joke.

He passed a cinema where they were showing a film he hadn't yet seen and, on the spur of the moment, he decided to go in and see it since there was a programme starting in fifteen minutes. As the auditorium lights went down on the icecream advertisements and the voice of the Duponts' macaw was heard, he decided what his first move would be; he must make sure he was as busy as humanly possible, fix up lots of social engagements, so that when Mademoiselle Iskarov next rang, he would be either busy or, even better, out. Although the seats on either side of him were empty, he squirmed round at the last minute just to check there was no one at all dodgy in the row behind him.

He had not expected her, frankly, to make her next move so soon. She must, he thought grinning, when he heard her voice on the phone, be desperate. She telephoned him on the Monday night straight after the dinner and she called him "Edouard". He had had no chance at all to fix up any social engagements, even if he had any means of doing so.

"Oh, hello, Mademoiselle Iskarov," he replied warily.

"I thought I told you to call me Irina," she said petulantly. "Are you always this proper?"

She had a great knack of casting Edward in roles he wanted to shed.

"Wait and see," he said provocatively, knowing, of course, even as he said it, that it was just the kind of repartee he should refrain from if he didn't want to encourage her.

She gurgled with laughter. "I was ringing to ask if you liked music?"

Edward hesitated; obviously a loaded question yet hardly one he could answer with a blanket "no". "Any particular kind of music?" he asked, trying to maintain the same level of jokey detachment.

"Russian music," said Irina, and there was something heart-felt in the way she said it, an endorsement, an emotional underlining, which made Edward answer quite spontaneously, "Well, yes, what I've heard."

"Would you like to hear some more?" Irina asked enticingly, as though she were offering him to remove layers one by one.

"Who, how, what, when, where?" asked Edward.

Irina giggled. "Who: a Russian choir, how: beautifully, what: oh my God, I couldn't tell you the names of composers of that kind of churchy music, when: Thursday night, where: the Russian cathedral, St Alexander Nevsky. And who with: me and my Great-Aunt Elena."

"Gosh," said Edward. It certainly didn't sound like a second seduction bid. He wondered whether Irina had got over his rebuff at the front door and decided to pursue a purely Platonic friendship, or whether she was just biding her time. Certainly, not even Irina, with her ever-present panoply of eccentric elderly relatives, could conceivably invite him to come and sit in a church alongside her and her great-aunt if she had any ulterior motives. "It sounds very interesting," he said guardedly.

"But you're not free on Thursday night," Irina said unexpectedly bitterly. *"Enfin*, it was just an idea."

"Hang on a minute," Edward protested. "I *am* free on Thursday night. I would like to come actually, if you don't mind."

"You would?" Irina exclaimed. "Well, then, I don't understand you at all. You seemed utterly unenthusiastic about continuing our acquaintance when we parted on Friday but now you agree to come and sit in a smelly church with a load of old fogies and listen to depressing religious music."

Her trill of laughter broke Edward's throttled silence. "Don't worry, Edouard," she said. "I'm only teasing you; I'm very pleased you want to come."

She embarked on directions and Metro stations and street names. They arranged to meet on Thursday at eight o'clock at the ticket windows of Metro Courcelles. The concert didn't start until nine but they would have to collect Great-Aunt Elena first from her apartment on the Boulevard de Courcelles and she was a slow walker.

Edward recovered from the telephone call over a large gin. He didn't see quite how Irina had done it but she had led him cleverly into saying and doing at every turn the exact opposite of what he had intended. As for her devastating frankness, he felt it was more than anyone could be expected to put up with in the long run.

For the next three days, he contemplated what he had let himself in for. At work, the main focus of interest was a visiting freelancer just back from an assignment covering the refugee story in Vietnam and Kampuchea. He was using their office as a base from which to extract follow-up information from the respective embassies. Habitually someone who worked on the move, he was indifferent to the territorial boundaries of office life and roamed in and out of the rooms, regardless of their occupants. Marie-Yvette and Aurore, and most especially old Monsieur Marchais, found him rather a hindrance but Edward welcomed his intrusions. His name was Geoff Burr and he too seemed to enjoy impressing young Teddy, as he rather off-puttingly called him, with his anecdotes from the great outdoors. Eventually, he so liked talking and Edward listening, that one early evening they went out drinking together.

It didn't take long before Geoff's anecdotes had roused Edward to a state of acute dissatisfaction. "God, if only you knew," he ventured, "how incredibly pissed off I was about getting sent to Paris."

Geoff looked at him from a huge distance comprised of genuinely different lifestyles and alcohol. "Ah, it's not that bad, is it?" he said.

Edward spluttered. "It probably isn't as a place to come back to after what you've just been telling me about. But imagine a year here. Or two."

Geoff took an enormous swig at his *vin rouge*. "Your time'll come," he said uncertainly.

To Edward's concern, there seemed to be something in his uncertainty to do with Edward's suitability for that life. To prove himself, there being no other way in a Parisian bar, Edward drank enormously and as the evening progressed, he was more and more affected by an upsetting vision of himself as a dreary, desk-bound hack, eagerly inhaling Geoff's whiff of the great outdoors.

Later, they went in search of a restaurant Geoff remembered where, he said, you could eat the best *soupe à l'oignon* in the world. As they wandered unsuccessfully through the redeveloped Halles, it seemed to Edward that the distinction between the inside of bars and the street had disappeared; he was just as much indoors in these pedestrian precincts as at any of the numerous marble table-tops they had visited in the course of the evening. He tipped his head back to glance at the purplish-orange night sky which he now abruptly perceived as a ceiling.

"Hang on a sec," he heard Geoff's voice from an unexpected angle. "Are you feeling OK, Teddy, my boy?"

They never found Geoff's restaurant but ended up instead in a rather seedy establishment where Geoff claimed to recognise a waitress. With the food, Edward's emotions settled somewhat and his jealousy of Geoff now, unbearably, planning a trip to West Africa, subsided to a pressing impatience to follow suit.

When they parted, Edward climbing carefully out of Geoff's

taxi on the corner of the rue Surcouf, Geoff, who was leaving Paris in the morning, gave him a large, vague wave. "See you in Phnom Penh, Teddy, my boy."

Edward tried not to register the depressing domesticity of his front door, his back copies of *Le Canard Enchaîné* beside the lavatory, and his toothbrush in its glass. He remembered to down three coffee mugs of cold water and went straight to bed, to dream, hardly surprisingly but nevertheless unfairly, of aeroplanes and take-offs and bumpy landings on air strips cut out of impenetrable jungle.

By twenty past eight, he had even wondered whether the whole thing was an elaborate punishment set up by Irina and she was going to leave him standing out of pique. He had been waiting at the ticket windows of Metro Courcelles for nearly half an hour. He had got there early, not to make a good impression on Irina, he assured himself, but simply because he couldn't yet judge his journey time with any degree of accuracy. It wasn't a very busy station and the home-going solid citizens of the eighth *arrondissement* gave him sideways glances of beady suspicion. He had mentioned to Marie-Yvette, not in any spirit of boasting but just so that someone at the paper should know he had an active social life, that he was off to an engagement on the Boulevard de Courcelles and she had wrinkled her nose and said, "Ah la la! So you're starting to move in all the *right* circles, I see." He felt himself a conspicuous, visibly alien figure on the draughty station. From watching successive waves of passengers emerging, he lazily drew up a list of characteristics which marked the species Parisian male: bottle-green overcoats with a pleat in the back, hunched head and shoulders, worry lines. And the women, not so many at this hour, all came trotting smartly through the exit, tight-lipped, diamond-hard, bristling, and bringing gusts of perfume which seemed to Edward, rather than seductive,

more like the defensive odour sprayed out by a skunk. Irina, he
realised, would stand out among them too. And when, finally,
at almost half past eight, she did emerge, hurtling from the
exit, her appearance had something arresting, quite dramatic
about it, which temporarily prevented him from expressing
his annoyance.

"Edouard!" she gasped. "I'm so sorry."

"What happened?" he asked.

Irina put her hand on his arm. It wasn't clear if she had done
it as an endearment or simply to help her steady herself. "So
stupid," she panted. "I was all ready. I was waiting for a friend
who was coming over to sit with Babushka and he didn't come.
I don't know what to do. I rang the bookshop where he works
and I rang his apartment, which I hate doing, but he wasn't
anywhere. I don't know what's happened; if he's forgotten
about it or if something's gone wrong. I couldn't reach you.
I was going frantic."

"Can't you leave her by herself?" Edward asked, aghast at
the thought of such a constraint on one's liberty.

"Of course I can," Irina answered scornfully. "How do
you suppose I go out to work every day? I lead my life.
It's just sometimes she gets these – ideas and it's best to
have someone there to discourage her from trying to carry
them out. Of course, she can hardly walk at all so it's not
really a risk but all the same I feel better if she's not on her
own. I just hope he shows up."

"What sort of ideas?" asked Edward.

They had left the Metro station and were hurrying along
a wide tree-lined boulevard. Beside him Irina, there was no
other word for it, was scurrying. Every few yards, she glanced
at her watch, tutted or clucked and scurried a little more. She
answered his question with a dismissive "Tchuh!" and a flick
of one hand. After a few moments, she added, "You couldn't
possibly understand. Specifically Russian delusions."

Edward hesitated, his curiosity aroused. "Try me and see,"
he suggested.

Irina gave a still louder "Tchuh!" "She tries to set out
on a journey," she said, almost resentfully. "Can you imagine? Eighty-seven years old, she can barely walk, and she
takes it into her head she's going to set out on a jaunt of a

89

few thousand miles. She couldn't get to the Metro on her own!"

"Where does she want to go?" Edward asked.

Irina gave him a malevolent sideways look. "St Petersburg," she snapped. "Leningrad to you."

She drilled on the bell of her great-aunt's apartment house and after the heavy, dark-green front door had clicked open in response, she hurried ahead of Edward down the deep entrance hall. The cavernous lift at the end of it was out of order, *"En Dérangement"* in Edward's favourite phrase. At the sight of the white card hanging askew from the lift door handle, Irina gave a little moan and plunged despairingly towards the staircase. By the time they reached the third floor, she was quite seriously out of breath. As they waited for the great-aunt to answer her bell, Edward felt suddenly acutely sorry for Irina, watching her struggle to control her panting and prepare her face into a serene expression of greeting. He had a half-formed intimation that getting older meant exactly this accumulation of worries, all the tedious constrictions and hindrances which had to be taken into account before you could do anything, and which culminated in his parents' fretful immobility.

"You'll be able to relax in church," he comforted her.

A high-pitched torrent of greeting became audible behind the door and the great-aunt opened it in mid-sentence, stretching out both hands in delighted surprise as though their arrival were completely unexpected.

Edward was relieved to see she was a lot more vigorous than the grandmother. A certain spherical sturdiness was obviously a shared characteristic of all the women of the family. In Great-Aunt Elena, as Irina hastily introduced her, it took the form of a fair amount of corseted girth and a pair of pink-veined, only faintly wrinkled cheeks which Edward incongruously imagined being featured in a promotion by the Apple Marketing Authority. She gestured enthusiastically for them to come in. Irina interrupted her flow to point out that they were very short of time. Great-Aunt Elena paused and gave Irina a majestic look. "Indeed?" she declared. "And whose fault is that, may I ask?"

Indignantly, Irina started to explain. As soon as she mentioned the grandmother, Great-Aunt Elena erupted into another stream of exclamations. "She was always impossible," she pronounced. "Always. Long before – even when she was a girl, she was always on the point of running away somewhere, you know." She turned to Edward. "Vera has suitcases on the brain."

"Don't drag him into it, please," Irina said tensely. "Where are your coat and hat? We really should be on our way."

Grumbling good-naturedly, Great-Aunt Elena went off into a side room. Edward tried to catch Irina's eye so he could give her a cheery conspiratorial wink, but she studiously avoided looking his way, seemingly embarrassed by this collective display of family oddity.

Edward was actually rather enjoying it. The small hall where they were waiting looked to him like a fly-blown model interior in a museum. Every inch of space was crowded with visibly venerable belongings and no anachronistic ephemera from 1980s Paris had slipped in to mar the yellowed authenticity. He felt he was standing in a hall in another city entirely.

After a moment, Great-Aunt Elena returned, wearing a highly feathered black hat and holding out an aged black astrakhan coat for one of them to help her put it on. Her voice had been just audible out of the other room, keeping up her running commentary on the evening's events. Now she paused in front of them, cocking her plumed head and looking winsomely from one to the other, waiting for them to compete for the favour of helping her on with her coat. Irina bustled forward and helped her a little roughly into it. Great-Aunt Elena pirouetted in front of a smoky mirror to judge the finished effect. She turned to Edward. "Irina lacks a gentleman's gallant touch," she said coyly.

As they went down the stairs, Irina and her great-aunt broke into Russian. Going down ahead of them, Edward tried to judge if the double chirruping conveyed discord or harmony but it was almost impossible to tell. Out in the street, they reverted smartly to French. He and Irina each giving Great-Aunt Elena one arm, which seemed unnecessary but which visibly gave her pleasure, they set off back up the boulevard. Edward glanced surreptitiously at his watch; it was just after nine.

He couldn't say he was taken with the actual music but as

91

an all-round experience the concert was certainly gratifyingly weird. A good quarter of an hour late, they turned into the rue Daru, a plain, grey street of dormant Parisian apartment houses, and halfway along it they arrived at the black and gold gateway to a scene from a Russian village, astonishingly resurrected between the drab apartment houses. It was such an incongruous sight, the gold onion-domed church of folklore standing in a courtyard planted with silver birch trees, that Edward involuntarily stopped and goggled up at it. Above the church door, there was an arch filled with a gold mosaic depicting a blandly sweet-faced male saint holding an open book. Edward tried to make out what details he could of the rest of the church in the dark but he was chivvied forward by his two companions. They obviously weren't the only latecomers, though, for there were other heavily coated figures ahead of them tramping up the flight of steps which led to the church door. In fact, the whole evening seemed to be running late because as they entered the church, a fat florid-faced man was only just announcing, in Russian and thickly accented French, the first item of the concert. The people who had come in ahead of them were engaged in a flurry of crossing themselves.

Since the music, an unaccompanied doleful chanting, didn't do much for Edward, he found his attention easily distracted during the first half of the concert by his surroundings and by the audience. On his left, Irina, for all her earlier scoffing at "depressing religious music", sat apparently rapt. Beyond her, Great-Aunt Elena alternately fidgeted and drowsed. The rest of the church was filled to capacity with an audience which appeared to be entirely in their seventies and eighties. Looking idly around, Edward could see an unparalleled concentration of silver hair swept into pin-studded buns, pink bald pates and ludicrously old-fashioned hats. There was also an impressive concentration of serious furs, reducing the number of short, stout figures which could be fitted into each row of unevenly assembled benches and chairs, and adding to the predominant reek of incense a background blend of mothballs.

"Well?" Irina turned to him when, eventually, one of the heartbreaking chants ended in a disconcerting silence and, without any applause, people laboured to their feet to go and greet acquaintances. "Are you enjoying it?"

Edward hesitated. "Well, the music's not really my idea of fun," he admitted. "But it is interesting. And actually I think this whole place is rather interesting; I am glad I came."

Irina considered the audience with what looked like bleak affection. "You should study this society while you still can," she said to him solemnly. "We're coming up to the middle of the nineteen eighties. By the middle of the nineteen nineties, this will be gone forever."

Undeterred by its imminent extinction, the aged community was battling towards a room off the vestibule where refreshments were being served.

Irina asked Edward, "Are you hungry? D'you want something?"

He shook his head. He had, slightly sordidly, eaten two Big Macs before taking the Metro to Courcelles. Eating Big Macs in Paris constituted a symbolic act of gastronomic rejection in which he still rather stubbornly took pleasure.

"Well, shall we go outside and breathe?" Irina suggested, "This incense gives me such a headache."

Great-Aunt Elena had disappeared into a multitude of nodding black hats. Dismissing her disappearance with an airy wave, Irina led the way outside. She looked distracted, Edward thought, as they stood a little aimlessly in the dark courtyard. She played with the bracelet on her wrist and glanced at her watch.

"How long does the interval last?" Edward asked. "What time will the concert finish?"

Irina threw him a look of amused disdain. "It's that bad, is it?"

"Why were *you* looking at your watch?" Edward retaliated.

"I was just hoping my friend had turned up," Irina explained. "To keep an eye on Babushka." She sighed heavily. "I don't want to have to spend my afternoon off tomorrow unpacking her suitcases."

Once again, Edward felt sorry for Irina, and slightly conscience-stricken. He was deeply glad that he had no one he needed to take into account. He asked, "Couldn't you telephone?"

Irina shook her head. "They're still pre-1917 here. I don't think they have a public telephone. It doesn't matter; I'll try afterwards from Elena's."

On their way back in, Irina was stopped at least half a dozen times to say hello to people. From their gestures, stroking her on the cheek, patting her on the head, Edward concluded that most of these old characters must have known Irina since she was a child and still viewed her as one. When they reached their row, where Great-Aunt Elena was once more ensconced, talking animatedly to a new neighbour in ear muffs, Irina breathed a heavy sigh of relief. "Sometimes I think I should go and live in Australia," she confided in a fierce whisper, "just to get away from them all."

The second half of the concert frankly dragged. Although the stencilled programme notes explained that these chants were of a completely different origin, Edward couldn't detect much difference. His attention freewheeled. He remembered Irina's remark, "By the middle of the nineteen nineties, this will be gone forever," and he wondered what it must feel like to be a historical curiosity. He wondered whether these sturdy old people in their furs even realised that they were a historical curiosity; meeting here only with their own kind, keeping up the language and customs of another country in another age, did the perceptions of the present day matter to them at all? He had entered a time warp. Subject only to the biological inevitability of ageing, the community was otherwise immune to change. He felt distinctly odd sitting in their midst, now he came to think about it; probably the only person who wasn't in the least Russian in the whole church. What exactly was he doing there? Beside him, Irina was far away inside her enjoyment of the music; she belonged here. It wasn't only her round face and the inherited ease with which she wore a fur coat. It was also a question of her nature. For all her flashy surface fashion, her coloured hair, the big brilliant green earrings she was sporting tonight, somewhere at her core it was still before the First World War. What worried Edward was that he hadn't noticed where the time warp first began; it had begun at the front door of the Iskarovs' flat.

Seeing Irina like this, in context, he felt much kindlier disposed towards her than at any time. Not only had she acquired

94

here a convincing carat mark of Russianness, even some of her quirks made more sense; for example, her abrasiveness, which he now saw as the ferocious struggle of a fly to free itself from the gluey golden amber in which it was trapped.

What had the old people made of him when they came up to say hello? He sincerely hoped they were all too old and proper to have put two and two together and made five. It was true none of them had seemed to show much curiosity about his presence as Irina's guest. But then, of course, he hadn't understood a word they said.

He felt cheered to be on thoroughly foreign soil for the first time since he came to Paris. The happy exhilaration of discovery enveloped him as he looked around at the dark icons watching over the silver heads. As a guide to her unlikely kingdom, Irina could certainly create a diversion.

It wasn't long before this transient optimism receded, washed away, doubtless, by the depressing music. It was pathetic to be reduced to feeling cheered because he had in a smelly church discovered a fossilised version of a country. He thought how totally ironic and back-to-front and sad it was that instead of travelling forwards into some dynamic and vibrant future, as he was meant to when he moved abroad, all Paris had been able to offer him was a journey sixty years backwards.

He greeted the end of the final chant with relief.

Irina scooped up her bag and gloves and said briskly, "Right, let's be on our way," as though to make up for the fact that she had visibly been moved by the music.

The goodbyes took a further ten or fifteen minutes and then they headed out onto the Boulevard de Courcelles again, pushing back towards Great-Aunt Elena's apartment house into what had become a bitterly cold wind. Neither Irina nor Great-Aunt Elena seemed especially troubled by the wind and Edward couldn't help admiring the way they kept up their conversation the length of the boulevard, shrieking their questions and answers at one another in the teeth of the wind. One of their exchanges caught Edward's attention. Although it was in Russian, he could understand it was about food because the food words were all in French; *quenelles de saumon, escalopes de dindon, pudding au riz*. His apprehensions were confirmed when Irina leant across her great-aunt and called to him, "Are you hungry, Edouard? We're going to eat at Elena's."

He began, "I didn't realise – " but Irina shouted cheerily, "I can't hear a word you're saying."

He tried again. "I didn't realise we were going to eat. I'm afraid I had something to eat beforehand."

Irina pouted. "You disappoint me yet again."

Great-Aunt Elena interrupted. "What? What did he say?"

"He's not hungry," Irina shouted at her. "We'll have to do something about that."

Great-Aunt Elena turned to Edward, full of acute concern. "Not hungry? What's the matter? Are you ill?"

Edward grinned sheepishly. "No, no, I'm fine. It's just I had something beforehand."

Great-Aunt Elena dismissed such a feeble pretext. "So what? You'll have something afterwards as well. At your age, one can."

With a dismal sensation of defeat, Edward realised he was not going to get out of this unexpected extension to the evening. What was more, he didn't like the way, for the second time now, these tough Russian women had got the better of him with quantities of food and drink. He, who was renowned among his friends as a bottomless pit; by their Slav standards, he acknowledged he was a non-starter.

Perhaps feeling slightly sorry for him, Irina added, "Great-Aunt Elena's gone to a lot of trouble. You mustn't disappoint her."

Before Edward could answer, Great-Aunt Elena squeezed his hand tightly. "He won't. Will you, *golubchik?*"

It must have been half past eleven when they sat down to table. By one o'clock in the morning, Edward's resentment had turned to admiration; Great-Aunt Elena was, by her own admission, eighty – "Eighty-one," Irina mouthed behind her back – but she wasn't flagging at all.

As soon as they entered the flat, Irina had gone to telephone home. Her friend had arrived, had talked the grandmother out of setting off for the Finland Station and was happy to stay there, watching the television, until Irina came home. Edward did wonder, briefly, what the nature of this friend (after all male) was, who was willing to do Irina such enormous

96

favours and wait uncomplainingly until all hours for her to come home. He even wondered whether all his anxiety about Irina's pursuit hadn't been misplaced. Maybe that was just her manner; maybe she behaved that way, ravenously, to all men? He observed her with pity.

Her face, in the better light of Elena's apartment, showed how tired she was; there were dark rings under her eyes and her complexion had a sallow tinge. When she returned from the telephone, having taken off her coat, her brilliant green earrings turned out to be accessories to a brilliant green top and skirt, whose lurid colour gave her, Edward found, a livid look. She plumped herself into an armchair and sighed, "Oich!"

"Hard day at the *lycée*?" Edward asked.

Irina shuddered. "Don't mention the name. The very idea of it makes me depressed."

"Ach, Irina, you exaggerate," Great-Aunt Elena commented. She was busy at the side of the room putting out a daunting number of dishes onto an already densely set small table. "You have less than one week of term left and then all that Christmas holiday."

"You don't understand," Irina retorted. It was obvious it was a disagreement they had had many times before.

Great-Aunt Elena appealed to Edward. "Tell me what *you* think. Don't you think she's lucky? She's got a post in one of the best, the very best *lycées* in Paris. Her pupils are mostly nice girls, no trouble-makers. And yet she goes on as if it were a prison."

"It *is* a prison," Irina said through gritted teeth. "When are we going to eat? I'm starving."

Great-Aunt Elena flung up her hands and then clapped them dismissively. The Russian exclamation which accompanied this sounded like someone incompletely bursting a paper bag. Then she bustled with busy dignity from the room.

Irina shut her eyes. Edward, observing her, remembered one of his friend Roland's observations on women. Roland, who fancied himself as something of a connoisseur, had once said that a woman's age showed most first thing in the morning. "Say you've had a fair bit to drink," he had said. "And you end up in bed with someone of your own age or younger, you'll both look about equally terrible in the morning. But say you've

97

picked up some eager older woman who might have looked perfectly acceptable under the party lighting the night before. Well, you'll probably wake up next to some absolutely awful old bag."

Edward was wondering experimentally whether the dictum would apply to Irina when she asked him, apparently without opening her eyes, "Why are you looking at me like that, Edouard?"

He answered flippantly, "Oh, just admiring you, I expect."

Irina's eyes popped open. "You didn't have an admiring look, let me tell you. You had that look as if I were a rare specimen of furry animal. You were observing the animal's sleeping habits."

"Oh come," Edward began unconvincingly.

Irina interrupted him. "Please don't just consider me as a geographical oddity for your journalist's notebook," she said with a display of rigid dignity obviously inherited straight from her aunt. "Remember I am a full person too."

Great-Aunt Elena bustled back in at this awkward juncture, bringing a dish of *quenelles de saumon*. Edward was glad of the excuse of his earlier dinner as the meal got under way, for it became clear that Great-Aunt Elena, in an effort to please the supposed tastes of her English guest, had prepared exclusively bland and stodgy dishes.

At first, the conversation centred on her preparations.

"I thought you would be homesick," she explained to Edward. "I discussed with my butcher what might be appropriate and he suggested *rosbif*. But I knew it couldn't wait during the concert so in the end I got *escalopes de dindon* instead. They're quicker and I know that turkey is a traditional Christmas dish in England, isn't that right?"

"It's very kind of you," Edward thanked her feebly, forking a bit of tasteless pink *quenelle* around his plate. He was marginally put off to notice that Irina was eating this unappealing dish with a hearty appetite; he had imagined that someone who was such a superlative cook would have been more discerning. But she seemed to tackle whatever was put in front of her.

"Have you been to England?" he asked Great-Aunt Elena politely.

She shook her head. "But I feel I know England intimately,"

she said. "You see, we had an English governess in Russia when we were children."

"Oh God," Irina groaned rudely. "Miss Macpherson. Here we go."

Great-Aunt Elena ignored her pointedly. "Miss Macpherson. She was an admirable woman. She taught us to read and write, she taught us English, she taught us to play the piano and to sing. She was a woman of profound culture and," she glanced defiantly at Irina, "great moral worth."

"Macpherson is a Scottish name," Edward said tentatively.

"Yes," Great-Aunt Elena said, "Yes, she was Scottish. But she taught us the most beautiful pure English." She sat a little straighter in her chair and recited:

> "I travelled among unknown men,
> In lands beyond the sea;
> Nor, England! did I know till then
> What love I bore to thee.
>
> 'Tis past, that melancholy dream!
> Nor will I quit thy shore
> A second time; for still I seem
> To love thee more and more.
>
> Among thy mountains did I feel
> The joy of my desire;
> And she I cherished turned her wheel
> Beside an English fire."

She spoke with an impeccable BBC World Service pronunciation but a distinct burring Scottish brogue.

While she was in the kitchen frying the *escalopes*, Irina explained, "Miss Macpherson is single-handedly responsible for Great-Aunt Elena's elevated view of the teaching profession. She thinks I'm carrying on a noble calling by dinning irregular verbs into the heads of my dear girls. Personally, I think Miss Macpherson must have been a terrible tyrant. She simply bullied them all into adoring her." Absent-mindedly, Irina impaled another *quenelle* on her fork from the serving dish and set about chewing it. "You should see her in their

99

photographs; bony, as straight as a soldier on guard duty, and with an expression – " she scowled ferociously into the middle distance. "They're all brown old photographs, of course, but Elena told me she had flaming red hair, so red that when she let it down to go to bed, they would cry out, pretending they thought there was a bonfire in their nursery."

Over the *escalopes*, served rather disconcertingly with dumplings, the conversation moved to Edward and from Edward, by way of his flat, to Volodya.

"Maybe we ought to give Edward Volodya's writing desk?" Great-Aunt Elena suggested to Irina. "Since he's a journalist."

Irina hesitated. "We could. But actually it's not that good for writing on for long periods, you know; it tips forward if you lean on it too heavily."

"What did he do?" Edward asked. "Was he some sort of a writer or a journalist?"

He saw a veil come down in front of Irina's and Great-Aunt Elena's faces. For a few seconds, both of them contemplated a past he could not share.

Irina answered, "He had several professions; he was too clever to allow himself to be limited by any one. He was in the import-export business for a long time and he was also an impresario; he put on shows with an optimistic element, you know, singing and dancing and plenty of jokes. He liked people to have a good time. And he had a lot of other interests too: stamps, perfume, *haute couture*, gastronomy."

Great-Aunt Elena came out from behind her veil to add, "At the time he lived in the rue Surcouf, he was planning to set up an antiques business. He wanted to conquer the new world with the treasures of the old. He went into partnership with an American woman – "

"That," Irina interrupted, "was a fatal mistake, literally fatal. Really, I don't know why you have to bring that up." She turned to Edward. "Dyadya Volodya was the most kind and generous man, you understand," she said insistently. "But frequently unlucky in matters of the heart. Certain sorts of women would take advantage of him."

Before Great-Aunt Elena could intervene with a rival version of events, Irina added teasingly to Edward, "You must beware the influence of his home."

"*Enfin*, Irina," Great-Aunt Elena protested. "Edward's far too sensible for that kind of thing; look at him. And in any case, poor Volodya suffered from a problem of disorientated people; he couldn't accurately place others in the category to which they belonged. He had become confused by too many migrations. He couldn't recognise the dangerous species. That couldn't possibly happen to Edward."

"I don't know," Irina said mischievously. "Edouard's going to travel the world for his newspaper too, you know. He's only here in Paris for a year. He could quite easily develop the emotional problems of a disorientated person."

"Only here for a year?" Great-Aunt Elena exclaimed. "You mean you let the flat to somebody who you know is only going to be here for a year? Whatever did you do that for?"

Simultaneously, both Irina and Edward volunteered, "It might be two."

Great-Aunt Elena shook her head in dismay. "I thought we'd agreed – "

"Look," Irina said, gesturing at Edward. "He seems fine, don't you agree? So what's the problem?"

Courteously, Great-Aunt Elena agreed that Edward did seem fine. But, embarrassingly taking Edward as a witness to Irina's fecklessness, she rolled her eyes heavenwards.

The rice pudding she produced next was a fitting end to the pre-digested dinner; it was milkier than an English one and enlivened by a few pieces of candied fruit but still a near relative. Unenthusiastically, Edward manoeuvred it around his plate.

Great-Aunt Elena, apparently intent on rebuking Irina for her rash behaviour over the flat, continued mercilessly. "Irina has the emotional problems of a disorientated person too, I believe. She doesn't like Frenchmen, she doesn't like Russians; she can't settle for anybody, it seems." She scooped up a bit of angelica and chewed it vindictively.

Irina said something grumpily in Russian, which she translated for Edward as, "What a marvellous song; sing it all over again from the beginning."

"Italians, Hungarians, Brazilians," Great-Aunt Elena went

101

on. "Never anybody too suitable, too close to home. Africans, Chinese – "

"I have *never*," Irina said with frigid dignity, "had anything to do with a Chinese."

They all three started laughing, including Irina, but she added, "Anyway, I have Mama and you to thank, don't I, for bringing me up such a sophisticated and cosmopolitan person that I can't find satisfaction anywhere on earth. I'm following in Mama's fine tradition; I'm sampling the fruits of the earth." She concluded, with an unnerving mixture of flattery and spite, "We can't all be as clever as you, Elena, and pick a saint like Borya first time round."

The teasing and bickering subsided as they scraped their pudding plates clean and simultaneously realised it was nearly one in the morning.

Irina announced, "In eight hours' time, I have to analyse Turgenev with my *Terminale*," and she shuddered.

Great-Aunt Elena was reluctant for them to leave. "No coffee?" she protested. "No *petit digestif*?"

She kept hold of Edward's hand in both of hers when they shook hands at the door. "It doesn't matter you're only going to be here for a year," she reassured him earnestly. "We shall still treat you as a member of the family so long as you're living in Volodya's apartment. I'll telephone you to make sure you've got everything you need. And maybe you can come over here from time to time and talk English to me. I'll look after you better than Irina."

Irina was uncharacteristically silent in the taxi on the way home. Edward said little either, browsing through some of the odder images of the evening: the grandmother's journey; the Scottish accent of a woman long dead incongruously preserved in Great-Aunt Elena's poem; Volodya failing to recognise a poisonous species of American woman and, in his gastronomic fervour, consuming her, with fatal results. He reflected drowsily how many of the evening's participants were in fact dead, yet how tenaciously they kept their places among the living.

Eventually Irina said, "I suppose you've had enough of my family now to last you the whole year."

"Why d'you say that?" Edward asked.

Irina gave a single hard laugh. "Isn't it obvious? Who, in their right mind, would put up with such a performance all year round? And you're so *much* in your right mind."

"I found this evening very interesting," Edward said feebly.

"Interesting!" Irina repeated bitterly. "Yes, I suppose for you it was *interesting.*"

They both stayed silent to appreciate the drive across the Pont des Invalides. The taxi entered the Boulevard de Latour-Maubourg. Edward briefly enjoyed the novelty of driving companionably between the dark shuttered apartment houses.

"You're sure you don't want to be taken home first?" he asked Irina. "You're sure you don't mind if he drops me off first?"

Irina shook her head. "You're sweet," she said bleakly.

The taxi pulled over opposite the rue Saint Dominique.

"Well, thank you again," Edward said a little awkwardly. "I did enjoy this evening." He extended his hand, uncertainly, to shake Irina's. She didn't even reach forward to take it. She raised hers in an offhand little wave. "*Au revoir*, Edouard," she said limply. "We'll be in touch."

He looked after her as he waited for the lights to change so he could cross the boulevard. Huddled in her furs, Irina was a gloomy but unmistakably a romantic figure as the taxi bore her away.

Henry and Mai's party, for the "holiday season" as Henry put it, for the *"fêtes de fin d'année"* as Marie-Yvette put it, was on the last Saturday before Christmas. Although there were still a couple of working days before the public holiday, Marie-Yvette and Aurore were both treating themselves to the following week off and as Edward overheard them discussing the party in the office, he got the impression that it was going to be quite an occasion for letting one's hair down, comfortable in the knowledge that most of them wouldn't have to face their colleagues for several days afterwards. He would have liked to ask them for further details – Henry's party was a hardy annual event – but it seemed undignified. From what he could hear, it sounded as though it would be a fairly smart event; there seemed to be a good deal of dressing-up on the cards. But from his three months' exposure to Parisian females and their propensity for dressing themselves up at the slightest excuse, he acknowledged wryly that this was not a reliable indicator of the smartness of the party. He noticed also that no one made much of its being Christmas. At first, he wondered if this were out of polite consideration for Henry's Jewishness, not that that seemed to consist of much more than a wicked sense of humour and knowing where the best restaurants were. Then he realised it was general; Christmas in Paris didn't seem to have the obscene quality of a sexless orgy which it had in England. There was a welcome lack of spray-can snow and piped carols. Monitoring the office conversation over the last couple of days before the party, and noting the absence of commentary on who was going to give what to whom, on who was going to eat which of the series of monumentally tedious meals at whose house, Edward decided that Christmas here had a non-committal cosmopolitan flavour to it, which he rather approved of.

He wore a tie, as a precaution, and arrived punctually half an hour after the time Henry had said, bringing a gift-wrapped box of *marrons glacés*. Mai, who opened the door to him, accepted it with a little giggle of amusement, "Oh, Edward, so *traditional!*" and while he was idiotically wishing that he had had the wit to bring something else instead, steered him down the picture-hung corridor, exclaiming, "Henry wants you to meet somebody here. Let me introduce you right away before I forget." Following her, Edward felt slightly ruffled; surely he wasn't such a pathetic figure that even his boss felt obliged to introduce him to single women? The now familiar living-room was already fairly lively with an intriguing assortment of guests, of whom he recognised only Marie-Yvette and Aurore, and an Indian couple whom he had met there once before at dinner. But the person Mai was enthusiastically steering him towards was not a woman.

"Arnold," she said to a large sun-tanned man, who was stooping, a look of forced attention on his face, to listen to the Indians. "Meet Henry's new colleague, Edward Wainwright." And to Edward, she added, "You may talk about work. Arnold is your man in Kabul."

With a whisk of silky Oriental fabric, she spun away to answer another ring at the front door, and Edward urgently tried to remember all he knew about Arnold Elgood. It didn't matter that this wasn't very much because Arnold, presumably relieved to be rid of the Indians, started to question Edward vigorously about himself.

He regretted afterwards, when they had been separated by the party, that he hadn't had a chance to put a few questions to Arnold about life in Kabul and maybe make a good impression on him. But the next arrivals turned out to be a couple, old friends of Arnold's, and the three of them plunged across the room towards one another with cries of recognition and delight.

Edward fell back on Marie-Yvette and Aurore. Marie-Yvette had made only a slight concession to the party, changing her perpetual jeans for a pair of black leather trousers and weighting her, Edward thought, singularly unsexy ears with a pair of immense, apparently scrap metal earrings. But Aurore was a vision; she was wearing a striking turquoise and navy jumpsuit, finished off with unbelievably high-heeled turquoise shoes and what looked like turquoise kitchen foil electrifying her hair. Edward would have paid her a compliment if she hadn't introduced a thickset West Indian man, standing beside her looking distinctly resentful and ill-at-ease, as her *fiancé*. The four of them stood and spoke stiltedly until Mai bustled over again, exclaiming, "*Alors*, Monday to Friday, nine to five isn't enough for you lot? Aurore, come and tell my friend Madeleine what she should know for her holiday in Martinique."

Idling across the room in the hope of refilling his glass, Edward came face to face with the Hirshfelds' daughter Dinh. She was standing by herself in the middle of the animated crowd, surveying her parents' party with an expression of serene aloofness. Both faintly embarrassed, she and Edward rather woodenly wished each other "*Bonsoir*".

'Great,' Edward thought sarcastically. 'First the secretaries from work, now the boss's infant daughter. I'm really doing well here.'

Without any loss of dignity, Dinh offered to refill his glass for him. "What are you drinking?"

When he answered, "Scotch", she wrinkled her small nose disdainfully.

She brought him back an exceptionally strong measure and, at a loss for anything else to say to her, Edward asked, "Have the school holidays started yet?"

"Of course. The *lycée* broke up on Thursday."

At the mention of the word *lycée*, Edward realised the girl must be a fair bit older than he had imagined. Simultaneously, a more complex thought occurred to him.

"Do you go to the same *lycée* where your mother teaches?"

Dinh nodded. A tense, defensive look came over her face. But Edward's next question was obviously not what she expected.

"Do you know the Russian teacher?"

She frowned in puzzlement. "The Russian teacher? I don't do Russian."

"Mademoiselle Iskarov," Edward volunteered, reproaching himself fiercely for what he was doing.

Dinh still frowned. "I don't know all the teachers. It's a big place."

"It doesn't matter," Edward said hastily. "I was just wondering."

"Wait a minute," Dinh added. "There is one foreign lady there. She's quite fat and fierce-looking." She blew out her utterly smooth cheeks and glared at Edward grotesquely.

Appalled, Edward stared at her; it couldn't be. Renowned as little girls were for nastiness, he simply couldn't believe they considered Irina "fat and fierce-looking".

Dinh's cheeks collapsed. "*Ah non*, I've just remembered; that's Madame Braun who teaches German. I don't know Mademoiselle Iks – Isk – the Russian teacher."

"Well, it doesn't matter," Edward repeated rather sternly. "It's of no importance."

After an awkward silence, Dinh asked, "Are you hungry? Maman's prepared the most tremendous self-service supper next door."

Only a Parisian child, Edward reflected ruefully, would have the *savoir-faire* to get out of a tight corner so skilfully. Before he managed to shed her in the developing scrimmage around the buffet table, Dinh asked, "How come you know our Russian teacher?"

"She's my landlady," Edward replied crisply.

Considering it was his first party for three months, he could hardly say he was making the most of it. All else failing, he scanned the sitting-room for fanciable women under thirty. There seemed precious few of them. As he perched on the arm of a settee to eat his second plate of supper, a lone press officer from the Japanese Embassy came up and gave him a beseeching little introductory bow. The man's French and English were both so cumbersomely accented that any conversation was

107

laborious. Later, Edward talked to a glamorous, flamboyant but middle-aged Greek woman, who asked him to find her an ashtray, and subsequently to a man from New Jersey with whom he thoroughly discussed Bruce Springsteen. He saw Aurore laughing uproariously and flirting with Arnold Elgood, while her sullen boyfriend watched her bad-temperedly from the wall. Edward didn't get near Arnold again.

Going over the party dispiritedly as he travelled home late with a silent taxi driver, he wondered about the factors behind his failure to enjoy himself as he had intended. There were, first and foremost, the well-known shortcomings of Paris. At the same party in some South American capital, he would, of course, have shone. But he hadn't put his back into it. Was it possible that after only three months he was getting rusty; out of practice at having a good time? There was something else actually, too, but he refused to admit that could be a factor. He had dreaded that Irina might be at the party and then was slightly let down when she wasn't. Perhaps he had hoped that he could prove in public that their relationship was merely that of landlady and tenant and thereby return it from now on to more manageable proportions. He felt done out of the opportunity. But, after all, it was silly to have expected Mai to invite her colleagues from the *lycée*. For that was all Irina was; Mai's daughter didn't even know her name. And it simply hadn't been the sort of party where Mai would include all and sundry from the staffroom.

Still he was concerned that he should be even the slightest bit disappointed. It wasn't as if he would have enjoyed the party any more if Irina had been there. He imagined how she would have flirted with Arnold Elgood, sweetly mispronouncing his name. She would have worn her pink dress no doubt, although maybe she had half a dozen others of that voltage. Out of discretion, surely, she would not have paid much attention to her tenant.

He was planning to fly home for a bare forty-eight hours, although he could easily have stayed for longer. The only way he could convey that his life in Paris contained anything of any importance, either professional or personal, was to fly hastily in and fly hastily back. Besides, the thought of a prolonged family Christmas filled him with such complete aversion that he thought he preferred the empty silence of the rue Surcouf. In the last couple of days before his departure, he made a few perfunctory preparations. He bought easy, unimaginative Christmas presents all round. He considered, just briefly, telephoning Guy and Roland to find out where they would be spending Christmas but decided against it pretty quickly. They were the only people from whom he knew he couldn't successfully hide how poorly Paris was turning out.

The night before he left, on an impulse, he telephoned Irina. He would warn her the flat was going to be empty for two days. He would wish her a Happy Christmas. As soon as the phone started ringing at the other end, he had second thoughts but hanging up seemed even more of a give-away. It rang for a long, long time. If Irina were out, why didn't her grandmother pick up the phone? He glanced at Volodya's clock on the bookcase. It was ten o'clock. Could the grandmother have gone to bed already? He counted six more rings; she was, after all, a very slow walker. Then he put down the receiver. He wondered where Irina was. He wondered what, in the unknown turbulence of her private life, she might be up to.

The vintage Brie had been in the fridge before, but he was sure the pâté hadn't. Nor had there been an unopened carton of milk in the fridge door and a fresh *baguette* on the kitchen table. Someone had been in the flat while he was away. Perplexed, Edward went from room to room, searching for further signs of the mystery visitor. Nothing seemed to have been taken; it definitely wasn't some sort of bizarre burglary. Had someone illicitly been staying here, a very transient squatter? Or had the Iskarovs sneakily put someone up while he was gone? He came to his bedroom. Had whoever it was been through his things? Nothing looked as though it had been touched, although it was true he did not have much here to go through. Had they slept in his bed? It all seemed pristine, but now the mystery presence filled the whole flat. He went back to the living-room and imagined who on earth might have been sitting in Volodya's chair, listening to the inordinately loud ticking of Volodya's clock, which he had forgotten was quite so ludicrously loud. It was only when the spooky nervous prickling had spread all over him that he went into the kitchen again to take another look at the only clues, noticed more gifts of food distributed around the room and realised that, of course, it could only have been Irina.

"Edouard!" she exclaimed joyfully, when she answered the telephone. "You're back!"

"Thank you for all the food," he ventured. "It is from you, isn't it?"

Irina gave an ever-so-slightly offended laugh. "Who else? Is there some other woman I don't know about who has the keys to your apartment?"

"Thank you very much," Edward repeated laughing. "It's really awfully nice of you. I noticed in the taxi on the way back here that most of the shops are still shut. But tell me, how did you time it right? How did you know when I was coming back?"

Irina marked a minute pause. "I took a liberty," she said. "I hope you won't mind. But as you left me completely in the dark like that, just going off without a word, I had no choice. I had to know for the post and the *concierge*. You didn't turn the gas off at the mains, you know. I telephoned Monsieur Hirshfeld to find out when you were expected back at work."

"I did try to let you know," Edward answered sorely. "I telephoned you the night before I went away. But you were out. Why doesn't your grandmother answer the telephone?"

"How could she?" Irina exclaimed. "She doesn't hear properly half the time and she's never exactly sure who it is at the other end. She wouldn't know who you were."

"But she's met me," Edward said indignantly. "And she knows I live in Volodya's flat."

"Don't flatter yourself," Irina said coldly. Marginally more gently, she added, "When you have that many generations piled on top of one another in your brain, it's easy to get them muddled up. She might have realised who you were, but she might have thought you were somebody completely different too: someone's nephew or some boy she remembered from somewhere you've never even heard of."

"Thanks a lot," Edward retorted.

Irina laughed. "Anyway, she doesn't like answering the telephone. She thinks it always brings bad news. Well, after all that's happened to her in her life, you can understand it."

They observed a brief truce.

111

"Did you have a good Christmas?" Irina asked. "How was *perfide Albion*?"

"Pretty terrible," Edward answered. "How was yours?"

He did surprise himself somewhat by his admission. He was sure that not so long ago he would have answered blithely, "Oh fine" or, "Great". But Irina's flagrant lack of restraint or pride when things went wrong encouraged him to come clean. He expected she would reciprocate with some tale of woe.

Sure enough, she gave a groan. "Mine was perfectly awful," she pronounced. "You want to know what happened? Great-Aunt Elena and her protégée, Varvara Stepanovna, came round for dinner on Christmas Eve, the same as always, and an old family friend called Nikolai Grigoriev, who was my mother's last attachment, and I slaved away to make them all a delicious dinner, the same as always, and what did they do? Just what they did last year, and the year before, and the year before that; down to the seasonal witticisms and the compliments about the meal – they always say precisely the same things to me even though the dishes are totally different – and they brought up the same dreadful subjects and had the same old squabbles. And in the middle of it all I went out to the kitchen and I thought, 'I can't bear this.' I couldn't even ring my good friend Lyova, the one who sits with Babushka, because he was shut up enduring his own hell with his dear ones. I thought, 'How much longer is this going to go on? How many more years of the same voices having the same conversations will I have to put up with? Will no one ever come along and get me out of this misery?'"

"Mine was pretty much a re-run too," Edward answered.

"Tell me about your family," Irina asked.

But he could think of nothing to say. When he recalled his two boring, married, elder brothers and his two boring, married, elder sisters, and his mother fussing over the whereabouts of the gravy boat, and his father making a pedantic performance out of sharpening the carving knife, they didn't yield a single worthwhile anecdote.

"Oh," he said. "They're not like your family. They're not *interesting*."

"Lucky you," said Irina. "So is that why you came racing

112

back to Paris so quickly? You were bored? You couldn't wait to get back to the excitements of the metropolis?"

Edward wondered what she was getting at. Had she come upon his humiliatingly blank diary during her visit to the flat? Did she guess he had come back to spend the weekend reading and watching television within his four walls and resorting to the old Nicolas gut rot if he thought he was going to get depressed?

"You could put it that way," he answered, and then he waited. Irina, he felt already confident, would make her meaning only too clear.

"Any particular excitements?" she pressed. "Or just the proximity of the Eiffel Tower?"

"Nothing special."

"Nothing special? You just prefer the air here, I suppose, the *ambiance*? And what are you planning to do with yourself all weekend, if I may ask?"

"Oh," he said. "Odds and ends."

"I'm still on holiday for ten days," Irina told him. "I've got plenty of free time, for once."

And, so he justified it to himself afterwards, at that stage it became quite impossible, unless he wanted consciously to offend Irina, not to suggest that at some point over the weekend they could perhaps see each other.

It did certainly change the whole prospect ahead of him radically to have a date for dinner on Saturday night. Whoever it was with, this would still have been the case. All that day, as he pottered around – taking his washing to the launderette only to discover it was still shut, greedily eating Irina's pâté and *baguette* for lunch – he was far more conscious of the rounded satisfaction of having an engagement at the end of the day than of any worry because the engagement was with Irina.

She had suggested they meet in the Taverne Tourville. Edward had never been inside it but he knew it well by sight; a big, solemnly respectable *brasserie* on the corner of the Avenue de Tourville and the Avenue de la Motte Picquet, almost exactly halfway between his and Irina's apartments. Unnecessarily early, he showered and got changed, making a midway concession between actually dressing up and going as he was. Unnecessarily early, he set out for the Taverne

113

Tourville. It looked both welcoming and at the same time faintly stand-offish in the winter darkness, as he entered the Place de l'Ecole Militaire. Warm light shone from its large windows, but the waist-high wooden barrier outside it, which fenced off a small enclosure where in summer there would be tables, gave it an aloof appearance, like a house in a suburban street set further back behind a bigger front garden than its neighbours. He wondered why, for all its useful location, Irina had suggested such a stuffy meeting place.

The interior was the explanation. Edward took a seat in the window and looked around in surprise at what turned out to be a perfectly preserved Art Nouveau museum. Even the other customers were talking to one another in the low reverential voices reserved for cultural haunts. The large restaurant was only discreetly lit by the most lush lamps: white-glass globes painted with bunches of grapes and vine leaves, and over the bar bunches of yellow-glass grapes with weak electric light bulbs inside them. The bar itself was an immensely long and curving one, which shone like glass. He ordered a double Scotch and he started to wait for Irina.

He had got there fifteen minutes early intentionally, of course, but now his good manners rebounded on him. He had ample time to sit, sip his drink, and ask himself what the hell he was doing there. What in God's name was he getting into? He had come early because he was certain Irina was the sort of woman, however she behaved herself, who wouldn't take kindly to being kept waiting alone in a café. But, though her old-fashioned side might be quaint, it wasn't the crucial aspect of her; the crucial aspect was that Irina was ravenous for manflesh and she didn't care to hide it. She was hungry and she was after him. Edward only now began to wonder, belatedly, why he was putting himself in harm's way. It couldn't only be that something was better than nothing, surely? OK, the tendency was not to pass up any opportunity so frankly offered, but in the whole of Paris, for Christ's sake, there had to be an opportunity less obviously fraught right from the start with the potential for farcical disaster. Was it possible that, so far unrecognised by him, he actually fancied Irina? Did the offstage chomping of the lioness's teeth excite him? Or was it just the unbelievably

114

bizarre domestic circus around her which drew him; Russia *c.* 1917 being intrinsically more interesting than Paris of the early eighties? Whatever it was, he had no doubt in a moment of unpleasantly cold lucidity that he was on the verge of doing something unbelievably stupid. He could, of course, not do it. But that would be the wimp's option.

By the time they had agreed on, he was ready for his second drink. He ordered it quickly before Irina put in an appearance. He wondered in what shape and form the moment of decision would present itself. And he did then allow himself to wonder, things having already gone so unwisely far, what it might be like; what it might be like if he just let things take their course and went along obligingly with Irina's transparent wishes. It would be, in a word, a catastrophe.

The catastrophe came in through the nearest stained-glass door. She stood there for a moment, poised, looking around across the tables for her prey, and she looked so elegantly in keeping, making her entrance between the spiky bamboo plants in their fancy white tubs that in that moment Edward's fears became schoolboy immaturity and Irina a graduation ceremony.

She was wearing her fur coat with a vivid silk neck scarf which, as she saw him and came sailing self-consciously forward, worked its way a little loose and fluttered at her chin. She reminded Edward suddenly of the Alphonse Mucha posters his elder sisters had been so keen on as teenagers; with just the same enraptured expression and porcelain complexion, they had gazed down on him from bedroom walls, enhanced as here by stylised vegetation and artificial harvests. Hugging her coat exaggeratedly close, Irina made her way past the hat stand and the glass cabinet displaying jaded desserts. People looked up as she passed their tables, and Edward hoped childishly that they would notice whose table she was heading for. She covered the last stretch of exposed aisle as though it were open sea, her fur toque bravely high, and her boots treading resolutely across the uncertain deck. She drew to a halt in front of him and beamed.

"You look very fetching tonight," said Edward.

"Do I?" asked Irina. She preened herself for a second or two, smoothing her fur-clad flanks with one hand as if wishing

115

symbolically to slim them down, and tweeking anxiously at her neck scarf with the other. She subsided, after the exertion of her entrance, into the chair opposite Edward and sat back with a satisfied smile. As she crossed her legs in the confined space beneath the table, the sharp, shiny toes of her boots emerged to the side of the draped peach cloth.

"You look especially Russian," Edward added. "The fur and the boots. It's great."

Irina laughed. "Babushka got so worried when she saw me going out dressed up like this. She wanted to know where I was going, whom I was going to meet."

"Did you tell her?" asked Edward.

Irina puckered her lips. "What d'you think?"

Edward hesitated. "Yes, I think you did. To reassure her it was a perfectly innocent meeting with your tenant."

"Well, I didn't," said Irina. "It wouldn't have stopped her worrying anyway, you realise. She worries the way other people breathe; it's a natural condition. And as for the private lives of people she cares about – do you know she's still worrying about marriages which finished in the divorce courts years ago?"

"You mean," said Edward, "if you'd told her you were meeting me, she would have thought that a cause for concern?"

Irina sized him up. "Would she have been so wrong?"

Edward beckoned to the waiter to order Irina's drink. She chose, a little surprisingly, a port and while she was waiting for it she took off her hat and scarf, like props whose scene was over. But a new scene seemed to be getting under way, for when the port arrived, she didn't set about it with characteristic gusto but just dipped her lip into it affectedly and set the glass down barely touched.

"So?" she said to Edward. "You're glad to be back?"

Before he had thought through the consequences of his answer, he shrugged. "Not especially, frankly, no. I'd just had more than enough of home."

Irina took it personally. She tossed her head and replied sullenly, "I see."

She ran the tip of her finger round the rim of her glass and sulked into its shallow depths. Then she lifted her head

116

and announced truculently, "Well, Edouard, *I'm* glad you're back."

He let the pause last as long as was charitable. "Thanks," he said. There was something he did which had always brought Rosie round, and one or two others before her; it consisted of enclosing her hand in a rough grip and at the same time looking intently but without any expression into her face. The lack of expression was crucial for into it, he had gathered, women tended to read whatever they wanted. Now, like a move he had long learnt in a martial art, he envisaged it and put it into practice on Irina.

It wasn't a move to use on a woman who wore so many big rings. Irina drew breath and snatched her hand back. "Oich, Edouard," she exclaimed, "you *hurt* me!" She shook her hand from the wrist, as if to return the blood to her fingers, and she added, with a mixture of reproach and admiration, "I didn't realise you were so strong."

They laughed. By misfiring, the move had turned out more effective than if it had come off. And, however botched, an advance had been made. The balance between Irina's side of the table, where all the advantages of age and sophistication and familiarity with Parisian practices were stacked, and Edward's had been perceptibly adjusted; it was he who had taken the initiative of touching her.

"Where are we going to eat?" he asked her. "Not here, I hope?" He showed her over her shoulder the dismaying contents of the glass dessert cabinet: frosted sundae glasses of greying chocolate mousse and slices of an inert white pudding sprinkled with chips of a bright-pink sugary substance which had bled alarming colouring over the long-dead slabs.

Irina shook her head. "No, not here. This is just for meeting and drinking our opening drink. No, I thought we should go somewhere a bit extravagant tonight, maybe in Saint Germain or somewhere, to cheer us both up."

"Fine by me," said Edward, and then he asked, "Are you feeling fed up too?"

Irina gave an eloquently gusty sigh. "Oh, Edouard," she exclaimed, "you don't want to hear about my problems, I promise you."

"On the contrary," said Edward, "I do. They make a change

117

from mine and, if it doesn't sound callous to say so, I think they're probably more interesting too."

"Interesting," Irina repeated bitterly. "That's twice now you've used that word about me. I suppose that's what I'll be to you in years to come, won't I? An 'interesting' far-away postage stamp stuck in your very full album."

"Say that again?" said Edward.

Irina shook her head but grinned. "You didn't hear what I said," she declared. "I have a talent for smelling an end before there's even been a beginning. So, where are we going to eat, then? What would you like best?"

On her much-ringed fingers, she ran off a list of names, none of which meant anything to Edward but all of which sounded deeply pretentious: Bacchus Gourmand, Le Sybarite, Chez Raffatin et Honorine.

"You choose," he said. "Really, I haven't the first idea – "

Irina tutted. "But I need to know what you feel like eating at least," she protested. "I can't just pick on somewhere."

"But you can," Edward assured her. "I don't have strong feelings."

Irina frowned. "Well, I think you should. This is an occasion, isn't it? You ought to have an image of what you want us to be eating at our first meal out." She flourished her hands evocatively. "Shellfish with pink flesh and claws, or artistic snippets of Japanese delicacies, or blood-red steaks."

Edward couldn't help laughing. "You know, you're a lot more French than you pretend to be."

"And you," retorted Irina, "are every bit as English." She sat straighter. "You should care about these things, you know, Edouard. Now tell me, what would you prefer; meat or fish, somewhere French or somewhere foreign?"

They ended up going to one of Irina's regular haunts.

"I can't get anything out of you," she concluded grumpily. "At least I know *I'll* be content there."

It was also somewhere she was known, of course; it wouldn't matter that on a Saturday night they hadn't booked. Now the decision was taken, she downed her port almost in one go and even hesitated when Edward offered her a second.

"No," she decided. "Let's go over to the Pré Geneviève now. We may have to wait at the bar there for a table."

As soon as they stepped out onto the pavement, an empty taxi sped into the Place de l'Ecole Militaire. Swiftly, Irina hailed it and as he climbed after her into it, Edward considered the novel sensation of events proceeding entirely according to his female partner's wishes. It wouldn't be something he would like in the long run. With minor but material acts, he would subvert it. But for the moment, he accepted it as an inevitable accompaniment to going out to dinner with a woman ten years his senior. Specifying their age difference like that, for the first time, he looked sideways at Irina and assessed her state of preservation.

She turned to face his inspection with a radiant smile.

"Are you hungry?" she asked him.

And because it was something he tended to do anyway, because her question seemed to him to be addressed to a needy child, he shunted along the back seat of the cab towards her and snarled in assent, avidly snapping his teeth.

The waiter at the Pré Geneviève showed them to a table almost at once, greeting Irina fulsomely and expertly relieving her of her heavy coat. Beneath it, Edward was almost distressed to see, she was more dressed up than ever before. She had on another six-cylinder dress, black this time, and decorated with an impressive collection of bruising silver bits and pieces, which matched the big rings he had earlier crushed on her hand.

She strutted ahead of him to their table, and despite his recurring dismay at what he had let himself in for, he couldn't help enjoying having someone swing their hips so consummately for his benefit. He reached the table in her wake, another novel sensation, and watched how skilfully she went through all the expensive-restaurant rituals: lowering herself onto the waiter's manipulated chair, responding politely to his briefing on the day's special dishes, and receiving gracefully her shaken linen napkin into her lap. Somewhere in the middle of all this, it occurred to Edward that the evening's likely culmination was as good a means as any of redressing the balance.

They read their menus diligently. The Pré Geneviève, Irina explained seriously, was a *nouvelle cuisine* restaurant. She liked it for the refined, ethereal quality of its cooking; you didn't leave the table weighted down by a ballast of sauces, doughs and creams. Your palate was exquisitely treated, but you could float away from table afterwards unencumbered by what you had eaten. Edward felt depressed. He also felt that, coming from someone as eminently material as Irina, this affected fondness for light, insubstantial meals was fundamentally dubious.

Around them, the restaurant was crowded with smart Saturday night diners. He had imagined, at some point, that getting to know Irina would bring him a share of Paris society. He now wondered whether this would be the case, for the distance between him and the other diners didn't seem to be reduced by Irina's presence. He sensed that she was just as alien and excluded from their midst as he was, and as if she sensed his misgivings but was determined to make a virtue of her predicament, she pronounced, "The only drawback is the *bons bourgeois* who flock here to eat without putting on weight."

Edward smiled appreciatively. At the tables to both sides of them, tidily dressed young couples were aping their parents' heyday. They were visibly well matched; socially and physically homogeneous, paired to perpetuate the status quo. To Edward and Irina's left, a sharp-featured woman lovingly fed yellow mussels from her fork to a sharp-featured man. It made Edward feel, just briefly, exceedingly uncomfortable. For he had an inkling of what he and Irina must look like to the biology-textbook couples; ill-assorted and incompatible, a pair plainly destined for a short, presumably carnal career and, should they be foolish enough to imagine for a moment otherwise, a sticky end.

Once they had ordered, the only remaining pretext for not facing the situation before them was gone. Irina took a great gulp at the white wine the waiter had uncorked before them with a flourish and treated Edward to a deep significant look.

"We discover each other in the depths of winter," she announced. "Such a cold, miserable time of year and yet in the middle of it such unexpected warmth."

'Jee*zuz!*' thought Edward. If there was one thing he couldn't bear in the embarrassing business of the emotions, it was a running commentary.

"You sound like a commercial for the Gas Board," he teased her.

Irina flushed. "I'm sorry, but I don't have your stiff upper lip, Edouard."

"I'll say," Edward agreed.

He hoped to discourage her from any further declarations but she tossed her pinkish hair and told him, "I say what I feel and I *feel* warm."

"Well, great," said Edward, and added meanly after a moment. "You look it."

One moment, he was chuffed and turned on by the splendid female achievement in front of him; the next he wanted to put her down. It seemed to him that only by periodically dropping obstacles in her tracks could he delay the onrushing advance of the female locomotive. Which was at the same time perverse, since he enjoyed the knowledge that its delivery was for him.

Irina made an exasperated tongue-slapping noise. Although it was not in any particular language, it reminded Edward unexpectedly vividly of her Great-Aunt Elena.

"How's your family?" he asked.

This time, Irina's sigh verged on a snort. "Edouard! Do we have to talk about my family? Just when I'm enjoying getting away from them and into a real *tête-à-tête* with you. How's *your* family?"

Edward grimaced.

"Why didn't you enjoy Christmas with them, actually?" She went on vindictively. "Let's talk about that."

"OK," Edward said. "Point taken."

But somewhere along the line Irina had felt insulted enough to want to get her own back. "No, I'm interested," she said, with a nasty artificial sweetness. "Remember you're only the second Englishman I've ever properly got to know. This is educational for me."

"Who was the other?" asked Edward.

Irina smiled archly. "Answer my question first."

"England's far too close," said Edward. "Do you understand that? I never wanted to get sent somewhere such a short distance away I could go home for Christmas. It rubs in how pathetically *near* I am. It makes being abroad at all seem a complete farce. You see, I wanted to get sent to South America, or somewhere radically different: new place, new climate, new culture. Being booted down the road to Paris was bad enough; going home made me absolutely desperate. There was everything and everyone I had wanted to get away from virtually next door."

Irina contemplated his troubles serenely. "Where will they send you after Paris?" she asked.

Edward cheered somewhat. "That is the sixty-four thousand dollar question," he answered. "Hopefully, after such a non-starter first time round, it'll be somewhere pretty decent next time. There are two schools of thought, really; either they'll send me somewhere French-speaking, but much further away, of course, maybe French West Africa or somewhere in Indo-China, to capitalise on what I've acquired here. Or they may just possibly look kindly on my fervently expressed desire and send me where I want. In which case, Rio de Janeiro, here we come."

"And that would be when?" asked Irina.

"Oh God, the sooner the better," said Edward. "The earliest possible would be next summer, I suppose. I mean, I wouldn't actually have been here a full year until September, but they'd have to give me a bit of notice to make the move, and for Henry's sake too. They'd probably let me know where I was going in July or August, with a bit of luck. Although in this game you never can tell, of course. They might just say, 'Want you in Brazil tomorrow, Wainwright.' Or there is the possibility, which I don't even want to think about, that they may want to keep me here for a second year. In which case, God – " he shook his head.

"The other Englishman was seventy-something years old," Irina said. "His name was Blenkinsop."

She recoiled, hurt and puzzled, when Edward burst out laughing. "What's funny about that?"

"Blenkinsop's rather a funny name," Edward excused himself.

"Is it?" Irina asked stiffly. "I don't think so. I think it's rather a soft and gentle name; if I had a Siamese cat, I would call it Blenkinsop." She caressed the name: "Blen-kin-sop."

"Who was he?" Edward asked conciliatingly. The trouble

was, he could all too easily imagine Irina owning a Siamese cat called Blenkinsop and it wouldn't be ridiculous at all.

"He was an acquaintance of the family's," Irina explained primly. "He was a business associate of my grandfather's in Russia, and after the Revolution he went back to live in England, by the seaside. When I was about fourteen, my mother sent me to stay with Mr Blenkinsop, to learn English. It was the most wonderful month; I have never forgotten it."

Two plates sparsely decorated with the elements of their *entrées* were set in front of them: each held half a dozen minutely arranged mouthfuls which symbolised rather than constituted a course. Edward's depression over the meal deepened and he felt irritated when Irina exclaimed, with what seemed a quite artificial brightness, "*Ah, comme c'est joli!*"

"Why was it so wonderful staying with Mr Blenkinsop?" he asked. "What happened?"

"Well, it was my first time abroad alone. I felt right on the edge of adulthood; it was terribly exciting. And Mr Blenkinsop behaved to me as if I were an adult, a grown-up woman, and there weren't sixty years separating us. Little things: he held the doors open for me, he helped me to put on my coat. No one had ever treated me like that before; I felt the belle of the ball. I think he had no notion really that I was still a child. He used to take me up to London to the theatre and to eat in restaurants and he behaved towards me just as if I were his partner; chocolates, compliments, flowers. Fourteen years old, imagine, I was in ecstasy!

"He lived in Brighton, in a big pink house, two or three streets back from the sea. I had never seen streets like that before in France with all the houses painted pastel colours: pink and yellow and blue. To me, it was the most exquisite thing imaginable to live in a pink house; I love the colour pink. It seemed the perfect setting for my idyll with dear old Mr Blenkinsop. One day I told him what a beautiful colour I thought his house was and I remember he got terribly excited. He kept looking at me and exclaiming, 'Good Lord! Well, isn't that a remarkable thing?' At first, he didn't want to tell me why it was such a remarkable thing. I don't know why he thought it might upset me. Apparently, *our* house was pink,

123

the Iskarov family house in what was then St Petersburg, and it had been a slightly unusual colour to paint it at the time, so it had caused a bit of comment and become a family motif. He couldn't believe that two generations later such a strong penchant for pink would crop up again. I felt awfully proud of my allegiance. Even though it was a much louder, shriller pink, I bought lots of that rock back as a souvenir. I told my mother about the pink house and she nearly burst into tears. She told me it was all she could really remember of Russia; our pink house. She was only two or three when they had to leave. She said the colour of the house had stayed in her memory all through the years, in all the dark apartment houses she lived in later; a very innocent pink, she said, like icecream or a birthday cake, beckoning through the silver birch trees or over the snow. During the last war, she said it sometimes came back to her, like a frivolous wave, when there was no frivolity left anywhere in the world. Dear Mr Basil Blenkinsop; we sent pink flowers to his funeral."

It had not previously occurred to Edward that Irina had at some stage been an adolescent, let alone once a child. She was so absolutely adult; she appeared to have come ready formed, complete with all her family's accumulated weary experience. In fact, now he came to imagine her as a child, it was a small-scale woman he imagined; just the smallest size of those stacking Russian dolls, which was in shape and facial features and character no different from the biggest.

"Have you always lived in Paris?" he asked her.

Irina nodded. "Yes. Well, almost; we had an experimental year in Geneva and another in Nice. But we always seemed to come back here in the end, don't ask me why. I don't think any of us was particularly drawn to Paris. I certainly wasn't."

"It's not the most hospitable of cities," Edward ventured.

Irina nodded vehemently. "There are times I hate it," she said. "Like now. I hate it now; so cold and dark and bare. It's not the dark and the cold I mind so much, but walking past the apartment houses full of smug *Parisiens* and looking up at their lighted windows and feeling eternally shut out."

"Hey," Edward said. "That's *my* fantasy."

They laughed. Virtually without noticing, certainly without

making any impression on Edward's appetite, they had eaten their *entrées* and the waiter brought the main course. Edward looked down at a small plump wedge of duck on which someone had painstakingly organised a floral arrangement of little slivers of carrot and leek. In the brown sauce, there was a single petal of cream. Wherever the evening might be heading, Edward hoped suddenly that he would finish it in his flat by himself if only so that he could fill up on pâté and bread.

"Yes, but it's not so surprising for you to be an outsider," Irina responded. "You're new, you know you're not going to be here for long, it's even part of your professional competence, isn't it? But I've lived here all my life, remember, I've got nowhere else in particular to go, and I still feel I don't belong. That's more brutal."

"Have you never thought of going to live somewhere else?" Edward asked her. "Why don't you get a job which would take you abroad?"

Irina looked at him resentfully. So fierce was her mascaraed hostility, Edward sensed she would be capable of emptying her dinner-plate over him.

"What am I supposed to do with Babushka?" she asked. "Put her in a home? And Great-Aunt Elena? She won't stay this valiant forever. And the properties, the Cité Etienne Hubert and the rue Surcouf; what am I supposed to do about them?"

"Oh come," said Edward. "You can't let your life be dictated by elderly relatives and flats."

Irina glared at him. Then she laughed and sat back. "You're awfully young, Edouard."

"Nothing I can do about that, I'm afraid," Edward said brusquely. He sliced and forked up his duck in silence.

"I suppose I envy you," Irina continued. "For the time being I have to confine my adventures close to home."

While they were reading the dessert menu, whose names, Edward thought gloomily, probably took up more space than the dishes themselves, Irina suddenly volunteered, "Don't be upset if I sometimes snap at you, Edouard. You do realise I'm just raging against the odds?"

Edward looked up at her. "The odds?"

Irina fingered the stem of her wine glass. "The odds against us being anything more than a joke which no one laughs at. You do realise I've been pining for you ever since we first met?"

"No," Edward answered. "I didn't. If you remember, our first meeting was a bit unfortunate."

"Of course I remember," Irina said. "How could I forget? Just my luck, I thought, to be favoured with such a colossal cold when somebody so absolutely charming walks in."

Edward's eyes escaped to the menu. Was she going to do it all herself? He supposed it was only natural that Irina should make the running. After all, left to his own devices he would never have come near her. She had offered the first invitation, she made the first admission. But was she going to decide everything?

"Don't be embarrassed," she told him.

Edward faced her for long enough to take in her practised yearning look and her right hand stretched far enough across the table for him to take it if he chose. He looked back to the menu. For the first time in what had probably been rather a happy-go-lucky sexual career, he envisaged a prospective sexual encounter as an act of subordination.

Irina chose the *Trois Sorbets nappés à la sauce Geneviève* and Edward a cake, which he felt was bound to have at least a certain mass.

In the longish pause before the sweets arrived, he teased Irina. "You don't really mean all that, do you? You're just having me on?"

She huffed gratifyingly. "Haven't I made enough of a fool of myself already? What else do I have to do to convince you?"

"You're not really interested in me," Edward persisted. "I'm just a callow trainee journalist, remember. You could have your pick of Paris's choicest specimens of Gallic manhood, Irina. I'm just your tenant."

Irina sat exceedingly straight. "Make fun of me if you like, Edouard," she said crisply. "But please, don't insult me; I wouldn't have anything to do with a Parisian male." She smiled distinctly nastily. "As for being my tenant, Monsieur Wenwright, let me inform you, you are not my first."

While Irina enjoyed the pink sauce poured over her icecream,

126

she pointed out to Edward a woman standing near the cash desk.

"That's Geneviève, the *patron*'s girlfriend. Isn't she beautiful?"

Edward saw a tall, aristocratically bony, black-haired woman, striking a lean, aloof pose. He looked back at Irina, whose enjoyment of good fare was now coming through her affectation of airier preferences. She was scooping and swallowing great gobbets with delight. Before he could answer anything, Irina said, "Look at her, so thin and smart and *narrow*; having sauces named after her to make women like me as fat as balloons."

Her cheeks were flushed with indignation and, maybe quite unconsciously, she drew herself up again, putting into prominence her black and silver bosom. It was the realisation that if he wanted, he could go to bed with a woman whose breasts were streets ahead of any of her predecessors which caused Edward to relent.

"But Irina," he said, "I don't think she's especially beautiful at all."

The bill, which he rather determinedly paid, was approximately twice what he had anticipated. To make sure Irina noticed how little it mattered to him, he put down a wad of notes instead of his credit card and left a hefty tip. As he followed Irina, now swathed again in her Anna Karenina furs, out of the restaurant, he struck himself as a man whose role-playing was about to go seriously too far.

Irina instructed the taxi driver, whom she hailed again without any problem, to take them to the Cité Etienne Hubert. When he heard her give the address, the back of Edward's neck prickled. Was this wise? No. Would it land him in more trouble than it was worth? Probably. Was it going to happen? Yes. They didn't speak much on the way. Just to express a preference, to show this was not simply happening to him, Edward reached out in the dark and took hold of Irina's gloved and strangely unresponsive hand. The taxi turned into the Cité Etienne Hubert and came to a stop unnecessarily abruptly in front of Number Nine. Irina withdrew her hand.

"Well, Edouard," she said, "it's been a lovely evening. Thank you so much."

A little stiffly, but he reckoned, churning it over later, this could well have been because of the taxi driver, she leant across and bestowed on him a cool, chaste kiss. She told the driver to continue to the rue Surcouf and she stepped out into the dark.

The names he used to describe Irina were short, uncomplimentary, and repeated in a chant for the rest of the weekend. The flat in the rue Surcouf seemed smartingly redolent of Irina when he was so summarily returned to it. Everything in it, from the new tablecloth to the armchair in which she had so luxuriantly snuggled, conspired to repeat her rejection, and he realised, lying in her bathtub on Sunday morning, helping himself to her milk and her butter from her fridge, that if that was as far as things were going to go between them, living in the flat would be one of the most humiliating experiences he had known.

He found pretty quickly that the character of Paris was also significantly altered by her trick. As he fumed over it from Monday to Friday of the following week, he became increasingly aware of a previously unrecognised aspect of the capital. It was a women's city. He supposed that, without explicitly acknowledging this, he had seen it. Women had all along seemed to outnumber men in the street. Now he realised that this was just because they were more dominant, more rapacious than the men. The men were tiddlers dodging cautiously among the shoals of plump, snapping pike. He thought he had never been a misogynist, but now he found himself noticing irritably the overwhelming numerical superiority of hairdressers, dress shops and beauticians over more manly establishments. The smell of perfume which had caught in his throat on his first evening in Paris returned to taunt him. With every passing whiff, he was reminded of Irina, plump, snapping pike *extraordinaire*, who had been prepared to gobble him up for breakfast, but who at the last minute had disdainfully spat out the pieces. Operating within her female bastion, according to skilled submarine ploys, no wonder she was capable of turning on him like that and dropping him with a silver stiletto tail flick.

On Wednesday, on an errand, he had to pass the end of the Cité Etienne Hubert. As his taxi drove by, he cast

128

a casual but hostile look along the street. Naturally, the pavements were empty. He did wonder, just in passing, whether he would have any dealings with Irina, beyond the payment of his rent, ever again. At the bottom of the Avenue Duquesne, the taxi was stopped by traffic lights. He could not resist turning round to take another look back at the end of the street. He saw something which prodded him into uncomplicated poignant longing and made at least part of him admit that if Irina were to make a come-back, he would not necessarily reject her out of hand. From the roof-top corners of the apartment houses on either side of the street, two stone nipples stood up against the cold winter sky.

He really could not make out what had happened. The major question was, of course, whether the deed was cancelled or only postponed. But the lesser problem of what Irina was playing at, and what exactly she hoped to achieve by it, preoccupied him too. The most likely explanation, he decided, was cold feet, with a dash of sadism. But, he kept wondering, maybe there was something else; some major unidentified obstacle, which he had simply failed to see? With so little to go on, how could he work out a strategy for the unlikely event of Irina's staging a come-back?

Which was why her telephone call caught him completely unprepared, stammering and embarrassed, when she finally got round to ringing him last thing on Friday night.

"So you let a whole week go by without telephoning me?" she asked aggressively. "Is that the sort of man you are?"

"Hang on a minute," Edward objected. "I rather got the impression on Saturday . . ."

"Yes?" demanded Irina.

"Well, look, don't get me wrong, but I got the distinct impression you wanted to call it a day."

"Did you?" Irina asked mockingly. "Well, spare me the expressions of the cricket pitch please, Mister Wenwright, and do tell me whatever gave you that impression."

"Is the phone the best place for this conversation?" asked Edward.

"Well, I don't see where else we're going to have it," Irina answered in an aggrieved voice. "I certainly don't see why

129

I should agree to meet you again before you've explained yourself."

"Believe it or not," Edward said hotly, "I feel rather the same myself."

He listened to Irina's stony silence. Into it, he eventually added, "If you remember, you did rather drop me from a great height outside your front door last Saturday night."

"Ah," Irina answered icily. "Is that it? How disgusting."

The silence which followed threatened to break all records. At last, in the depths of it, Edward thought he heard a chuckle.

"What are you doing tomorrow night?" asked Irina.

This time, he deliberately didn't take her hand in the taxi on the way back. He wasn't going to give her the least pretext to recoil. Instead she reached over and took hold of his, squeezing it conspiratorially as their taxi driver, one of the garrulous school, held forth on the rampant evils of socialism currently clutching France in its tentacles. He was displeased with the size of Edward's tip, which Edward made deliberately small as a reproof. When the taxi driver had reversed vindictively fast and noisily the length of the Cité Etienne Hubert, expressing his displeasure with a mighty revving, Edward started to explain his action to Irina, but she appeared to have something else on her mind.

"Let's take a walk before we go in," she suggested to Edward. "To digest our dinner."

At Edward's instigation, they had not gone back to the Pré Geneviève, but to a less pretentious Armenian restaurant where they had, indeed, both eaten heavily.

It seemed to Edward the moment to take Irina's hand, as they paced in silence under the trees of the dark Avenue Duquesne. But he still hesitated for Irina had an abstracted look on her face, and he worried that any move on his part which could be construed as pressure might tip the balance of her doubts against him.

Finally, when they had reached the top of the avenue, cast affectionate glances at the Taverne Tourville, and turned round again, Irina said, "I have a matter to discuss with you, Edouard."

He thought dismally, 'Here goes.'

130

"You must not let my family know to what extent you are seeing me," Irina said. "Babushka and Great-Aunt Elena and Varvara Stepanovna, if you ever meet her; they mustn't find out that we are – friends. Do you accept that?"

Edward grinned. "Yes, of course I do. I mean, it's pretty unlikely they'd ever grill me on the subject, isn't it? I'll go along with it, though, if that's what makes you happy. But why?"

Irina made one of her "Tchuh!" noises. "Isn't it obvious? We're not what you'd call ideally suited, are we? You must remember, they've still got the outlook of another time and another place. They have these ridiculous old unrealistic dreams for me; they want me to be happy."

They walked along a façade or two in silence.

Perhaps embarrassed by her explicit relegation of their romance to the rank of doomed endeavour, Irina went on, "And also the fact they know you're going away in a year or two; they'd be shocked."

Edward said, "OK, point taken." He felt an unmistakable relaxation at Irina's having mentioned his departure just at this juncture.

They turned into the Cité Etienne Hubert. The stump of a street for once seemed long, and as they walked down to Number Nine, Edward was aware all the way of the big wall at the end of the street, looming over them, closing off the distance.

At the double front doors, in the brief pause between Irina pushing the brass bell and the right-hand door springing open in response, she glanced at Edward. He saw she had, miserably, as many misgivings as he did.

The lift came down clanking, and they stepped inside. While they waited for it, looking upward through the lozenged wire mesh for the small wooden box to come into view, neither of them said a word. They transferred their taut apprehension to the arrival of the lift, staring as if it mattered at the two quivering ropes which ran the length of the lift shaft. Irina pressed the button for the fifth floor and, with a jolt followed by a shivering moan, they set off.

Confined for the first time, the two of them, in a small oblong space, they were enclosed in a sudden inescapable intimacy. As the lift rose, swaying and shuddering, through the red-carpeted tiers of the staircase which encircled it in a long embrace, they exchanged their first frank look of mischievous complicity. But Irina looked away almost at once and fixed her eyes seriously on the struts of the door. Not to be outdone, Edward concentrated on the safety instructions. Ascenseurs Roux-Combaluzier gravely informed passengers that unaccompanied children were forbidden to use this machine. Accompanied, they were to be kept well away from the passing walls of the lift shaft. The lift, till then an absurd spoof of a vehicle, took on an uncertain, treacherous quality. Behind them the thin, hairy ropes hissed. At each passing floor, the lift cabin acknowledged the possibility of stopping with a little lurch.

Edward read on automatically until he came to a sentence which filled him with profound pleasure, and a childish wish to grab Irina by the arm, to point and share the joke. The sentence read: "*Pour provoquer le départ, appuyer sur le bouton de l'étage désiré.*" He had always had a soft spot for Parisian lifts; ungainly spiders laboriously spinning their webs. Now he relished the new erotic connotations they would shortly acquire. Having pushed the requisite button to provoke their departure, he and Irina were rising, side by side, to the floor they desired. With a final audible exertion, the lift covered the last few feet, slowing disturbingly and drawing level with the fifth-floor landing only inch by inch. As they waited those ultimate inches, Irina's hand ready to yank back the sliding inner door, she caught sight of Edward's broad grin, due solely to the phrase "the desired floor", and as the lift bumped home, she responded with a quick nervous smile.

She looked at her watch as she opened the front door and murmured, "Ah good, Babushka will be long in bed. But don't make too much noise, just in case."

She didn't hang their overcoats in the hall cupboard but took them and went to put them in another room. She gestured to Edward silently to go and wait for her in the sitting-room and a moment later she came in, reperfumed he was sure, and shut the sitting-room door behind her.

"The one thing to be thankful for," she said, "is that

Babushka goes to bed really early, at nine or ten o'clock. It leaves me room to manoeuvre." And she laughed.

Edward was about to tell her what had happened at her dinner; how he had been on his way back from the lavatory at twelve o'clock or one and had encountered Babushka, horror-struck, in the doorway of her room. But it seemed pointless to unsettle Irina by such a suggestion. If the aged grandmother found out what they were up to, what did he care?

"What sort of thing would you like now?" Irina asked him, in a way which seemed somehow so explicit, Edward was almost embarrassed. "Coffee? Whisky? Vodka?"

She displayed herself in front of him and on an impulse, really, he had not intended to take the initiative, Edward stood up, walked towards her smiling, and enfolded her in a hug. There was more of her than he had expected; every woman he had hugged before had been distinctly smaller and thinner than he was. That had even been part of the enjoyment; wrapping up and squeezing someone he could contain. Irina was of undiscovered dimensions. She was a short woman, but as she leant forward appreciatively into his hug, he felt fleshy parts of her meet him the whole way down. She not only had splendid breasts, she had a tummy and soft round thighs. He might have expected her substance to repel him – when all was said and done, she verged on the fat – but quite the opposite happened. As he eagerly took her tighter, Irina burrowed her head into his chest as if she were embarrassed. Edward ran his hand down her back, to reassure her and encourage her, and he felt the robust bottom which completed her figure. They stood for a few moments, embracing in the middle of the dark-red rug and then they seemed simultaneously to decide it was time to proceed to the kiss.

He was about to prise Irina's head up towards him when, of her own accord, she lifted it. She had her eyes shut but there was no mistaking her willingness. As he put his lips tentatively towards hers, they immediately opened and his tongue could make its way into a warm rotating welcome. Her hands, which had been fairly neutrally around his shoulders, moved into action; one frisked around the back of his neck,

133

making little delightfully ticklish forays into his hair, and the other slipped down to the small of his back where it exerted a most enjoyable pressure. For one moment, he thought there was a third hand cradling his right ear but then he realised it must be the frolicsome hand from his neck which had moved up. Reluctantly, they had in the end to draw apart and breathe, reluctantly also because it meant opening their eyes and looking each other in the face. Irina's eyes only came open slowly and gazed at Edward, as if in amazement or dismay.

He said, "Howdy."

What he did not expect were the two small tears which rolled out of the corners of her eyes and trundled down her cheeks.

They went to sit on the deepest settee. Irina rubbed the two tears away and beamed at him moistly.

"Ach, Edouard, I feel very happy."

"You could have fooled me," he teased her.

"No," she said. "Don't worry. I always cry when I'm happy."

"Oh, great," laughed Edward. "Thanks for warning me."

Irina smiled, a smile of profoundly sad, sweet tenderness, which, despite her flushed face and her crumpled clothes, made her look in passing a little like the Mona Lisa. She laid one hand on Edward's leg.

"Do we know what we're doing?" she asked him earnestly.

Having embarked on his flippant mode, Edward found it hard to switch out of it. Also, he had little wish to.

"Nope," he replied. "But does that matter?"

Irina sighed, just slightly. "No," she agreed. "It doesn't matter tonight."

Edward pulled her towards him by the scruff of her neck. "Don't let it matter at all," he urged her. And because he had been wanting to for some time, he bent and nibbled her sweet pink ear.

They were not a lot further on when Irina sat up and in a way which Edward actually found disconcertingly business-like, said, "OK, let's go to my bedroom. It really is better there."

He did not like being led to the bedroom and, when they got there, he found he did not really like the bedroom either.

It was a narrow, high-ceilinged room, in which Irina had visibly lived for years. It was full of mementoes of a younger Irina, décor, knick-knacks, books, and against one wall stood a virginal single bed. Edward felt for a minute he was coming with evil intent upon a schoolgirl. Irina closed the bedroom door behind him and resolutely locked it. "Just to be on the safe side," she said. Then she stood a little way away from him waiting and he realised with alarm that in the chaste, lamplit bedroom all his desire had gone.

He was about to say, "Let's just sit and talk for a minute, shall we?"

Irina, not coming any closer to him, but not taking her eyes off him, unbuttoned the waistband of her skirt. A few seconds later, the skirt, of soft coffee suede, slipped to the floor and Irina, wearing a lacy slip which crackled with static, stepped deftly out of it. She began, slowly and methodically, to unbutton the matching waistcoat, little brass button after little brass button. As she shrugged off the waistcoat, which followed the skirt to the floor, Edward could not stand it any longer and stepped forward to give her a helping hand.

Irina held him at bay. "You get undressed as well," she said. "I don't like to be the only one who's naked."

Edward wasn't used to a woman who stated so baldly what she wanted. Her knowledge came, presumably, from extensive experience and, at the thought of it, Edward again felt his own desire retreat. But he was locked in now; there could be no running away. He would rely on what had always been reliable in the past; bare bodies, eyes shut, on sheets.

At the completion of a straight-faced ritual, they stood in front of one another naked. Edward was not at ease with his own nudity but, worse, Irina's seemed to him unapproachable. It was like looking at an Old Master's fleshy white fantasy; you might experience a passing flicker of fun but you would never in a million years imagine reaching out to fondle it. So he stood in front of Irina now, admiring her classic painter's proportions, and he feared he couldn't lay a finger on her.

"How do you do?" she said wryly. For she could see, of course, that she was not having the expected effect on him. She came towards him and did what Edward probably least

135

expected. She took him by the hand. She led him soberly to her bedside.

He was relieved and proud at how little time, in fact, passed between their lying down and matters righting themselves. The touch of Irina's fingers, the feel of her bare skin soon did the trick. But, even so, he waited for quite a while before beginning. It occurred to him that he had never been to bed with a woman on this scale before. The single bed, of course, reinforced her proportions. But even so he realised he had never slept with a full-scale woman; someone with such unashamed undulations, with such fruitily pigmented nipples. He wanted to be jolly sure he made the most of them.

Everything went extremely successfully. Irina had a good time too, of that there was no doubt. At the height of their straining, panting, grappling and eventual groaning, he even wished for a second she would pipe down. He feared the grandmother's slippers shuffling down the passage, and the door handle rattling. It speeded up his pleasure, and afterwards as they lay in silence, sweaty and gasping, he was aware that he was still listening out for the grandmother. Neither of them said anything for a long time, and in fact Edward thought he must have dropped off for a few moments because Irina seemed to be saying something to him which made no sense.

"Not fallen," she was saying. "Not degraded. Do you believe me?"

"What d'you mean?" he asked sleepily.

"It is the truth," Irina insisted. "Always before I have felt abused and degraded afterwards, as though I'd been pulled over and dragged through the dirt in my nice clothes. But not now; with you I feel quite equal and clean and comradely, you know, like two children lying here together in all innocence."

Edward fondled the nearest part of her at random.

"What about you?" she persisted. "Are you contented?"

"Yup," Edward said. "It was great."

"For me it was excellent also," Irina said unnecessarily. "But just lying here now is actually even nicer; I feel we've played a match without a winner and a loser. No victory, no defeat; just two schoolchildren who both came first in the same race." She giggled. "I'm starting to use your sporting expressions, Edouard."

He spoke much less than she did. He would have been happier to lie still and not be constantly reminded with whom he was in bed. In the end Irina fell silent. He thought she was asleep, but she kept one arm proprietorially across him. He couldn't get to sleep. He thought he'd finished with single beds at university. He rolled and shifted uncomfortably on the sticky sheets. In doing so, he managed to throw off Irina's arm. But sleep eluded him. The next thing he knew Irina was shaking his shoulder and saying, "Wake up, Edouard. It's half past six. You must go home before Babushka gets up."

In the unlikely days after he first spent the night with Irina, Edward was greatly cheered to see what a difference she made to Paris. He experienced an inevitable lapse into depression straight afterwards, dismayed by the futility and possibly unattractive aspect of what he was doing. The unrelievedly drear grey Sunday which followed it was the worst. He went straight back to bed in the rue Surcouf and woke around midday with the unmistakable feeling that something had gone awfully wrong. When he remembered what, he wanted to burrow even deeper under his bedclothes. He had to go out and eat a sizeable solitary lunch to raise his spirits. But walking back, the bare, empty streets in the winter weather so depressed him that he was forced to acknowledge the worst of it; in this frozen, miserable, empty January, he and Irina were sure to stick together, to keep each other company.

So it was a relief to realise, as the working week progressed, that having Irina in the background improved certain aspects of Paris considerably. The knowledge that he was having at least a slight sexual adventure here seemed somewhat to validate his presence. Lovers on benches ceased to be distressing. At the paper, he was able to portray himself as an enigmatically sexually active person. Naturally, no one there was ever going to find out who it was he was seeing. But he could at least convincingly hint at fully booked nights. Best of all, perhaps, he knew he was now enjoying one of the fundamental pleasures of travel; untrammelled and cosmopolitan sex. He only faintly regretted the women of South America, who would have writhed, he felt, without speaking, or if they had spoken, he would not have understood.

On principle, he did not telephone Irina until Thursday, and the way she answered the telephone convinced him he had done right.

"Edouard! I've been dying for you to ring. What have you been doing with yourself all week?"

"Oh," he said vaguely. "This and that."

"You haven't," asked Irina, "you haven't regretted what occurred?"

As non-committally as he could, Edward answered, "Nope."

There was a silence.

"What have *you* been up to?" he asked.

Irina sighed. "Oh, not a lot. Term doesn't start again until next week, you know. I've been sitting here, waiting for you to call."

"Don't do that," he said, more sharply than he had intended. And then, placatingly, "I mean, I don't want you languishing for me when I'm not there, OK?"

After what he took to be a hurt pause, Irina laughed. "Certainly, sir," she said.

He suggested, as casually as possible, that they could see each other again the coming Saturday. To his dismay, Irina had assumed this would happen, and she presented him with a ready-planned programme of activities. It started with tea at Great-Aunt Elena's at four. "She wants to talk English to you again and her protégée, Varvara Stepanovna, is longing to meet you." It went on conveniently to one of the cinemas not far away on the Champs-Elysées and after that to dinner *à deux*. Irina even recited the titles of the films she wanted to see.

Edward consented to the programme for two not especially creditable reasons; the Russian family was one of the key attractions, and they cut down on the amount of time he spent perilously alone with Irina.

This time, Irina arrived absolutely punctually at Metro

Courcelles. It was an afternoon of nasty diagonal drizzle and as they came out of the Metro station onto the Boulevard de Courcelles, almost as a reaction against the weather, Irina took Edward's arm and snuggled up against him. He was surprised; he had assumed that in view of the secrecy Irina had stipulated, this was something she wouldn't do, especially on the way to visit a member of her family. However, it was a much more pleasant way than usual to walk around Paris and, besides, he was fast becoming blasé with Irina's inconsistencies. He passed his arm around her shoulders and they walked companionably up to Great-Aunt Elena's.

She opened the door to them in a froth of happy anticipation. But the perpetual anxious bustle of the night of the concert remained; welcoming them, taking their coats, exclaiming at their cold fingers all generated a welter of activity in the small hall, and it wasn't for several moments that Edward noticed another woman standing watching them from an open doorway. The sight of her rather startled him for he was smartly on guard to conceal any signs of his new relationship with Irina, and here was someone who had been watching him without his noticing.

Great-Aunt Elena saw him look at the woman and whirled into a new preoccupation.

"Varvara Stepanovna," she clucked at the woman bossily. "What are you doing, hanging back there? Come over here and meet Mister Wenwright."

The woman came forward and Edward shook her extended hand with a mixture of revulsion and pity; he thought she was one of the fattest, flabbiest, palest people he had ever seen. 'It was about you,' he thought, 'that poem was written:

> O fat white woman whom nobody loves,
> Why do you walk through the fields in gloves?'

As if she were aware of his condemnation, the woman offered a pale, pleading smile and murmured, *"Enchantée."*

Great-Aunt Elena swept them all forward into the sitting-room. In her unexpected Scottish burr, she announced, "Come in, come in. Make yourselves at home."

"Look here," Irina interrupted her ungraciously in French.

"School doesn't start for me until Thursday. I hope we're not going to speak English all afternoon."

"You can speak to me," Varvara Stepanovna said quickly. "My English is terrible."

Great-Aunt Elena gave a first-rate Iskarovian snort. "Those who are capable of it will speak English," she replied disdainfully. "And those who are not will have to make the best of it." She took Edward by the arm. "Come and sit beside me, dear boy. I don't hear very well any more and I want to have you right next to me." She cast Varvara Stepanovna another patronising look. "The spirit is willing, but the flesh is weak."

She questioned Edward avidly: about the paper, about his training, his education, his home, his family. To every answer, she gave a little vigorous nod, or cocked her round head on one side and considered it beadily for an instant or two. Some of her follow-up questions were bizarre: did his family eat kedgeree for breakfast? At their "property" in Kent – Edward imagined their short lawn – how many acres did they own? Did they have domestic servants? Big dogs? Her vision of England appeared fixed before the First World War: red double-decker buses laden with bowler-hatted passengers still lumbered along Piccadilly. For breakfast, every Englishman had Frank Cooper's Oxford marmalade and *The Times*. When Edward told her about *The Times*' forthcoming move to Wapping and the imminent demise of Fleet Street, she was quite horrified. "Really?" she kept exclaiming. "Really? How are the mighty fallen!"

Across the room, a conversation of sorts was puttering along between Irina and Varvara Stepanovna. Edward caught stray and rather scientific-sounding phrases: "*cellulite*", "*lipoaspiration*". He wondered what on earth they were talking about.

Once he intercepted a look of Irina's. Despite her stress on secrecy, she frankly ogled him. Perhaps her conversation with Varvara Stepanovna was not all that engrossing; she called across to Great-Aunt Elena, "*Alors*, are you going to give us something to eat, or do we go hungry?" She turned back to Varvara Stepanovna and giggled. "Here we are talking about slimming and then straight away clamouring for cakes!"

Great-Aunt Elena stood up, grumbling good-naturedly, and went to the kitchen. Conscientiously, Varvara Stepanovna went after her and he and Irina were left on their own in the living-room. In an instant, Irina swooped on Edward and seized him in a starved embrace.

"For Christ's sake!" he protested. "What are you *doing*?"

Irina clung onto him. "I couldn't help it," she whispered. "Sitting there watching you; I was beside myself."

And, with totally devastating accuracy, she began to lick at his neck.

Edward had not had occasion to find out before what a powerful stimulus the risk of discovery could be. To his profound embarrassment, he felt himself responding urgently to Irina's caresses. In the middle of an eighty-year-old lady's afternoon teaparty, he was ready to leap on her between the nest of occasional tables and the bookcase.

Luckily, Varvara Stepanovna's return could be heard from some way off; her careful, heavy tread bringing a clinking tray. They let go of each other reluctantly and Irina bent away to separate the nest of occasional tables.

Wistfully, Varvara Stepanovna set out their silver-handled tea glasses and plates, and a china basket of little biscuits.

"Elena has bought such lovely things," she said sadly. "But I know I shouldn't touch them."

Great-Aunt Elena followed her into the room, bearing two proud cakes. "Bring the tea and the hot water, please, Varvara," she said crisply, and as soon as the sad, fat lady had left the room, she whispered maliciously to Irina and Edward, "'Shouldn't touch them!' You watch her; she'll eat more than the rest of us put together."

Edward was disappointed to see that, once again, Great-Aunt Elena had catered to his supposed English tastes. Instead of the luscious *pâtisseries* he had been looking forward to, Great-Aunt Elena had managed to lay her hands, in Paris, on two pale, bland sponge cakes and a dish of plain biscuits.

She poured everyone tea. Edward was pleased at least to see it was lemon tea, which was, he felt, authentic.

Varvara Stepanovna passed round the cakes, looking down at them with a fearful longing. "I have only to look at a piece of cake and straight away I put on a kilo," she said miserably.

Great-Aunt Elena, who was already well into her slice, snapped at her, "Then eat it with your eyes shut, *ma chère*."

Irina and Edward giggled, and Varvara Stepanovna, almost defiantly, helped herself to two slices and started to gobble them, chewing and swallowing very fast and vindictively.

Irina perhaps felt sorry for her, or perhaps she felt guilty at forking up her own slice. "I suppose I shouldn't be eating this either," she commented.

Edward looked across at her and wondered suddenly what she would look like when she was Varvara Stepanovna's age, which he took to be approaching fifty. Would she also be bloated and shapeless, desperately guzzling cakes because they were the only source of sweetness in her life? He felt actually queasy. He faced the fact that he was having an affair with someone much further on down the road of ageing and decay.

"If you prefer," Great-Aunt Elena snorted, "next time, I shall offer radishes all round."

While Varvara Stepanovna was despatched to the kitchen to get some more hot water, it occurred to Edward to ask if she was a member of the family too.

Great-Aunt Elena shook her head even more than usually vigorously. "She worked for my husband, Boris," she explained. "He had a business and, as a favour to her really, he took Varvara Stepanovna on to keep the books. When Borya died and the business was sold, Varvara Stepanovna transferred her allegiance to me. She's a poor soul, you see; she hasn't got anyone else in the world. We look after her, don't we, Irina?"

As if content to be reminded of her own generosity, Great-Aunt Elena was noticeably more amiable to Varvara Stepanovna when she came back in, even going as far as encouraging her to help herself to a handful of biscuits, saying, "*Allons, ma fille*, it's too good to waste."

Edward very much wanted to ask Great-Aunt Elena about her past. The amount of history she had lived through was bound to yield some stirring stories. But he hesitated. Would it mean good stories or would it mean trauma, stirred up trouble and a row?

Finally, when Irina and Varvara Stepanovna had gone into

143

another room where Irina was going to try on a dress Varvara Stepanovna had promised to alter for her, he raised the subject delicately. Great-Aunt Elena was threatening to embark on another interrogation, this time about where in the world the paper might one day send him, and that provided him with an easy transition.

"You must have seen a fair bit of the world in your time?" he asked her.

Great-Aunt Elena shook her head wistfully. "I haven't seen the places I wanted," she answered. "Only the ones I didn't: Berlin, Geneva, New York, Nice. I haven't seen the Pyramids or the Great Wall of China or the Taj Mahal." She brightened somewhat. "Maybe I still will, though; they organise the most splendid trips for pensioners nowadays, you know. Although, I must say, I don't like the idea of going somewhere with a whole group of senile old dears in a bus. I'd rather travel independently." She gave another vigorous head shake. "It gets me so angry when Vera tries to set off with her suitcases to places that don't even *exist* any more, when the world is so full of the most marvellous sights we've neither of us seen. If she would only concentrate more on *those* places, she'd have a much better grip on reality. I keep giving her books about China and about Egypt, but I don't think she even opens them."

"What d'you mean?" Edward asked. "Places that don't exist any more?"

Great-Aunt Elena gave him a fond but faintly condescending smile.

"Russia," she said.

"But Russia still exists," he argued.

She shook her head. "Unfortunately not."

For a moment, Edward felt himself floundering. "You'd better explain that one," he said.

Great-Aunt Elena was terse. "The Russia we knew no longer exists. It has been replaced by a country called the USSR; that is a completely different place." But it was clear she didn't want to dwell on this sorry state of affairs. "Tell me, Edward, where would you most wish to be sent next?"

He had to insist. "Where in Russia did you live?"

144

Her round face began implausibly to lengthen. "St Petersburg."

He wanted to say, "Tell me what it was like", but he sensed he was pushing in a perilous direction. Instead, he asked, "How old were you when you left?"

"Twenty-three," Great-Aunt Elena answered.

This was followed by a reflective pause, in the course of which a devastating thought came to Edward. Great-Aunt Elena had been three years younger than he was when she left Russia; to all intents and purposes, she had been his age. At that moment, her intended future had been sliced off. Her life had been in many respects halted. For here she was, eighty-something years old, still harking back to the time and the place before the amputation, and her whole being, everything about her, was still determined by that vanished world. He wondered whether anything comparable could conceivably happen to him, here and now, which would slice off his intended future the way hers had been sliced off, and result in his spending the rest of his life stopped short, in many respects, at the developmental stage he had reached now. It was such an appalling thought, he had to keep quiet to assimilate it.

Great-Aunt Elena had apparently taken off in another direction during the pause.

"I had a son," she said.

Edward flinched. The use of the past tense in this sentence moved him more than anything else he had encountered in his embryonic journalist's career. "I had a son." He didn't think he had ever heard the sentence spoken in the past tense before.

"I carried him out of Russia in my arms. He was only a baby, younger even than Irina's mother. I hoped he was small enough to be spared; he wouldn't remember anything, he would grow up in France or in Switzerland, wherever we ended up, and he would become a thorough citizen of that country, free of all our severances and dislocations. Maybe he would have; he was a stable boy. Although, look at Irina, one generation further on and still just as dislocated and confused. His name was Kiril. In France, it became Cyrille. And he was exceedingly French in a great many ways. We used to make fun of him. He was fussy about his clothes in a particularly French

145

way; everything had to be just so. And he was especially fussy about his food, *mon Dieu*, a real *gourmet*. We used to joke whether he would open his own restaurant or go into *haute couture*. As it turned out, he decided to study law. Well, he was a serious person at heart. I remember how he used to set off to the rue d'Assas each morning, with his armful of books and his fresh cravat, and Borya and I would watch him go and marvel at this impeccable Frenchman we had created. Then the second war came and Kiril was such an impeccable Frenchman, he escaped to London to join De Gaulle. He was more of a Frenchman than many of his compatriots, I can tell you that. He was killed outside Amiens."

The lovingly preserved past of her living-room revealed itself as a memorial. Edward stared down at the carpet ahead of his feet, unable to come up with any worthwhile response. After a moment, he risked a sideways look at Great-Aunt Elena and saw her face had retreated behind a veil as it had on the night of the concert. For perhaps the first time, Edward had encountered an appropriate use for the adjective "tragic".

In that most unfrivolous of moments, Irina and Varvara Stepanovna bounced back in, Irina parading the dress which Varvara was altering for her. She gave a model's pirouette for their benefit, only pausing for fractionally longer in front of Edward than in front of her great-aunt.

"Aren't I magnificent?" she pealed.

Varvara watched, her podgy hands clasped and her lunar face tipped to one side. The dress was a red and black sheath, which enclosed Irina like a capsule. Just a few pounds more, Edward thought, and Irina would not be able to squeeze into it. But, for now, it moulded her contours alluringly with its red and black pattern. There was unmissable longing in Varvara Stepanovna's eyes, and Edward found himself thinking briefly, between admiring Irina, how insensitive of her it was to set the poor fat lady to work on sewing a dress like that for her. It was a dress to go out and shine in, to seduce people and to be lingeringly unzipped. None of these things would ever happen, had maybe ever happened, to Varvara Stepanovna, and lurid vicarious imaginings of them were painted all over her face.

There was a busy discussion of seams and hems and linings

146

among the women, during which Edward walked over to the nearest bookcase and browsed along its length. He found that the books themselves were, as in Irina's own flat, largely out of bounds since they were almost all in Russian. But along the top of the bookcase, he found rich pickings: family photographs in old silver frames, including one, in pride of place, of a young man posing on some academic steps, whom he took to be Kiril, and slightly shockingly among the dead faces, one unmistakably of Irina as a little girl. She had been an unequivocally stocky child, seated slightly pompously on a donkey in the Jardin du Luxembourg.

It was, he thought, typical of Irina that she should succumb to jealousy of a bookcase. She dropped the discussion of her dress and bustled over to him.

"Are you getting bored?" she asked. "Are we neglecting you? I think you and I should leave soon."

There were protests in the background from Elena and Varvara Stepanovna.

"You've been here for barely an hour and a half!"

"Why are you so keen to hurry away? Are we not entertaining enough?"

"We're going to see a film," Irina told them. "The *séance* starts at six fifteen."

"Ah, what film?" asked Varvara, a glazed expression, which Edward only subsequently realised must be artistic appreciation, descending over her face.

Irina told her a name.

Like the little increasing speech bubbles in a strip cartoon, Edward saw himself thinking, 'Well, huh, thank you for letting me know; that's the first I've heard of it.'

When they were outside on the Boulevard de Courcelles again, Irina hugged him extravagantly.

"Thank you, Edouard. You were wonderful."

"Meaning?" he asked, wrestling her jokingly away.

"You behaved so well towards my impossible family. I know it can't be anybody's idea of a good way to spend Saturday afternoon, sitting discussing English domestic traditions with an eighty-one-year-old fusspot, but you behaved so beautifully to her. I was watching; I was touched."

Edward was about to tell her that he found her family

perfectly amazing; that he was more than happy to spend the odd Saturday afternoon soaking up their eccentricity. But he didn't; he realised in time that Irina would take it wrong. She would object to her near and dear ones serving, as she put it, as curious postage stamps for his stamp album and, more to the point, she might query what it was that had attracted him to her in the first place.

The film she had mentioned was showing up and down the Champs-Elysées. It had Alain Delon and a strong love interest.

"We don't *have* to go and see it," Irina said as they approached the cinema. But, once they were there, of course, it seemed too much trouble to seek out an alternative.

Edward had his first opportunity to fondle Irina in the dark of a cinema, to hold hands and entangle across the upholstered arms of the seats. But, to his dismay, Irina strongly objected to this, and at his first encroaching hand in the dark – slipping matter-of-factly round her thigh – she gave a little shocked gasp of disapproval.

"*Mais enfin*, Edouard, what are you doing?"

"Isn't it obvious?" he whispered flippantly.

Irina snorted. "But not here," she scolded him. "Not in the cinema."

She sat very straight and stiff after that and stared fixedly at the cinema screen without acknowledging his presence for about twenty minutes. He sat beside her, feeling resentful, but at the same time, that being the unfair way with these things, a steadily increasing amount of desire.

They came out of the cinema into a Paris evening tuning up. The queues for the next programme of the film were already penned behind their metal barriers the length of the pavement: smoking, chattering, flirting, putting on a self-conscious parade of Parisian attitudes. Edward and Irina strolled down towards the Rond Point des Champs-Elysées, discussing the little there had been to discuss in their film. On a traffic island, Irina impulsively seized him and treated him to an extensive kiss.

"Why here?" Edward asked her afterwards, faintly irritated. "But not in the cinema?"

Irina twined her arm through his as they continued strolling.

148

"In the cinema, it's dark and distasteful," she explained. "And the contrast with the couple embracing on the screen is too dismal."

They had agreed to eat in the Marais. They went down into the Metro at Franklin D. Roosevelt and rattled their eight stops in near silence.

Despite the proliferation of new restaurants in the Marais, the streets were quiet as they made their way to the one Irina had chosen. Edward had not made any serious suggestions when they were discussing it. He didn't feel confident, even after four months' residence, to submit his judgement to Irina's Parisian scrutiny. So she had opted, after lengthy deliberations, for somewhere called the Soucoupe Musicale, just recently opened and apparently well recommended.

As they spotted the lifesize waiter's silhouette holding the menu outside it, Edward suddenly worried that Henry and Mai might be eating there; a well-recommended new restaurant right in their neighbourhood. He wondered, in a panic, how ever he could explain away the fact that he was out having dinner with Mademoiselle Iskarov, his landlady, on a Saturday night. It seemed fairly clear that he couldn't. While Irina read the menu in the silhouette's graciously outheld hand, he considered the problem; even though Irina had sworn him to secrecy *vis-à-vis* her elderly relatives, he could hardly ask the same of her as regards his colleagues. The sensibilities of working journalists were not those of well-bred eighty-year-old refugees, and the implication that he was embarrassed about her was unavoidable.

"It looks fine," Irina concluded. "They even have *blinis*."

Henry and Mai weren't in the restaurant and they enjoyed a thoroughly relaxed dinner. As they were drawing out the last remains of their desserts, Edward summoned his courage and asked Irina, "Would you mind coming back with me to the rue Surcouf tonight?"

Irina looked startled. "Why, Edouard?"

He hesitated, drawing out a trail of chocolate cream into a long question mark across his plate. "Well, we wouldn't need to worry about your grandmother hearing us. And, remember, I've got a double bed."

Irina looked distantly disgusted. "Babushka's deaf," she

149

replied. "And besides I *liked* the two of us so close together in my single bed. We were like Hansel and Gretel."

One of Edward's cartoon bubbles shot up, filled with expletives.

"But, Irina," he said beseechingly, "can't you see it's more comfortable for both of us if we have a bit more room?"

Irina pouted. "It seems disappointingly soon for you to be concerned about things like that, Edouard. Anyway, I have to be there when Babushka gets up. I have to make her breakfast. D'you want me rushing back across Paris at crack of dawn?"

"Well, I had to," Edward answered roughly.

Irina looked at him as if he were, he thought, a lesser form of insect life. "I know you are very young, Edouard," she said with leaden dignity, "but please don't be quite so uncouth. Just because I ask you to do something, it doesn't mean you may automatically expect the same thing of me."

To Edward, who had grown up in times of notional equality, this statement was at first staggering. He was on the verge of answering back when he realised abruptly there was no point. Irina operated by different rules. If the truth were told, he found her pompous little airs and graces to a certain extent appealing. After partners who drably put up with almost any indignity, there was something rather, if shamefully, entertaining about a woman who expected and performed a pantomime.

So they went back to the Cité Etienne Hubert. This time, they began to embrace in the lift and arrived at the fifth floor ready to proceed directly to Irina's single bed. It was therefore especially frustrating that Irina should hiss, "Shush!" as she opened the front door, listen for a minute before whispering to Edward, "Babushka's on the prowl" and tell him to wait outside on the landing until the coast was clear. He waited, fuming, for almost fifteen minutes. The peep hole in the door of the apartment opposite watched him with fishy humour. At last, Irina let him in, her finger to her lips, and led him in silence to her bedroom.

The delay had, as it turned out, only heightened their impatience. There was none of the previous Saturday's slow motion undressing. They toppled, grappling with one another's clothing, onto the pastel bedcover and what eventually

150

followed was one of the all time greats of Edward's sexual career. Beneath him, he registered Irina coming twice in close succession and he himself forgot all thoughts of the prowling grandmother and bellowed his exultation like a ship's funnel.

In the quiet which came afterwards, he still lay on top of Irina, relishing the feel of her small, warm mountain range, simmering like a recently erupted volcano. His pleasure was barely touched by the slippers which this time did pass down the corridor, and by the thought that he had never intended to like Irina this much.

The second time he spent the night with Irina, and the third, she did not throw him out in the early morning. Instead, she told him to stay secretly in bed while she made Babushka her breakfast and settled her for the day in her room. Then she would come back to him. He expected to sleep thankfully, lying across the warm space Irina had vacated. But it felt so extremely odd to be lying in bed in someone's apartment, without their even knowing you were there, that for quite some time he didn't go back to sleep. He listened for sounds of Irina and her grandmother moving about the apartment, but he couldn't hear a thing. He wondered, slightly jealously, how Irina was able to sally out in her dressing-gown, as though nothing had happened, and sit quite calmly chatting to her grandmother, without giving away any sign of the action-packed night which had passed between them. Out there, it must be as though he didn't exist. He lay feeling swallowed up by the large flat, a small object digested in one of the plural stomachs of a cow. Apart from Irina, no one in the world knew he was there. He drew the sheets over his head; he had disappeared. As he breathed in the remains of Irina's perfume with short shallow breaths, it seemed to him the silence of the apartment had deepened. Had Irina taken her grandmother out for a Sunday morning stroll? She hadn't come back in here to get dressed. But maybe she kept clothes somewhere else in the flat too? He folded the sheets down and strained to listen. In his own personal cul-de-sac, within the greater cul-de-sac, the silence was absolute.

He had fallen sound asleep when Irina came back to bed. She pushed him gently over towards the wall and slid in again beside him. They lay for a while, drowsy, undecided between the relative merits of sleep and each other. But gradually Irina's touch woke him and they rolled into an action replay, although this time it was unlike the volcanic activity of the night before. It was low key, slow and affectionate. Afterwards, they slept for the rest of the morning, curled in cramped but happily sweaty proximity.

At lunchtime, Irina said he should shower and dress while she diverted her grandmother's attention, and then "arrive" for lunch by tiptoeing out through the front hall and ringing the door bell. It was an uncomfortable meal. The grandmother spoke hardly at all, only to Irina and only in Russian. But her eyes flickered back and forth between them, suspecting, Edward was certain, all there was to suspect. In spite of this, he and Irina kept up a pretence of formality, passing one another dishes and saying pointedly, *"S'il vous plaît"* and *"Merci."* It didn't do anything to improve Edward's appetite for what was a disappointing meal of meat rissoles and red cabbage.

When they had eaten, Irina wanted to go out for a walk but it had started raining heavily. Despite her energetic efforts, Irina could not persuade her grandmother to go back to her room for her usual after-lunch nap. Instead the grandmother stayed sitting bolt upright in the living-room, not participating in Irina's and Edward's severely stilted conversation, but presumably monitoring it for indiscreet nuances.

Edward took the coward's option. "I have to push off now," he said to Irina. "Please do excuse my staying such a short time."

Irina's forlorn grin hid her obvious disappointment.

"When are we going to see each other again?" she whispered at the front door.

"Soon," Edward promised her, but he escaped with one-hundred-per-cent relief into the dark-grey wintry afternoon.

He had been greatly looking forward to getting back to his sanctuary in the rue Surcouf, but when he let himself in, it struck him that the flat was perceptibly changing its character. The more involved he became with Irina, and the more she told him about her catastrophic family, the less this place was his and the more it belonged to her Uncle Volodya. The three inter-connecting rooms, which he had appropriated with such pleasure in October, were being taken over again by somebody else. Their previous owner, slowly through Irina acquiring a face and a history and habits, was reinstating his claim. It struck Edward especially forcefully that Sunday afternoon; he was coming back to someone else's home.

Dyadya Volodya was Irina's mother's elder brother. There had been another brother too, Igor, but his whereabouts were unclear. Edward seemed to remember Irina mentioning he had gone to live in Brazil, but frankly the number of family members the Iskarovs seemed to have misplaced was such, he really couldn't be certain. In the absence of Irina's own errant father, Volodya had taken over the paternal role in her upbringing. As long as his marriage to the awful Aunty Ada had lasted, it sounded as though the relationship had never gone much beyond big birthday presents and trips to the Jardin des Plantes, sitting on her favourite uncle's lap and extorting franc pieces from his pockets. Volodya had been a big, genial, meatily male presence in small Irina's otherwise lopsidedly female life. But with the disappearance of his hindrant wife, it seemed Volodya, who must have been particularly keen for female company himself at that time, had begun to play a far greater part in Irina's life. This change had coincided with Irina's teenage years and must, Edward thought, be responsible for her predilection for older men *à la* Mr Blenkinsop. Until he himself had come on the scene, that was, and here he came up against the most awkward aspect of the whole situation. He was living in Volodya's flat; but was he also stepping into Volodya's shoes? He had wondered at the time whether Irina's reluctance to come and spend the night with him in the rue Surcouf concealed anything more than material reasons. Did she feel uncomfortable about misbehaving with Edward in a flat which was so reminiscent of Volodya? Could she not face the thought of sleeping with

Edward in Volodya's bed? At this point in his suppositions, Edward stopped every time. He had no reason at all to imagine that Volodya had been anything more than Irina's favourite uncle. So why did his mind keep coming back to the idea in this sick, obsessive way? He might as well admit why: he was concerned that it wasn't him at all that Irina was having an affair with, but the inhabitant of Volodya's flat.

Edward made himself a cup of coffee and put on a cassette. Volodya's presence was actually strongest, not as you might have expected in his bedroom, but in the living-room. Edward sat and listened to Bob Dylan and to the winter rain lashing down. He wondered whether the not unpleasant melancholy he felt might be characteristically Russian. As soon as it was permissibly late, he went to the kitchen to open a bottle of Nicolas plonk. There was a picture over the kitchen table which he had stared at vacantly often enough, but which he only now really took in. Who had chosen that picture? It was an oldish engraving, Edward didn't know much about these things; maybe salvaged from Volodya's antiques business which had never taken off. It was of a couple; a young woman in a long flouncy dress sitting in a swing. Her face, turned flirtatiously up towards a portly man standing watching over her, half-hidden by some shrubbery, bore an unmistakable resemblance to Irina. Edward wished he hadn't noticed. She was doubtless going to swing over his breakfast every morning from now on. He took the bottle and his glass and went back into the living-room. He only hoped it wasn't going to be the first of a string of similar discoveries; the walls and furniture of the flat shedding their surface appearance week after week to show him who was really who.

He imagined that it was Volodya Iskarov, instead of himself, sitting in the prime armchair, with his feet up on the battered footstool. It was of course Volodya Iskarov's feet which had created the twin depressions in the cracked green leather where his own now rested. Edward looked warily around the rest of the room. As on the day, a fortnight ago, when he had found Irina's food in the kitchen, he searched for clues which might reveal Volodya. He sensed somehow that many of the things in the flat were gifts from women. Although Volodya had ultimately been unlucky with women, he seemed

155

to have always had plenty of them on tap. The clock perhaps, with its over-loud, fussy tick, that seemed to be more of a woman's choice than a man's. Or the profusion of cushions, which Edward had always had difficulty with; surely they had been scattered by the hand of an Iskarov female. It was, of course, impossible to tell what had been in the flat beforehand, when Volodya had lived there, and what had been added since by Irina for her tenants. But the durable, old-fashioned ring holders on the bathroom wall for a shaving-brush and a mug, they undoubtedly dated from Volodya, and in the bedroom the incontrovertible evidence was the bed. For there was no way Irina would have gone to the expense of buying a new bed for her tenants. The broad, dark, wooden bed had also housed Volodya.

In the course of the evening, Edward had dinner, in the form of a number of successive forays to the fridge. He twiddled the television dial and drank considerably more than he had intended of his plonk.

Fairly late that night, the telephone rang. Irina's voice said, "Edouard, darling, I am miserable without you."

More churlishly than he meant to, Edward told her, "It's the weather."

"Don't be like that," Irina said. "This is genuine; I miss you."

"I enjoyed being with you too," Edward answered, he was aware, lamely.

"What are you doing now?" Irina asked.

He said, "Getting pissed."

Irina tutted. "Drinking alone?" Then she added triumphantly, "You see, you do miss me too, Edouard."

Her logic escaping him, he changed the subject. "What have you been doing with yourself today?"

He was rewarded by a full-scale sigh. "Trying to drum some sense into Babushka. Making afternoon tea and then supper for Babushka. Putting Babushka to bed. I tell you, Edouard, it's just as well her state is not infectious. I'd be raving mad by now." And then, with no apparent connection, she asked him, "Are you doing anything on Wednesday evening?"

Across his hesitation, she went on, "I'd like my friend Lyova to meet you. You remember, the one who came to

156

be with Babushka that time, who works in a bookshop? I'm going to visit him in the shop on Wednesday after school and I thought you could come with me."

The ominous advances which this represented, seeing Irina at a time other than on Saturday night and presumably for a purpose other than on Saturday night, and being presented to one of her friends, were sufficient to make Edward hesitate even longer. The cons quite definitely outweighed the pros, so the only explanation he could think of for the fact that, after a moment or two, he accepted was Lyova's Russian name. It was a day or two, in fact Wednesday, before the remainder of the explanation occurred to him; natural curiosity about this other man in Irina's life, combined with the far-fetched idea that setting eyes on Lyova might somehow illuminate Volodya.

Irina had given him the address, Number Eleven, rue de la Montagne Sainte-Geneviève, and said they should meet directly at the bookshop, "rather than one or other of us having to wait at the Metro in this cold". As things turned out, Edward was for once delayed in leaving the paper – an important telex was coming in from Yaoundé – and it was a good quarter of an hour after their arranged meeting time that he emerged from the nearest Metro station. It was one of his favourite names, Maubert-Mutualité, and he savoured it on the station signs before trying to identify the probable direction of the rue de la Montagne Sainte-Geneviève. It took him a while longer to find it – it wasn't a neighbourhood he went to often – and so by the time he actually arrived at the bookshop and opened the door, setting off a quavering bell, Irina and her friend were long cosily installed drinking tea at a table at the back of the shop, looking a contentedly domesticated couple.

But Irina jumped up gratifyingly quickly when he came in and hurried forward to greet him. There were only two or three customers left in the shop, which was about to close, and none of them appeared to pay the slightest attention when in the middle of the shop Irina gave Edward a quick but audible kiss. They were all elderly characters, muffled so elaborately in woollen scarves and fur hats that perhaps they simply didn't hear. They were reading with absorption, apparently from cover to cover.

Irina led Edward, holding his hand, to meet Lyova. He admitted that his first emotion was hostility, for Lyova, rising lazily to his feet to shake hands, looked down on him with scarcely concealed entertained surprise. He was a big man, who extended one spade-like hand and muttered a gruff, "*Enchanté*" before disappearing into the back of the shop to bring Edward some tea.

Irina squeezed Edward's knee under the table but he shook her off; he did not want consoling. He did feel slightly less aggressive when Lyova came back with his glass of tea and sat down opposite him for, seated, the disparity in their heights at least was gone. But Lyova still possessed a number of irritating advantages. In the first place, he looked like a hero; his was the face you saw in newspaper pictures of dissidents, *refuseniks*, unbreakable men coming out of years in camps. He had a jutting jaw and a long Pinnochio nose, stern brown eyes which conveyed the impression they had daily witnessed scenes not entered in your English schoolboy's catalogue of horrors. He also had, which would have been an affectation on almost anybody else, collar-length hair and what Edward thought of as a Russian peasant smock, a dark woollen affair, buttoned down one side and held in by a mammoth belt. The last straw was he smoked; a potent, foul-smelling Cyrillic brand.

The only option open to Edward was to take the offensive. "What is this place?" he asked.

It sounded like a poor joke when they answered simultaneously, "The YMCA." The shop was a dimly lit barn. Hanging neon strips overhead shed insufficient light across the lino floor and the crammed shelves of plainly bound books. The air smelt of cheap paper and cheaply bound books. Even when there was no one smoking in the shop, you knew there would be a nostalgic whiff of foreign cigarette smoke. It was a place for futile governments in exile and revolutionary plots doomed to extinction.

"Come off it," Edward said.

Lyova laughed. "Not *your* YMCA," he said. He told Edward about the press which published the works of Russian dissident writers and, wryly, he pointed out the Russian emblems around the room: the heavily gilded orthodox calendars, the photographs of wooden huts in the snow.

158

"You have entered the realm of retrospection," he explained in thickly accented French. "You see these dear old people browsing? Never, incidentally, do they buy a book. They are like the statue turned to salt, forever looking backwards. They have been here in France, Edouard, for fifty or sixty years, but you should hear the way they speak French; they speak as if they arrived here yesterday. I, who *did* arrive yesterday, speak better than they do."

"You didn't arrive yesterday," Irina contradicted him.

"Seven years?" objected Lyova. "Seven years *is* yesterday, especially in terms of fifty or sixty years' residence. They make me weep, you know. They are so hopelessly nostalgic. They have no word for 'tomorrow' in their vocabulary; only 'yesterday'."

"How long have you worked here?" Edward asked.

Irina interjected, "Lyova's an artist. He only works here sometimes."

Lyova grimaced. "An artist," he repeated with affected horror at the pretentiousness of the term. "And you, I understand, are a journalist?" With which he bestowed on Edward a frankly disdainful smile.

"That's right," Edward answered hotly. He wasn't sure if Lyova's disdain was directed at his profession or at the notion that someone so young and inexperienced could be a journalist. Either way, Edward's indignation was roused.

But Lyova wouldn't gratify him with the wherewithal to have an argument. He just nodded, smiling infuriatingly, and contemplated a highly entertaining middle distance.

Edward knew his rejoinder, "What's funny about that?" sounded squeaky and childish. He regretted it as soon as it was out of his mouth, especially when Lyova answered ironically, "Nothing funny at all, I assure you. It is a noble calling." He stood up a little abruptly. "Please excuse me. It is time for me to close this circus."

He went to the front of the shop, clapping his hands and calling out in Russian to his elderly customers. Gradually, over several minutes, he chivvied them, protesting and apparently querying the accuracy of Lyova's watch, out of the shop, turned the "Open" sign over to "Closed" and switched off some of the lights.

159

While he was doing this, Irina again tried to take Edward's hand, but he withdrew it bad-temperedly. What had been the point of bringing him here, just to be made fun of?

"Are we going to have a drink together?" Lyova asked when he returned.

"Why not?" Irina exclaimed brightly. "What time are you expected back?"

Lyova ran a harassed hand through his hair. "Anna's at one of her classes tonight," he said gloomily. "The kids are with my sister-in-law. I should pick them up before eight, I guess."

This revelation came as a heaven-sent bounty to Edward. So Lyova, his taller, bigger, braver, better rival for Irina's affections, Lyova who he was now quite convinced must remind Irina of Volodya, Lyova was married to someone else! Just briefly, he reproved himself for his immaturity in not having thought of this option. It did, of course, explain everything: the equivocal nature of the friendship and the way Lyova was sometimes on the scene and sometimes inexplicably not. Edward found it in himself to feel sorry for Lyova; no wonder he felt provoked to savage Edward. He must be eaten up with envy, poor bugger. For the fact was Lyova must at some stage have been Irina's lover, but he wasn't a free agent, shackled with a wife and puling kids to boot. He wasn't a free agent but Edward gloriously was.

"Sure," Edward agreed magnanimously. "Let's have a drink."

When Lyova had left reluctantly early, managing, Edward observed with disgust, to look vaguely dashing even in such unpromising circumstances, going off with the collar of his leather jacket turned up against the drizzle to collect his two little girls, Edward turned on Irina and asked, "What was all that in aid of?"

"What d'you mean?" she asked. "And why have you been so unpleasant this evening? Didn't you like Lyova?"

Edward gave a sour laugh. "I'm sure he's a fine, upstanding chap. What's the score between you two?"

"Edouard!" Irina exclaimed indignantly. "I've told you before, I will not have these sporting expressions. Lyova is my best friend."

160

Edward scoffed. "A likely story."

Unexpectedly, Irina did not erupt. She shook her head glumly.

They sat in sulky silence for a while and then Irina explained, "I wanted Lyova to see what you were like. It's hard not being able to talk about you to anybody."

"You must let me hear his verdict," Edward answered nastily.

Irina sighed. "It's really not what you think, Edouard. Lyova and I are *allies*, that's all; I complain to him about my terrible family and he complains to me about his, that's all."

"You're not going to convince me that's always been all there is to it," Edward said.

Irina drew herself up. "I'm talking about the present, Edouard," she told him. "Not the past."

Lyova as old boyfriend, which was the category Edward consequently filed him under, was a lot less problematical than Lyova as an ongoing proposition. Edward relented a little while they ate a quick dinner – Irina had to be home early too – and he asked her in an offhand way, "So how often do you see each other, then? And what does his wife have to say about it?"

Irina's reply was not at all reassuring. She snapped, "Anna has no right to reproach anybody for anything, I can assure you."

Edward let the subject drop and called for the bill. He decided that, even if Irina offered, he would not go back with her that night to the Cité Etienne Hubert. It seemed an undesirable admission of dependency to start to spend nights with her during the working week. And he didn't like the smug smile which his earlier display of jealousy had left on Irina's face.

Great-Aunt Elena telephoned him the following Sunday to invite him to lunch.

"Oich!" she exclaimed, even before she had told him why it was she was ringing or gone through the elaborate Parisian hello-how-are-you formula. "It has such an effect on me, dialling Volodya's number, you can't imagine!"

"I'm sorry it's only me on the other end," Edward said a bit lamely. Straight away, he wasn't sure if the crack was in good taste.

Great-Aunt Elena made the exclamatory noise he had previously compared to the partial bursting of a paper bag. "Ach, Edward," she said. "I'd much rather you than some of the people we've had in there in the intervening years."

He wondered whether Irina had been responsible for choosing those people too, and also, just quickly, about what naturally followed on from this question.

"You are a perfect treasure, I can assure you," Great-Aunt Elena went on, "compared to some of the tenants we've had."

"I heard about the American," Edward volunteered.

"American!" Great-Aunt Elena said dismissively. "But I bet she hasn't told you about the Italian or the Hungarian or the Brazilian, has she?"

162

"You had a Brazilian here?" Edward asked.

"Yes, we did," Great-Aunt Elena answered. "He worked for a bank with a most suspicious name, I remember: the Banco Espirito Santo e Commercial." She repeated the name dubiously. "And I believe he was a fundamentally unprincipled man."

'This flat,' thought Edward, 'is becoming more and more of a liability all the time.'

"The Italian was a decent person," Great-Aunt Elena continued. "And then there've been a few others I never met, who were apparently perfectly all right. But the Hungarian!" She interrupted herself. "Tell your newspaper to keep you here for as long as they possibly can," she said. "Really, you're the most delightful tenant we've had since I don't know when."

"I'm afraid it's out of my hands," Edward said.

"And I know it's not what you want anyway," Great-Aunt Elena said hastily. "Well, that's quite right; you should travel and see the world while you're young." She changed tack with the kind of French conversational manoeuvre which still always made Edward feel like clapping. "We must just make the most of you while we can. Will you come and have lunch with me next Sunday?"

The feeling that this bizarre Russian family could one day get beyond a joke had been at the back of Edward's mind all along, of course. He welcomed Irina's relatives as an engaging diversion which could – who knew? – turn out to be professionally useful to him. But at that moment he sighted the day when they would cease to be the free gift which came with Irina, the joke in the cracker, the oddity in the gumball, and become the one thing he would flee from anywhere in the world: merely surrogate family ties and domesticity.

He said, "Um, I'm not sure if I can make it."

"Sunday the thirty-first," Great-Aunt Elena said encouragingly. "A week from today. Oh please, do come; it would give me such pleasure."

"I'll just look in my diary, if you'll excuse me," Edward said, playing for time. He knew his diary gaped, utterly empty for weeks ahead, apart from the few single exclamation marks which were his jokey way of recording dates with Irina.

The telephone receiver was still chirruping into empty

space when he came back to it. Great-Aunt Elena didn't seem to have realised he had walked away. She was holding forth with great vehemence about something or other into the blue.

Mischievously, Edward picked up the receiver and listened for a moment without saying anything.

" – worried at all because, really, she's a wonderful girl, wonderful, it's just her manner. People have, I am afraid, on occasion, misinterpreted her manner, but I know you won't. You're far too wise and intelligent to make such a primitive mistake. I was telling Vera only the other day: you have a wisdom beyond your years, I can sense it."

"I'm sorry," Edward said. "But I had to leave the phone for a minute to get my diary. I think I missed the last thing that you said."

There was a confounded silence.

"Which thing?" Great-Aunt Elena ventured.

She sounded so uncharacteristically crestfallen, Edward answered hurriedly, "Oh, just that very last bit. Who was it you were talking about?"

He heard her thwarted intake of breath, and then there was what seemed a deeper silence.

At last she answered coyly, and enigmatically, so that Edward was left not knowing if his interpretation was anywhere near accurate, "I was telling you not to be afraid it would be a boring *tête-à-tête* with me. I've invited Irina too."

In the end, he said he could come. It seemed counterproductive not to and, besides, the alternative was just one more bleak Sunday spent watching some mediocre film at the cinema or with his feet up on Volodya's footstool.

Since he spent the night beforehand with Irina in the Cité Etienne Hubert, setting off for lunch with Great-Aunt Elena presented certain problems. For a start, it had been another highly energetic night and neither of them had the least inclination to get up and dressed, or to go out into the frozen greyness and put on a charade of distance. Irina had come back to bed after making Babushka her breakfast and woken him with such a frank request with her fingers that, instead of catching up on sleep, the remainder of the morning had gone the same way.

164

Edward showered in their antediluvian bathroom, convinced that even Babushka must guess from the raucous plumbing that Irina wouldn't take two showers. He dried himself on the unprepossessingly pink bath towel Irina had given him and took advantage of the privacy to have a snoop through the compromising contents of the bathroom cabinets. Their rows of little mucky bottles containing medicines and cosmetics were thoroughly off-putting. He wished he could be certain that all the really stomach-turning ones belonged to Babushka – the tonic for dandruff, the horrid little khaki pills for flatulence – but, frankly, it was hard to tell whose cupboard was whose. This unnerved him. The faint stirrings of revulsion he had felt when he imagined Irina the age of Varvara Stepanovna revived. He closed the doors of the last cupboard hastily on a glimpse of something unidentifiable made of yellowed latex and told himself firmly it was, of course, his own fault for having gone snooping and, also, that last cupboard must be Babushka's.

Leaving the flat was a ridiculous rigmarole. Irina went in to occupy Babushka while Edward sneaked out and he waited for her on the landing while she made her goodbyes and followed. But she seemed to take so long coming, and the situation struck him as so unnecessarily undignified, that he was tempted to fling the front door open – he had left it ajar so as not to make any noise closing it – and to yell in, "Come *on*, Irina!"

"I'm quite sure your grandmother's tumbled to the fact there's something fishy going on," he grumbled as they travelled down in the lift. "I can't see why you insist on carrying on with this cloak-and-dagger stuff."

"She has no idea," Irina said haughtily. "And please make sure she doesn't get one."

"I don't know what makes you so sure," Edward said unpleasantly. "I can think of a hundred and one ways she could have found out."

"I think," Irina answered sarcastically, "I know her a little better than you do."

The lift came to the ground floor with an unnerving mechanical settling and an exhausted sigh.

"Well," Edward finished belligerently, "I still think the whole thing is ridiculous."

Irina glared at him. "I'm not sure what *you* think is the crucial consideration, Edouard."

They added bad temper to their other accumulated problems of lack of sleep and muzzy heads, and travelled across to Great-Aunt Elena's in a bleary, tousled-feeling trance.

Her greeting was uncomfortably to the point. "*Mon Dieu!*" she exclaimed. "What a pair of washed-out-looking faces! You both look in need of a good lunch."

She had laid this on with evident forethought. "This time, you shall have *rosbif*," she said triumphantly to Edward.

When they were seated in the living-room, with aperitif glasses at their elbows, she lifted hers and declared proudly, "Cheers!"

Irina lay back in her armchair and closed her eyes, looking rather green, Edward thought. He couldn't tell if she was sulking or if the previous night had caught up with her. He was relieved when she picked up her glass and answered aggressively, "*Na zdorovye.*"

Great-Aunt Elena determinedly repeated, "Cheers!" and then, with a wicked giggle, "Bottoms up!"

Edward laughed. "I bet you didn't learn that one from Miss Macpherson."

"Indeed not," replied Great-Aunt Elena. "I learnt that expression from a young fellow who was a business associate of our family's in Russia. His name was Blenkinsop."

"Oh yes," Edward said. "Irina's mentioned him to me before."

Great-Aunt Elena and Irina exchanged a suspicious and a respondingly hostile glance.

"Of course," Great-Aunt Elena said, "Irina only knew him in later life, when he was well past his prime."

"Miss Macpherson was far too much of a prude to teach them anything fun," Irina retaliated. "She only taught them nursery rhymes and silly songs."

"They weren't silly songs," Great-Aunt Elena answered sharply. "They were charming."

Unexpectedly she warbled:

"Bobby Shaftoe's gone to sea-ea,
Silver buckles on his knee-ee,

He'll come back and marry me-ee,
Bonny Bobby Shaftoe!"

"Ah, *ça suffit*," snapped Irina. She stood up rather abruptly. "I'm going to the bathroom if you're going to start singing those maudlin melodies."

As she stamped past Edward, he was taken aback to see her chin was trembling, as if she were on the verge of tears.

"I don't know what gets into Irina sometimes," Great-Aunt Elena commented. "She can be so moody and sharp. I think it must be the shortcomings of her life which distress her."

She misread Edward's non-committal look, with which he tried to wipe any traces of responsibility or guilt from his face, as incomprehension.

"She leads in many respects an unsatisfactory life, of course," Great-Aunt Elena explained. "But, I keep telling her, she only makes it worse for herself, the way she behaves. People get the wrong idea about her. She's a dear girl, a – "

"Don't," Irina called out, reappearing unexpectedly quickly in the doorway. "Don't poison his mind against me. I forbid you to." Her voice was disturbingly strained and shrill.

Great-Aunt Elena snorted. "Precisely the opposite of what I was doing," she declared. "Precisely the opposite."

She stood up and bustled indignantly towards the door. "I shall serve you lunch, although you, Irina, don't deserve it."

For a few moments, Edward and Irina stayed, not communicating with each other at all. Irina had slumped back deep into her armchair, her eyes shut and a profoundly miserable expression on her face.

"Hey, cheer up," Edward whispered to her. "It's not that bad, surely."

Irina's eyes opened and he saw they actually were glinting with tears.

"It is," she retorted. "And worse."

The cock-a-leekie soup and the *rosbif* seemed to restore the spirits of Irina and her great-aunt. They had rather the opposite effect on Edward. The heavy, bland food settled in his stomach like a leaden depression. He hadn't come to Paris, he reflected, to experience this ersatz England. There was something profoundly dismal about watching these last survivors of a dead empire dotingly mimicking another empire in its death throes. Was it, in fact, some sort of unrecognised affinity which had brought him here, to eat rice pudding and to listen to "Bobby Shaftoe"? Did he have some fatal English fondness, which he had not till now noticed, for what was old and crumbling and *passé*? Rather than enjoying a private laugh at their expense, was the joke actually on him?

Great-Aunt Elena's little chipolata of a forefinger poked out and plucked him on the chin.

"Why so glum, Edward?"

He said hastily, "I'm not glum, am I? I'm sorry; I didn't mean to be. Probably I was just concentrating on this lovely lunch."

He saw Irina raise one finely shaped eyebrow.

"*Mais enfin*," Great-Aunt Elena exclaimed, "what's got into the two of you today? You didn't at all have the look of someone quietly enjoying his lunch, you know, Edward. You looked as if you were plunged in gloom. What's the matter?"

"I can't speak for Irina," Edward said. "But I'm really not feeling down at all. Maybe eating this sort of food reminded me of England, that's all."

"And that made you feel sad?" Great-Aunt Elena asked. "Why? Surely you aren't homesick?"

Irina gave a harsh laugh. "Homesick? Edouard? Haven't you realised he's longing to get as far away as possible from England, from Europe, from all of us? He wants to go to the jungle and find himself a girlfriend who wears flowers behind her ear."

"And quite right and proper at his age too," Great-Aunt Elena reproved her. She turned to Edward. "Visit the jungle while you can," she instructed him. "At my age it's too late." As an after-thought, she added, "Send me postcards."

"Postcards?" Irina scoffed. "From the jungle? You amaze me with your never-ending wanderlust, you know, Elena. One would have thought that after all the migrations you've been through in your time, you'd finally be quite glad to stay put in one place. You're really no better than Babushka with her perpetual suitcases."

Great-Aunt Elena drew a very deep and, Edward felt, menacing breath.

168

"Well, I think it's tremendous," he chipped in.

Great-Aunt Elena, far and away the shortest person at the lunch table, managed to look down on Irina with a regal glare. "I am astonished that you, Irina, of all people, should dream of comparing opposites. What do you suppose our travelling had in common with Edward's? How can you make such a frivolous comparison between forced, joyless displacements and gadding about?" She turned graciously to Edward. "I do not wish to make light of what you do, Edward, but it is a game, isn't it?" She rounded on Irina. "If you cannot perceive the difference between Edward, who propels himself around the world, notebook in hand, and we, who were propelled, then, *milaya moya*, really I do not know what the last thirty years have been in aid of."

"Oh, I'm sick and tired of this litany," Irina burst out. She dropped her knife and fork in disgust. "Tell me, how many times have I had to sit through the recital of the sufferings of the Iskarov family from A to Z? Since I was a child, year in, year out; never let little Irina forget how much we all suffered so that she could have her donkey rides in the Jardin du Luxembourg and get the bean on the Fête des Rois. Well, little Irina had enough! She didn't see why she should carry the burden of all that inherited suffering into the next generation: inherited complexes, inherited disorientation, inherited weather! Little Irina decided a long time ago she was going to have a good time. So there's no point going into it all over again, for Edouard's benefit, thank you very much. Let's just let the matter drop."

There was a short, very sultry silence. Edward wished himself anywhere but in the midst of this family confrontation.

"I'm quite sure the distinction is clear to you, Edward," Great-Aunt Elena continued provocatively. "For your generation, travel is just a ride on a fairground carousel or a Ferris wheel; you know, barring a disaster, you'll come safely back to the place you set out from and you can sit back and enjoy the sensations of the voyage. You don't need to worry that the station you started out from won't be there any more when you get back."

"You can tell her when you've had enough, you know," Irina interrupted rudely.

"I think it's extremely interesting," Edward answered defiantly.

For a moment, he and Irina faced one another, all their extensive differences exposed.

"For us, of course, it was another matter entirely," Great-Aunt Elena went on. "Only a very few people were fortunate enough in those days to sample exotic travel: the jungle or the Himalayas. For most people, travel was something that was forced on you quite against your will. It came, frankly, in the category of natural disasters; like an earthquake or a hurricane. It uprooted you, blew you in a turmoil halfway across the world and then dropped you down quite arbitrarily somewhere you hadn't chosen at all, and you had to make a go of it as best you could. Travel meant essentially loss, not the acquisition of colourful experiences and mementoes. It meant the loss of people, of places, of ridiculous irreplaceable things like smells and sounds and colours. And the loss was absolute, irrevocable; those things weren't just mislaid or temporarily out of reach, you understand. They were gone for good." She hurried herself a little, as if she realised that Irina's forbearance would only last so long. "Considering what a catastrophe it was, it is remarkable how quietly, how unnoticeably it began. The day of a disaster, and I suppose the day of your death, dawns just like any other, you know. Yes, the day on which your life is totally changed or utterly ruined begins with a perfectly unremarkable banality. Afterwards, looking back at that day, at the events which preceded the catastrophe, it is their very banality, their failure to foreshadow what followed, which astonishes you. You remember, not waking up and knowing that today the chain of events would start which will end in you and your family fleeing your native land, taking with you only what you can carry. No, you remember waking up and feeling pleased because you have a new blouse to wear. You remember very clearly the colour and the feel of that new blouse because it was the last new garment you had for a long, long time. You remember lying in bed in the early morning and listening to the familiar noise outside of the ice floes splitting and creaking as they float down the river. You have lain in bed in the morning and listened to that same strange noise every spring. It is just

170

one of the familiar seasonal phenomena of your youth. But you will remember this ordinary, annual phenomenon with such clarity, such intensity, because you will never hear it again."

"Bravo!" Irina said tartly. "Now, if the show is over, perhaps we can go on to the cheese?"

"Why are you being so vile to her?" Edward whispered when Great-Aunt Elena had left the room, maintaining a dignified silence.

Irina heaved a giant sigh. "Please, Edouard, don't take sides in a battle you don't understand."

"Oh, come off it," said Edward. "I don't need to *understand* anything to see you're giving her a hard time. I think you're being unbelievably mean."

Unexpectedly, Irina capitulated. "You're right," she agreed. "I'm an utter cow."

She stood up, her face distorted with remorse, and went out to the kitchen, presumably to make her peace with Great-Aunt Elena. They were gone for a fairly long time, during which Edward ambled around the cramped living-room, reviewing the photographs on the bookcase in the light of today's stories. When they returned, bringing a platter of Double Gloucester and Stilton, both of them had pink eyes.

The rest of the meal passed relatively peacefully. Afterwards, they sat drinking numerous cups of coffee and talking innocuously about the relative merits of Costa Rican and Brazilian blends. Edward felt the first pins and needles of boredom. But Irina insisted on going to the kitchen to do all the washing-up in a lather of amends and, while she was gone, Great-Aunt Elena repeated to him what a dear girl she was. All she needed was someone who would show her the direction of proper happiness, instead of pursuing chimeras.

By the time they left, it was five o'clock. Outside, it was already dark; the brief winter's day seemed to have lasted barely a couple of hours. Although Edward had expected it would be uncomfortable to be on his own again with Irina, after the interval of suppressed disagreement, in the event no argument surfaced. They walked in silence down the Boulevard de Courcelles, sculpted in a particularly severe Sunday stoniness. Since Irina didn't round on him or begin

171

to scold him for taking her great-aunt's side against her, he gave her hand a tentative squeeze.

"Why are you so fed up today?" he asked.

Her sigh was a classic of its kind. She gestured at the gold-tipped black railings of the Parc Monceau.

"Why? Because of this."

Automatically, Edward cast a glance at the deserted gravel paths and the empty green wooden benches dripping with moisture.

"Anything in particular?" he teased her.

She looked around bleakly and settled on an elderly couple creeping down the opposite side of the boulevard towards them. She jutted her chin in their direction. "For example."

As seriously as he could, for Irina's moods always seemed to him faintly farcical, Edward considered the pair. They were moving at the slow precarious pace of brittle bones on slippery pavements, their arms crooked for mutual support at the elbow, their grey heads bowed in the struggle. They looked, as they shuffled forward, welded by long years of similar, painstaking companionship.

He considered Irina. With the collar of her fur coat turned up against the weather, and the dark rings of gloom around her eyes, she really did look exceptionally dramatic. She reminded him of the woman glimpsed through mist or cigarette smoke in a Forties film. He tried to decide whether he had ever fantasised about partnering such a woman. He couldn't say he ever had. It really did just seem to be a stroke of ridiculous luck; Paris depositing this superlative booby prize in his lap. In that spirit, of grabbing your luck while it lasted, he reached for Irina's hand again as they came to the Metro station and asked her, "Why don't you come back with me to the rue Surcouf?"

She glanced at her watch and his spirits rose; the proposition was not rejected out of hand then.

"I don't know," she said. "It's getting late."

"Oh, go on," Edward urged her. "You don't need to stay for long."

Irina giggled, apparently titillated by the implication. Still she hesitated. Then she sighed. "Sooner or later," she said,

172

"I suppose it has to happen. But, in that case, we're going by taxi and not on the Metro."

The act was quite distinctively different in the bigger bed. As they came in through the inter-connecting rooms, Irina seemed to lose her usual cocky self-assurance. She tagged behind Edward in the direction of the bedroom, but stopping all the way to examine things wonderingly, as if the circumstances had given them a new dimension. In the bedroom doorway, she came to a complete standstill and Edward had gently but firmly to propel her the final stretch down onto the bed.

As he had expected, the constricting anxieties of the Cité Etienne Hubert were lifted here. There was nothing furtive in the way they engaged beneath the bedclothes. But, freed of the oppressive constraints and the fear of discovery, it seemed they might at the same time have lost an element of their usual excitement. Things were much slower getting off the ground. It was almost as if in the broad space of the double bed, everything had been somehow diluted.

Nevertheless, the upshot was well up to the mark. They lay afterwards, a little way apart, and Edward was glad to notice that he felt just slightly more detached from Irina than he might have expected at that juncture. She didn't prattle anxiously either, holding onto him and repeating in the most sickly sentimental terms what a great performer he was. The bed seemed, if possible, to have put more than physical distance between them. It had taken them out of the grotesque nursery universe, in which one or other or both of them were always children, and returned them to a cool adult environment, where their encounter took place amid antecedents, consequences and inhibiting implications. To his considerable surprise, Edward realised that although comfort would certainly dictate more frequent use of his bed in future, he would not mind in fact if, from time to time, they still went back to the Cité Etienne Hubert.

Because Irina still didn't say anything and because her eyes were closed, Edward assumed she was asleep. He had a sudden spitefully mischievous wish to whisper something to her in Russian, to confuse her. He hoped perversely that in this bed she might give the game away by muttering Volodya's name in her sleep.

173

But he didn't know how to say anything. He reached for his watch and he noticed again that it was January 31st. February was invariably such a foul month, but he reflected contentedly that, contrary to all expectations, this year it looked as if he was going to get through it rather well.

Irina announced the idea to him like a premium bond she had won. They had met in the Taverne Tourville, for what Edward had pleasurably anticipated as another enjoyable evening of eating and drinking, winding up cosily on the fifth floor of Number Nine, Cité Etienne Hubert. They were on their first drink, Scotch and a *kir* respectively, and the only decision Edward had contemplated was how many drinks they might have here before moving on to a new restaurant and where that restaurant might be. They had already got into the habit of sitting at the same table, the one beside the glass dessert cabinet, and one of the waiters even knew what drinks they ordered.

Irina leant forward, propping her forearms across the peach cloth and trying to diffuse her excitement by playing elaborately with the silver-plated cruets. Lyova had asked her a favour. She darted Edward an apprehensive glance, in case Lyova's name had had a detrimental effect. Lyova had to go away for a few days. A gallery owner in Nice had offered him his big break, an exhibition of his own, and Lyova obviously had to go down there to arrange it. The problem was, Lyova's horrendous wife, Anna, had walked out on him yet again, this time it looked serious; she had taken up with some ghastly, vulgar advertising man, just her type, and if Lyova went to Nice, there would be no one to look after the little girls. Irina broke into a broad grin. By a wonderful coincidence, though, it just happened to be when half-term fell at the *lycée*. When Lyova had put the problem to her, at his wits' end, wanting to ask her to help out, of course, but knowing it would be impossible, she had at once been able to say yes, yes she would, yes with pleasure.

Edward tried to work out where in this story lay the key fact which was making Irina so delighted, and what, in any case, it had to do with him.

"So are you going to?" he asked cautiously.

Irina beamed. "Naturally. I shall stay in Lyova's apartment for four days from Monday to Thursday. Elena will come over to be with Babushka and you and I will be free."

"Oh yes?" Edward asked. "Where do I come into all this?"

Irina squeezed both his hands, unable to restrain her excitement any longer. "Don't you see? Those two little girls are far too small to go spreading gossip and, anyway, if we take care, they won't find out. Don't you really see? You can come and stay there with me, of course. Lyova won't mind. We can have four days and four nights to ourselves." She raised her eyebrows and rolled her eyes at him with a luridly overdone suggestiveness. At the same time, she gripped his hands so tightly he had to extricate them.

"Hang on a minute," he said. "I don't want to come and stay at Lyova's place and look after his children, thank you very much. You're perfectly welcome to, if that's your idea of a good time. But I'm afraid you can count me out."

Irina's face fell an incredibly long way. "I don't understand you."

"Nothing not to understand," Edward said briskly. He was polishing off his Scotch at a fair lick. "It doesn't appeal to me, that's all. Sorry."

Irina let go of his hands. "But Edouard," she protested. "Maybe I haven't explained myself; I'm inviting you to come and spend four days and four nights with *me*."

Behind her head, a pot plant stood on the café's white piano. Edward suddenly saw the two in juxtaposition: lady's head and pot plant, a blandly decorative painting from his Paris period.

176

The vision enabled him to give Irina an absolutely calm look and to answer levelly, "Yes?"

Irina began to grow fretful. "This is a joke, isn't it, Edouard? Although not a funny one."

"Depends how you look at it," Edward answered flippantly. "I think it's rather a joke your suggesting that I come and help babysit for Lyova for four or five days."

Irina glared at him. "You seem to be missing the point. I can't tell if it's because you're really obtuse or if you're just doing it to provoke me."

"A combination of both?" Edward suggested.

He suddenly felt he didn't want to lose the pleasant evening in prospect because of one of Irina's whims. He squeezed both her hands hard and added, "Don't get me wrong, Irina. I really enjoy spending time with you, you know that. Only not in Lyova's flat, and not surrounded by kids."

"Why not Lyova's flat?" Irina asked petulantly. "What's wrong with Lyova's flat? You yourself complain that we have to go on tiptoes in my flat and you know it's difficult for me to come to yours. So here's someone offering us another flat, where we can be perfectly at peace, and, really, I don't see where's the problem. And, in any case, Lyova only has two children."

Edward laughed at her. "Two too many."

Irina's patience expired in an exasperated snort.

"What's *wrong* with you?" she exploded. "Katya and Solange are the dearest, sweetest little things. They wouldn't get in our way at all. And if they did, we could always take them to Anna's sister for a bit during the day. It's not a kindergarten I'm inviting you to; it's a little holiday, just the two of us."

"That's not what it sounds like," Edward countered.

"I never thought," Irina said stuffily, "that I would have to criticise you for behaving too much like an old person. But, really, this hesitation, this caution; what are you worried about? Why can't you just take a golden opportunity when it arises without fussing about how it might possibly go wrong?"

"Hang on a minute," Edward objected. "Who's saying this is such a tremendous opportunity? It sounds like purgatory to me. And anyway, I thought we'd worked out rather a good compromise, haven't we; your place at night and mine during the day?"

Irina's face flushed furiously. "You're so unromantic, Edouard," she declared.

She downed the last of her *kir*. "I'm not going to beg you," she announced loftily. "If you're too much of a fuddy-duddy to recognise a stroke of good fortune when it comes your way, then I don't see why I should make the effort to persuade you."

They went to a modest Provençal restaurant. Throughout the meal, Edward had to try to scale the barricade of injured pride Irina had erected. It was tiring and irritating but he knew full well that unless he surmounted it, Irina took her dignity seriously enough to shut her front door in his face at the end of the evening, and that did seem an awful waste.

Towards the end of the meal, to secure his position, he raised the subject again conciliatingly. "Have you babysat for Lyova before?"

"Once or twice," Irina said sulkily, and he saw he still had a man-sized grudge to work on.

He asked himself then if it were really worthwhile; all this uphill slogging when there must be no shortage of women in Paris who would give approximately as good a return for half the effort. An answer came to him which was almost mathematical in the simplicity of its logic; it had taken him over three months to land Irina. In three months more, with any luck, his time in Paris would be coming to an end.

"It's very generous of you," he said.

Irina looked at him suspiciously. "Lyova babysits for Babushka," she said. "That's much more of a favour."

"When is it?" Edward asked. "When are you going to stay there?"

"You're not interested," Irina said resentfully. "Don't pretend you are. What's the point of my telling you when it is since we're not going to see each other that week anyway?"

He only said it in a last-ditch attempt to save the evening: "Oh come off it, Irina," he said. "There's no reason why I shouldn't come and *see* you at Lyova's."

What was all this about, he wondered increasingly uneasily over the intervening fortnight. He concluded it was about one thing and one thing only: Irina's body in a variety of positions and a variety of lights. He had had no intention of setting foot in Lyova's flat. The whole plan sounded preposterous to him. But somehow, somewhere, between their *tarte tatin* and the next morning's croissant, he found he had agreed to do more than look in on Irina there. It was perfectly insane, but it seemed he had agreed to spend the night.

It was about the ghosts of breasts billowing in the dark; twin white ghosts which, when you touched them, turned out to be joyously warm and full and fleshy, equipped with little red lights at their tips which appeared to glow at you welcomingly. It was about sharing a too-small bed with a female mountain range, a chain of peaks and valleys which sprawled magnificently in relaxation and when aroused, spewed forth hot lava and elemental sighs. He derived nearly as much pleasure, although of a naturally more subdued kind, from covertly observing Irina naked as from getting down to business with her. He found the astonishing contrast between her calm, almost prim Old Master's shape and what it so readily gave way to incredibly stimulating. Possessing Irina was like being admitted to a connoisseurs' club, where everything, from the furniture to the refreshments, was embossed with a seal of venerable appreciation. He discovered too that sexual excitement could be triggered by inanimate objects which he would never have dreamt were capable of provoking such an effect. He felt a distinct anticipatory pleasure at the mere hissing of the lift ropes, and riding up in the cabin, even on his own, without Irina, he found the oblong box so charged with erotic associations that it reminded him of Woody Allen's Orgasmatron in *Sleeper*. The Iskarovs' flat was full of things which were in themselves utterly unexciting, even off-putting, but which, as accompaniments to what now took place there, had become positively indecent. Throughout the flat, there were a quantity of scattered leather pouffes, plump, over-filled, yet promptly yielding when someone sat on them. They let out little anguished sighs as they took your weight and they retained the imprint of your backside for hours and hours. Edward could not remember at what point he had had to stop sitting on the pouffes because of the embarrassing effect the yielding leather under his buttocks immediately had on him. In Irina's bedroom, there was a dressing-table with three long mirrors which, even though he found it a hideous piece of furniture, still had the most potent effect on him. It was painted a pale saccharine pink, as if it had been hewn from a block of strawberry icecream, and it was always packed with the countless bottles and jars of Irina's beauty regimen. Even though Edward loathed the jostling bottles, the cotton wool and the Kleenex, they grotesquely triggered an unmistakable response in him. Coupled with their faint, rotting-flower smell, they were horrid objects. But, linked to the reflection of Irina triplicated in the mirrors, they still had an almighty effect on him, even when Irina wasn't there.

The fixtures and fittings of his own flat seemed tame by contrast, and what took place there was, in fact, often less highly charged. But, even in the rue Surcouf, on the rare afternoons when they managed to get away from the demands of one or another of Irina's relatives, there were accompaniments which endowed the proceedings with a richness quite new to Edward. It was daylight for a start, a winter daylight which gave no indication of what time of day it was and filled the bedroom with an opaque, ghostly light. In that light, Irina's body would sometimes catch a more concentrated ray of light, emerging somewhere from between two clouds, and an unexpected part of her would be briefly highlighted in the gloom. The ease with which she moved, even quite naked, through the inter-connecting rooms convinced Edward more and more that she had known them in that state before, and this intuition, the mystery, and the apparent uncle who was there along with them, all gave their afternoons a grainy, marvellously sophisticated complexity.

None of it, Edward acknowledged, was probably reason enough to go and stay at Lyova's.

"Teach me how to say something in Russian," he asked Irina.

They were sitting in Lyova's unbelievably squalid living-room after a late supper. Edward had refused to come over until the two little girls were safely tucked up in bed and it wasn't until nearly ten o'clock that the telephone had rung in the rue Surcouf and Irina, sounding flustered but exceptionally happy and triumphant, had informed him that the coast was clear.

Lyova lived in a distinctly seedy stretch of the twelfth *arrondissement*, quite close to the Gare de Lyon. As he walked down the long and increasingly unsavoury rue de Charenton, Edward reflected that Irina really was slumming it. The building in which Lyova lived could have been some sort of industrial premises, from its appearance. The low front door was set in a filthy small façade, hung with the nameplates of what seemed to be resident business operations. There was nothing to indicate that anyone actually lived there at all. Edward hesitated for a moment in front of the building, wondering if he had picked the wrong place. Then he noticed an unobtrusive, rather mucky-looking bell in a recess beside the front door and rang it on the off-chance. The door clicked open in response and he looked inside, into a long, barely lit yard, at the other end of which was, as Irina had told him, a small staircase going up into a three-storey, yellow-ochre building. He crossed the yard cautiously, still not absolutely convinced that this shabby forecourt, full of dismantled bits of unidentifiable machinery, really could be where Lyova, romantic Russian dissident and avant-garde artist, lived with his wife and children. He was prepared for a savage Alsatian, hopefully chained, to dash out at him at any moment or a burly figure, flashing a torch, to challenge his intrusion. Nothing of the sort happened, no one appeared, and when he got to the bottom of the staircase, he heard music coming from the lit windows on the second floor of the yellow-ochre building.

He was preparing to greet Irina, 'What kind of a dump is this?' But she looked so extraordinarily transformed by happiness when she opened the door to him that he momentarily lost track.

"So you found it OK?" she beamed. "No problems getting here?"

"No," Edward answered. "No," but then, recollecting himself, "What kind of a dump is this?"

"A cheap dump," Irina said crisply, pulling him inside.

Her answer put him to shame, of course, reminding him with a pinprick that Lyova, engaged in his worthy struggle, was desperately hard up. Edward reminded himself that it was perfectly possible to live somewhere poor but not ridiculous, and to show Irina that he was not humbled by her reproach, he persisted, "No, but what *is* it? A factory? An abattoir for *Deux-Chevaux*?"

Irina giggled. "Ach, Edouard, don't be so silly. It belongs to a Russian who imports refrigerators from Eastern Europe, and he rents out the two upstairs floors to people in trouble. Lyova has this floor and downstairs there are some very charming Cuban refugees. Really, no one is supposed to be living here at all, because they aren't residential premises, so the rent's very low. D'you want to have a peep at the girls sleeping?"

Edward shook his head vigorously. "I waited on purpose until they were asleep. The last thing I want is to risk waking them up."

Irina looked crestfallen. "But, Edouard, they're so *sweet*. They've got stripey black and white pyjamas like zebras, and Katya goes to bed with a rabbit and Solange with a woollen snake."

"I'll take your word for it," Edward said rudely. "I want something to drink."

He assumed Irina's radiance was anticipation of the liberated fun and games ahead and he wanted to get into the right frame of mind to enjoy them. He could see no reason why she should want to dwell on the drawbacks. But, to his annoyance, she concluded, "Well, never mind, you'll meet them in the morning anyway. I've told them not to come into the bedroom without knocking. But actually, you know Lyova's set-up; the bedroom door has a very crucial lock and key."

It was all really thoroughly off-putting, Edward found, and he couldn't help wondering, as he followed Irina through into the small and quite phenomenally messy kitchen, what the upshot would be or whether, in these increasingly unpromising surroundings, there would actually be any upshot at all.

Irina had prepared a rather hasty meal. The girls, she explained (Edward felt not sufficiently apologetically, considering she had lured him here on the pretext of an idyll), the girls had kept her busy all day; she hadn't had a moment to prepare for tonight. She had only finally got them into bed ten minutes or so before Edward arrived. When she had rung to say they were in bed, in fact she had only extracted a promise from them that they would be in bed by the time Edward arrived. It had been touch and go; they were terribly curious to meet Irina's "friend".

At least there was no shortage of vodka. Edward used it to subdue his growing feelings of discomfort and dismay. He had expected to feel distinctly odd visiting Lyova's flat. Of course, the oddity of the flat itself didn't help; that sinister entrance and these little, close, low-ceilinged rooms, all absolutely packed with Lyova's assortment of weird belongings. But what actually struck him as oddest in the set-up was the way Irina was behaving. Dressed, he could not help noticing, with far less than her usual smartness, her hair all dishevelled, she was still glowing with a completely uncharacteristic and apparently inexplicable elation. Moving about the little kitchen, setting out the bits and pieces of their slapdash dinner, she behaved as if she were taking part in some uniquely special celebration, and when they were ready to eat, she raised her glass over the assortment of greaseproof-paper-wrapped offerings and jubilantly toasted their "dolls' house".

Edward really could not see what in the circumstances should have put her in such an outrageously good mood. They were hardly going to be able to let fly with two sleeping infants in the room next door. There was precious little he could see in this sordid setting to make anyone feel romantic. It annoyed him that Irina should feel so evidently at home here when he felt totally excluded. Everything, from the Russian magazines left food-smeared around the kitchen to the subjects of the canvases Irina had shown him in Lyova's small studio, was closed to him. Even some of the food on the supper table had to be explained. He hated being at such a disadvantage, in precisely the role Lyova had patronisingly cast him when they first met; the naïve young Englishman with whom Irina had amusingly taken up. Across the table, he resented Irina's exuberance and when, for the second time, she got up to check that the sleeping girls were quite all right, he snapped at her, "Oh, for God's sake, Irina, can't we even eat in peace?"

After the meal, they moved to the equally jam-packed living-room, having added their plates and glasses to the stack of washing-up waiting in the sink. Irina put on one of

183

Lyova's smuggled cassettes of Russian underground ballads, the singer Vladimir Vysotsky. Something in the way she sprawled contentedly on Lyova's kilim-covered sofa to listen to the music, one hand extended, almost incidentally, to caress Edward's knee, made his exclusion suddenly intolerable. Was he to sit here while she got into the bedroom mood, listening to songs he couldn't even understand? He knew, of course, he had no place here and he had been pretty certain he couldn't care less. But it was unmistakably in a bid to gain a toehold in the boisterous Slav universe Irina and Lyova and Volodya and all her relatives shared that he turned to her and asked, "Teach me how to say something in Russian."

She considered his request. "What? What d'you want to say?"

He shook his head. "Anything. I don't mind. You decide. Just teach me how to say something."

Irina thought for a quite unnecessarily long time. "What sort of thing? Something affectionate? Something funny?"

"I told you, I don't mind," Edward repeated impatiently. "I'd just like to be able to say something, even 'fuck off'."

"Oich!" Irina exclaimed. She recoiled a little along the settee. "I'm certainly not going to teach you anything like that, Edouard."

He resisted replying, 'Why not? It may come in useful one day.'

"OK," he said. "Well, teach me something else then. Come on."

Irina contemplated a rosy middle distance. At last, she pronounced slowly and clearly:

> "*Ya pomniu chudnoye mgnovenye:*
> *Peredo mnoi yavilas ti*."

"For heaven's sake," Edward objected. "Does it have to be so long? Couldn't you just teach me something short and simple like 'hello', 'goodbye', 'thank you'? What does it mean?"

"First say it, then I'll tell you," Irina answered archly.

"Are you pulling my leg?" Edward asked. "Does it mean something really rude?"

"Certainly not," Irina humphed. "It's the beginning of a poem by Pushkin. Go on, say it."

"You'll have to say it again, more slowly," Edward told her, "if you want me to start spouting poetry straight away."

Laboriously, word by word, she taught Edward to repeat what she had said. He had always thought Russian sounded caressingly smooth spoken by Irina, but the words he pronounced with difficulty sounded throttled, quite unlovely.

Irina heaved with suppressed laughter at his efforts. "*Chudnoye*," she ticked him off, "not *choodnoyeh*, really!"

It was his first acquaintance with Irina, the Russian teacher, and he couldn't honestly say he took to her.

At last, on the fifth or sixth repetition, he managed to get his mouth round the lines.

"What does it mean?"

Irina looked unbearably smug. "It means: 'I remember the wonderful moment when you (female) appeared before me'."

"Oh, for God's sake," Edward protested. "Talk about fishing for compliments! Can't you teach me to say something sensible?"

Again, Irina thought quite unnecessarily long and hard.

"OK, this is shorter," she decided. She declaimed, "*A schastye bilo tak vozmojno, tak blizko.*"

"What's this from?" Edward jeered. "*War and Peace*?"

Irina threw him a crushing look. "*War and Peace*! It's another very famous quotation from Pushkin, from *Evgeny Onegin*. It is a more appropriate comment."

"A more appropriate comment on what?" Edward asked suspiciously. "And I'm not going to the trouble of saying it until you tell me what it means."

Irina's good mood seemed to be spoiling slightly too. She answered drily, "It means: 'happiness was so possible, so close.'"

"Oh great," Edward retorted. "Depressives of the world unite! Can't you just tell me something short and snappy – and useful? Cut the heavy hints."

Irina must have been spoiling for a fight. Or perhaps she had gone so far on her Pushkin kick that it was impossible to disengage. Without pausing, she began to recite line after

185

line of similar-sounding poetry, directing it almost vindictively at Edward. When she finished, she said, "An excerpt from Tatyana's letter to Evgeny Onegin, for your benefit. I shall just translate the first line: 'Why did you come to visit us?'"

Edward stood up. "OK, I've had enough of this game," he said. "I'm going to bed."

Where, in the end, it wasn't up to much. In the morning, the bedroom door handle rattled urgently and a piping voice called in French, "Reena, Reena, let us in!"

Edward woke, confused, in time to see Irina bounding out of bed, again with that beatific smile on her face, and this time he knew for certain it could not have been caused by the delights of the night before.

Irina slipped out of the room without looking back at him and, for the next half-hour, the flat resounded with peals of girlish giggles, shrieks, and the urgent scampering of excited feet.

Edward had half-hoped to get back to sleep for a bit; it was only seven. But that was out of the question. Failing that, he wondered if Irina might come back to bed again. By eight o'clock, it was clear she wouldn't, and he had to admit he was hardly surprised. At the same time, he couldn't help feeling a little resentful because it was she who had got them, quite against his wishes, into these uncongenial circumstances. He put on the pyjamas, which Irina had insisted he bring with him for the sake of the little girls, and ventured out apprehensively in the direction of the bathroom. Almost at once, there was a scuttling noise behind him and two tiny, shrill, sharp-faced girls leapt at him, shouting competitively, "*Bonjour! Bonjour!*" It was the worst way of starting the day he could possibly imagine.

The little girls scampered around him, keeping up a squeaky running commentary on his name, his age, his unshaven face and, most amusement-inducing of all, his flapping pyjamas. He waved his hands rather helplessly around them. "*Allez, allez*, I need to get washed and dressed." But they barred his way to the bathroom, giggling, and insisting he answer their questions.

Irina appeared in the kitchen doorway and he turned to her, hoping she would call them off. But, instead, she merely beamed at them, and then at him, and said, "Aren't they adorable?"

"Not," Edward answered in English, "at bloody eight o'clock in the morning. I've got to go to work, you know. Can't you keep them out of my way, at least until I'm washed and dressed?"

Irina flinched at his bad temper. Still in her shapeless and horribly mumsy dressing-gown, which he had never seen before, she bustled forward and scooping up a little girl by each hand, she hurried them away in the direction of the kitchen as if out of reach of some savage wild beast.

"Come along," she clucked. "Edouard will come and have breakfast with us when he is ready."

That was the culmination of his ghastly visit. Breakfast was never his forte. All he needed was to restore his caffeine level and, here in Paris, he had rather taken to the affectation of a croissant. But a meal at that hour was more than he could cope with.

Katya and Solange ate, in varying degrees of sloppiness, cereal, yellow *biscottes* and eggs. The decibel level in the kitchen was perilously high for someone who had consumed the amount of vodka he had the previous evening and, feeling distinctly delicate, he had to watch the horrible hit-and-miss encounters between Katya and Solange's mouths and clumsy spoonfuls of cereal and egg yolk.

The fact they continued to squeak at him non-stop made matters considerably worse, of course. He supposed he could see that they were very energetic, vivacious children, but what seemed to him their shrill, spiteful dedication in interrogating him, plus the fact of course that they were Lyova's children, made them appear precociously shrewish. Katya, the elder one, looked out at him quizzically from under miniature replicas of Lyova's eyebrows and asked him needling questions about his friendship with "Reena". Solange, who was too young to look quizzical, just stared intently from the safety of Irina's lap, as though he really were some savage wild beast. He answered in monosyllables and, once, when Katya thrust her dribbling egg shell at him, demanding to know whether he thought there were any chickens inside, he turned on Irina and protested, "Why don't you get them to pipe down?"

Irina sat, still radiant, amid the chaos. Inevitably, Edward's bad temper focused on her. She seemed to be in her element in this revolting domestic quicksand. For the first time, he thought that she looked utterly unappetising. Her dreadful dressing-gown was now splashed with traces of infants' breakfasts. In the Cité Etienne Hubert, she wore a green and black kimono. Her hair needed washing and, unmade-up, he thought cruelly, her face showed her age. But it wasn't the deterioration in her looks which made him stand up, as soon as he had drunk his first cup of black coffee, and announce, "I'm off": it was her obvious, transparent pleasure in her come-down which he could not forgive her. Sleek, vampish, seductive in the late afternoons of the rue Surcouf, or breathing elemental sighs at night in the Cité Etienne Hubert, Irina had never looked as unequivocally happy as she did now. It confirmed all Edward's prejudices against children that two such small ones could wreak that much havoc on Irina in twenty-four hours.

She did not get up to accompany him to the front door. Solange was still sitting on her lap. It irritated Edward unreasonably that, when she was looking the worst he had ever seen her, she should seem to care least about his leaving. Normally, her anxiety would surface at every one of his departures. Today she merely, nauseatingly, made Solange wave goodbye. So it was much easier than it might have been for him to say casually, "I shan't be coming over tonight."

She did look disturbed at that, despite her beatitude. "Why not?"

He gestured at the kitchen. "It's hardly conducive – Anyway, I've got something on."

"What?" Irina asked. "You didn't tell me,"

He shrugged. "Didn't I?"

"What about tomorrow?" Irina demanded. "It's the last night."

Edward pretended to check his watch. "I'll call you," he said. "Look, I've got to go. I'm late."

"Oh, do come," she called after him. "Do, please, Edouard."

And Katya and Solange took up a mocking chorus. "Do, please, Edouard. Please, Edouard, please."

He came for dinner, to keep the peace. He was adamant

that nothing and no one would lure him into staying the night. Although, as things turned out, he had no need of this resolve because a ready-made excuse arrived soon after midnight in the shape of Lyova returning unannounced a day early.

Edward had been strongly tempted not to go back to Lyova's flat at all. What persuaded him was Irina's probable retaliation if he didn't. For, however much below par she had looked in that dressing-gown, with kids crawling all over her, he could still conceive of her looking desirable in another context.

She seemed to have made a slight effort, although she did look very much the worse for wear. He had waited again until he got the all-clear that Katya and Solange were in bed and then he waited a little extra, just to be sure. It was after half past ten when he came in through the dark yard and climbed the staircase up into the yellow-ochre building. Irina opened the door immediately he rang, as though she had been waiting right behind it. She had dark circles under her eyes and her welcoming smile looked an effort.

After their rather perfunctory kiss, he teased her, "Glad it's nearly over?"

She looked at him defiantly. "You know, I've really enjoyed staying here?"

"I know you have," Edward answered. "Quite beyond me. In fact," he lied, "that was part of the reason I didn't spend much time here; I felt I was superfluous."

"Oh no!" Irina exclaimed, falling so promptly for his ploy, he felt almost ashamed. She must be very tired. "Not superfluous, Edouard." She cuddled his shoulder but then, with quite unexpected vitriol, she got her own back. She pulled a stiff, pained face, imitating Edward fending off children. "Just awfully English."

They observed a delicate truce over dinner, which consisted again of a hurried trip to a *charcuterie*. Afterwards, they sat together on the sofa and Edward wondered how far he could let things go before Irina would assume he was going to spend the night there. At one point, it crossed his mind that even if they went the whole way, there was no reason why he should necessarily spend the night. It was at approximately that point that a thin wailing started in the girls' bedroom. Irina left what

189

she was doing with insulting alacrity and hurried towards the wailing, calling soothing messages. Edward lay back on the sofa and wondered whether sex with Irina would ever be free of some form of familial disturbance. Wherever they were, it seemed, there would always be someone in the background whom she couldn't quite shake off. The grandmother's slippers would keep on shuffling, Volodya, the avuncular question mark, would continue to hang over them and, even in the neutral flat of a friend, she would acquire children who would wail at the crucial moment. There would always be someone who prevented them from finally letting go.

This thought had sufficiently deterred him from continuing that he was no longer so enthusiastic when Irina came back.

"A nightmare," she explained briefly, before proceeding to resume.

Edward's apathy only dawned on her slowly and she took even longer to give up. They were sitting, more than lying, in a position of arrested stalemate when they heard the front door open.

Both of them sat upright. Edward, even more than Irina, readjusted his clothes. They heard a low whistle and Lyova appeared in the living-room doorway.

"What's happened?" Irina greeted him. "Why've you come back early?"

Lyova looked at them wryly. "I'm sorry to intrude. But Monsieur Lvov and I concluded our business agreement today over a splendid lunch and I caught the early evening train back." He gave a brilliant smile. "My career as an artist of renown has begun. Let me find the vodka."

While he was in the kitchen, Edward said, "I'll be off," but Irina exclaimed, "No, no, you must stay and drink to Lyova's good fortune."

When Edward hesitated, she grabbed his wrist and repeated, "You *must*."

Lyova brought in what Edward and Irina had left in the bottle and three glasses, held in a cluster on his fingers. He deposited them all carefully on the low table and, as he poured, he asked, "How have my little devils behaved?"

The fact he took Edward's presence so absolutely for granted paradoxically made Edward feel especially uncomfortable. He

190

didn't like his unexpected liaison with Irina to be so publicly acknowledged. He wondered who else, for all her stress on secrecy, Irina might have put in the picture. And he didn't like the image of himself he saw reflected in Lyova's wry smile. Irina's amusing aberration was not a role he relished.

At the beginning of March, Henry and Mai went away for a week's skiing and Edward was left temporarily in charge of the paper's Paris bureau. It was the most exciting moment to date in his work experience; hoping desperately for some story of epic proportions to break, he stayed in the office until all hours, much to the amusement of Marie-Yvette and Aurore who irritatingly made it clear in subtle ways that they believed they were keeping the office running. This didn't stop them scooting off early every day as five o'clock approached. Edward stayed alone late in the empty office, willing the phones to ring or the telex to burst into chatter, bringing the news that would jump-start his career. He didn't ring Irina once all week.

When the weekend arrived, and he realised the key week had gone by without so much as the suggestion of a story, he felt severely disappointed. It was in search of consolation that he decided on Saturday afternoon to go and pay a surprise visit on Irina. On the way, he began to feel guilt and remorse for his week-long neglect and he wondered whether he wasn't going to walk straight into a mammoth Iskarovian sulk. A florist's shop at the bottom of the Boulevard de Latour-Maubourg suggested a remedy and, feeling distinctly self-conscious because he had never made a habit of buying women flowers, he went in to get a bouquet for Irina.

The choice of flowers was so manipulated by the crafty old assistant that he ended up with a much bigger, more flamboyant bunch than he had intended. He felt completely idiotic, toting it down the Avenue Duquesne, and he wondered what he would say if by some freak he walked into someone he knew. The assistant had asked a number of delving questions about *"Madame"* and then scientifically selected the flowers accordingly, and he couldn't help thinking, as he shifted the sheaf from one arm to the other, that she really hadn't done too badly. There was an encircling ruff of greenery and ferns and in the middle a whole assortment of various flowers which he couldn't identify since, apart from the roses, he had no idea of the names of flowers, but pink predominated. As he turned into the Cité Etienne Hubert, he felt pretty confident that this bouquet would be a match for any sulk.

It only occurred to him in the hall downstairs that of course Irina might be out. The idea of trying to explain himself and his bouquet to her grandmother was so awful that he hung around for a minute or two, wondering how on earth he would deal with it. Abstractedly, he looked about at the lozenge-patterned tiled floor and the double glass doors of the *concierge's loge*. Would she know by any chance whether Irina was in or out? He considered the impenetrable net curtains and the angry handwritten notice Sellotaped to the doors, one in a long-running series. What made the inhabitants of Paris so professionally peevish? Rejecting any idea of turning to the *concierge* to help him out, he headed for the lift. With any luck, if the grandmother were alone at home, she wouldn't answer the door.

It was answered by Irina. For a moment she simply stared at Edward with no discernible expression. He was preparing to thrust the bouquet at her, jauntily saying something like, "Hello, stranger" or "Long time no see" when her eyes distressingly gelled with tears and she exclaimed, "I thought you were never coming back."

Edward jabbed the flowers at her jovially. "Whatever gave you that idea?"

Irina pulled him into the flat and fell on him desperately. He had to hold the flowers out to one side while they embraced. It would be an awful waste to squash fifty francs.

"You don't need to tell me," she said, with quavering self-control, "where you've been or what you've been doing. I just want you to know I'm very happy that you've come back."

"Irina!" Edward protested. "What are you on about? I didn't get in touch for a few days because I've had a very busy week at work. I hardly think that calls for this kind of tearful reunion scene."

Irina gave him an appraising look, her tears gone. "Ah," she said. "Work."

He realised with amazement that she did not believe what he said and, as she conveyed her wounded suspicion by lifting her chin and adopting an expression of obviously faked unconcern, he asked himself helplessly in what extraordinary scenario she was living.

She hung his coat in the hall cupboard, along with the furs.

"Would you like some tea?" she asked him, obviously still maintaining a major effort to keep calm.

"Sure," he said.

He patted her placatingly on the bottom as he followed her into the kitchen.

"I think you should put the flowers in water first, though," he said.

He almost wished he hadn't come. Ever since that distasteful episode at Lyova's, he had taken advantage of the additional distance he felt from Irina to remind her at every opportunity of how temporary all this was; how, come the summer, he would almost certainly be on his way. It seemed to be producing the opposite effect to the one he intended; Irina clung onto him more and more every week. Even though it was already plain that once she had made her point, this afternoon was going to turn out the way he had hoped, this further evidence of Irina's dependence on him depressed him terribly. He wondered, as he watched her piling a dish with sufficient little sticky cakes for a junior school, whether he wouldn't be wiser to begin to disengage now.

She carried her overloaded tray into the living-room and served him with exaggerated care. She sat down in an armchair close enough to his to touch tips of shoes, should it be appropriate, and she said, "So what kept you so busy at the paper?"

He told her about the Hirshfelds' skiing holiday (well, that she could check up on easily enough at the *lycée*), and his consequent new responsibilities. He didn't tell her, since it seemed to undermine the whole story, that in the end nothing had come of them; that he had sat for five days beside a silent telephone and that when Henry reappeared on Monday, he would have nothing in the least impressive to report to him.

Irina listened politely. "And this weekend?" she asked, with patently feigned nonchalance. "Are you busy this weekend too?"

"Well, it looks as though I'm here, doesn't it?" Edward teased her.

Irina's eyes narrowed just slightly. "I meant the rest of this weekend," she said impatiently. "What are you doing the rest of this weekend?"

Since he clearly had the upper hand here, Edward thought it fairly safe to suggest, "Well, I thought maybe we could go out and do something together tonight?"

"I can't," Irina snapped.

Her ferocity took him aback.

"Why not?" he asked.

Instead of the haughty explanation he expected, about some other more suave escort, she answered mournfully, "Varvara Stepanovna and Nikolai Grigoriev are coming to dinner, curse them."

He managed to play down his disappointment pretty well, he felt. He supposed it had been a bit arrogant to roll up at the front door at five o'clock and just assume Irina would be waiting for him. But it was irritating that she should be busy on a Saturday night with such a mundane chore.

"On a Saturday night?" he objected. "Why've they got to come to dinner on a Saturday night?"

Irina looked resentful. "They always come on a Saturday night," she said. "It's a tradition. It goes back to before Mama died."

"But Irina," Edward protested. "What d'you mean? We've been out together almost every Saturday night for the last two months."

195

"That's the whole point," Irina answered bitterly. "They've been grumbling, saying I've been neglecting them because of the high life I'm leading. And so, this week, when I thought you weren't coming any more, I rang them and I said to come over tonight. Such lovely fun."

"You mean normally they come over here every Saturday?" Edward asked aghast. "But what excuse have you been giving them for all these Saturdays in a row when you're suddenly no longer available?"

Irina's smile forewarned him. "Not every Saturday," she said. "Just maybe once or twice a month. But, you understand, every Saturday it's a possibility, especially if they didn't come the Saturday before or the one before that. One or other of them will ring me without fail on Thursday or Friday, not to invite themselves straight out, of course, just to sound me out. Great-Aunt Elena comes too, if she's free, but she's not such a no-hoper as those other two and she has things of her own to go to quite often. She's not coming tonight. But she's been ringing me much more ruthlessly than Varvara or Nikolai, on their behalf, telling me how sad and lonely they are and how I really should make the effort, whatever's occupying me."

"But what have you been telling them?" Edward insisted.

Irina drew a coy little circle with the tip of her shoe. "I told them different things on different occasions," she said evasively. "The first couple of times, I was very vague; I just said I was busy, I had something on, without going into any details. They didn't fish for any because of course they promptly imagined I'd met some ideal, respectable man who might do them all the huge favour of marrying me. Only, naturally as time went by, their imaginations started to run short of material and they started to ask me all sorts of questions about this implausible person. Well, you can imagine how difficult it was, having to bear the burden of their expectations when I knew full well there was nothing of the sort to look forward to. So sometimes I said I had an invitation to dinner from some teacher or other at the *lycée*, sometimes I said I was being taken out by a man I'd met recently, and sometimes I did say I was seeing you."

"You what?" Edward exclaimed. "I thought all this was supposed to be top secret."

196

Irina laughed. "Oh, don't worry. I didn't say anything which could give the game away, to use your favourite phrase. I made it sound as if, you know; our new young tenant, all by himself in Paris, it's rather a bore, but I feel I ought to extend the hand of friendship."

"And you think they believed you?" Edward asked.

Irina bridled. "Of course they believed me. Why shouldn't they believe me?"

Edward hesitated. He had come upon one of those fault lines between fact and fantasy which riddled the Iskarov universe. Tread upon it at your peril.

'They shouldn't believe you,' he wanted to tell her, 'because it's the most see-through story I've ever heard. Why do you always imagine things which are glaringly obvious aren't visible to the naked eye, simply because you don't want to acknowledge them?'

Instead he answered rather lamely, "It doesn't sound all that convincing to me."

"Oh no?" Irina challenged him. "You mean they think I'm having a love affair with our tenant, a boy ten years younger than me, and that I'm parading him in front of them; bringing him to Sunday lunches and to concerts right under their noses?"

Edward laughed at her unkindly. "But Irina," he said, "you *are*."

Her glare stripped his smile like a blowtorch.

"If you think it's so visible," she retorted furiously, "if you think it's so obvious that I would do a thing like that, then please stay to dinner tonight and see for yourself how very wrong you are. You can say whatever you like, behave as indiscreetly as you wish and, I can assure you, nobody will harbour the least suspicion."

"No thanks," said Edward.

Irina changed tack unexpectedly. "Well, what are you going to do if you don't stay to dinner? You said yourself you've got nothing else planned; you were expecting to spend the evening with me."

"Oh, don't worry," Edward said. "I'll find something."

He imagined what that something would in all likelihood be; the cinema and more vinegary Nicolas plonk.

Irina glanced at her watch and stood up in a bustle of indignation. "You'll have to excuse me anyway," she said. "It's nearly six o'clock and I have to make dinner."

Edward followed her into the kitchen. Even if he didn't stay for dinner, he didn't want to go off, leaving her in a huff. He watched her at work for a while, trying to keep up a conversation on innocuous topics. It looked as if she were creating one of her *chefs-d'oeuvre*: three intricate courses of pastries and sauces and creams. He had to admit that his eventual capitulation to stay for dinner was due primarily to what he saw taking shape on the kitchen table.

Nikolai Grigoriev posed the only possible problem. Varvara Stepanovna, got up in a dinner-dress of black and white lozenges which reminded Edward in its immense expanse of the entrance hall floor, was familiar with Edward's supposed place in the scheme of things. She was in any case patently naïve. But Nikolai Grigoriev, a rather frail but dapper old dandy in his early seventies, whom Irina had described as her mother's "last attachment", seemed to Edward pretty speedily to smell a rat.

He perched on the rim of one of the deep armchairs as if he were scared he would otherwise never be able to rise out of it again. He measured Edward with piercing pale blue eyes and cross-questioned him about his activities with an arthritic wit.

"So Paris is just a staging post for you, then?" he quipped. "*En route* to the *tristes tropiques*?"

He did his best to subdue his quivering suspicions; his stiff neck kept swivelling alertly from Edward to Irina and back, but it was obvious he was hoping anxiously not to catch any collusion between them, not to spy any grounds for his suspicions.

When they moved to table, despite his frailty, he offered Babushka his arm to lead her into the dining-room and, despite her vagueness, Babushka rose alertly to her feet to be led. They formed a delicately anachronistic pair. Following behind them, Edward was bemused yet again by the bizarre universe he had got himself into and, for the time it took to shuffle behind them to the table, he found himself yearning to be out of it.

198

Varvara Stepanovna said, "Remember, this was Volodya's favourite dish," when Irina brought in the main course.

Irina gave her a withering look. "Of course I remember. Why do you think I made it today? Do *you* remember it's his birthday?"

Varvara and Nikolai exclaimed.

"Isn't that awful?" Varvara lamented. "I'd forgotten all about it."

She eyed the dish remorsefully. "Punish me with a specially small portion, Irina."

Irina shrugged rudely. "Why? You'll only use it as an excuse for an even bigger second helping."

She smacked portions of the dish, a lavish blend of pork and beetroot and rye breadcrumbs which, she instructed Edward, was called *Vereshchaka*, onto people's plates. Ignoring the others, she told him, "If Volodya were alive today, he would be sixty-seven years old."

"A stripling!" Nikolai Grigoriev interjected.

Irina served herself last and sat down, pulling her chair in under her resolutely. She added maliciously to Edward, "Yes, and you'd be homeless."

Her tartness to him must have helped dispel any doubts there were about their relationship. But it hardly made a sticky situation any easier. From her silent spot, Babushka's eyes continued to patrol the dinner-table. With splintery laughter at his own jokes, Nikolai Grigoriev continued to probe Edward's intentions. And poor old Varvara Stepanovna, singing for her supper, kept up her well-meaning but monotonous conversation.

Edward had considered the most favourable outcome; he would stay after everyone else, earning plus points by publicly offering to help with the washing-up, he would wish Babushka goodnight, close the front door audibly, and go and lie in wait in Irina's bedroom. The trouble was, as the evening advanced, that outcome seemed steadily less attractive. What he most wanted to do, he discovered, when this wretched farce was over, was get the hell out of here.

"Volodya loved sausages, didn't he?" Varvara Stepanovna reminisced. "I'll always remember Borya and Elena taking Volodya and Ada and me to a German *Bierkeller* once, after a show, one of Volodya's shows. And Volodya was so enraptured by their sausages, he ate a dozen in a row. Ada gave him such a telling-off!"

"He didn't especially like sausages," Irina contradicted her. "You've got it muddled."

"I'm sorry, Irina," Varvara disagreed. "But I think I'm right. I still remember Ada's words: 'Volodya, you are digging your grave with your teeth.'"

"That cow!" Irina snorted. "I don't want to hear what that cow said." She delivered her trump card. "If he liked sausages so much, how come he never served them himself? You know he could make anything he liked."

'He's dead, for God's sake!' Edward wanted to interrupt. 'Who gives a stuff whether or not the man liked sausages?'

Around him, the debate raged.

"Sausages are a terrible bother to make yourself," Varvara protested. "Nobody makes their own sausages in Paris."

"Excuse me," Nikolai corrected her. "Princess Berberova made her own sausages. They were not, I have to admit, pinnacles of the gastronomic art, but they were home-made."

"He didn't like sausages," Irina insisted petulantly, like a child. "He didn't, I'm telling you."

She stood up and started to gather the plates. "I wanted to remember Volodya's birthday in harmony," she said truculently. "Not squabbling over sausages."

She was gone so long fetching the dessert that Edward excused himself and went out to the kitchen after her. He found her with her head on her arms amid the debris of the kitchen table, crying furiously.

"I hate it," she burst out. "I hate it, and I hate you seeing it. I should never have asked you to stay to dinner. I should never have let you meet any of them. I know you'll go off me now because I'm part of that."

Hard as it was for him to contradict her, Edward did his best. He patted her gingerly on the arm.

But Irina dismissed him contemptuously. "There's no need to pretend, Edouard," she told him. "I'm not a little girl."

After dinner, as they sat in the living-room, Edward due to the number of people forced to sit on a pouffe, he writhed over the outcome. He had got himself into a situation where both staying and leaving would lead to even worse problems next time round.

Varvara Stepanovna had latched onto him; he hadn't heard her sad stories all before. As he struggled to see a way out of the cul-de-sac, he realised to his dismay that Varvara seemed to be telling him the story of her life.

"I don't know how old you think I am, Edouard," she simpered, her cheeks flushed with the contents of her midget glass of liqueur. "An ancient old maid, I shouldn't wonder, ha ha. But don't forget that I was a gay young thing once too, you know. My youth was just rather different from some other people's. Perhaps I didn't have the same degree of frivolity some other people had, that's all. You understand, I lived with my parents until they died. I was an only child and perhaps some people might say they cherished and protected me too much. I was born to them rather late in their lives; my mother was forty-three. So by the time I reached an age to go out and gallivant, ha ha, they were old people already. And, in any case, the way they'd brought me up, I didn't really have the personality to go out and gallivant. You see, they were always very cautious. They warned me a great deal about all life's dangers. They worried dreadfully. If I were late home, they'd think straight away that I'd been kidnapped or assaulted. The local *commissariat de police* actually forbade them to come in any more and report me missing. They worried especially about men; the ways they lured you, all the myriad tricks and traps. Really, I think I grew up perceiving men as a grave risk, ha ha; an untrustworthy species which might at any moment turn and devour you. You can imagine, it didn't make for a great career as a flirt, ha ha. I was always on the look-out for those snapping jaws. My parents taught me there was one sure sign to watch for, though; the configuration of a man's mouth. His eyes might be kind and gentle and adoring, but you could tell his true character by his cold, chiselled lips. Only I don't know if you've ever tried judging the world's character by mouths alone. The world is full of greedy mouths, cruel mouths, wicked mouths, mean mouths, but I never yet saw a mouth which was pure and saintly and good. Every man I met, my eyes would go straight to his mouth and I would see squishy, sensual lips or a narrow, selfish strip, which would

201

distract me from his kindly brown eyes or his jovial red cheeks. I never found the perfect mouth. Though let me say that when I met you, Edouard, your mouth raised my hopes. Not for me, naturally, there's no need to look so terrified, ha ha, but I felt sure you have the perfect mouth for someone."

She plunged precipitously at an adjacent table, which held one of Irina's black and red lacquer trays of sticky cakes, and almost convulsively, she began bolting them very fast, one after another, into her mouth, cramming, plugging, punishing that vile offending orifice.

Any remaining desire to stay demolished, Edward decided to make a virtue of his departure. If he left before anyone else, they would all of them see him going and safely reach the wrong conclusion about him and Irina. This was also the excuse he would use in justifying his exit afterwards to Irina.

She followed him out into the hall, on the pretext of fetching his coat from the cupboard.

"Why are you leaving so soon?" she whispered. "What's the matter?"

Edward whispered back: "I want all of them to see me leave."

Irina looked relieved. She nodded understandingly. "But you'll come back, won't you?" she whispered. "When all of them have gone?"

She took his head tenderly in both her hands and, despite the open living-room door, despite the assembled listening ears, she administered a near-disabling goodbye kiss.

Once out on the Avenue Duquesne, Edward told himself that he had not said yes or no. He had not committed himself. If, after a walk and a chance to clear his head, the idea of a return trip to the Cité Etienne Hubert appealed to him, then the option was open.

He turned into the Avenue de Breteuil for a change and walked out onto the Esplanade des Invalides. In the dark, it looked especially big and bare; a vast, deserted drawing-room with its furniture of lampposts and benches, across which he made his way, a conspicuous trespasser. It brought home to him that, in all these months, he had got no closer to Paris than he had been in those early weeks when he had had nothing to do but walk. Thanks to his landlady, he had remained in a queer sort of cosmopolitan limbo; in Paris, but not of it, of Russia perhaps, but not in it, a place which, when you came down to it, existed only in the imagination of its absurd inhabitants.

As he came out onto the *quai* and his feet, instead of turning left, back towards the rue Surcouf, instinctively turned right, in the direction of districts where there would still be life and things going on, he found himself wondering how he would remember his Paris period in years to come. Would he remember it at all, or would it have been submerged beneath years of stays in more exciting places? Would he remember his cold walks and his loneliness and the week he saw five films on his own one night after another? One thing was for sure; he would not remember the living, daytime geography of the city because he realised now he had never really got to grips with it. He had been immersed all winter long in another nocturnal geography, whose landmarks and inhabitants and customs bore no relation to any *Guide Michelin*. Would he remember Paris as a city of bulky women in fur coats, chirruping together in a sibilant language?

He walked, enjoying the freshness of the night air, along the opposite pavement overlooking the river. At the corner of the rue du Bac, he witnessed a shouted altercation between an irate driver and a man in a grey raincoat almost invisibly walking his wife's minute dog beside the kerb. Edward drew level with the dispute in time to savour their climactic shouts of *"Imbécile!"* and *"Ordure!"* In search of further Parisian scenes, he followed the *quais* right round to the Place Saint Michel, repeatedly giving the view ten out of ten as he walked. The rue Saint André des Arts was still brilliantly lit and wide awake. Edward enjoyed the spectacle of the strolling crowds and the half-intriguing, half-repellant window displays of the Tunisian cake shops. A man was suddenly ejected from the doorway of one of them, pursued by a minute Arab in a skullcap who screamed after him, *"Il est interdit d'insulter les races maintenant!* Understand? It's forbidden to insult a person's race nowadays! Forbidden! Forbidden!"* His elderly customer, noticeably unsteady on his feet, staggered away into the shadows, mumbling insults not yet in Edward's vocabulary. He caught the comments of a passing couple, though, a conservatively dressed, middle-aged

203

pair, picking their way distastefully down the busy street after an expensive dinner off the Boulevard Saint Germain. It was the metallic carapaced wife who turned to her pudgy husband and commented acidly, *"Des gagas comme ça, on devrait les abattre tous.* Nutcases like that one ought to be put down."

It was extremely late when Edward got back at last to the rue Surcouf, but the phone still rang twice. He didn't answer it. It only occurred to him just as he was about to fall asleep, and it put a wry smile on his face, that Irina would doubtless deduce that he was off spending the night with someone else.

He rang her late on Sunday afternoon and told her about his outsize walk, extending it by an hour or so as a safety measure. He could sense her smarting resentment. She said very little and what she said was sharp, shrewish. He had intended to invite her out to dinner that evening, to put an end to their hostilities, but naturally he didn't now. He had to show Irina that nastiness would get her nowhere.

Henry reappeared on Monday morning, tanned and good-humoured. He listened to Edward's inevitably anticlimactic account of his week's absence, and he laughed.

"You mean the New Zealanders didn't retaliate by dumping radio-active waste in the forecourt of the Elysée Palace? Chirac didn't disembowel Giscard in a television duel?"

Then he looked considerably more serious. He stirred his cup of Marie-Yvette's truly terrible coffee, as if contemplating whether or not to drink it.

"You're not being stretched nearly enough, are you, Edward?" he commented. "Isn't it about time we found something sensible for you to do?"

Edward hoped fervently that, in his fifties, he too would develop a similar network of creases around his intelligently avuncular eyes.

It was the prospect of a week away which enabled Edward to put up unprotestingly with two of Irina's more wearing weekends. Henry's "sensible thing", which he came up with remarkably quickly, before the week was out, turned out to be at first sight pretty idiosyncratic. He wanted Edward to go down to Marseilles to do some spade work and fix up some interviews for a feature he was planning on Jean-Marie Le Pen and the rising National Front. "And while you're down there," he had added, "why not take a few days' vacation in the Midi? Unless I'm much mistaken, you've got a fair amount owing, haven't you?"

Edward had wondered, although not for long enough to spoil the pleasure of the news, whether this was a real assignment or just a jaunt dreamt up by Henry out of the goodness of his heart to give Edward a break at the paper's expense. Even if it were only that, he concluded, it was more than welcome. He felt a warm rush of affection for Henry Hirshfeld at the realisation that one could so easily suspect the man of such a deed.

Bucked up by the prospect of a departure, even five or six hours on the train to Marseilles, he rang Irina from the paper the day he heard the news. He didn't make a habit of ringing her from work. For a start, she was usually out at work too and, even though he was painstakingly careful never to call her by her name on the phone (thereby improving his image by letting people know he was involved with someone, but avoiding the embarrassment of anyone finding out who), he was well aware he was running a risk. There was nothing to stop Irina from starting to ring him there, and although there was nothing at all suspicious about getting the odd phone call from his landlady, he wouldn't put it past Irina to raise suspicions, especially since Aurore, who frequently took incoming phone calls, was such a fertile breeding ground for them. It was Friday afternoon, Irina's afternoon off. She answered the telephone very promptly and gave a little gratifying cry of pleasure at hearing Edward's voice.

"Guess what?" he said playfully.

Not in the least playfully, Irina answered, "You're leaving work early and coming over here to visit me."

"Sor-ree," said Edward. "Don't you remember I'm having dinner with the Hirshfelds this evening?" And, this time, the excuse was genuine. "I thought we were seeing each other tomorrow anyway. No, this is to do with me and work."

After a noticeable pause, Irina asked in what Edward thought was a quite unnecessarily anguished voice, "Where?"

"What d'you mean: where?" he laughed.

"Where are they sending you?"

"Marseilles," he said. "In ten days' time. Isn't that great?"

"*Marseilles*?" Irina exclaimed. "But I thought – how long for?"

"Oh, just for a week," he said. "Though I may tack on a few days' holiday. It's a special assignment for Henry. I don't think I ought to discuss it on the phone."

He thought for a moment Irina was laughing at him; making fun of his top-secret assignment which couldn't be discussed on the phone. But her high-pitched laughter was directed at herself. She explained: "I thought this was it; they were sending you to Marseilles for good."

"Christ, that'll be much further than Marseilles, I hope," said Edward.

He didn't know whether to be pleased or perturbed that his departure was already so much on Irina's mind.

He agreed to her arrangements for Saturday, although he

206

could hardly pretend that they were to his liking. Their evening together was to be prefaced by yet another visit to Great-Aunt Elena. Now the novelty of the Russian *milieu* was wearing thin, Edward found the lengthy afternoons closeted with endlessly reminiscing females, frankly, pretty tedious. It was true that, every now and then, their stories did throw up some gem, some weird historical insight which, remembering Irina's jibe, he might or might not jot down later in his notebook. But, by and large, he simply found them depressing. He felt in sympathy with Irina's outbursts of impatience: so much grief, so many losses. Behind them, across Europe, they had left, if they were to be believed, pastel-coloured mansions, other better furs, serious jewels and close relations. Edward was not sure when another aspect of the family had struck him. As they sat here in Paris, painting their past in recollection pink, these women were all palpably strong and stout and, in keeping with their Parisian environment, tending to the predatory. But their menfolk had all fallen by the wayside. It was when he noticed this that Edward knew for certain he had no regrets that his days in Paris were numbered.

They found Great-Aunt Elena somewhat below par. Varvara Stepanovna was at home with flu, and Elena seemed slightly at a loss without anyone to order around. She suggested busily that the three of them went for a walk in the Parc Monceau before their tea. Although it was an unpleasant day, with a raw wind scouring any area of exposed skin, and the complexions of the Parisians and the stone façades both the same washed-out, end-of-winter grey, Irina agreed readily. When Edward pointed out that it wasn't a very nice day outside, she retorted that exercise was always beneficial.

He had walked countless times now along the gold-tipped black railings of the park, which formed one side of the Boulevard de Courcelles, but he had never yet been inside. It was, not surprisingly, pretty empty and as they walked at Great-Aunt Elena's processional pace along the wide gravel paths, he thought how Iskarovian it was, and how appropriate Irina and Great-Aunt Elena looked, bundled in their furs, and stepping with the same intrepid tread over the crunching gravel. He had noticed before the enjoyment with which Irina wore her high-heeled boots. Once, when they were undressing, he had teasingly persuaded her to keep them on till last and even though in the end she had grown indignant and protested, "I suppose next you want me to do circus tricks with a whip?", to start off with she had enjoyed the game and had admitted that she was exceptionally fond of her boots. They gave a welcome boost to her otherwise undeniably short, round shape and she strutted in them, acquiring straight away, Edward felt, an additional ingredient of seduction. Now, of course, he had Great-Aunt Elena's black lace-up shoes between them to prevent him from properly enjoying the spectacle. She had held out an arm to each of them as they set off down the Boulevard de Courcelles and, even though Edward felt incredibly self-conscious about walking through Paris like this, she had maintained her firm grip.

Because they walked so slowly, and because Irina and Great-Aunt Elena had lapsed into one of their prolonged exchanges of chirruping, he had a good chance to look around the park. He suspected that, in summer, you wouldn't find here the poseurs of the Jardin du Luxembourg, with their tortoiseshell-rimmed spectacles and *recherché* periodicals. It was a park for old ladies in black astrakhan coats, old gentlemen who raised their wilting hats, and possibly fey children escaped from an Impressionist painting with hoops and sticks. There was something overwhelmingly arch and toy-like about the park. Even the paths had names; the one they were walking along was called the Avenue Ferdousi. Near the entrance stood a fake domed temple and, not far off, a small fake aqueduct. Edward was wondering facetiously whether the hillocks in the neatly manicured green lawns were the product of deliberately coy landscaping or huge mutant moles which were running amuck under this enchanted garden when he heard Irina break into French to say, "Well, I think we should drop the subject anyway. It's dreadfully boring for Edouard."

"Only because we're not speaking French," Great-Aunt Elena answered. "Excuse me, Edward. We were discussing yet again Vera's infuriating *idée fixe*."

Edward heard Irina give an ominously gusty sigh so he just gave a non-committal, "Uh-huh?"

"Maybe," Elena continued provocatively, "maybe I should explain to Edward the basis of this *idée fixe*?"

"Maybe you shouldn't," snapped Irina.

Ignoring her niece, Elena turned to Edward. "I think you ought to know about this, Edward. It may help you to understand the world.

"The meanings of certain words have changed this century. We have talked about travel. Also teaching. The meaning of the word 'lost' has changed too. For people of your age, and also Irina's, 'lost' is no longer such a serious word as it used to be. You lose handkerchiefs, all right, wallets, luggage on aeroplane journeys. But, for you, 'lost' isn't such a terrible thing any more. It contains the possibility of 'found again', doesn't it? Your world today is equipped with a perpetual lost property office; the police return your wallet, the airlines retrieve your suitcase from the ends of the earth. Nothing is really gone for good any more. If your child-bearing abilities are lost, they provide you with someone else's. If your heart loses its power to pump, they give you a new one. Everything can be replaced. If your marriage fails, you simply pick another partner. For us, things were very different."

He heard Irina sigh, "Ah-la-la," and saw the toe of her boot impatiently scuff at the gravel.

"For us," Great-Aunt Elena continued, "'lost' meant precisely that; no possibility of 'found again'. You lose your handkerchiefs and your wallets and your luggage. We lost each other. You cannot imagine today how total that loss was; how total and how permanent. All right, there were the stories of miracles; forty years later in Sao Paulo, in New York. But they were exactly that: miracles. For most people, there came a revolution, a war, another war, dispersal half way round the world, and the people you had left behind were lost forever. You couldn't go back to look for them and even if you could have, you wouldn't be able to find them, because they would have moved somewhere else too and changed their names, their occupations, their appearances. Well, losing playmates, servants, familiar faces from your childhood; that's sad, but you can live perfectly well without them. In fact, maybe, I have sometimes thought, looking on the positive side, in some cases you were spared a deterioration by losing them in their youth; you never had to see them grow old and fat and ill-humoured. But losing a sister; that you never recover from."

209

"She wasn't a sister," Irina interrupted. "Tell the truth if you're going to."

Elena scowled at Irina. "In spite of what Irina says," she went on, "the person in question was a sister; not by birth, but in every other respect a sister, and I think it must be a sign of some emotional insufficiency in Irina that she can't recognise that two people may perfectly well be sisters even though they were born of different mothers. This sister grew up with us from an early age, she shared our lessons with Miss Macpherson. She was as close to Vera as I was. In fact, because they were the same age and I was the baby, seven years younger, in many respects they were closer. Sophia Solomonovna was the daughter of our family doctor. Her mother had died when she was a baby and our mother always took a great interest in her upbringing. When her father, who was a very active political man, a social reformer, was sent to prison, Sophia Solomonovna came to live with us. His sentence was so severe and he was sent so far away that, as the years went by, Sophia Solomonovna became part of our family. At least we thought so. But when the Revolution came, and we had to leave, Sophia Solomonovna chose to stay. Naturally, she could hardly leave her father, even if he was hundreds of miles away in Siberia. And she imagined she saw a future for herself under the new order. Lots of the Jews did. So we lost her.

"Of course, it affected all of us profoundly. But if you break your leg, you don't feel so acutely the chilblain on your foot. In the agony of the greater loss, the pain of the lesser one is masked. I know Vera never stopped thinking of Sophia Solomonovna, wondering what might have happened to her. She wrote to her for years, but of course the letters were never answered. At every calamity in her life, the loss of her husband, the premature death of her son Volodya, I know she thought of Sophia Solomonovna and imagined what life might be inflicting on her. Well, this became a very bad habit. Vera has always had trouble keeping her narrative tendency in check. In time, the life she imagined for Sophia Solomonovna came to seem quite real and convincing to her. Whereas, of course, the chances of Sophia Solomonovna even being alive any more must be minute. She has had so *many* chances to die: the purges, the Nazis, the war, not to mention natural, God-given sickness and old age. She could be dead a hundred times over. But Vera has got it into her head that she is still somehow miraculously living in St Petersburg, like your Dorian Gray, with not a white hair on her head, and she will keep packing her bags to set off to their reunion."

Edward left for Marseilles with unalleviated relief. The complication of Irina had been oppressing him all week. He wondered how he could have been stupid enough to make such an elementary mistake; on the verge of a career of single, unfettered travelling, unintentionally to form a tie. Certainly, the walk in the Parc Monceau had been a prelude to a particularly splendid night at the Cité Etienne Hubert. As if provoked by the onslaught of family misery to assert her independent pursuit of happiness regardless, Irina had been at her most unbridled. They must undoubtedly have alerted the grandmother, he thought, in the last few exquisite seconds before sleep; their performance had been tumultuous. But when he told Irina on Sunday morning that he was going back to the rue Surcouf to read up on the National Front, she had virtually thrown a tantrum.

"We have so little time left together," she had raged. "And you want to spend it *reading*."

"Yes," Edward had answered stubbornly. "I do."

And he had gone back to the rue Surcouf through the chilly grey silence of a Sunday morning, leaving Irina glowering after him from her front door, a tableau of outraged offence.

Again, he didn't ring her all week and when she rang him (three times) he fobbed her off with patently fabricated excuses about pressure of work and preparations for Marseilles. Still, since he was leaving first thing on Sunday morning, he saw no harm in seeing her on Saturday night. But their evening was overshadowed by his departure and nothing went as well as before.

He promised Irina a present before telling her that he would, in the end, be adding a few days' holiday to his week. As deliberate policy, he didn't specify on which day of the next week but one he would come back, pretending dishonestly that he hadn't yet made up his mind. He couldn't help detecting a trace element of guilt as Irina nevertheless

211

swamped him in a long, thorough and highly effective goodbye embrace.

He expected to enjoy Marseilles, of course, but he was unprepared for the euphoria which came over him when, having dumped his bag at the once grand old hotel off the Canebière which Henry had recommended, he set out to discover the city on his first evening. He felt liberated. For a start, it was a good ten degrees warmer than in Paris and at six o'clock in the evening still not yet dark. The streets, busy with the home-going evening rush hour, lay unexplored ahead of him. Best of all, he was on his own. He had worked out from his map up in his hotel room which was the direction to head in, towards the Vieux Port. But he had left the map behind; if there was one thing he couldn't bear it was to be seen consulting a map in the street, a blatant advertisement of helplessness. As he started out, he relished the sensation of casting himself adrift into the evening, peopled, he realised within the first few blocks, by a largely Arab population. He had read about this, of course; he had done his research. But the visible evidence of finding himself walking among short men in skullcaps, sunburnt men with handlebar moustaches, and hearing every few yards incomprehensible Arabic instead of French still excited him. There were little stalls like a *souk* in one of the streets he passed through and merchandise and haggling scenes and strong food smells, all of which vividly evoked North Africa, not that Edward had ever been there. He had obviously walked straight into one of the districts he had read about, where the influx of an immigrant population was being used to fuel the vicious backlash Henry wanted to write about. But instead of eyeing the scene professionally and memorising useful detail, he let himself aimlessly enjoy it and went on walking in his heady euphoria. He felt he had travelled much further than Marseilles; yes, that he was somewhere in North Africa or Arabia, and his real career had at last begun.

He stopped to have a pre-dinner drink or two on a café terrace in the vicinity of the Vieux Port. In his mood of indulgent *bonhomie*, he had bought a couple of postcards to send to people and as he sat enjoying his first drink and the new view, he decided generously to send one of them to

212

Irina. There she was, stuck up there in that icebound winter, and he was so free. She would still be stuck up there when he left for good and he felt sincerely sorry for her.

"Dear Irina," he wrote. "Arrived without any problem in Marseilles. The place has elements of *1001 Nights*. But never fear; nothing to rival Parisian nights so far. Love Edward."

Then he felt annoyed because he realised that, having written that, he would need to send the card in an envelope and he didn't have one with him. He put the card in one of his jacket pockets and decided he would only post it if he happened coincidentally to come across an envelope.

Because he was on expenses, he had an especially good dinner and, afterwards, for all his bravado about not needing a map, no longer quite sure of his bearings, he took a taxi back to the hotel.

He dreamt that night that he was in a shop on the Boulevard des Capucines, not far from the paper. It was a shop which he had always found rather depressing previously, a big dark emporium which went by the preposterous name of "Old England". But, in his dream, he was thrilled to be in there because he was kitting himself out for the tropics. He was buying, ridiculously, a solar topee and a mosquito net, khaki shorts and bush shirts. He half-woke at this point in the dream, troubled by his overloaded digestion, but he made himself continue the dream when he got back to sleep. In this second part, he was already travelling and, dressed in his shorts and bush shirt, he was cutting a fine figure as he reported to the television news in front of a landscape of desert sands and palm trees.

Despite his reluctance to confront the shortcomings of his life there once again, and despite the drop in temperature, Edward did feel certain positive anticipations on returning to Paris. He had a fat file of material and contacts to give to Henry; diligent, intelligent, impressive. And he did look forward to springing the happy surprise of his return on Irina; telling her all his various adventures and delighting her with her present.

No one had been in his flat while he was away this time, distributing edible gifts all around the kitchen. There was a modest pile of mail untouched on the doormat, with a particularly outrageous card from Roland uppermost. Reading it standing in the hall, still with his coat on, Edward received an unwelcome surprise. Roland wrote, cryptically, that he had been trying to reach Eddy on the phone for days but not having any luck – what the fuck was he up to? – he was resorting to a card because he wanted to let Eddy know he was coming to stay on the second. Checking the date on his watch, Edward's annoyance was reinforced; it was Thursday and Roland was coming to stay the day after tomorrow.

His immediate reaction was to leave the rest of the mail, and his luggage, and to go and telephone Irina. If they only had two days ahead of them before Roland's arrival, he may as well make the most of them.

Irina answered the telephone in formal mode: "*Allo oui?*"

Deepening his voice, Edward said, "*C'est toi, chérie?*"

"Ah," Irina said flatly, not entering into the spirit of the game at all. "Did you have a good time, Edouard?"

"Great," he answered. "Great. I just got back this minute, in fact. I wondered whether – you're not free for dinner tonight, are you?"

Her sigh was so slight, he wasn't even sure he had heard it. He expected her to say no but instead she said, just as flatly, "Yes, I am."

"Is anything the matter?" Edward asked cautiously. The last thing he wanted to bring him down to earth was an evening of Iskarovian histrionics.

In a sharpish tone of voice, which made him even more apprehensive, Irina replied, "No, Edouard, nothing's the matter; everything is just marvellous."

He liked the sound of that even less, of course, but it was too late to withdraw now.

"Let's go to that Russian restaurant you were telling me about," he suggested placatingly, "shall we?"

In the shower, absorbing the disappointment of Irina's low-key reception, one of Roland's maxims on women came back to him. It stated: "Never get involved with a woman who's got more problems than you have." He wondered what Roland would make of Irina, if he allowed their paths to cross. (On balance, he thought he wouldn't.) Roland would doubtless be savagely comic about the whole thing; inform Edward what

214

the oddity of the relationship spelt out about him. On the other hand, had Roland ever been seen with anyone as rampantly a *femme fatale* as Irina? And, with his eternal bloody maxims, wasn't Roland just the sort of person who would be impressed by their age difference?

He speculated on the possible encounter as he dressed, seeking out the tie Irina had given him for good measure. There was no doubt Irina would want to meet one of his friends from England. There was no doubt either that, should Roland decide to act the buffoon and make any of his tasteless quips about him and Irina, Irina could certainly look after herself.

She greeted him, dressed in black and an assortment of angular modern jewellery which looked jarring in the Iskarovs' antiquated front hall. His spirits rose; even if Irina were in a bad mood, she had gone to the trouble of dressing up for him.

"You look fantastic," he whispered. The grandmother was undoubtedly within earshot. He gave her a quick minor hug and one of the angles of her jewellery prodded him in the solar plexus.

"So what d'you feel like doing?" he asked her. "Shall we go to the Datcha?"

Irina shrugged ungraciously. "If you want." Then, as if determined to run counter to the grain of Edward's good mood, she added, "First come and say hello to Babushka. She needs cheering up."

"Oh Christ," Edward whispered. "Do I have to? I'm really tired, Irina; I've been on the train all day."

She chilled him with a look.

"OK," he muttered to her back in the doorway to the grandmother's room. "Just hello."

As if she hadn't budged during the fortnight since he had last seen her, Babushka sat immobile in the same armchair. When Irina showed Edward in, she responded with the merest trace of a tremor. Edward resisted a mad impulse to open the innings with a jokey reference to St Petersburg and after Irina had announced, "Edouard's just back from Marseilles," he added rather moronically, "Yes, I've been sampling *bouillabaisse*."

215

"Bouillabaisse!" Irina repeated loudly. "It's been a long time since you ate that, *n'est-ce pas*, Babushka?"

This time, there was no missing the impression which Edward had often thought he caught before but now unmistakably registered; Babushka impaled Irina on a long beady look. The look darted to Edward and Babushka drilled with the same silent accusation into him. Then she gave a tiny, almost inaudible, perfectly genteel sniff.

Irina bundled Edward out of the room so speedily, he wondered if it had been worth dragging him in there in the first place. The encounter was, he thought wryly, rather like paying a skimpily ritual visit to a shrine. It had not done anything for Irina's mood either; she collected her coat and her bag and came out after him to the lift without a word.

He tried to fondle her in the lift; there was a well-established precedent. But, wearing an insultingly martyred expression, Irina merely let him and didn't respond at all.

Edward cursed inwardly; he would have been better off in the rue Surcouf with a bottle of wine.

"Irina," he said irately, "I don't see what's the point of us spending the evening together if you're going to be like this the whole time."

The lift reached the ground floor. In a retaliatory gesture that was frankly childish, Irina's forefinger jabbed out and pushed the button for the fifth floor. With a long-suffering exhalation, the lift rose again.

"Oh, for God's sake," said Edward.

Irina stared stonily ahead of her. The first and second floors moved laboriously past them.

"Is this it, then?" Edward asked furiously, between the third and the fourth.

Even as he said it, he was painfully aware of how ridiculous the pair of them were, riding up and down in this cantankerous journey by lift.

The lift bumped home. Irina had the presence of mind to prop the lift door ajar with one hand to stop someone else summoning it from another floor, but she didn't get out.

With as much dignity as someone in that position could expect to muster, she said to Edward, "If you wanted to go out with someone all sunshine and high spirits, tra-la-la, then you shouldn't have chosen me." Whereupon, letting the lift door fall to, she flung herself around Edward's neck and burst into noisy tears.

Edward prodded the door ajar again with his foot but then, fearing that either Babushka or the lady who lived behind the fish eye opposite might overhear Irina's sobs, he let it close and reached awkwardly around Irina to push the button for the seventh, top floor.

The lift rose again, wearily.

"I'm sorry," Irina sobbed. "I'm so sorry to be like this, Edouard. You're quite right to get angry with me. But I can't help it."

"What's the *matter*?" Edward asked.

If they hadn't been ridiculously yo-yoing up and down in the lift like this, he would have felt really sorry for Irina; she was shuddering against him so pitifully. But he was simply exasperated.

Irina attempted to regain control of herself. She scrabbled in her handbag for a very lacy handkerchief and dabbed only somewhat affectedly at her eyes. Rather sweetly, she appealed to Edward, "Has my mascara run?"

"No."

"Ah good," said Irina. With one of her disarming transitions, she added, "It's not *meant* to. I chose it specially. A girl like me needs to wear tear-proof mascara."

She gave a little gulping laugh, which sounded dangerously as though it might turn back into a sob. But she pressed the button decisively to take them down to the ground floor again and squaring her shoulders, which were anyway padded in a militaristic jacket, she announced, "The storm is over. The weather forecast for the rest of the evening is set fair."

"But tell me what's the matter," Edward insisted as they walked up the Cité Etienne Hubert. "You can't greet me like you greeted me tonight, burst into floods of tears, and then just carry on as though nothing had happened."

He didn't add, 'And, frankly, I would rather have you all Slav and soulful than putting on this horrible pretence of synthetic happiness, which isn't in the least convincing.'

After a worryingly lengthy pause, Irina confessed, "I'm depressed."

217

"Well, I guessed that much," Edward teased her. "But *why?*"

Irina said, "Ach, you don't want to hear that, Edouard. Concentrate on now and have a good time and don't worry what happens afterwards; you live the right way."

"I *do* worry," Edward said, largely insincerely, but it seemed the best way to salvage the evening. He squeezed Irina's hand. "Especially where you're concerned, believe it or not."

Irina's high-pitched laughter sounded almost disturbing on the empty avenue.

Edward gave her a startled sideways look. He hadn't said anything that was so funny.

For a few moments, they walked in silence in the direction of the Boulevard des Invalides. In a last-ditch attempt to cheer her up, Edward began to do a silly walk, plunging his hands deep in his trouser pockets, squaring his shoulders, and pretending to saunter in a ludicrously debonair stroll along the avenue.

Irina made a supreme but unconvincing effort to smile.

"Are we going to the Datcha?" Edward asked her. "Shall we take a taxi?"

Once Irina had summoned one, with her usual skill, out of the night, Edward felt reasonably confident that the evening was back on an even keel.

"You know what you need?" he said to her in the back of the taxi. "A couple of stiff vodkas."

Irina snorted, in itself probably a sign of recovery. "Not that remedy," she scoffed. "Not for me. Oh, I've seen it in practice often enough; one of our traditional Russian specialities. You drink to drown your sorrows but you end up drowning any chance of happiness along with them."

In spite of which, no sooner were they installed at their rather rickety table in the Datcha, than she started to drink steadily. Edward did not point this out to her, however, since he thought it could only improve the prospects for the evening if Irina did get slightly drunk.

The Datcha was in the rue de l'Eperon, a dingy, not even properly lit lane off the rue Saint André des Arts. Irina had mentioned it to him many times – "And then afterwards Volodya used to take me to dinner at the Datcha", "Lyova

218

went to the Datcha and he came face to face with his wife Anna and her horrible barbarian" – and Edward couldn't think why it had taken them so long to get round to eating there.

It was not a particularly grand restaurant; that was a polite way of putting it. It consisted of one not very large, awkwardly L-shaped dining-room, so that the owner had the option of neglecting his customers in the back part of the L or not hurrying forward immediately to welcome new arrivals at the door. To alert him, a rather loud bell jangled when they came in and almost everyone looked up. After they had stood slightly uncertainly for a moment or two, waiting, and Irina had given a fluttery wave in the direction of one of the tables, the owner bustled forward out of the hidden part of the L and greeted them by flinging his hairy arms aloft and calling, "Irochka! It's been ages!"

He was built on the same lines as Lyova, Edward noticed with dislike. He was a coarser, burlier version, but he shared the same excessively broad shoulders and mammoth legs, encased, presumably to fit the folksy décor of his restaurant, in immense boots. He looked down at Edward with the same amused query in his eyes.

'Fuck you too,' thought Edward.

Irina simpered at the colossus. "I've been unbelievably busy," she said. "But I didn't forget you, Sasha." The next sentence was in Russian, after which she added, "This is Edouard."

Edward and the colossus shook hands and the colossus said, "Listen, I'm afraid the only table I've got is this one right near the door. D'you mind that, Irochka?"

Irina shook her head but asked Edward with a pretty display of submissiveness, "Do *you* mind, Edouard?"

Once they were seated, the owner excused himself, tramping off to attend to the rest of the restaurant, and a pretty, visibly harassed waitress brought them two red tasselled but worn menus.

"First of all, vodka and *zakuski*," Irina instructed her. "Since I know you would like that, Edouard. And then we'll order in a little while."

"*Za* – what?" asked Edward.

219

"*Za-kus-ki*," pronounced Irina, the Russian teacher. "Say it after me."

"I'll *eat* it after you," Edward answered guardedly. "What is it anyway?"

Although it had been his idea to come here in the first place, he swiftly regretted it. The Datcha was only too obviously another cell in the cosy network of collusion in which the Russians sustained their imaginary universe and he was as much a sore thumb here as he had been in the church, in the YMCA bookshop, in Lyova's fiercely alien flat. It was short-sighted of him not to have thought of it. A combination of gastronomic curiosity and that weak wish to placate Irina on the telephone had made him suggest a meal he doubted he was going to enjoy.

The *zakuski*, which the waitress brought immediately on a little platter, together with an alarming amount of vodka, turned out to be assorted dollops of smoked fish, caviar, meat patties and salads. Their purpose, Irina explained, was to form a buttress against the vodka, a purpose which she began amply to illustrate. It annoyed Edward even further that although he, in spite of nearly six months of practice, still couldn't down his glass of vodka as you were meant to, in one go, Irina stylishly did so. She munched happily on a bit of herring. Edward felt an unreasonable wish to get back at her.

"So this is the famous Datcha then," he said patronisingly. "I must say, I did think it would be a bit smarter."

Irina looked around vaguely at the modest restaurant, its walls decorated with varnished logs split lengthways, to create the effect of a log cabin. She shrugged and helped herself to a meat patty.

"I mean, this is one of your favourite old haunts, isn't it?" he persisted meanly. "It looks a bit tacky to me, if you don't mind my saying so."

Irina focused reluctantly on some of the more sentimental touches, the rose-coloured views of Russian scenes, the *matrioshka* dolls turned into the bases of table lamps.

"Yes," she agreed serenely, "this sort of *pastiche* Russia is ridiculous, isn't it? But that's not why we come here, of course. We come for the *ambiance*, for the familiar faces: for Sasha," she nodded in the direction of the proprietor, "the Solovyovs over there, say, those people I said hello to when we came in. And this place has pleasant memories attached to it too; I feel at home here."

She was taking her second glass of vodka more slowly, with small pensive sips, but getting through it just the same. She gestured at the round-cheeked face of the table-lamp doll; "I despise this garbage," she said calmly. "It's what Lyova refers to as the debris of the Union of Sentimental and Retrospective Republics." With just the slightest edge of antagonism in her voice, she concluded, "I thought you liked this sort of thing, though. I thought my old world heritage amused you. Otherwise I'd never have dreamt of bringing *you* in here."

The emphasis on *you* annoyed him. "Why not?" he asked, with illogical indignation. "You've gone on about it often enough. It's obvious it's important to you."

Irina gave him a slow look, which was either steeped in the sorrows of ages or the first blurring of alcohol.

"Everybody knows me here," she explained. "Whoever I come in here with, the whole world will know about it before the week is out."

Edward felt slightly sick. Before he could say anything, though, the owner materialised massively beside Irina and protested, "Irochka, nobody is looking after you! What would you like to order?"

As soon as they had chosen, and the owner had solicitously refilled both their glasses, Edward asked hastily, "Who is there here tonight to spread the word, then? D'you think anyone will realise?"

"Don't worry about it," Irina said soothingly. "It's too late now anyway."

For a short while, they drank sullenly, and neither said anything.

Then, goaded by the distinct impression that he had been rewarded for his good intentions with an underhand trick, Edward complained, "But what made you decide it was OK to come here now, if you knew we'd run the risk of being found out?"

Irina sighed.

Edward was terribly tempted to snap, 'Stop bloody sighing, can't you? Just tell me what the hell's going on.'

221

Before he could work out a gentler way of saying the same thing – was the vodka getting to him too? – he noticed the earlier desolation had returned to Irina's face. He was terrified that she might start weeping again in the middle of the restaurant, so he quickly said jokily, "Oi, don't accidentally over-salt that pickled herring, will you? It's bad enough as it is."

Not a giggle in response, not a grin; they were in trouble.

"I mean," he back-pedalled, "not that I'm not pleased you did bring me here. I'm just puzzled. If you felt it wasn't a good idea before, what made you change your mind?"

Irina stared at him in what seemed to be amazement. "*Mais enfin*, Edouard, isn't it perfectly obvious?"

"Sorry, not to me."

Irina reached for her refilled glass and started to sip at it just a little too fast for Edward's liking.

"What does it matter now?" she burst out. "What does it matter? Who cares if we're found out or not found out when you're going away so soon anyway?"

Edward felt himself break into a sweat. He was aware that he must have gone extremely red in the face.

"I think it still matters," he said as mildly as he could. "I mean, your family will be just as upset if they find out now as if they'd found out three months ago, won't they?"

"My family – " Irina said bitterly.

She stared into a middle distance which seemed to be filled with nothing but barren despair. She opened her mouth to go on but she couldn't; a sudden choking sob stopped her and she pressed her serviette to her lipsticked mouth with a white-knuckled force which alarmed Edward.

"Hey," he whispered urgently. "Don't, Irina, please. Please not in the restaurant."

With a tremendous, visible effort, Irina restrained herself. Now, she frankly gulped at her vodka.

"What does anything matter?" she asked wildly. "I have wasted far too much of my life taking notice of things I thought mattered and, actually, I found out they don't matter at all. Only one thing matters to me now, Edouard. Don't you realise? It's almost April. Soon the school Easter holidays will be starting. And after the holidays it will be the summer term. And in the summer you're going away."

Only a complete cretin would not have been moved by a statement of such devotion from a woman as striking as Irina looked at that moment. She had gone quite white, which made the dark rings show up beneath her eyes, and together with her plum purple lipstick, her dark eyes formed three deep pits in a chalky theatrical mask.

Edward was so confounded by guilt, he was temporarily incapable of offering any helpful platitudes in response.

The waitress brought their main courses at this opportune moment and the two large plates of steaming meat confronted them with a crude reminder of the obvious.

Although, uncharacteristically, the last thing Edward felt like was eating, he was relieved at first to see Irina take her knife and fork and begin on her Chicken Kiev. Only after a moment or two he noticed there was something seriously amiss in the way Irina was eating; apparently quite oblivious to the contents of her plate, she was mechanically slicing, forking up and chewing her dinner in rote, automatic despair. She was eating like Varvara Stepanovna.

He had to stop her. At the risk of triggering the scene to end all scenes, he reached across the table and took her hand.

"I know it's true I'm probably leaving in the summer," he said desperately. "But I want you to know you've been the best thing that's happened to me in Paris." Recklessly, he added, "I won't forget you, you know."

Irina shook off his hand fiercely enough for some drops of garlic butter to splash his cuff.

"Thank you, Edouard," she said with icy hostility. "Perhaps I might have liked to be a little more than a thing which happened to you."

Although his major reaction to that meal was to renew his policy of avoidance, he had to give Irina credit for a fine performance. For most of the meal she did control her tears, but she had grown steadily more drunkenly maudlin on the Georgian wine which succeeded the vodka, and he couldn't help being grudgingly impressed by the authentic picture of a tragic heroine which she presented.

Even as she gestured censoriously at the shelves of assorted vodka bottles rising behind the till, she was starting to slur her words.

223

"Ah yes, we're Russian, aren't we? We have to have – to have vodka, don't we? We can't have a Russian restaurant without the where-where-thall to drink ourselves into oblivion."

Edward was shocked but slightly titillated; he had never seen a woman he knew get that drunk before.

And when it was time to go, when Irina and Sasha had chirruped away at each other in Russian for long enough for Sasha to clap one spade-like hand on Irina's shoulder, and confide to Edward in French, "Look after this lady. She is one among millions," he couldn't help but be turned on by the sophisticated figure she looked leaving the restaurant, walking very upright, a lady from Toulouse-Lautrec, he thought, balancing on the edge of an abyss of alcohol and despair.

It was true alcohol was supposed to affect performance but the effect it had that night Edward had never encountered before. Irina had obviously dismissed all idea of caution anymore. She spoke to him at the top of her voice in the hall of their flat and when a light came on behind the door of Babushka's bedroom, she called a greeting nonchalantly in Russian and turned to give Edward a juicy wink.

In bed, it was another matter, though. Because of the fumbling uncertainty caused by the alcohol, they both had to concentrate rather hard on what they wanted to do, and they fell silent as they tried to focus on the ways and means. A silent Irina in this situation was a new and not entirely welcome experience. Without the encouragement of her volcanic gasps and moans, Edward felt slightly at a loss, working away in silence in the dark, and since everything took rather longer than usual because of the alcohol, he even had the bizarre impression for a while that Irina was no longer there. He would turn out, when this dream was over, to have been making love to a woman whom he had only imagined. Beneath him, there was really no one at all.

This bizarre sensation caused him to lose his stride and Irina's hands emerged from the dark to reassure him that she was there with him after all. His head spinning with the motion and the vodka, he embarked once more. It seemed to him in the end that he and Irina had managed to break loose after all, that they were rocking across Europe, the immense international night spinning around them, rocking across a nocturnal geography of the Arc de Triomphe and the Sacré-Coeur, of Central European fairy-tale wooden houses, and hallucinatory onion domes.

He did in the end show her to Roland. His reasoning was twofold: she looked so low, lying all white and wan and wretched when he left her early on Friday morning. He felt genuinely sorry for her. It seemed only fair, in the few months remaining, not to abandon her entirely. In Roland's presence, it would be time spent quite innocuously too; there was no risk of Irina exerting her nefarious influence on him and his capitulating to anything more than the absolute minimum. His other motive was not altruistic at all; he wanted to show her off to Roland. For, thinking it over during Saturday, while he waited for Roland to arrive, he was confident old Roland would be pretty impressed by Irina, if only because she was so startlingly different from anyone who had preceded her.

The three of them went out for a meal together on Saturday evening. Afterwards, as Edward settled down with Roland in the rue Surcouf for a long night of catching up on news and drinking, Roland volunteered the opinion that Irina knew her stuff. It was her accumulated years of experience which seemed to have made the strongest impression on Roland. He dwelt rather gratifyingly on the skills which a woman acquired with advancing years and it was obvious to Edward that, despite a rather snide reference to Irina's weight, Roland was undoubtedly seriously impressed by the worldly sophistication of Edward's Parisian affair. This gave Edward great pleasure. For, in the past, Roland had always had the reputation of being sexually much more adventurous than Edward.

Against all the odds, it began to feel as though it might one day be spring. Paris hardly stirred; there was no uprush of seasonal sap along the avenues. But there came a slight slackening. Unexpected curtains flapped at the open windows of the seven-storey façades and the minute lapdogs rushed at one another on their circumscribed outings, frenziedly tangling their hair-fine leashes.

Irina drew Edward's attention to the premature flowering of skimpy, high-summer dresses in the shop windows.

"That one," she had pointed at a lime-green slither which tied, what there was of it, in a flamboyant bow on one shoulder. "Do you think I would look nice in that?"

Edward couldn't say he relished the prospect of Irina in revealing summer dresses. She wasn't really made for clinging, emphasising scraps of fabric. They would, he suspected, only highlight her flaws. Already he missed her enveloped in her furs and her boots. He distrusted the enthusiasm with which she latched onto the summer clothes in the shop windows. It was shrill, over-excited, and quite artificially girlish. He hoped she was not going to be someone who ran amok at the first days of sunshine, scantily dressed and demanding immediate picnics and parties and armfuls of flowers. He imagined her, apprehensively, in outfits that were strapless, backless, low-cut, vaunting all that she had to vaunt, and vaunting also a revamped summer personality to go with them: polka dots perhaps, teetering high heels in ridiculous rainbow colours, and outsize *fantaisie* earrings and necklaces, laden with plastic tropical fruits.

They had already had a disagreement over the very word *fantaisie*. Irina had bought Edward a shirt. He was dismayed, beyond the purchase, that Irina should have found out his correct collar size. Apart from the unsought attention, he didn't like the idea that Irina had looked into his clothes without his knowing, or maybe even gone secretly through his cupboards on a visit to the rue Surcouf. It was potentially disastrous, of course, that she should have to have the keys to his flat. The shirt was pink, a colour he had never worn and furthermore had no intention of ever wearing. Irina described it as *fantaisie*.

He asked her, rudely, how a plain, unpatterned shirt, with no particular frills to it, could be called *fantaisie*, simply because it happened to be a particularly unprepossessing colour.

Flinching, Irina had, not for the first time, cast aspersions on the limitations of an Englishman.

"You really haven't any idea about dressing," she had reproved him. "I didn't want to say anything before, but now the spring's coming. You'll be on your way. I want you to leave Paris looking smart, Edouard; showing, please, some signs of having known me."

She had torn the shirt from its wrapping and in a way which was infuriating but at the same time physically difficult to resist, she had draped the *fantaisie* shirt about him and effusively embraced both him and the shirt.

Shrinking from a new display of effusiveness, Edward had scowled disparagingly at the lime-green dress in the shop window.

"Not you at all," he had said.

And he had noted with impatience the ambulating sulk he had then had beside him for the next few blocks.

He saw more of Irina than he had probably intended because of her Easter holidays. Apart from a few days spent, reluctantly, with family friends near Nice, she didn't go away from Paris at all and, every day, Edward was conscious she was there in the Cité Etienne Hubert, available, expectant. It seemed excessively callous just to leave her there. He reassured himself increasingly frequently with the reminder of his departure. Only, occasionally, he would panic that there might not be a departure. He had no guarantee, after all, that, come the summer, some marvellous destination would materialise and he would be effortlessly airlifted out of this implausible situation he had got himself into. He was getting on so well with Henry Hirshfeld; maybe they would decide to keep him on in Paris for a second year. Then he would leave Irina to pine in the Cité Etienne Hubert for days on end, until she rang him, with tears in her voice, and pleaded with him to come and rescue her. He told himself that he owed her at least this consolation. For, reluctant as he was to admit it, he supposed that the main reason Irina didn't go away from Paris was him.

One afternoon in the rue Surcouf, he realised he was ceasing to enjoy even her redeeming qualities. They were lying in bed and Edward was only half-listening as Irina, draped partly over him, was spinning one of her whimsical post-coital fantasies. Outside, the Duponts' macaw, newly put out on the window-sill to enjoy the milder weather, was warbling a new advertising jingle and Edward was straining to work out what the product was. "*L'artichaut,*" he thought he could hear the bird proclaiming, "*Le légume de l'été!*" But there seemed to be no brand name. He was vaguely considering this puzzle when, beside him, Irina also started to sing, she and the macaw clamouring in a sort of insane competition for his attention, and what Irina was singing sounded at first like some cloying advertising jingle too.

She was singing:

> "*Il était un' dame Tartine,*
> *Dans un beau palais de beurr' frais,*
> *Les muraill's étaient de praline,*
> *Le parquet était de croquet,*
> *Sa chambre à coucher*

228

Etait d'échaudés,
Son lit de biscuits,
Les rideaux d'anis."

"There was a sliced bread lady,
In a beautiful butter palace,
The walls were made of praline,
The parquet of brandy snaps,
Her bedroom was made
Of tiers of tea cakes,
Her bed of biscuits,
And the curtains were aniseed."

Then she rolled giggling against Edward and started nuzzling and nibbling at him with exaggerated noises of enjoyment.

"Mm, *délicieux*."

"Oh, what are you on about?" Edward asked her wearily.

He liked to enjoy the peace and quiet at these moments. It irritated him intensely that as soon as Irina had regained her composure, she would invariably start to prattle away on the perfection of the act, the perfection of Edward, her supreme happiness at their lying there together. He had learnt to switch off when she started and this had, in fact, led to a couple of nasty squabbles when he failed to hear particularly significant compliments or confessions and Irina was forced, humiliatingly, to repeat or retract them.

She wallowed luxuriantly amid the new flowery sheets which she had recently provided.

She gurgled.

"I feel like a *dame Tartine*," she announced happily. "This is my beautiful butter palace. That wallpaper could easily be praline, don't you think? And that lampshade looks incredibly like a meringue from this angle, doesn't it?"

Edward said nastily, "I'm afraid this literary allusion is lost on me."

Irina bravely ignored his tone of voice.

"It's a nursery rhyme I used to love when I was little," she explained. "Mama would sing it to me sometimes. She had a lovely voice."

229

She started up again:

> *"Elle épousa Monsieur Gimblette,*
> *Coiffé d'un beau fromage blanc – "*

"She was wed to Monsieur Gimblette,
In his hat of champion curd cheese – "

"OK," Edward interrupted her irritably. "OK, I've got the point."

He rolled over, turning his back on Irina but, enchanted by her fantasy, she went on, "Really, that's exactly how I feel about being here, Edouard. It's just like some nursery rhyme make-believe; too beautiful, too delicious to be true."

She warbled: *"Le palais sucré du bonheur."*

Looking around the room, she enumerated, "Those curtains are of course completely the wrong colour for aniseed. What would they be? *Café au lait*? Demerara sugar?"

"It's a more appropriate analogy than you realise," Edward murmured meanly into his pillow.

Irina heard him and paused.

"What d'you mean?"

"Well, all the edible metaphors," Edward retorted. "We've virtually guzzled our way through the whole scenario, haven't we? Nothing much left now."

He wondered when might be a reasonable time to raise the subject with Henry. They had lunch together regularly at least once or twice a week these days, and Edward supposed that one day over lunch he would screw up his courage and ask Henry where his future lay. Not that Henry was himself in the least daunting, of course. More than once, he had made throwaway remarks which made his sympathy for Edward perfectly plain: "I'm not letting them bury you in Bonn, that's for sure," and on one immensely satisfying occasion he had prefaced a description of the work of a Vietnamese artist by saying to Edward, "When you're in Saigon". But, apart from the obvious considerations of career strategy, it seemed discourteous to remind Henry of his impatience to be off any earlier than necessary.

After all, Henry had no idea of the grotesque mess Edward had got himself into here. He probably assumed that there was likely to be a woman; he would hardly expect a celibate twelve months. But he probably assumed as well that it would be nothing more than the kind of practical relationship which could be painlessly terminated whenever the needs of the paper dictated it. He wasn't to know what increasingly wild scenarios Irina was threatening.

One Sunday afternoon, Edward came to the Cité Etienne Hubert to take Irina out for a walk. He had not spent the previous night with her and the walk was to be her booby prize. He tacked between such small concessions and a consistent hardline cold shoulder. As part of his campaign of emancipation, he took the stairs to the fifth floor instead of the lift. It must have been at around the fourth floor that he became aware of female voices somewhere in the building raised in dispute. The voices echoed shrilly through the stairwell, sounding particularly strident in a house that was normally silent. But it wasn't until he reached the last flight of stairs leading up to the fifth-floor landing that he realised the furies' voices were, in fact, coming from the Iskarovs' flat. He stopped on the final steps. He could immediately identify Irina; a high-pitched petulant tirade of what sounded like defiance and rebellion. A second voice sounded like Great-Aunt Elena; a puttering volley of brown-paper bags being busily burst one after another. But, for some seconds, he couldn't work out who the third voice would be; quavering, beseeching, now rising to a near wail. Then it came to him; of course, it had to be Babushka. In six months, he had hardly ever heard her speak, certainly never raise her voice or show any emotion stronger than suspicion. She would very occasionally say something in Russian to Irina in front of him, but only in response to something Irina had already said. She never started a conversation. Yet here she apparently was, virtually wailing, and certainly giving as good as she got in what sounded to Edward like an absolutely monumental row. What on earth were they arguing about?

He waited, wondering whether to interrupt the row by going ahead and knocking at the door or prudently retreating and explaining his non-appearance tactfully to Irina over the telephone later. As he hesitated, the *minuterie*, the time switch on the stairs, clicked off, leaving him in near darkness in

231

which the raised voices sounded somehow even louder and more anguished.

Edward felt he was eavesdropping on some larger-than-life drama: screeching, tearing of hair and beating of large, flapping breasts. A minor, despicable part of him even enjoyed it. Whatever else, what was going on behind the Iskarovs' front door was at least meaty. In this chilly prim city, it was a hot-blooded eruption from elsewhere. He only enjoyed it for a very brief moment, though. One after the other, two unpleasant factors impinged on him: under the front door of the apartment opposite the Iskarovs', a strip of yellow light shone out into the hall. Someone could be standing there eavesdropping too. And it occurred to him with foreboding that it was not beyond the bounds of possibility that the Iskarovs were fighting about him.

He debated his options, the most attractive of which was undoubtedly heading back down the stairs, taking them in giant, enjoyable leaps, and saying goodbye to any idea of a walk. Alternatively, he could wait there until the row was over and then knock. But, from the sound of it, that would be a very long wait. The voices weren't even alternating any more but frequently rising all together. He deliberated. The third option was the one which required the most nerve. But, frankly, he didn't like the idea that he could be chased away by a trio of strident women and the prospect of a confrontation with them. It really wasn't a flattering image of himself; pelting headlong down the stairs just to get away from three highly-strung women, two of them in their eighties. A floor or two below him, the staircase light clicked on. Even though it was probably just some other old lady coming out to summon the lift, the light galvanised him into action. Funnily enough, it was the thought that this was his chance to shut these Iskarov women up which, in the end, prompted him to cross the landing and to ring decisively at their bell.

Complete silence followed, and in the very long pause before Irina came to answer the door, Edward had ample opportunity to regret the option he had taken.

Irina looked a little flushed, and her eyes were glinting, but, otherwise, she showed no signs at all of what had been going on. She was very dressed up, presumably for their walk, and Edward couldn't help being slightly impressed by the stylish composure with which she posed for him in the doorway, showing off her new outfit, regardless of all she must have been through in the last ten minutes. Just as he had imagined, she had gone for something very eye-catching for the spring. He supposed it was basically a suit, but its colour scheme of crimson and mauve brushwork on a white background was so bright, it did away with any connotations of buttoned-up office efficiency. Irina waited for long enough to see the involuntary admiration in Edward's eyes and said briskly, "Well, come on in."

"Should I?" asked Edward.

Irina exclaimed, "Why ever not?"

"Well," Edward said, "I just heard – "

Irina gave a curt "Tchuh!" She tugged at Edward's hand defiantly. "Come in. All you heard was idiocy."

There was absolutely no sign or sound of Babushka and Great-Aunt Elena. Edward waited in the hall while Irina collected her bits and pieces and listened keenly for some low murmur of Russian dissent: nothing. He supposed Great-Aunt Elena must be too distraught to make an appearance. Maybe she was calming Babushka. But he was still a little put out that, considering all her repeatedly professed affection for him, she shouldn't even stick her perfectly spherical head round whichever door she was hiding behind and say hello.

They walked up to the Quai Anatole France and across the Pont Solférino, Irina keeping up a conversation on assorted anodine topics. It wasn't until they were strolling under the trees of the Quai des Tuileries in a leisurely, relaxed promenade that Edward eventually asked her, "What was the row about? It sounded like the beginning of the Third World War."

To his surprise, Irina laughed. "Oh no, it wasn't the Third yet. You know we're always behind the times in my family; we're still on the First and the Second."

Then she shrugged dismissively. "It was nothing, I told you. It was ridiculous."

"It didn't sound like nothing," Edward insisted. "You know one could hear you right the way down the stairs? I was standing out there for quite a while, because I didn't know whether or not I ought to interrupt. In the end, it got so bad I thought I'd better come in to rescue you."

"Sweet," Irina commented absent-mindedly. "You know that swimming pool I pointed out to you as we came over the bridge, the Piscine Deligny? Shall we go swimming there together in the summer, when the weather's warmer? You know you can swim topless there?"

"OK, I'll try another approach," Edward said, "Twenty questions. Was it to do with: money matters, morals or men?"

Irina frowned. "Why d'you keep going on about it, Edouard? Why spoil our lovely walk too?"

"It intrigues me," Edward answered. "And I care about it if it upset you."

Irina stared away over the river for so long, Edward wondered if it wasn't a strategy for hiding tears.

"I told you," she finally said wearily, "Great-Aunt Elena and Babushka came up with this ridiculous notion. It's not the first time. They're always doing it, although I must admit they used to do it a lot more often than they do now. Maybe now they're so old, their energy is running out. Or maybe they've just given up hope. They want to introduce me to a man."

It was all Edward could do not to burst into astonished laughter. He concentrated on the Pont Royal coming up ahead of them.

"A man?" he repeated.

"Oh, one of these deserving cases Elena comes across on her rounds; a bald, fat, Russian widower," she added viciously, "with diabetes."

"And they want you to go out with him?" Edward asked.

Irina scoffed. "Go out with him? The marriage papers are as good as drawn up."

"Oh, for God's sake!" laughed Edward.

He felt a sense of tremendous relief.

"That's not the worst of it," Irina went on. "Naturally, I got annoyed. And, as tempers were heating up, they started telling me what a source of deep distress my way of life is to them. Babushka made an allusion."

But that was as far as she was prepared to go. Abruptly drawing the line, she put a finger on Edward's lips.

234

"I promise you, Edouard," she assured him, "You don't *want* to know any more."

They had walked as far as the Pont des Arts. Ahead of them the Ile de la Cité jutted up in its magnificence. For a while, Edward was content simply to stroll through the fine spring afternoon and enjoy the trite pleasure of walking arm in arm with a woman as glamorous, as noticeable as Irina in her spring finery.

But Irina's new mauve shoes were starting to give trouble. Edward noticed her pace gradually slowing from a stately promenade to the tiredest of saunters. Eventually, they were on the slim bridge between the Ile de la Cité and the Ile Saint Louis, Irina gasped out, "I have to sit down. My feet are killing me."

They found a timely bench a little way along the Quai d'Orléans and Irina flopped down and kicked off her shoes. She sat back and shut her eyes, quite obviously exhausted.

Edward reflected in the long silence before Irina felt recovered enough to speak to him, how absolutely typical of her it was to set out for a long walk in new shoes which she hadn't yet had a chance to walk in. He looked down at the shoes, kicked beyond her blissfully wiggling toes, and grew impatient at how unsuitable they were for a walk. They were little dainty, mauve canoes, with narrow, pointed toes and on each heel a frivolous, mauve rosette. The moment summed up, Edward thought, in microcosm, the disadvantages of setting off anywhere with a woman in tow.

Irina had opened her eyes without his noticing.

"Spring isn't my favourite season, in fact," she announced. "I prefer autumn. In autumn, I am at my best. Everything fits: my colouring, my melancholy nature. It will be one of my lasting regrets, you know, when you are gone, that we won't have known each other in autumn."

Because this was one of Irina's frankest acknowledgments yet of his likely departure, Edward said nothing, so as to let it resound and really sink in.

They were sitting in silence when Irina, who was gazing pensively past him towards the quieter eastern end of the *quai*, exclaimed, "*Tiens!* Look who's coming!"

Edward turned round to see, not far away and vigorously

235

approaching, the distinctive, ill-matched shapes of Henry and Mai Hirshfeld. Rooted as he and Irina were to the bench, by their visibility as well as by Irina's bare, swollen feet, they could hardly up and run for cover, a possibility which did pass just very briefly across Edward's mind. In the last moments left before the Hirshfelds reached them, his concentration on contingency maneouvres was distracted by trying desperately to remember whether or not he had actually been touching Irina when the Hirshfelds came into view and by the paralysing glaze of horror which set over the whole picturesque scene.

Irina, the one who had been so keen to keep everything secret in the first place, waved and called, "Ooh-hooh!"

Mai's arm shot up and fluttered a jerky wave in response, and she turned to Henry, who was short-sighted, obviously telling him who it was.

Henry raised an arm too and, as soon as they were close enough to speak, called expansively, "Isn't it a marvellous day?"

In a situation so hopelessly beyond his control, Edward did what he could to retain a grip. He stood up and asked Henry, "Do you know my landlady, Mai's colleague, Mademoiselle Iskarov?"

"No, I haven't had the pleasure," Henry answered, and he held out his hand to shake Irina's warmly.

"Such a beautiful afternoon," Mai enthused. "We usually come this way on our Sunday afternoon outing. It's our favourite walk. But it's especially beautiful today, isn't it? The sunlight, the reflections."

Her small composed face gave not the slightest sign of surprise at finding Edward and Irina together on a bench in the middle of a Sunday afternoon. But there was no need to go on quite so much, Edward thought, about the scenery.

"Ah," Irina said playfully, "listen to the artist talking," and all four of them laughed over-heartily.

"Yes, Mai compensates for my myopia," Henry remarked jokily. "She's forever pointing things out to me which have escaped my notice."

"A perfect team!" Irina exclaimed, horribly gushingly, Edward felt. "You should go into print together: your words, illustrated by Mai's pictures."

Again, everyone laughed, slightly laboriously.

"Well, we should be on our way, I guess," Henry said. "We want to take in the exhibition at the Pompidou. Nice to meet you, Mademoiselle Iskarov. 'Bye, Edward."

Mai flashed them both a bright perfunctory smile, and the Hirshfelds continued on their way along the *quai*.

Edward and Irina looked after them for a few seconds in individual states of dismay. Edward had barely begun to assess the damage when Irina, who had hastily slipped on her shoes at the approach of the Hirshfelds, sat down again abruptly and kicked them off.

She looked up at Edward, who was still standing at a loss beside the bench, and she hissed at him in a voice which actually seemed to contain hate, "Are you ashamed of me or something?"

He asked stupidly, "What?"

"You know what I mean. Why did you do that, you – you swine?"

"Irina!"

"Go on, tell me why. I've never been so humiliated in all my life. 'Mademoiselle Iskarov, my landlady.' How *could* you?"

Edward looked down at her in disbelief.

"Irina," he said, "I thought all this was supposed to be secret. You were the one who said it had to be in the first place, remember? *I* didn't get offended. Henry's my *boss*. Haven't I got the right to keep things secret from certain people too?"

Irina glared at him furiously for a moment or two. Then something within her seemed to snap and, putting her face into her hands, she collapsed into the most acutely miserable, heartbroken sobs.

Edward reproached himself that his overriding emotion at that moment was embarrassment because a crocodile of Japanese tourists was coming their way along the *quai*.

For a long time afterwards, for as long as Edward thought of that period of his life, he wondered what had determined the sequence of events. Had it been simply chance which had then set things in motion, or had that meeting with the Hirshfelds actually determined his future?

He had agonised until the Monday morning over what Henry would have deduced from it. He acknowledged this was ridiculous, since Henry was far from stupid and there was only one conclusion any sensible person could have drawn from it. But a craven, completely unrealistic hope made him pretend that if he told Henry Mademoiselle Iskarov had been pestering him for so long to go out for a walk together that on that fine Sunday he had been forced reluctantly just once to agree, Henry might believe him. It was easy enough to paint Irina as a man eater. Of course, this cast him in rather a feeble light. He wondered what Henry would think of him if, as seemed a foregone conclusion, he and Mai had tumbled to the truth. He realised, gradually in the later evening, that it wasn't inevitable that Henry would think the worse of him. It was a rather schoolboy reaction, in fact, to imagine that he automatically would; Wainwright caught by the master up to no good. Of course, Henry wasn't the sort of man to be impressed by sexual trophies. But he was characteristically far from conventional. He would certainly have been more

238

disappointed in Edward if he found him on a bench with some seventeen-year-old office temp with highlights in her hair. For all Edward knew, Henry and Mai had gone on their way, metaphorically raising their hats to him; good for Edward, he didn't miss a trick, not only had he found himself a place to live but while he was about it some high-class female company too. The Hirshfelds were, after all, Edward thought, what the French called *soixante-huitards*; the generation imbued with the ideals of 1968. With their life-long commitment to being broad-minded, they maybe even approved of a liaison which went in the face of all conventional expectations. Look, Edward thought, at their own.

He was still appalled at the thought that they knew about it. When Monday morning came, he adopted a policy which he knew to be pure cowardice, although he kidded himself lamely that it was nothing but discretion. He made no allusion at all to the weekend meeting, he didn't say a word, and Henry, for whatever reason, did the same.

Irina wouldn't, or couldn't, stop crying. Still crying, she had at last stumbled into the mauve shoes and set out to find a taxi. She said she didn't care whether or not Edward came with her, but he had, because it was the only way he could retain some control over what she did next. He thought he had never seen such extravagant despair and it seemed only wise to keep tabs on it.

In the taxi, Irina said she forgave him. She understood what had motivated him to deny their association and although what he had done had hurt her deeply, for the sake of the time remaining to them, she was prepared to put it behind her. This annoyed Edward considerably for, as far as he was concerned, he had done nothing which merited such a fuss. But he restrained his annoyance, only wincing slightly when Irina started to caress his cheek despite the taxi driver's reflected stare.

Once he had seen her safely in at the front door of Number Nine, Cité Etienne Hubert, he felt his duties were discharged, and he went back to the rue Surcouf to begin worrying in earnest about Henry's reaction.

Nothing happened on any front for a month. Irina went

back to school and had less time to dwell on Edward. She still rang him far more often than their relations warranted, related all her little pieces of news, and pumped him avidly for his. He did his best not to be rude to her. The safest course seemed to be a stern regimen of metered meetings, no hostility which might cause her to flare up, and only when there was absolutely no way round it, the rare concession of an overnight stay in the Cité Etienne Hubert.

It was in the second week in May that the development occurred which led Edward to wonder whether the meeting beside the Seine had, in fact, been without consequences. It was in the league whose exact circumstances you remember long afterwards: the weather, your clothes. Edward remembered it was a Friday and Henry had taken him out to lunch. He was almost certain it was raining and that was why they had gone to the pricier Japanese, which was closest to the paper.

Henry had asked him, and he remembered the saké fermenting abruptly in his throat, "How quickly do you think you could learn Russian?"

Edward had blushed abominably, with the combination of saké and embarrassment, and only after a long moment's strained scrutiny of Henry's apparently well-disposed face, had he decided to brazen it out and replied, "What are you getting at, Henry?"

Henry grinned, as though acknowledging that Edward had decided to parry his oblique approach with oblique hedging of his own, and good-humouredly agreeing to it.

"Well, have you ever studied it, for instance?" he asked. "Have you any knowledge of it at all?"

Edward was amazed; coming from Henry, this indelicate probing was so completely out of character. Could it mark an advance in their relationship; man-to-man confidences over the lunch table? Deciding that he wanted at all costs to rise to the occasion, Edward looked Henry squarely in the eye and asked, "Is this to do with Mademoiselle Iskarov?"

Henry gaped, frankly gaped, and then broke into a grin so broad, his highly amused face looked as though it might literally disintegrate amid the resulting creases.

"No," he had answered, nearly laughing. "No, it isn't, I assure you. It's to do with your next job."

240

The surge of adrenalin almost drowned Edward. He had to make a supreme effort actually to hear what Henry was saying above the crescendo of his own circulation.

Obviously delighted to be the bringer of such resounding news, Henry beamed down on Edward, enjoying every moment of Edward's flushed, taut face.

"You remember meeting Arnold Elgood at our home at New Year? Well, Arnold is moving to Moscow. He told me on the phone that he was looking for someone capable to go out there and assist him. I suggested you."

"Gosh" was a farcically inadequate response but it was what Edward came out with.

"Did – does Arnold remember who I am?" he asked falteringly.

Henry's grin grew unmistakably mischievous. "Vaguely," he said. "I gave you a great write-up, though. By the time I was finished, Arnold couldn't wait to get hold of you." Teasingly, he added, "Poor old Arnold. He never stopped to ask himself why, if you were such a *Wunderkind*, I was so eager to get you off my hands."

"Thank you," Edward said formally. "Is it definite, then? I mean, are you – am I being offered the job?"

"If you want it," Henry answered flippantly. "You can always turn Arnold down."

"I do want it," Edward assured him. He added hastily, "Though I shall be sorry to leave. It's been really great working for you."

Gravely, Henry replied, "I shall be sorry to say goodbye to you, Edward."

He lifted their little saké jug, found it was nearly empty, and signalled to a waiter to bring them another. They toasted Edward's destination.

"*Na zdorovye,*" Henry pronounced, with a strong American accent. Then he gave another gleeful grin. "May I say, Edward, I was intrigued by your earlier reference to Mademoiselle Iskarov?"

Edward left the paper at the end of the afternoon and walked the whole way back to the rue Surcouf in a march of triumph through the streets of Paris which he would be leaving in less than six weeks' time. He had a tremendous urge to tell people his excellent news but since, apart from Irina and her family, he had made no friends in his nine months in Paris, he had no one to tell. He was naturally reluctant to tell Irina. He wondered briefly, coming over the Pont de la Concorde, whether his destination would make any difference to Irina's reaction, which was bound to be dreadful. He couldn't think that it would. It wasn't South America and it wasn't Africa but it was still a long way away and access was peculiarly difficult. He thought he remembered Irina saying once that Russian officialdom made a point of being particularly unpleasant to people like her, the offspring of Russians who had chosen to leave the Communist motherland. He suspected that, like most Iskarovian political pronouncements, this one was mistaken but, so long as it kept Irina from trying any crackpot scheme of coming to visit him there, he wouldn't contradict her. He remembered how impotently irritated he used to get listening to the elderly Russians voicing their deep-seated distrust of Mitterrand's socialist government. He looked down towards the Piscine Deligny as he passed it and he thought, on a wave of cruel euphoria, that he would after all be spared the sight of Irina in a bikini.

He stopped at the local Nicolas to buy a better-than-usual bottle to celebrate. But when he got back to the flat, he felt frustrated by the limitations of celebrating on his own. It was a real shame that he couldn't tell Irina. He knew that when he did, he would open the floodgates to an all-time torrent of tears. He quailed at the thought of it. It was doubly a shame because, of course, Irina could help him get ready for Russia in these last few weeks. She could give him a crash course in Russian, her family could fill him in on all sorts of useful background information.

He rang England; he told the exciting news to Guy, who answered the telephone in his old house, and to his parents. He had the open bottle by the phone and he drank as he told them.

In the middle of the night, when he woke with the consequent thirst, he found himself first dwelling on Henry's role. Had Henry understood straight away what was going wrong and decided to provide him with a way out? Or had it maybe been Mai, indirectly responsible for the whole grotesque,

242

misconceived match in the first place, who had spotted the self-evident and told Henry what to do? Or was all that, he thought in the morning, paranoia and what had happened only the better luck he deserved?

Because there was a definite limit now on the time left with Irina, he found the tendency was to be a little more generous to her than of late. She responded eagerly. They spent two successive Saturday nights at the Cité Etienne Hubert. With a premature foretaste of nostalgia, Edward enjoyed those enduring aspects of Irina. He did feel, intermittently, that he was cheating her by keeping from her that the death sentence on their time together had been pronounced. But the mere idea of her despair was enough to convince him he was doing the kinder thing. He would tell her only when he had to, at the last minute. In this new-found benevolence, he even agreed to see some more of her family on whom he had placed an absolute embargo in recent weeks. There was a useful, practical purpose to be served by seeing them now; circumspectly, he questioned them about Russia.

Considering the concession he had made in coming back to see them, yet one more to Irina's temperamental potential, he could hardly have said that they welcomed him with open arms. Over tea, on the second of the Saturdays, Great-Aunt Elena seemed distinctly distant to him.

He put up with the rather frosty formality and what seemed to be pursed lips, making the most of things by asking what the Russian word was for all the objects on the tea trolley: cups, saucers, spoons, cake forks and *choux à la crème*.

Three days later, Great-Aunt Elena telephoned him, in the evening at the rue Surcouf, and invited him to come and have a drink with her. The invitation puzzled him. Naturally not particularly enthusiastic, and playing for time, he had asked what the occasion was, who else was coming, apart from, presumably, Irina?

Great-Aunt Elena's answer was brisk: "No one else is coming, Edward. This is a *tête-à-tête*; just you and I."

By which stage, he had unfortunately already expressed too much interest to be able to back out. Grimly, he headed up the Boulevard de Courcelles two or three evenings later, wondering what the old woman had in store for him. Even the positive prospect of being able to question her freely about things Russian without any risk of alerting Irina's suspicions didn't compensate for what felt increasingly like trouble.

Great-Aunt Elena greeted him with apparent goodwill. She had loaded her little trolley with an array of fierce-looking liqueurs and both savoury and sweet snacks. A cynical voice within him warned Edward that there must be quite some trouble coming up. But, to begin with, all was utterly amiable; Great-Aunt Elena poured him a bilberry liqueur with the power of a paint stripper and set a plate at his elbow piled with a solid stack of goodies. They talked about Edward's work, a feature he was preparing on the increasingly vocal ecology lobby, and then Elena announced, "I wish to talk to you about my great-niece."

For a ridiculous moment, Edward couldn't think who it was she meant. Then, with a sickening certainty, he understood: Irina.

Great-Aunt Elena sat very upright, her small, stoutly-shod feet crossed at the ankle and her plump hands clasped in her lap.

"Edward," she began, "I have a very high opinion of you. I have always had a very high opinion of you. I think you are, for one so young, an exceptionally wise and serious person. But there are certain things you do not know about. For example, I know you have become extremely friendly with Irina. But there are certain things you do not know about Irina. I wish you did not need to know them. They are neither pleasant nor happy things. If matters had gone otherwise, you need never have found them out. Certainly, it gives me no pleasure to have to tell you them. But tell you I must. We hoped maybe your friendship was slackening, you see. Several weeks went by and we had the impression you and Irina were seeing less of each other. But maybe we were mistaken; maybe things had just moved underground. I am afraid Irina would be capable of just this kind of deceit. Please take note; we do not blame you for anything which has happened. This is, I am afraid, not the first time something of this kind has taken place. We hoped that when you stopped visiting though perhaps, with your exceptional perspicacity, you had sensed something was not right and you had thought better of the whole business.

244

But then last Saturday she brought you back, and Vera and I realised the friendship wasn't slackening. Maybe, we worried, it was even being revived more strongly than before. So, we decided, you must be told.

"Irina has led perhaps an unusual life. I do not know if it was unusual from the beginning; if maybe the way we brought her up had some deficiencies we didn't realise. Although I can't see what they could have been; she always had a surfeit of everything. But, at any rate, since she has been grown-up and independent, managing her own life, I am afraid it has grown steadily more unusual. She has never found herself a serious and constant partner. Excuse me, this comment is not intended in any way as a reflection on you, Edward. What I mean is, Irina has somehow never settled on anybody who could last. She has had a series, oh dear, a long, long series, of highly unsatisfactory encounters. And, in this sorry series, Volodya's apartment has played a most unfortunate part. We let her manage it because, after all, she is young and capable; a modern woman, a woman of the world. She could handle all the paperwork, the bureaucracy and the bank, much better than we could. We never dreamt of the way it would be exploited; how Irochka would use it, I am afraid quite scandalously, for her own purposes. Over the years, she has always chosen the tenants. We let her; we saw no harm in it. I think we were blinded to her intentions not only by our affection for her; I think she actively misled us. But eventually, of course, we realised what was going on. It was when the Italian moved in that we first had our suspicions, and then when he moved out rather suddenly and she replaced him with the Hungarian, the suspicions were reinforced. But, you see, we could scarcely believe it; our little Irochka up to such a thing! I am afraid it was the Brazilian banker who confirmed our darkest fears. Do I need to spell it out? Irina was using the apartment to house men whom she wanted to be close to. I'm sorry, but that is the case. We had a most unpleasant discussion. I said that from then on *I* would choose the tenants. I'm afraid the first person I chose was perhaps not entirely suitable, an American who turned out to be a follower of Hinduism. How was I to know? We never touched on religion in the interview. Anyway, we agreed

245

the next tenant would be a woman, and Varvara Stepanovna found us a very appropriate Norwegian woman through her self-help group. And then, just at the last minute, all we were waiting for was her bank reference, Irina suddenly came up with you. At first, we were adamant: no, not again. But Irina insisted; it was via the *lycée*, she couldn't refuse a favour to her colleague, Madame Hirshfeld. And she told us how young you were. Excuse me, we thought nothing could possibly go amiss. But it seems we were mistaken, yet again.

"Edward, I must ask you, please, to stop seeing Irina. I know it will create difficulties for you. I know Irina can be a terribly tempestuous person. But, for her sake, please, be hard on her. She will ruin her life, I know, the way she is going. Please, tell her now, tell her no."

Edward sat stunned, with over his head the inky black exclamation marks of a cartoon strip.

"Listen," he said at last. "You don't need to worry. I haven't actually told Irina yet, but I've already heard about my next job. I'm leaving Paris in less than a month."

"Oich!"

Some quite abstracted part of Edward's brain reflected calmly how remarkable it was, the way these exclamations were inherited within the Iskarov family. How many times had he heard Irina make exactly that same winded little "Oich!" when he shocked her and by some uncouth act incurred her displeasure.

Elena leant forward, her face a frozen conglomeration of absolutely round, shocked cheeks, eyes and mouth.

"Less than a month?"

"Yes," Edward said. "I'm sorry about the notice for the flat. But you can understand how, in the circumstances – "

Elena shook her head for a second or two helplessly. But then she seemed to brighten, realising that, however brutally, her aim had been achieved.

"Tell me," she asked him eagerly. "Where is it to be? Which 'land beyond the sea' are they sending you to?"

"Brace yourself," Edward told her. "Russia."

Elena gaped at him with what looked very like awe. Yes, it was a little as if he had announced he had been picked for a moon shot. Elena stared at him as if he had acquired a new and heroic stature.

"You're going to *Russia?*"

"Yup."

Once again, her head wobbled from side to side in astonished admiration. Then came a new exclamation: *"Molodyets!"*

This one was not a burst paper bag; it sounded to Edward more like the cluck of extreme glee a hen might make upon laying an egg.

"Meaning?" he asked.

"Clever you!" Great-Aunt Elena exclaimed. "And can we claim a little of the credit for having switched your thoughts in that direction? Was it your Russian experiences here in Paris which made you choose Russia in preference to South America?"

"Oh," Edward blurted tactlessly, "I didn't *choose* it. It's just happened. Though," he added quickly, "of course I'm terribly pleased."

Elena sat back slightly, just a trifle disappointed.

"Well," she declared, "I've sensed it all along, but now my feelings are confirmed: you are the future."

Edward started to say, "Oh, come – "

Elena dismissed his objections. "You represent the new unfettered era," she informed him. "There is no reason why you should not go anywhere. For you, all countries are as one. There are no taboos, no closed doors any more. The world is a self-service restaurant."

There was more than one assumption in this speech which displeased Edward: the suggestion that he maybe didn't distinguish deeply between one country and another, and the implicit comparison with the type of journalist he so despised, for whom a destination was only as appetising as its restaurants. But he thought he should be satisfied that Elena had taken this awkward news so positively, and not press the point.

"Of course," he said, "I do intend to tell Irina. But I want to leave it as late as I can, you understand, so as not to upset her any sooner than necessary."

Great-Aunt Elena seemed to look doubtful.

"Please," Edward insisted. "You won't tell her, will you?

I really think it's important, in the circumstances, that the news comes from me."

Elena still looked unhappy. "When will you tell her?"

"Oh, very soon," Edward assured her. "As soon as I've got an actual date for going."

"How will you go there?" Elena asked. "Will you go back to London first or will you travel directly?"

"I thought," said Edward, "it might be rather fun to go by train, across Poland; a good introduction. But, of course, it depends how urgently I'm needed there."

Great-Aunt Elena gazed at him. "You know why I've always liked the Boulevard de Courcelles? It reminds me of the palaces in St Petersburg on the banks of the Neva."

"I'll go and look at them," Edward said earnestly. "And I'll think of you. And you know what; I'll send you a postcard of them."

He returned to the rue Surcouf on an ebb tide of bilberry liqueur and fell almost immediately into a sound, satisfied sleep. The noise which woke him had the inexplicable and relentless quality of a nightmare and, for several seconds, he couldn't work out if he were dreaming it or if it were really happening. Someone was battering on his front door. Thinking first of fire or some medical emergency, he scrambled out of bed and as he fumbled his way into the nearest pyjamas, he managed to focus on his bedside alarm clock and saw it was two o'clock in the morning. The pounding on the door didn't let up during the few moments it took him to get to it.

He called, "*J'arrive, j'arrive. Qu'est-ce qu'il y a?*"

Irina's voice howled back, "Let me in, Edouard."

He did, for a moment, hesitate to open the door but he cringed, in what he acknowledged irritably was a very English way, at how his neighbours were liable to react if the noise continued.

Irina plunged in at him.

"Is it true?" she demanded.

"For Christ's sake!" he protested. "What d'you think you're doing? Is what true?"

"You're leaving," Irina panted. "They're sending you to Moscow in a fortnight's time."

She looked so ghastly, Edward experienced an instant of

248

sheer revulsion: staring-eyed, livid-faced, and every incipient wrinkle of her thirty-six-year-old face starkly accentuated by her panic.

"Is this why you've come round now?" he asked her angrily. "Do you realise it's bloody two o'clock in the morning? You must have woken up every single person in the building, banging on the door like that."

Irina grabbed him by the arm and tugged at him fiercely.

"Tell me!" she shrieked.

He saw in her panic-stricken eyes black depths of desperation he had never seen before and he became gradually scared.

"Look, come in and sit down," he said roughly. "We need to talk this over together quietly. There's no point getting in such a state."

As he tried to reach around Irina to close the front door discreetly behind her, she whirled round on him, pinning him against the door, which at least slipped securely shut beneath their combined weight.

Grimacing into his face from point-blank range, Irina breathed, "If you don't tell me this instant – "

"OK," Edward said furiously. "It's true. I'm being sent to Moscow and I'll be leaving in three or four weeks' time. Now, if you don't let go of me and calm down and stop behaving like a lunatic, I promise you, you'll regret it."

But he was already speaking to a deflated balloon; Irina released him in the process of clutching her own face and doubling up as if in unbearable pain. Gasping, she held her face and her stomach, as if with terrible difficulty holding herself together.

Edward didn't move an inch to help her, for his predominant emotion was outrage.

Irina reared up, proving that her seizure was either short-lived or, more likely, a sham.

"*You'll* regret it!" she screamed. "Not me; you'll regret it, Edouard Wenwright! You thought you could cheat me, didn't you; deceive me and cheat me, and I wouldn't find out? What was supposed to happen, tell me; was I supposed to wake up one fine morning and discover you were gone? Or would you have left me a little goodbye note maybe? 'Cheerio, it's been nice knowing you.' Was that what was supposed to happen? Well, I tear up your little goodbye note and I spit on it. I spit on *you*, Edouard. You've disappointed me more than I ever thought was possible. You know, I was stupid enough to think you were a decent man, my first-ever properly decent man. I thought you believed in all those fine English values: being a good sport and fair play. But you're really a specimen of something else English, aren't you? It's true what they say about *perfide Albion*. If it needed to be proved, you've just proved it." Two or three times, in a quavering voice, she shrilled, "*Perfide Albion! Perfide Albion!*"

Edward was just considering some act of violent assertion to lower the noise level when Irina paused to summon breath for a final onslaught.

"You thought you'd steal away like a thief in the night, didn't you?" she shrilled. "Take what you wanted and then sneak away, *filer à l'anglaise*. But you're going to find out life's not as easy as you thought. I'm going to teach you a lesson, Edouard Wenwright, which you'll never forget."

"I was going to tell you," Edward said. "You weren't meant to hear this way from Great-Aunt Elena. I asked her specially not to tell you."

The tempest redoubled in volume.

"Of course!" Irina screeched. "And I know why! I may have been stupid, but not *that* stupid."

"Actually," Edward started vaguely. But he almost no longer cared. What appeal was there in retaining the goodwill of someone so hideously transformed?

"When I have done what I intend to do," Irina announced, "I hope you can still have a nice life as you travel around the world. I wish you *bon voyage*."

She strutted towards him and although he could easily have restrained her at the front door, tried to talk some sense into her, he stood aside and held the door open with ironic courtesy. He was too outraged to make even the least conciliatory effort.

Irina stalked out. In the very last second before he closed the door completely after her, Edward saw her stop and begin to turn. He finished closing the door immediately, for the last thing he wanted was Irina coming back.

The rest of the night was of course a write-off. For hours, he turned furiously, fuming, thinking of cleverer, more conclusive responses than the ones he had given, and from time to time ruthlessly squashing a recurring uncoiling of anxiety over what dramatic act it was Irina was planning to perform. In the end he grew calm enough to sleep. He concluded, with a callousness which frankly surprised him, that Irina had at least solved the problem of how to say goodbye to her.

Reading up on his next country, plus the acquisition of the many indispensable objects which Arnold warned him over the telephone would be unobtainable in Moscow, enjoyably filled the rest of Edward's time in Paris. He liked the sound of Arnold's voice on the phone; albeit in the fruitiest of English public-school accents, it seemed to convey the same jovial, robustly cynical outlook as Henry's.

Of course, he did worry about Irina, resentfully. But his worry tended to focus on the most likely form of her threatened revenge rather than on her plight. He realised he was, in fact, waiting for it, and every day of what should have been this splendidly happy countdown period was being subtly spoilt by the oppressive awareness that every day which elapsed free of drama only meant it was more likely the following day. He supposed there were two forms the reprisal could take; it would either be directed against him (sneaking into the flat while he was out and sabotaging his belongings, for example; lying in wait and somewhere publicly leaping at him; or possibly contacting the paper and causing him some monumental embarrassment) or else it would be directed against herself (suicide). Each drama-free day which passed in silence made this second dreadful option seem the most likely.

He dealt directly with Great-Aunt Elena over the business of relinquishing the flat and he realised he was ringing her more often than was strictly necessary to sort out the inventory, the documents and the bills because he assumed she would tell him if anything awful happened to Irina. He wondered whether Elena and Babushka were adequate guardians under whose protection to leave Irina and he couldn't help feeling that, with their track record, they were not. For his own peace of mind, as much as anything else, he wished there were someone sensible he could tip off, who would keep an eye on Irina in the coming weeks and guarantee that his start in Moscow was not marred by the arrival of some ghastly black-edged envelope. It was at this point that he remembered Lyova and, much as he thought he disliked the man, a week before his departure decided to go and see him. It took him a while to identify the Russian bookshop in the telephone directory as *Les Editeurs Réunis* and he thought with reflex irritation how typical of Irina it was never to have called the shop by its proper name. The first time he rang, Lyova wasn't there and a woman with a near-incomprehensible accent told Edward she didn't know when he would be back. With some relief, Edward left it till the following day. He wondered whether it was really such a bright idea to contact Lyova after all. It was true Great-Aunt Elena had referred to him during that last dramatic truth session as one of Irina's few trustworthy male friends, a "noble soul" she had described him. But Great-Aunt Elena's judgement had hardly been brilliant, by her own admission. How was Edward to know that Great-Aunt Elena's version of their friendship bore any relation at all to reality? She had portrayed Lyova as a much persecuted individual whose own suffering had enabled him to understand other people's, and who magnanimously allowed poor, childless Irina to mind his little ones. This interpretation alone seemed to Edward to cast doubt over her whole reading. But there was no one else he could turn to and he knew that, even if something ghastly were to happen, he would sleep more peacefully if he had warned Lyova before he left.

The next day, it was Lyova who answered the telephone. He sounded only slightly surprised to hear from Edward, his predominant tone as usual being faintly aloof amusement. But what caused Edward most indignation in the circumstances was that, to start off with, Lyova didn't seem at all sure who he was. They arranged to meet at seven when the bookshop shut and Edward, just so as to keep his end up and not appear straight away as the helpless supplicant, suggested on the phone that they went for a drink at a different, he implied more congenial, café than the one the three of them had gone to before.

He and Lyova shook hands, probably with more sincerity than either of them felt, and set off in the direction of Edward's preferred bar. It was only when Lyova, to break what was already a wary, awkward silence, asked, "How is Irina?" that it occurred to Edward that perhaps Lyova didn't know what had happened. This was a possibility which had not crossed his mind. He had assumed Irina would have gone running straight to Lyova and sobbed what a pig, or possibly perfidious wretch Edward was and how, from now on, she would have nothing whatsoever to do with Englishmen, who, whatever people said about them, weren't actually gentlemen at all. He had expected this conversation to be mainly self-justification, defending what Irina would already have portrayed as despicable behaviour. But if Lyova really knew nothing, he gained an immediate advantage.

He gave Lyova a careful sideways look. His face was, if anything, distracted, clouded in smoke from one of the pungent cigarettes he had offered Edward as soon as they began walking.

"When did you last see her?" Edward asked.

Lyova shrugged. "Not for a while. You've been keeping her too busy, I guess."

"Listen," Edward said precipitously. "I think there's something you ought to know."

He acknowledged he came out of his version of events, delivered somewhat hastily over red wine on the terrace of the bar, better than he would have out of Irina's. But he felt he was fair.

"You see," he concluded, "she seems to have got hold of the wrong end of the stick completely. There was never any question at all of this thing having a future."

He was relieved that Lyova continued to smoke tranquilly.

Eventually Lyova shook his head with weary amusement. "Don't worry," he said to Edward.

"I *do* worry," Edward contradicted him, aware that he was exaggerating this worry in order to appear a more admirable person. He told Lyova, in a considerably censored version, about Irina's threat of retaliation. "I'm afraid she may be thinking of doing something silly."

To his astonishment, Lyova gave a rich roar of laughter.

"You mean suicide? Irina? Really, don't worry!"

"But you didn't see the state she was in," Edward protested, now defending his own abilities as a judge of human nature as well. "She was – beside herself."

Lyova crushed his cigarette butt in the metal ashtray. He took a large swig of his wine and sat back, crossing his arms.

"Listen," he began patronisingly as though, Edward thought crossly, he were just sixteen rather than twenty-six. "I've known Irina for seven years. She was one of the first friends I made here when I came out. She wanted it to be otherwise; I mean, more than friends only. She was terribly keen on me. But I was still genuinely married then. The West hadn't yet corrupted my marriage along with everything else. By the time the marriage started to come undone, by the time Anna decided that an advertising executive was a more appropriate partner than an artist in the West, I knew Irina too well to want to be anything more than the best of friends. Irina bore this disappointment very bravely. She was at that stage – otherwise engaged. I think she saw the benefit to both of us of having a good, close friendship that was free from complications. You see, Irina lives under the tyranny of her imagination. For her, the distinction between what she dreams and what she does is none too clear. She won't commit suicide. She's just in love with the idea of it."

"Honestly," Edward interrupted him, "she did seem dreadfully distraught."

Lyova stroked wisely at his beard.

"I believe you," he agreed. "From time to time this happens, inevitably. What Irina represents is the triumph of imagination over tedious reality. When reality insists on barging in, she is always deeply shocked and hurt. She really believes things which aren't true in the least, you know. I don't know if she has ever talked to you about her beloved Dyadya Volodya. She has? Well, to listen to her, wouldn't you agree, she and Volodya were the perfect couple, scandalously more than uncle and niece. Complete rubbish. I met this Volodya just before his death and, believe me, there was nothing to it. A spoilt little girl humoured by an incurably weak man. Irina had made the whole thing up. It would be a comedy if it weren't also a tragedy."

He took another cigarette from his battered Cyrillic brand packet.

"You can fly away to Moscow with your mind at rest," he concluded ironically. "*Anna Karenina* may be Irina's favourite book but, I can assure you, she's not about to compose a sequel."

He breathed out smoke loftily.

"If you like, I can give you some names and addresses in Moscow. I know a woman there who'd love to make your acquaintance."

In his last days, Edward reflected that what had happened to him in Paris was the opposite of a plot. All the lurid dimensions which he had imagined lay behind Irina's half-coloured-in life turned out to be only that: imagined. None of them, it seemed, had ever existed at all. The relationship with Volodya, which he had invested with such sinister overtones, was, if Lyova was to be believed, nothing out of the ordinary. So what had given him the idea? Was it only Irina's wishful thinking? Or did he have a conventional imagination which meant that when something was wrong, he expected it to be the obvious? Whereas, in the case of the Iskarov family, it was something more submerged and subtle, which had eluded him. And her friendship with Lyova himself, which, Edward had been convinced, was much more than Irina admitted, turned out to be the most innocent of friendships. Had he perhaps wanted all these sordid things to be true because they made dumpy, chaos-saddled Irina seem a more spicy and wicked partner? On the other hand, could everything really be as bland as Lyova suggested? He began to suspect Lyova's motives in playing it all down, in attributing everything to Irina's over-active imagination. What lay behind Lyova's eagerness to promote a cover-up? Although he did not intend or now expect to see Irina again, Edward could not suppress a slight, perhaps professionally inspired regret that he might not get to the bottom of this story.

They held a small leaving party for him at the paper. Everybody, Monsieur Marchais included, went out for a celebratory dinner on Edward's final day, toasted his destination and offered him a variety of jokey parting ideas.

It was Aurore who, in innocent goodwill, delivered the most disturbing.

"I hope you find yourself a gorgeous Slav girlfriend," she declared. "A ravishing beauty of the steppes, and one day you will bring her back to Paris and introduce her to all of us."

Frankly drunk afterwards, Edward walked part of the way back to the rue Surcouf. He felt the decisive triumph of departure struggle with his usual feelings of helpless hostility between the dark apartment houses. How unyielding they looked, with their stone nipples, and their windows which he now, for the first time, saw looked vividly like architectural vaginas: long narrow slits with their narrow shutters forming prim labia on either side of them. He grinned drunkenly at the vision. The windows epitomised this prudishly exclusive female city. A vague depression settled over him as he walked, for he realised it could be said that he had failed here. The city had, not even on a grand scale, administered the first of the dents by which, he supposed, you eventually attained the battered cynicism of a Henry or an Arnold. If he could only view this Parisian dent as a battle scar, honourably acquired, then the time he had spent here would not have been only a setback.

He thought of Henry raising his glass at the party and repeating once again, "*Na zdorovye*" and he concluded, with a rush of real affection for the man, that knowing Henry Hirshfeld had made his stay in Paris worthwhile.

Irina

I saw my happiness sail past and out onto the open sea. I was left, standing on a shore which bore a strong resemblance to a pavement, watching him disappear. He didn't know I was standing in the neighbouring entrance watching him, that I had been standing there since two o'clock, waiting to see him go. Elena had inadvertently let me know his plane left that evening, but for these geriatric Slavs I know the evening can begin at four, and I didn't want to risk missing my last chance of looking at my happiness.

So finally, a little before five, I saw the taxi arrive, the ugly driver go in to fetch him, and I saw him come out of the house, weighted down with his luggage, and supervise the driver as he piled it into the boot. I saw him run his fingers in nervous irritation through his curly hair as the driver incompetently tried to jam everything in, and I nearly cried out because that last sweet curl on the top of his head stayed crooked and, as he jokingly congratulated the driver on fitting everything in at last and turned briskly to open the rear door of the taxi, he looked so like a young boy playing at the importance of a man. The driver swung round dangerously in the narrow rue Surcouf, against all the traffic regulations, intending to set off again in the direction from which he had come. I was sure Edouard would see me as the driver rammed his bumper up onto the pavement nearly at my feet. I crushed myself right back into the corner of my doorway, as thin as a blade, although actually I do not think I would have minded if he had seen me. For the last brief spurt backwards of the driver's perilous turn, I saw him through the window. The taxi's police number on the window near his head gave him a remote official look, as if I were seeing his face on a passport photograph or – a suddenly seductive thought – reported dead in a newspaper. He was looking straight ahead, already concentrating on his future, and that was how he vanished from my life; his face set resolutely on the route ahead but that little crest of curly hair still sticking up as if from recently rumpled sleep.

His was not the first departure I had watched in hiding from that doorway. I saw Anibal leave too, although then I was not spying on him in expectation of his departure, but catching him in the early morning together with the other woman whom I suspected he was bringing to Volodya's apartment. I saw them go away together; Anibal handing her with his gangster's elegance into their get-away car. I crossed the road right in front of their car. The friend who was driving it had to brake abruptly. I expect he would have pulled the window down or even leapt out to yell at me if Anibal hadn't panicked and urged him to speed away. That was how I saw him as the car accelerated forward; hunched over the front seat in a cowardly panic, screaming at his friend to get him away from the terrifying monster called Irina Iskarov. I had no intention of intervening. I stood on the kerb, having finished crossing the road at my leisure, and I surveyed the pathetic spectacle he made quite calmly.

But Edouard's was without any doubt the departure which wounded me the most, Edouard's was the one which I believed might kill me. It could still kill me now. He was the youngest of all my tenants and he was the one I loved the most. I loved him the most *because* he was the youngest. My love for him was not only the love for a man but also for a boy, a child.

Thus the remainder of my life began, my mourning a gaunt incongruity amid the insolent radiance of the city in summer. Although internally dead, I carried on mechanically with my daily duties, so demolished I did not even notice the sequel there was to be. My dulled brain revolved around two topics only: July and August as if Edouard were still there beside me – his constantly remembered company in the Tuileries and passing the Taverne Tourville and in my bedroom – and recapitulating again and again and again the wonderful winter we had shared.

To tell the truth, I was not really interested when he first telephoned about the flat. We had that Norwegian female settee selected by Varvara Stepanovna lined up, and it was only out of nostalgic curiosity that I decided I might as well look him over. I thought then that the apartment's days as my love nest were over. I thought on the phone that he had bad manners. But when I saw him, I understood; he was so terribly young, of course. He hadn't yet learnt any better.

I remember that dreadful day. I had such a disfiguring cold, it is still a mystery to me how he was straight away attracted to me. When I opened the door and saw him standing there, what with my flu and my shock, I really thought I might collapse. He looked so young and innocent, standing on my threshold. He had come to me, and I knew it was more than I could do to send him away. Young, physically ripe, and unspoilt; those were the characteristics which struck me first. His fresh pink cheeks and his particularly red mouth and, of course, his candid blue eyes; these were all virtues which I only distinguished singly later. But what was most astonishing, apart from the sheer unexpectedness of the encounter, was that so very soon I realised he was also captivated by me.

I prayed, all the time he was away looking at the flat, that he wouldn't want to take it because, if he did, I knew without any doubt what would follow. But at the same time, of course, I was desperate for him to take it, desperate for this, perhaps my last chance of happiness, not to evade me. I was already preparing all the reasons I would give, all the lies I would tell, why we had to let it to him.

When he came back, I wouldn't let him see me again; one horrible glimpse of my raspberry of a nose and my albino rabbit eyes in the bathroom mirror had been enough to convince me that was the only possible solution. I thought it might intrigue and tantalise him also to be denied admission.

Once he was installed in Volodya's apartment, I proceeded with exemplary restraint. I allowed three weeks and a day to go by before I telephoned him and, even then, I invented some domestic pretext to make sure he suspected nothing.

Seeing him settled in Volodya's interior did give me quite a turn. Of course, in the interim it had since been Giorgio's interior, and Imre's, and Anibal's. Perhaps it was simply the shock of seeing someone new installed there once again and realising that the whole wicked business of plucking my pleasure from the circumstances created by Volodya's untimely death was about to begin all over again. I had to sit down. I worried that the place was now simply too steeped in shadows for any more adventures to be possible there. The inhibiting ghosts literally over-populated the place. But I concentrated on Volodya; that was how I had originally overcome my scruples when the idea of exploiting his apartment first occurred to me. I knew Volodya would have been pleased that, as he was no longer there to care for me, his apartment continued to provide solace after his death. He would have been a bit jealous, certainly, but I found a little way of getting round this. Mentally, I would present my tenants to his inspection when I had them displayed on his bed. Only if they met with his approval would I proceed. Luckily, because Dyadya Volodya and I were in the essential ways so similar, he did not object strenuously to any of them. I knew he would like Edouard the best.

The sheer pleasure of Edouard's proximity soon did away with my anxieties. I busied myself with all my domestic excuses for coming: light bulbs and tablecloths and keys. But really I was dwelling on the delightful details of his appearance which I was now noticing one by one: there was a sprinkling of freckles over his high-coloured cheeks, still a soft cushioning of puppy fat to his smile, and that curly hair which I already longed to rumple. I know this awakening appetite was mutual because he spontaneously invited me to stay for coffee and then subtly changed the invitation to whisky instead.

It might seem implausible to say it but when I left Volodya's apartment that night, I know I was already halfway in love with Edouard. Over the next fortnight before our dinner, I must have thought of little else. The warming knowledge enabled me to cope more bravely with the increasingly gloomy aspects of my existence: Babushka's continuing journey into aberration, the burden of responsibility which I have to bear for her and Elena and, for Mama's sake, for Nikolai Grigoriev; those turgid Saturday-night dinners, and over it all, the suffocating awareness that my time is running out, that if I am not able to break free and create a future for myself, this is all I shall have.

Our dinner did not actually go quite as well as I had anticipated. Babushka, bless her, cast a chill over it right from the start by refusing to greet Edouard and treating us both to an icily suspicious stare; before anything remotely deserving suspicion had even taken place! It infuriated me. Edouard seemed determined to play hard to get too. I don't know whether it was merely boyish panic or a more calculated strategy, but he had the nerve to ask me at the outset if I had also invited other people. I was indignant. As if I would have gone out and bought that abominably expensive dress for "other people"; tidied the apartment from top to bottom and cooked all afternoon for "other people"! It took the atmosphere a little while to recover from that blow. Apart from anything else, I was disconcerted to discover that Edouard wasn't entirely the sincere, straightforward person he appeared, that he was prepared to play hard-hearted games with me.

But in due course things did revive; we spent a most delightful evening. I knew it was too soon to expect a move from anyone so young and so British. I didn't try to hurry him; I knew the quarry could be scared away. But I was disappointed, bitterly disappointed that he didn't even kiss me goodnight.

These are dreadful days. It is as if my life stopped the day he drove away, yet I am still perversely, quite against my will, alive regardless. I am alive for the fulfilment of a purpose which transcends me. For I myself, ex-Irina Iskarov, am finished. I received one blow too many in the delicate region of the heart and this time I shall not recover. Never again another lover, never again another afternoon sailing aboard my ghost ship from the rue Surcouf. I remain alive for one reason only and it is not a reason which can be spoken publicly.

After the dinner, I was a little desperate, I admit it. I was worried that Edouard's failure to kiss me goodnight signalled some serious impediment which I had not yet uncovered. (Maybe the English disease?) I telephoned him sooner than was sensible, on the very next Monday. I invited him to come to a concert, any old concert; today, I cannot even remember any more what the music was. It was the slimmest of pretexts of course. My only aim was to set eyes on him again as soon as possible. As a means of deflecting suspicions, both his and my dear family's, I made it the least seductive occasion I could possibly imagine; a concert in the Russian church, and I dragged Elena along too for good measure.

Naturally, no progress of any significant sort was made that evening. But my purpose was achieved to the extent that Edouard did seem to relax a little about the prospect of our acquaintance and Great-Aunt Elena, the old flirt, took such a shine to the well-bred young Englishman that her suspicions melted like her favourite English fudge.

From then on, I felt considerably more confident. It was only a matter of time, it seemed, until Edouard was won over, and my days went by in a glow of happy anticipation.

How harsh it is to recall that happiness from the perspective of my sorry present. Harsh, but it seems I cannot help it. I keep reliving that time again and again for weren't even the bad bits a thousand times preferable to this state of affairs?

Without telling me, he went home to England for Christmas. And I had been looking forward to our spending it cosily together in a deserted Paris! It reminded me again how very young he was; going home to his Mummy and Daddy for the holidays. Only when he came back, it seemed it hadn't been like that at all.

We met immediately, unable to stay away from each other, and united in our miserable Christmases behind us and our isolation in that stone-cold Paris January. I sensed then that we were on the verge of fulfilling my dearest desires. But because I didn't want Edouard to get a mistaken impression of me, I deliberately delayed that last sweet course. I knew it would drive him wild, and that was all to the good. Only to my amazement, the dear naïve chap misunderstood my tactics. He thought that because I hadn't invited him to somersault straight into my bed at the first available opportunity, I wasn't interested in him after all! I was really rather dismayed by his interpretation. It took us only a short time, though, to recover from this upset and, within days, we were one.

Oh, my little boy, you were beautiful in bed! You didn't know you were beautiful and that was probably the greatest part of your charm. As you reared above me, perfect and pink in every detail, preparing to possess me, I assure you, you were Grecian in your perfection. And your enjoyment of me was so wholehearted, so wholesome; the glee of a child at play or once, forgive me, the image did come to me, a pig at truffles. For me, who had long become used to sexual complications, your simplicity was the height of pleasure. I was released by it from the obligation to feign, to simulate, to tailor my pleasure to the other's design. With you, Edouard, I was more satisfied than with anyone ever.

The memory arouses in me another irrepressible craving for sweet consolation. Although I know I will find Babushka in the kitchen, defending the fridge and the cake tins from my ravenous attacks, I must go there. Must. Now. Babushka doesn't seem to understand what it is which is driving me to these bizarre feasts of *mille-feuilles* and *crème caramel*. It is biological, but she doesn't seem to see that. Or if she does, she is pretending that by not seeing it, it will go away. Well, it won't. It is all very well, she and Elena going on and on at me about how fat I am growing, how unbecoming it is, and how, unless I diet, I will never find a husband now. They won't be able to keep up this prudish pretence for very much longer. I will burst. Yes, that's it; I will burst!

I do wonder sometimes how Edouard would feel if he found out. Probably panic-stricken, and even more panic-stricken now it is too late for anybody to insist on a common-sense remedy. Do not worry. In one respect, I am really quite happy, you see. All my life, I have hated common sense, and now, at last, I have the opportunity to do something which flagrantly contradicts it. I am turning what was a fantasy into real flesh and blood.

Edouard and I were, according to the loathsome tenets of common sense, ill-suited. Yet we achieved greater complicity, greater joy than most pedestrian, sensibly assorted pairs. Could there have been a moment of greater joy than when Edouard, tossing his heels at the winter grey, suddenly walked on his hands in front of me in the Bois de Boulogne? Or when, one night, he crept up on the peep hole of the apartment opposite ours, from which an indiscreet light was shining, and waggled his fingers from his ears and stuck out his tongue? All winter long we were ecstatically happy with one another, so ecstatically happy that it is not surprising Babushka and Elena became suspicious. Our happiness must have been painted all over us. I suppose I knew I was paving the way to a terrible denouement. On the one hand, Babushka and Elena were bound to find out what was going on. Their fury at this repetition of scandal, coupled with the further deception, was bound to be dreadful. On the other hand, I knew Edouard would eventually go away and leave me. You could say, I suppose, I was knowingly risking everything for the known prospect of nothing. That is certainly what a dull, common-sense person would say. But, somehow, I overcame these trite considerations. Regardless of mere probabilities, I had the winter of my life.

It was when the autumn came round again, when signs in the streets started to repeat all the accompaniments of the year before – the return of oysters to the stalls of the rue Saint Dominique and then the chrysanthemums of mourning – that the effort of maintaining my false composure became too much for me. The clockwork which had kept me functioning like a well-behaved, varnished wooden toy ran down. In the silence when its ticking stopped, I noticed a new mechanism starting up.

I remember the first time we made love in Volodya's apartment. It was after a Sunday lunch at Elena's. We were both burdened with familial gloom and the sepulchral silence of Paris's wealthy neighbourhoods on a winter Sunday afternoon. It was Edouard who suggested it, with his habitual boyish mischief, his knack of leap-frogging out of oppressive solemnity. I went warily, fearing the resurrection of evil memories. But, in the event, we entered a new kingdom there in which we were emancipated and my ghosts became guardians of the kingdom, watching protectively over our bed. I felt so loved then, so profoundly at peace that afterwards I said not a word so as not to break the spell.

I remember having breakfast with Edouard and the two

little girls at Lyova's and pretending privately that we were a family. Although he was in a fearful mood, incensed by this ersatz family, I still relished every moment of it. In a way, his bad temper made the game seem even more real; my husband would be grumpy as he hurried off to his day's business and his children frolicked around him and delayed his departure.

Lyova warned me that what I was up to was silly. I think he did not have a high opinion of Edouard. But I dismissed his warning as obvious jealousy.

I cannot pinpoint the day when my happiness began to draw to a close. It is important for me not to dwell on distressing topics in my condition. (All topics are distressing.) In March, when Edouard let a whole week go by without contacting me, it did fill me with a fatal foreboding, but I did my best to believe his explanation about added responsibilities at work. I tried to overlook the proliferating omens of disaster.

Only when he went away, he said to Marseilles, did I start to sink. For then I had a foretaste of what my life would be like when he was gone for good. I did not imagine this development, of course; I imagined myself sinking alone into a choking black bog of despair and demanding elderly relatives from which no one would ever again appear to extricate me.

To make my predicament worse, it was around that time too that Babushka's and Great-Aunt Elena's suspicions sharpened. They started to spy on me and I was forced to resort to all sorts of clandestine stratagems like in one of their own wartime stories.

When Edouard came back, I could not conceal my depression from him, even though I knew it was wrong, even though I risked alienating him. To hang onto him for as long as possible, I knew I should be a source of light-hearted entertainment, not troubles. But such are not my gifts.

Naturally, Edouard wanted to know what the matter was. My depression got in his way like a large black bat blundering lost in the wrong context. And I, fool that I was, I told him. But would things, in fact, have turned out any differently if I hadn't? I sometimes suspect that the two alternative happy endings I had imagined were neither of them really plausible. In one of them, Edouard took me away with him on his travels and, in the other, which I admit was less likely, he renounced his desire to travel and opted to stay on in Paris instead with me, like Monsieur and Madame Hirshfeld. Although that ending was the less plausible, it had the advantage that I would still be able to look after Babushka and Great-Aunt Elena.

In the short term, though, my rash confession didn't seem to have any very serious consequences. Of course, the monster rat, misery, was gnawing away at my "*palais sucré du bonheur*" from underneath. But only I could hear its teeth. Edouard was oblivious to them.

I envy him his selfishness. I envy him the dedication with which he went in pursuit of his own happiness. And I think that, on balance, I wish him a good life. I like to think of him in Moscow, in a rabbit fur hat with ear muffs to protect him from frost-bite, ice-skating, or on a fine summer weekend going out to the woods with his beery Soviet chums to pick mushrooms.

Only occasionally, I have a treacherous dream in which he has fallen into the clutches of the KGB and they are interrogating him in the Lubyanka prison. And I have another dream, too, just very rarely, in which he is dead.

My first symptom was the most obvious one, but I ignored it. I attributed it, if I thought about it at all, to my state of upset since Edouard's departure. For I have been very low for a long time now, and it seemed only natural that my physical functions should be depressed too. It actually took more than one repetition for me to realise, in amazement, what the cause of it must be.

We were discovered. I am not quite clear any more what the ultimate piece of incriminating evidence was, which led Babushka and Great-Aunt Elena to confront me. All I know is that they chose the worst possible day; a day which was intended to be one of carefree spring spirits, walking hand-in-hand with Edouard along the *quais*, and they combined to spoil it. I refused to stoop so low as to deny it. I took the irrefutable line that all their accusations were quite accurate, only there was simply absolutely nothing wrong in it. Their facts were right but their conclusions were hopelessly, farcically wrong. As was their suggested remedy, the diabetic widower, whom I furiously rejected.

The day would have been spoilt anyway. For, on the Quai d'Orléans, whom should we meet but the Hirshfelds, and my beloved Edouard rejected me. These were his words, surely still legible in scar tissue on my heart: "Do you know my landlady, Mai's colleague, Mademoiselle Iskarov?"

Each word was branded there, I am convinced, for ever. In such spring sunshine, in such friendly circumstances, my edifice of sugar, undermined from within by the rat, crashed in ruins. Somehow I managed to maintain outward appearances. Already nothing but a cheerful automaton, I joked and laughed with the Hirshfelds. But inside, Edouard, didn't you realise, you had destroyed me? And when the Hirshfelds had walked on, a happy pair, a married pair, walking in step on their American rubber shoes, I lost the last of my fragile self-control and screamed at Edouard and from then on we didn't see each other nearly as often any more.

Secrecy, I see with hindsight, was the malign underside of our relationship. Everything that was pernicious and evil flourished there and we ignored it. By keeping our great happiness a secret, each for our own more or less respectable reasons, we allowed the poisonous mushrooms of neglected dark places to multiply. We should have declaimed our happiness from the rooftops, climbed up together to that slate-grey realm of mansards and stone members rearing against the winter sky, and yelled our happiness down on all their heads.

Far from feeling agitated, once the first shock was past, I welcomed it. It was like an unbelievable reward which compensated me for all the rejection, the deprivation, the loss. There is a satisfying justice, when you think of it, about the outcome of our magic winter being something which can in no circumstances remain a secret.

He left in June. But, frankly, it may as well have been midwinter for all the pleasure I could take in the season. Ever since our disagreement beside the Seine I had been waiting for his departure, dreading it, because it seemed to me the disagreement would inevitably have brought it closer. If there were any chance at all of his hastening the decision, he would surely do so now. I had already begun to lose my concentration at the *lycée*; easily done at the best of times, but then beginning to assume disturbing proportions.

271

Disturbing enough for one of my pupils, the especially smug and odious Clotilde Ponomarev, to complain to her parents and her parents to complain in turn to the headmistress. I was able to prevaricate satisfactorily, but I was aware that this complaint now lay in wait in my *dossier*, ready to re-emerge when the time came. It was one more small element of the disaster that was about to overwhelm me.

What I cannot forgive Edouard, what I shall never forgive him, is that on those last two or three occasions we did spend a night together, he should have deceived me; that he should have lain with me, knowing he would soon be gone, and not said a word. It is that which made my fury erupt in the end. For he was lying, because silence can also be a lie, and if he was lying in word, or rather in lack of word, then how do I know he was not lying in deed as well?

One thing is certain; I was never meant to find out. He was intending to sneak away from Paris while my attention was elsewhere and, at best, I would have received a scribbled postcard. So I am, oddly enough, grateful to Elena for her cruelty in telling me. Whatever her misguided motives may have been, she at least spared me the greater cruelty of waking one morning to find my Edouard was gone.

There is a German woman living in Volodya's apartment now. Volodya would be horrified; he couldn't stand Germans. It is another *coup* by Varvara Stepanovna, who met the woman in a beauty salon where the German pulls out hair. A beauty salon; Varvara Stepanovna! Allow me to laugh. Although it is true that as I am subsiding into this necessarily sluggish period, Varvara seems to be growing ever more active. As Elena never tires of reminding me, Varvara has now lost seven kilos.

If Volodya hadn't died, my life would, of course, never have gone askew. He would have continued to protect me and care for me, the way he always did, and I would never have needed to seek out lesser men.

But, oh, my little Edouard, I did love you! I don't think I will ever stop regretting you, you know. I wake in the morning, in this room where we lay and laughed together. I wake missing you. I hear your breathless voice saying, "Wow!" And when I do go out, not often now, for obvious reasons, I keep imagining that I see your curly head in front of me in the street, so strong is my yearning for you.

My breasts have swollen to unbelievable dimensions. And sometimes I feel sick. That is further proof, if proof were needed, that this is not, as Babushka and Elena would unkindly imply, all in my head. It is not in one's head, *mes chères*, that one conceives a baby. It is not true that I am becoming like Varvara Stepanovna, cramming myself with cakes in place of affection. That is not the reason why I am swelling, swelling shamelessly now for all to see. Believe it or not, I am carrying Edouard Wainwright's child.